WILLIAM SHAKESPEARE

*

HAMLET

EDITED BY
T. J. B. SPENCER

WITH AN INTRODUCTION
BY ANNE BARTON

PENGUIN BOOKS

PENGUIN BOOKS

Published by the Penguin Group
Penguin Books Ltd, 80 Strand, London WC2R 0RL, England
Penguin Putnam Inc., 375 Hudson Street, New York, New York 10014, USA
Penguin Books Australia Ltd, 250 Camberwell Road, Camberwell, Victoria 3124, Australia
Penguin Books Canada Ltd, 10 Alcorn Avenue, Toronto, Ontario, Canada M4V 3B2
Penguin Books India (P) Ltd, 11 Community Centre, Panchsheel Park, New Delhi – 110 017, India
Penguin Books (NZ) Ltd, Cnr Rosedale and Airborne Roads, Albany, Auckland, New Zealand
Penguin Books (South Africa) (Pty) Ltd, 24 Sturdee Avenue, Rosebank 2196, South Africa

Penguin Books Ltd, Registered Offices: 80 Strand, London WC2R 0RL, England

www.penguin.com

This edition first published in Penguin Books 1980
Reprinted with revised Further Reading 1996
41

Set in Monotype Ehrhardt
Printed in England by Clays Ltd, St Ives plc

CONTENTS

NOTE	6
INTRODUCTION by Anne Barton	7
FURTHER READING	55
HAMLET	59
COMMENTARY	205
AN ACCOUNT OF THE TEXT	362

NOTE

Except for the Introduction, this edition of *Hamlet* was almost complete at the time of Professor T. J. B. Spencer's death in March 1978. His typescript has been edited and seen through the press by Dr Stanley Wells, with the help of Mrs Katharine Spencer.

INTRODUCTION

Towards the end of the twelfth century, a Danish chronicler collecting information about his country's past wrote down the story of Amleth, Prince of Jutland. Although Saxo Grammaticus, the author of the *Historiae Danicae*, obviously shaped and elaborated his material, he did not invent it. Amleth's revenge upon Feng, the uncle who had treacherously murdered Amleth's father and married his mother, was part of Saxo's Northern inheritance. Probably he also remembered the Roman legend, retold by Livy at the end of the first century B.C., of Lucius Junius Brutus, a forebear of the Brutus in Shakespeare's *Julius Caesar*. Ironically, considering that they were later to become attached to two of Shakespeare's most cerebral and meditative characters, the names 'Hamlet' and 'Brutus' both signify 'the stupid one'. Neither Amleth, however, nor the original Brutus was really witless. Both escaped death after the murder of their fathers only because they cunningly pretended to be fools, boys not worth killing. They concealed their true natures behind an antic disposition, a madness that had method in it, and in time avenged themselves.

Even in Saxo's Latin, Amleth's story has the universality, the capacity at once to satisfy and disturb, of the great world myths. The primal sins of fratricide and incest, hints of a seasonal or vegetation rite, sexual initiation, the emergence of a dark wisdom from riddles and apparent folly, a son's revenge for his dead father, and the cleansing of a polluted house: these potent and dangerous

7

elements were all gifts from the myth to Shakespeare's play. They persist there in subtly altered forms, as do many of the characters and incidents of the old Icelandic legend. Equivalents, not only for Hamlet himself, but for Claudius, Gertrude, Polonius, Horatio, Ophelia, even Rosencrantz and Guildenstern, appear in Saxo. There are no ghosts – nor any need for one, because it is public knowledge that Feng slew his brother – no travelling entertainers, no Laertes or Fortinbras. There are also no pirates. After killing a spying councillor in his mother's chamber, Amleth completes his enforced voyage to England. He delivers the forged royal commission which seals the fate of his false companions, coolly collects blood-money by pretending to be outraged by their deaths, and then marries the king's daughter. A year later, the time at last being right, he returns home, resumes his feigned idiocy, and with the help of his repentant mother not only kills Feng but fires his palace, having trapped all the members of the court inside. No one, not even Saxo, seems to disapprove. Amleth has come of age. After explaining his actions to the people, he is elected ruler of Jutland. He dies in battle some years later, not because his actions necessitate any moral retribution, but simply because he has incurred the enmity of a neighbouring and more powerful king.

As told by Saxo, the story of Amleth is simple, irrational, and obscurely gratifying – like some savage stone, wave-worn but intact, cast up anonymously from the sea. There are no questions to be asked, or at least none that cannot be answered in their own terms, which are those of a primitive but consistent world of craft and heroic individualism. Some four hundred years later, however, when François de Belleforest set himself to re-tell it as part of his collection of *Histoires tragiques*, Saxo's

tale had become altogether more problematic and re-
fractory. Belleforest was obviously both fascinated and
made uneasy by what his early-seventeenth-century
English translator (1608) was to call *The History of
Hamblet*. He felt obliged to make excuses for it on the
grounds that it all happened long ago, in a cruel and
barbarous age, before Denmark became Christian.
Baffled to discover anything in Saxo that might be
described as a moral purpose, Belleforest tries desperately
to introduce one by way of a prolonged and quite gra-
tuitous assault upon the worthlessness and deceit of
women. Hamblet's mother, who in Saxo had been the
innocent victim of her brother-in-law's ambition and
lust, becomes in Belleforest an adulteress all too willing
to marry the lover who assassinated her first husband.
Saxo's Ophelia figure, loosed to Amleth in the forest as
part of a ruse to test the supposed imbecility of her foster
brother, remained scrupulously loyal to him afterwards,
despite having been dragged off by the Prince, and virtually raped, in the middle of a fen. Her equivalent in
The History of Hamblet is positively eager to be seduced
and, Belleforest manages to hint, disappointed of her
wish. When Hamblet finally does yield to what the translator terms 'concupiscence', it proves to be his undoing.
The Prince of Jutland becomes a bigamist in both accounts but it was Belleforest who imagined, characteristically, that Hamblet's new and beloved Scottish wife
not only callously married Wiglerus, after this rival king
had killed Hamblet, but conspired with him before and
during the battle. Wiglerus was another of Hamblet's
uncles, on the maternal side, so that in this reading of the
myth it almost seems as though Claudius ultimately was
revenged.

Belleforest's misogyny, shrill and unattractive in itself,

is also puzzling in the way that it deliberately seems to divert attention from what, in a late-sixteenth-century Christian writer, might seem to be a much more obvious and expected centre of moral blame: the revenge code itself. Belleforest is clearly aware, as Saxo appears not to have been, that Hamblet's actions need defending. The Prince may be admirable in his constancy of purpose, courage, and invention. He has trespassed nonetheless against the biblical injunction forbidding private revenge: 'Vengeance is mine, I will repay, saith the Lord'. Belleforest's nervousness emerges in his claim that 'if vengeance ever seemed to have any show of justice, it is then, when piety and affection constraineth us to remember our fathers unjustly murdered'. This is special and emotional pleading. He also brands Hamblet's uncle as a tyrant, and invokes the authority of both the Old Testament and ancient Athenian law for the idea that 'where the prince or country is interested, the desire of revenge cannot by any means (how small soever) bear the title of condemnation, but is rather commendable and worthy of praise'. This last argument, inappropriate to the saga world of the original Hamlet story, is also highly questionable in Christian terms. It was, however, essentially that of the 1584 Bond of Association, a document which thousands of pious and conservative Englishmen signed. In doing so, they pledged themselves 'to take the uttermost revenge' on all persons conspiring to overthrow Elizabeth I, and also upon any monarch succeeding to her throne by such means. As Helen Gardner has pointed out, this vow made before 'the eternal and ever-living God' violates one of the most explicit commandments received from that God. To ask how it was that so many of Elizabeth's subjects could put their names to such a document is to confront an enigma. It is also to penetrate to the heart of that contradiction in attitude towards private revenge upon which a number of plays in the period, including *Hamlet*, are built.

As a structural and thematic centre for tragedy, revenge has much to recommend it. It is not mere coincidence that the first truly great tragedies which have survived from ancient Athens and from Elizabethan England – the *Oresteia* of Aeschylus and *Hamlet* – should be revenge plays. It is unlikely that Shakespeare knew Aeschylus in any form, although he was certainly acquainted with the complex of tragic myths upon which the *Oresteia* draws. Analogies between Greek and Shakespearean tragedy are notoriously treacherous. There is, nonetheless, an uncanny resemblance between the opening of *Hamlet* and of the *Agamemnon* (458 B.C.), the first play in the Aeschylean trilogy. In both, an apprehensive and mysteriously dispirited sentinel, a watchman on the roof of a royal palace in which there is something obscurely but terribly wrong, scans the night sky for a portent. This sign, when it comes, serves to unleash the pent-up violence of the past upon the present. Both tragedies involve the shameful killing of a great king and the adultery of his consort. Both impose upon the son of the dead man a task which either way (if he fulfils it, or if he does not) will cost him dear. Like Hamlet after him, Agamemnon's son Orestes is both a passionate and a decidedly reluctant avenger: a man who needs to be spurred on at the last moment by the command of Apollo. His hesitation is entirely understandable. Although Hamlet may feel tempted to kill his mother as well as her lover (III.2.399–406), this is never, for him, an obligation. For Orestes it is, and the consequences are grim.

Most important of all, *Hamlet* and the *Oresteia* are alike in the way they juxtapose a primitive ethos in which personal retaliation for injuries is not only acceptable but mandatory, with a rival code in which 'civilized' considerations complicate what was once a relatively straightforward issue. Matricide is a terrible action, but the uncertainty of Aeschylus's hero also reflects the anguish of his position in a kind of no-man's-land, poised between the old, family-based law of blood vengeance and a new, essentially civic, order. The *Oresteia* is, among other things, about how an impersonal court of law, the Areopagus, finally superseded the claims of private revenge in historical Athens. It remembers a time, long before Aeschylus's birth, of transition and conflict between contradictory systems. But what Francis Bacon was later to call the 'wild justice' of personal vengeance can never really be legislated out of existence. When Euripides, in his tragedy *Orestes* (408 B.C.), retold the story of the revenge for Agamemnon, he imagined that the official court to try homicides which emerges only at the end of the *Oresteia* was already in existence at the time Agamemnon was killed. His Orestes has simply ignored the means of legal redress available to him, for reasons which have something to do with the kind of person he is, but also with the ineradicable belief of human beings that only the man who actually suffers in a situation has the right to deal with that situation: that the very impersonality which, in certain respects, constitutes the strength of criminal law renders that law emotionally inadequate.

In Elizabethan England, too, the conviction that retaliation for murder was solely the prerogative of the state and its legal institutions clashed with an irrational but powerful feeling that private individuals cannot be blamed for taking vengeance into their own hands, for ensuring that the punishment truly answers the crime. This response, arguably always latent in criminal cases, was likely to become especially forceful when, as sometimes happens, the law proved impotent or else too corrupt to pass sentence. As Bacon conceded, 'the most tolerable sort of revenge is for those wrongs which there is no law to punish; else a man's enemy is still before hand, and it is two for one'. Reasoning of this kind presumably gave the 1584 Bond of Association what shaky justification it had. It was also likely to generate clandestine sympathy for avengers who found themselves in the position of Shakespeare's Hamlet: unable to obtain legal justice for the premeditated killing of a parent, sibling, or child because of lack of circumstantial evidence and/or of a court prepared to deal with the culprit.

For Shakespeare at the turn of the century, when he addressed himself to the Hamlet story, contradiction and ambiguity of attitude towards revenge would have been part of the air he breathed. He must also have been familiar with a considerable body of literature, much of it dramatic, in which revenge was a central preoccupation and motif. Aeschylus, and possibly Euripides, were not known to him, but the revenge plays of Seneca certainly were. By 1600 there was a considerable accumulation of native English tragedies dominated by the idea of 'paying back' an injury or a death. Some of them were imitations of Seneca. In others, such as Sackville and Norton's *Gorboduc* (1562) or Pickering's *Horestes* (1567), classical elements mingled with an indigenous Morality play tradition. *Horestes* is especially interesting because its recasting of the archetypal story of Orestes' revenge for the murder of his father provides a virtual diagram of the Elizabethan perplexity about vengeance. Pickering was careful to personify Revenge as an agent of hell, a Vice figure tempting Horestes to an unnatural and forbidden deed. At the end, this villainous seducer is ritually cast out of an ordered society which has formed itself around Horestes as king. Revenge is clearly wrong. But the revenger himself can be exonerated. Horestes does not have to shoulder moral responsibility for his actions, let alone be punished for them.

Although it is certainly ingenious, Pickering's formula in *Horestes* was too special and evasive to be of use to other dramatists. It also happens to be fundamentally anti-tragic. Revenge for merely social injuries can and often does motivate comedy plots – as in *The Merchant of Venice, The Merry Wives of Windsor, Twelfth Night, The Tempest*, or Marston's *The Malcontent*. Retaliation for an actual death, however, is never a laughing matter. It is inherently tragic, not only because blood will have blood, but because of what it usually does to the life and person-ality of the virtuous avenger: a man cruelly isolated from society by the nature of the task he has undertaken. The revenger's position, necessarily secretive, solitary, and extreme, is conducive to introspection. It encourages meditation on the anomalies of justice, both human and divine, on past time, and on the value of life and human relationships. Many revengers become bitter satirists of the society from which they have severed themselves. Some slip into madness, not simply because the dramatist needed to spin out and delay the revenge action, but because the strains imposed upon them by the period of lonely preparation and waiting become psychologically intolerable. When Pickering (who probably had a political axe to grind) chose to use the Vice as a scapegoat and allow Horestes to emerge from his ordeal unscathed, he rejected tragedy. His response was unusual. For most Elizabethan dramatists, the attraction of revenge plots lay precisely in their tragic potentiality.

There is no evidence to suggest that Shakespeare had

read about Hamlet in Saxo, and only a remote possibility that he was familiar with Belleforest. His principal source, almost certainly, was a lost Elizabethan play – the so-called *Ur-Hamlet* – probably derived from Belleforest, and quite possibly the work of Thomas Kyd. Little is known about this work except that it was in existence by 1589, was still being performed in the 1590s, and that it added a ghost to the story. In 1596, Thomas Lodge referred to 'the ghost which cried so miserably at the theatre, like an oyster-wife, "Hamlet, revenge".' Further speculation as to the nature and quality of the *Ur-Hamlet* depends in part upon certain features of the 1603, or 'bad', quarto of Shakespeare's play. This first, unauthorized, edition incorporates material which seems to come from another and older tragedy on the same subject. The same may be true of a debased German text of 1710, *Der Bestrafte Brudermord*, or *Fratricide Punished*. This seems to have been a legacy from English actors performing a version of Shakespeare's *Hamlet* on the Continent early in the seventeenth century. Most important of all – especially if Kyd, as his contemporary Nashe implied, was the author of the *Ur-Hamlet* – there is the evidence supplied by Kyd's extant and immensely successful revenge play, *The Spanish Tragedy* (1587).

A brilliantly inventive piece of theatre, *The Spanish Tragedy* was still being remembered and paid the tribute of parody well into the Jacobean period. The play is remarkable on a number of counts, but not least for its prophetic awareness of the dimensions of revenge as a tragic theme. Although Kyd's hero Hieronymo is himself a magistrate, he cannot obtain justice for the murder of his only son. Slowly, he retreats from the corrupt daylight world of the Spanish court into introspection and darkness, a questioning of the meaning of existence, madness, and at last into a frenzy of retributive killing crowned by his own suicide. In 1601 someone (perhaps Ben Jonson) added to the original text a series of passages elaborating Hieronymo's psychological anguish and frustration. These impressive additions may or may not have been the work of a man who had seen Shakespeare's *Hamlet*. What matters is that they take up and extend themes and pre-occupations already present in Kyd's play. On a far more majestic scale, this may have been what Shakespeare did as well when he transformed another, and now lost, revenge play by Kyd into *The Tragedy of Hamlet, Prince of Denmark*. In doing so, he created the first tragedy for over two thousand years which invites and also can support comparison with the *Oresteia*.

*

Hamlet is, by a significant margin, the longest of Shakespeare's plays. The two authoritative texts, that of the second Quarto (1604) and of the 1623 Folio, differ from one another in a multitude of individual readings. Each text also contains a substantial amount of material not present in the other. In terms of stage performance, even the shorter Folio version remains formidably long. The entire tragedy, on the rare occasions when it is attempted in the theatre, is likely to constitute an endurance test for performers and audience alike. Probably Shakespeare knew at an early stage that what he was writing would inevitably require playhouse abbreviation. Even if Elizabethan actors delivered their lines at what would seem to us break-neck speed, it would still seem impossible during much of the year to fit an uncut *Hamlet* into the number of daylight playing hours available during an ordinary afternoon at the Globe.

The impractical length of *Hamlet*, together with the

existence of varying authoritative versions, suggests a protracted period of composition. Shakespeare may have added to the tragedy over a period of time. Certainly *Hamlet* has always registered as a mysteriously personal play: the sort of work an author composes primarily to please himself. For hundreds of years, readers have been recognizing themselves in the Prince of Denmark, as they do not in Lear, Othello, Brutus, Romeo, or Macbeth. But they have also been tempted to identify Shakespeare. T. S. Eliot went so far as to claim that the tragedy represented an unsuccessful attempt on Shakespeare's part to drag material deeply submerged in his own unconscious to light. Neither Eliot's idea that Hamlet is an artistic failure, nor his theory of the 'objective correlative', developed in an effort to characterize that failure, has worn particularly well. (Eliot's notion that Hamlet's emotional disturbance is insufficiently motivated by his circumstances has been brilliantly parodied by Tom Stoppard in the first act of *Rosencrantz and Guildenstern are Dead*.) Yet Hamlet himself, partly because of his obviously Oedipal situation, partly because he is a character about whom we are told so much yet understand so little, continues to be subjected to Freudian analysis. Such investigations tend to begin with the fiction and end with a diagnosis of the psychological problems of its creator. They have not proved very fruitful.

Like the *Essays* of Montaigne, with which it has other features in common, *Hamlet* marks a cultural and historical watershed: the moment when 'modern' man – sceptical, complex, self-lacerating, uncertain of his relationships with other people and with a possibly bogus world of heroic action – achieved artistic embodiment. This may or may not imply a self-portrait. What does seem clear is that the play occupied a special and important place in Shakespeare's artistic development: a new departure that was also a culmination. Certainly it seems more than any other play he wrote to provide a kind of retrospect on his previous work, gathering to itself many of the themes and preoccupations of the tragedies, histories, and comedies he had already produced. There is a sense in which they, quite as much as the *Ur-Hamlet*, provided a basis for Shakespeare's *Hamlet*.

Chronologically the first of what it has become customary to refer to as Shakespeare's 'great tragedies', *Hamlet* must have been written shortly after *Julius Caesar* (1599), another if very different revenge play. At two significant moments in *Hamlet* (I.1.113-20 and III.2.112-13) the killing of Caesar is remembered. *Julius Caesar* had contained a vengeful ghost. It also adumbrated, existing between Caesar and his protégé Brutus (and, in another form, between Caesar and Mark Antony), a troubled father–son relationship which, for some reason, seems to have occupied Shakespeare's imagination to a considerable extent around the turn of the century. (His own father died in September 1601.) This is a theme worked out in the second sequence of English histories as well, by way of Henry IV, Northumberland, and Falstaff, and their 'sons' Hotspur and Prince Hal. *Hamlet* complicates the motif by directing attention to three linked father-and-son pairs: old Hamlet and the prince who has inherited his name but not his kingdom, old Fortinbras and a son (again a namesake) whose situation parallels that of Hamlet but whose character is very different, Polonius and Laertes. All three fathers die by violence. All three sons feel it incumbent upon them to exact a revenge, but the response of each to his task is wholly individual.

Although the character of Brutus has attracted what is perhaps a disproportionate amount of attention, *Julius*

Caesar might plausibly be sub-titled 'or The Revenge of Mark Antony'. It seems to have been the third tragedy Shakespeare wrote, at least according to the groupings established by Heminges and Condell in the first Folio. Its two predecessors, *Titus Andronicus* and *Romeo and Juliet*, were also revenge plays. In the early *Titus Andronicus* (*c.* 1594) Shakespeare had experimented successfully with the type of play made popular by Kyd: classicizing, rhetorical, beautifully patterned in terms of stage action, and coolly horrible. Titus himself, a father with two dead sons and a raped and mutilated daughter to avenge, produces many of the reactions of Hieronymo. He demands justice both from men and from the gods, and gets no response from either. Genuinely and incapacitatingly deranged during much of Acts III and IV, he is essentially mad in craft at the end, when he takes advantage of a 'play' devised by his enemy Tamora and her children (they visit him disguised as characters called Revenge, Rapine, and Murder) to destroy his persecutors at the cost of his own life. *Romeo and Juliet* (1595) may seem to push the revenge theme, in the form of the senseless vendetta between the Montagues and the Capulets, into the background. It is, nonetheless, the cause of the tragedy. The exceptional love which unites the children of the two warring houses does what all the threats and legislation of Verona's prince have failed to accomplish. It begins by over-riding Romeo's and Juliet's hereditary responses to incidents in the feud. Then, by way of their tragic fate, a calamity which accuses Montagues and Capulets alike, it puts an end to what Greek dramatists liked to describe as the virtually unbreakable chain of violence, retribution, and fresh violence in the city.

These three early revenge plays obviously prepared the way for Shakespeare's full-scale consideration of the revenge dilemma in *Hamlet*. But the English histories that he was writing throughout the 1590s also seem to have left their mark. The contrast between the reign of Richard Coeur-de-Lion and his younger brother John, between Richard II and his pragmatic successor Henry IV, or between Hotspur and the Machiavellian Prince John of Gaultree Forest, reappears in the distinction drawn between the vanished, chivalric world of the elder Hamlet and Fortinbras and the hard-headed, unglamorous court of Claudius. In the Denmark to which Prince Hamlet returns from his studies in Wittenberg, hired Swiss mercenaries guard a king more renowned for his drinking exploits than for any heroic achievement. International disputes are no longer settled by single combat but through the medium of ambassadors. Even the gentlemanly exercise of fencing (itself a trivialization of something the old Hamlet had done in earnest) is brushed aside by the new King as an accomplishment 'Of the unworthiest siege ... A very riband in the cap of youth' (IV.7.74–6).

At the end of *Richard II* (1595), Shakespeare had made it apparent that the medieval world of heraldry, honour, gages, oaths, and ceremonial combat within which the action began was now obsolete and even faintly absurd. Prince Hal's threat to appear in the lists at Oxford wearing a whore's glove as a favour may scandalize his father: it reflects his characteristically shrewd understanding of the change of climate in the new reign. In *Hamlet* too the new reigns in Norway and Denmark appear to have closed the door on a heroic past. Despite Ophelia's encomium on his 'courtier's, soldier's, scholar's, eye, tongue, sword' (III.1.152), the Prince himself, as he ruefully admits, is no Hercules (I.2.153). But his father apparently was.

There is more than mere filial loyalty and pride in Hamlet's comparison of the former King to Mars and Hyperion, or his sad recognition that 'I shall not look upon his like again' (I.2.188). For other people as well, the dead Hamlet is already becoming a legendary and distant figure. In *Julius Caesar* Antony began the myth-ologizing of the dead conqueror by identifying a mantle as the one he put on, new, 'on a summer's evening in his tent, | That day he overcame the Nervii' (III.2.173-4). Horatio creates the same kind of icon, a curious com-bination of the epic and the minutely personal, when he recalls the frown of the warrior king long ago when, 'in an angry parle' (I.1.62), he smote his weighted battle-axe on the ice.

Although he may seem to approximate to this vanished heroic past more closely than Claudius, Hamlet, or his own 'impotent and bedrid' uncle (I.2.29), young Fortin-bras is really no substitute for it. The son of the king killed by Hamlet's father in single combat, he seems to have been nudged aside from the succession in Norway much as Hamlet has in Denmark (although, presumably, he was younger than Hamlet at the time). At the be-ginning of the play, Fortinbras has 'Sharked up' (I.1.98) a band of lawless and irregular soldiers. He hopes to recover by force the disputed lands his father surrendered to Denmark by agreement, as a result of his defeat. Significantly, young Fortinbras has waited for the death of King Hamlet before making this attempt. When Clau-dius's ambassadors complain to old Norway, Fortinbras, rebuked like a naughty boy, has to abandon his project. To keep him out of mischief, his uncle then gives him an annuity of three thousand crowns and packs him off to harass the unfortunate Poles – who seem to have done nothing whatever to provoke such hostility. The enterprise itself, as one of Fortinbras's own captains volunteers, is completely pointless:

> We go to gain a little patch of ground
> That hath in it no profit but the name.
> To pay five ducats, five, I would not farm it;
> Nor will it yield to Norway or the Pole
> A ranker rate, should it be sold in fee.   IV.4.18–22

It is characteristic of Hamlet that he should punish himself by transforming Fortinbras's activities into something they are not, and the Norwegian prince he is fated never to meet into a 'spirit, with divine ambition puffed' (IV.4.49). In his dialogue with the Norwegian captain only seconds before, Hamlet had matched the soldier's cynicism with his own. He assessed the Polish expedition then, quite accurately, as the symptom of a disease: 'th'imposthume of much wealth and peace, | That inward breaks, and shows no cause without | Why the man dies' (IV.4.27–9). Only when he is left alone does he invent a Fortinbras who is a type of honour, a man whose ability to find quarrel in a straw rebukes his own inaction. The exercise is dubious, but also familiar. Hamlet did something like this in Act II, with the Player whose tears for a purely fictional Hecuba seemed to inform against him as the procrastinating son of an actual murdered father. Fortinbras, although doubtless competent enough to pick up the pieces in Denmark after the final holocaust, is neither the idealized Renaissance prince of Hamlet's panegyric, nor a genuine reincarnation of the lost heroic past. He stands to the world of Hamlet's father much as the bastard Faulconbridge had to that of Coeur-de-Lion, the dead crusader king in *King John*. A kind of Henry V, he too conceals hard-headed opportunism beneath the chivalric surface of a military adventure which, in large measure, represents a politic distraction.

Behind *Hamlet* there lie, not only three revenge plays and the English histories, but at least nine of Shakespeare's comedies. *Twelfth Night* (1600), with its revenge sub-plot involving Malvolio, seems to have been composed at about the same time as *Hamlet*. *All's Well That Ends Well* (*c.* 1602?) and *Measure For Measure* (1604) probably succeeded it. The other nine plays which critics agree to call comedies (as opposed to 'romances') were all written before *Hamlet*, and their legacy can be felt in that play to an extent unmatched in the later tragedies. On the most basic level, *Hamlet* contains many more comic characters and episodes than *Othello*, *Lear*, *Macbeth*, and their successors. The elder statesman Polonius, garrulous, self-important, and fussy, is funny in a way that makes his death behind the arras doubly shocking: this is not the kind of fate that normally overtakes characters of his type. Rosencrantz and Guildenstern, Osrick, and the gravedigger are all creators of a somewhat sinister comedy, while Hamlet himself seems to be the only one of Shakespeare's tragic protagonists (apart from Cleopatra and her Antony) who possesses – and demonstrates – a sense of humour. Like the witty characters of the comedies, he likes to play games with language, to parody other characters' verbal styles, and he has a predilection for puns, bawdy double entendres, and sophisticated badinage which links him with figures like Petruchio, Berowne, Benedick, or even Touchstone and Feste.

Hamlet's situation at the beginning of the tragedy seems, to the other members of Claudius's court, to be like that of the Countess Olivia at the opening of *Twelfth Night*. Wilfully persisting in what Claudius denigrates as 'obstinate condolement', 'unmanly grief' (I.2.93–4), he refuses to bury the memory of his dead father. Olivia had done exactly this when she imposed seven years of deprivation and mourning upon herself in the effort to keep a dead brother's love 'fresh | And lasting, in her sad remembrance' (I.1.32–3). The impulse itself is not foolish or contemptible (Henry James handled it with great poignance and sensitivity in his story *The Altar of the Dead*), but it is something to which comedy, whether that of *Twelfth Night* or Chapman's *The Widow's Tears* (1605), has always been a mortal foe. Comedy insists that life must go on, that the dead must be forgotten, and the means is always the same: sexual love. In comic terms, it is quite right – although it is also a little sad – that Cesario/Sebastian should oust the dead brother from his place in Olivia's heart. The process itself is inevitably somewhat shaming and undignified (comedy admits this), but there is never any doubt as to its fundamental rightness and excusability.

Apart from *Timon of Athens*, where the issue never arises, and *Romeo and Juliet*, where, ironically, it precipitates the catastrophe, *Hamlet* is the only Shakespearian tragedy whose hero is unmarried and eligible. The play advances comedy's usual solution in the form of Polonius's daughter, Ophelia. Ophelia dutifully informs her father that the Prince has 'of late made many tenders | Of his affection to me' (I.3.99–100). The phrase 'of late' can only mean since the death of the old King and Hamlet's return from Wittenberg. During this period of about a month, he has written her love letters, given her presents, and tried to use her youth and beauty as a way of surmounting death and loss. The attempt has failed, for a number of reasons. In the first place, although her situation is potentially that of a comedy heroine, Ophelia herself is no Julia, Rosalind, Portia, or Helena – let alone a Juliet or a Desdemona. Naive, passive, and dependent, she accepts without demur what her father has to say about Hamlet's intentions, and her brother Laertes's stress on disparity of rank. She is wrong to do so, not only because, as Gertrude later reveals (V.1.240), there would in fact have been no objection to this alliance, but because comedy heroines worth their salt have always remembered that King Cophetua married the beggar maid. Even more important, her childish obedience to her family prevents her from giving Hamlet the kind of loyalty which even Miranda in *The Tempest* – who has never seen a man except her father – instantly gives young Ferdinand. Miranda disobeys Prospero and seeks Ferdinand out. Ophelia, by contrast, docilely returns the Prince's letters and refuses to speak to him. When a distracted Hamlet finally forces his way into her presence, she apparently sits staring at him in terrified silence, and then runs immediately to tell Polonius. In the third act she will allow herself, without asking any questions, to be used as a pawn against him.

Exactly why Hamlet should have intruded upon Ophelia in her closet, and paraded before her all the conventional symptoms of love melancholy, is one of the unresolved problems of the play. It is linked to the question of his madness: is his lunacy real, like that of Titus and Kyd's Hieronymo, feigned, or a mixture of the two? If, however, his appearance did constitute some kind of appeal, Ophelia was unable to rise to it. Later, when she is loosed to Hamlet by pre-arrangement in the lobby, she can think of nothing better to do than to blame him for a separation which she and her family have enforced. With feeble coquetry, she insists upon returning his love tokens: 'For to the noble mind | Rich gifts wax poor when givers prove unkind' (III.1.100–101). The trite little couplet is recognizably Polonian. It is also rather baffling: what unkindness there has been in this relationship so far has certainly not emanated from Hamlet. It is true that he is about to even the account, violently, but a modicum of exasperation might well be forgiven him.

When her father is killed, and hastily interred, Ophelia's quiet world crumbles around her. Unable to endure her situation, even for the time it takes Laertes to hasten back from France, she disintegrates into a plangent and gentle madness. Her involuntary disclosure, at this point, that she has secretly committed to memory the words of a rude song about how young men behave themselves on St Valentine's day (IV.5.48–67) seems especially pathetic. It offers a sad testimony to her hidden curiosity about precisely those areas of adult sexuality from which Polonius would protect her – not to mention her brother, who is convinced that 'The chariest maid is prodigal enough | If she unmask her beauty to the moon' (I.3.36–7). Characteristically, when Ophelia falls into the stream by accident, she makes no attempt to cry out for help, or save herself: she simply yields to the current, as she has always done in her life. This is why both the Clowns and holy Church suspect suicide. Long before that happens, Hamlet has outgrown his youthful attachment, much as he learns to put away the adolescent jests and persiflage of his university days. Ophelia's death shocks him, briefly, but it seems significant that he can respond to it by producing a wild parody of Laertes's histrionic grief: he does not offer her anything of his own, nor does he mention her again.

Even if the love between Ophelia and Hamlet had been made of stronger stuff, and he had not spoken with the Ghost, another powerful factor in the play must have militated against comedy's normal solution for cases of obstinate sorrow. This, of course, is the fact that Gertrude herself, after only one month of widowhood, has already embraced that solution with a precipitant haste that degrades comedy's process of natural healing to ugly farce: creating that askew and distorted face which Claudius smoothly conjures up, with one laughing and one weeping eye, 'With mirth in funeral and with dirge in marriage' (I.2.12). Gertrude's plea to her son to abandon his black clothes and his dejection –

> Do not for ever with thy vailèd lids
> Seek for thy noble father in the dust.
> Thou knowest 'tis common. All that lives must die,
> Passing through nature to eternity –   I.2.70–73

is, in itself, the counsel of comedy and, as such, un-impeachable. Unfortunately, she has contaminated it, not only by the unseemly and callous speed of her remarriage, but because of the suggestions both of incest and of adultery implicit in her union with Claudius. Hamlet is presumably thinking of Ophelia when he accuses his mother of having done something that 'takes off the rose | From the fair forehead of an innocent love | And sets a blister there' (III.4.43–5). For him, the words 'frailty' and 'woman' have become synonymous (I.2.146). In this equation, the wretched Ophelia inevitably comes to bear the burden of Gertrude's inadequacies, as well as her own.

*

Shakespeare had often, in the plays he wrote before *Hamlet*, considered the nature of poetry, the imagination, and the actor's art. *Love's Labour's Lost* and *A Midsummer Night's Dream* are both self-conscious in this way. In *Julius Caesar* the actors who played Brutus and Cassius were made to speculate in mock innocence how the 'lofty scene' of Caesar's murder might appear on the stage 'In states unborn, and accents yet unknown' (III.1.111–16). *Hamlet*, however, is unique in the density and pervasiveness of its theatrical self-reference. The glaringly topical and, in some ways, uncharacteristic passage about the 'little eyases' and the 1601 War of the Theatres which embroiled the adult companies with the children's troupes (II.2.338–61) is acceptable in this play as it would not be in another precisely because *Hamlet* as a whole is so concerned to question and cross the boundaries which normally separate dramatic representation from real life.

Those tragedians of the city who arrive so opportunely at Elsinore in Act II provide a focus for extended disquisitions upon acting, and for two inset plays. Kyd's *Spanish Tragedy* had also relied upon plays within the play, although the actors there were all amateurs. There seems no way of knowing whether the travelling players were present in the *Ur-Hamlet*, or whether they derive from the troupe which so perplexed Christopher Sly in Shakespeare's own early comedy *The Taming of the Shrew* (*c.* 1594). The stage imagery of *Hamlet*, however, exists independently of the professional actors who appear in Acts II and III. It is there from the beginning, and it remains important in the final movement of the tragedy. The ghost of Hamlet's father comes in the 'shape' or 'form' of the buried majesty of Denmark, as though he were an actor in a doubtful part. Alarmingly, this may be exactly what he is: an agent of hell impersonating the dead King. Hamlet himself, after having contemptuously repudiated those 'actions that a man might play' on his first appearance (I.2.84), confronts this ambiguous ghost, decides that henceforth he will play the part of madman, and proceeds to devise a lethal little dramatic entertainment in which to 'catch the conscience of the King'

(II.2.603). Later, on the voyage to England, Rosencrantz and Guildenstern are sent to death by way of a stratagem which Hamlet can identify as that of a revenge tragedy (V.2.29–31). He is conscious again of the playlike character of events when, at the very end, he addresses the silent and horrified court of Denmark as 'mutes or audience to this act' (V.2.329).

There are a number of reasons why the Prince should deal obsessively in images of the theatre, and why the chance visit of some strolling players should have consequences so far-reaching. Polonius, it seems, like many an Elizabethan schoolboy, was an amateur actor in his youth. He played Julius Caesar and, prophetically, was stabbed to death in the Capitol. Hamlet is a devotee of the newer, professional stage. As a university student in Wittenberg, he memorized speeches from his favourite plays. He can give a creditable recitation, without book, of Aeneas's speech to Dido, addresses the First Player familiarly as 'old friend' (II.2.421), and chaffs the company's youngest actor because he is demonstrably outgrowing his childish line in female parts. A connoisseur as it seems of revenge plays, well acquainted with their conventions and character types, Hamlet is adept at parodying the melodramatic excesses of the genre: 'Come; the croaking raven doth bellow for revenge' (III.2.262–3). It is only natural, when he finds himself swept against his will into a real-life revenge action, that he should remember his fictional experience of such situations, and turn to the stage for assistance. Illusions perhaps can be penetrated by counter-illusions. For Hamlet, the theatre becomes a means of deciphering a treacherous world in which Claudius can 'smile, and smile, and be a villain' (I.5.108), and everyone, except Horatio, may be acting a part.

When the First Player weeps real tears for the fictional

sorrows of Hecuba, Hamlet is reminded by them of how thin the dividing line can be between life and art. The speech for which he has asked, a rhetorical and highly wrought account of Pyrrhus's vengeance upon Priam for the death of Pyrrhus's father Achilles, comments on Hamlet's immediate situation in ways that go beyond a common concern with the slaying of fathers. Although he has raged like a tiger through the burning streets of Troy, Pyrrhus hesitates strangely before letting his sword fall on the defenceless old man before him: 'So as a painted tyrant Pyrrhus stood, | And like a neutral to his will and matter | Did nothing' (II.2.478–80). Hamlet will later lecture the players on the importance of a naturalistic acting style, one capable of showing 'virtue her own feature, scorn her own image, and the very age and body of the time his form and pressure' (III.2.22–4). His strictures are obviously governed to some extent by anxiety lest *The Murder of Gonzago*, in performance, prove too bombastic and artificial to probe Claudius's guilt. The aesthetic principle itself, however, is a Renaissance commonplace – and essentially didactic. Sir Philip Sidney had justified comedy and tragedy in his *Apology for Poetry* (before 1586) in similar terms. What Hamlet does not reveal to the players is his private, and more unorthodox, understanding of how art may acquire a temporary and unpredictable dominion over life: how dramatic fictions can comment upon the situations in which individual members of the audience find themselves in ways far more complex and disturbing than any mere exemplary tale.

The momentary indecision of Pyrrhus, a vividly realized fact, in itself neither bad nor good, presents Hamlet with an image of his own, mysterious inactivity. Then, in the next instant, Pyrrhus decides. Priam falls, and Hecuba runs wild in a tragic grief which, unlike that of Gertrude, cannot be doubted or assuaged. For Hamlet, the speech has acquired new and alarming resonances since he heard it last, back in that vanished world of his university studies, when old Hamlet was still alive, and Gertrude apparently innocent. In Philip Sidney's sonnet sequence *Astrophil and Stella*, Astrophil relates how Stella, although unmoved by her lover's real anguish, has wept bitterly over a fable 'of lovers never known' and non-existent. He concludes wryly by imploring her to respond to him as though he were a character in a tragedy: 'I am not I: pity the tale of me' (Sonnet XLV). Like Astrophil, Hamlet broods on the complex and disturbing ways in which art and life may invade each other's territory. Because he himself has become 'the son of a dear father murdered' (II.2.581), the familiar account of Pyrrhus's revenge upon Priam suddenly looks different. The speech becomes an uncanny gloss on his own situation. The emotion it generates is compounded when he notices how, as with Stella, a purely fictional sorrow has brought real tears into the eyes of the First Player. These inexplicable and disproportionate tears seem to accuse Hamlet, by comparison, of producing only a meagre response to his father's actual murder. He stands condemned, in his own eyes, as 'a rogue and peasant slave' (II.2.547). But they also remind him of related, and potentially useful, ways in which art and life can exchange places.

Guilty creatures sitting at a play, so he has heard, have sometimes been forced to confess their hidden crimes through the power of theatrical suggestion. This might happen to Claudius. If it did, Hamlet would have something more substantial than a mere ghost story on which to base his revenge. Indeed, the killing of Claudius would transform itself from a wild and dubious thing to a judicial and open necessity. Accordingly, Hamlet arranges for a special performance of *The Murder of Gonzago*, another favourite from his theatre-going past that he remembers now with a difference. Unfortunately, although this tragedy shadows the facts of the situation at Elsinore more closely than Aeneas's tale to Dido, its effect upon Claudius and his court is inconclusive. This, of course, is the problem with using works of art as didactic instruments: unless they are very simple indeed, their interpretation must be conditioned to a considerable extent by the personal experience and predilections of the audience. Polonius, Rosencrantz, Guildenstern, and the city actors had all listened with Hamlet to the tale of Priam's slaughter. But it was only for the Prince that Hecuba, the 'mobled Queen' whose husband lies murdered, both was and was not Gertrude, the cruel Pyrrhus an avatar of Claudius the fratricide, and Pyrrhus's indecision (strangely) Hamlet's own. *The Mousetrap* turns out to be similarly private and enigmatic.

There is no way of knowing how the original Claudius at the Globe spoke the crucial line 'Give me some light. Away!' (III.2.278) and broke up the inset play. Subsequent actors have run the gamut between hysteria and controlled disgust. Hamlet announces, after the King and Queen have retired, that he would 'take the ghost's word for a thousand pound' (III.2.295-6), but even Horatio – who has seen the Ghost, and been admitted into Hamlet's confidence – is non-committal in response to the Prince's excited appeals. He offers no corroboration that the King's guilt has indeed unkennelled itself. For the rest of the Danish court, it seems only that this exasperating and tactless young man has carried resentment at his mother's second marriage to a socially unpardonable extreme. Given that Lucianus, the villain and poisoner of *The*

Murder of Gonzago, is the nephew, not the brother, of the man he kills, the play is likely to be regarded by an ignorant court (and in some measure even by Claudius himself) as Hamlet's scandalous threat to the life of an innocent and long-suffering uncle.

Claudius, of course, is guilty. The moral blow registered in that heart-struck aside earlier in the act, a reaction to Polonius's comment upon man's ability to 'sugar o'er | The devil' (III.1.48-9), is exacerbated by this mysterious re-enactment of his crime. Left alone afterwards, he struggles vainly to repent and pray. It is important, however, to remember that both the King's incriminating aside and his subsequent soliloquy in III.3 are available only to the theatre audience: not until Hamlet unseals the royal commission entrusted to Rosencrantz and Guildenstern, on the voyage to England, does he or anybody else in the play have positive proof of his uncle's villainy. This is the evidence which finally persuades Horatio to exclaim: 'Why, what a king is this!' (V.2.62). But for the greater part of the tragedy Hamlet possesses only the word of a possibly unreliable ghost, plus his own instinctive dislike of Gertrude's second husband, as a basis for revenge. It is not much justification for suddenly stabbing a man in the back as he kneels at his devotions. Hamlet's excuse for sparing the King at prayers – that Claudius's soul, released under such pious circumstances, would be likely to go straight to heaven – is characteristically devious and opaque. As with his encomium later on Fortinbras, it is difficult to believe that he really means what he says, as opposed to concocting the argument as a means of rationalizing his perfectly natural hesitation. It is true that Brutus, in *Julius Caesar*, persuaded himself to kill a head of state on similarly intangible and slippery evidence – but, significantly, the decision there was a mistake.

Hamlet has pursued his university studies in Wittenberg, the city where Luther nailed his ninety-five heretical theses to the church door. His father's ghost, however comes from a surprisingly detailed and specific Catholic purgatory. Deprived by Claudius of the last rites of the Church, 'Unhouseled, disappointed, unaneled' (I.5.77), it haunts the earth by night and fasts in fire during the day until the sins committed during its lifetime have been 'burnt and purged away' (I.5.13). Just exactly what this supposedly penitent and suffering spirit is doing when it enjoins its only son to undertake a revenge action for which the orthodox theological punishment would be not purgatory, but an eternity of hell, never becomes clear in the play. All four of the characters who actually see the Ghost (Hamlet, Horatio, Barnardo, and Marcellus) have doubts as to its purpose and credentials. Hamlet himself is intelligently aware that demons can assume pleasing shapes, that the Ghost may be an infernal tempter playing upon his depression and his loathing of Claudius in order to lead him into mortal sin. During the oath-taking which concludes Act I, he shouts to it under the stage with a hysterical levity more appropriate to a nervous conjurer than to a bereaved son miraculously in touch with his father beyond the grave. Confronting the apparition in the Queen's closet, on the other hand, Hamlet is reverent and tender. Yet neither he nor Horatio ever formulates the question which seems implicit in the situation: if the Ghost really is the repentant soul it claims to be, how can it ask the Prince to usurp God's prerogative and kill Claudius?

Critics have sometimes argued that the inconsistency between the Ghost's account of its eschatological state and its very un-Christian injunction to Hamlet confirms its diabolic origin. But this reading seems untrue to the complexity of the play. It does not, in any case, explain why Hamlet – for whom the situation of 'a father killed, a mother stained' (IV.4.57) prompts the most extraordinary, various, and far-reaching series of intellectual speculations – never articulates this particular, and glaring, problem. Perplexingly, he altogether avoids the issue of God's prohibition of revenge, although he has a good deal to say about what there may be in the afterlife, and about the Christian sanction against suicide. This silence seems odd in a play where even the unreflective Laertes admits that to exact revenge for a father's death is to 'dare damnation' (IV.5.135). But it must be intentional. In *The Spanish Tragedy* Hieronymo had explicitly weighed the biblical text forbidding private revenge against his own extremity and frustration before deciding to act. There is no way of telling how the issue was handled in the *Ur-Hamlet*. It seems likely, however, on the evidence of other Elizabethan revenge plays, that the original Prince Hamlet paid at least some attention to the question. After all, even in the non-Christian Rome of *Titus Andronicus*, in an alien society where human sacrifice appears to be accepted quite as a matter of course by everyone except the victim himself and his mother, the idea that vengeance belongs to heaven and that Titus ought to wait patiently for divine retribution was painstakingly expressed (IV.1.129–30).

In general, it is true of revenge tragedy as a form that the virtuous revenger (as opposed to villainous Machiavels like Iago or Marlowe's Barabas) attracts audience sympathy up to the point at which he resolves his predicament and actually kills. A sense of dissociation then supplants the earlier feeling of involvement. This distancing of audience from hero springs from the fact that the avenger, however sorely tried in the earlier sections of the play, almost inevitably becomes the deed's creature in accomplishing his vengeance. He may turn bloodthirsty and berserk, like Hieronymo and Titus. Or, like Vindice in Tourneur's (or Middleton's) *The Revenger's Tragedy* (1606), he may metamorphose slowly into a man who takes a suspect delight in the mechanics of murder. Even in *Antonio's Revenge* (1600), a tragedy singularly tolerant of blood vengeance, Marston makes it plain at the end that his hero has become so warped and abnormal that he cannot continue to live in the very society his vengeance has helped to purge. Only in Shakespeare's *Hamlet* does the audience retain sympathy for the hero from beginning to end. This was no mean dramaturgical feat, considering that Hamlet is responsible, either directly or indirectly, for the deaths of at least five other characters in the tragedy before he finally kills Claudius.

There is no equivalent in Shakespeare's play to that moment characteristic of other revenge tragedies when we realize that the hero ought now to turn back, committing his cause to God, to the state, or to a political revolution like the one Titus's son Lucius plans to unleash upon Rome. As one of the senators in *Timon of Athens* (1607) puts it, 'To revenge is no valour, but to bear' (III.5.40). This position will be vindicated in the end, regardless of the provocation, or the seemingly intolerable nature of the revenger's situation. Elizabethan dramatists enlisted powerful emotional support for the virtuous avenger, up to a point, but they almost invariably turned on him in Act V. In doing so, they acknowledged that the man who persists and actually does the deed must be contaminated by it, that he cannot really be approved of or saved. It was an ingenious way of dealing with the contemporary ambiguity of attitude towards private revenge. Shakespeare adopted it himself in *Titus Andronicus*. *Hamlet*, however, creates a complex variation on the pattern, deliberately shifting attention away from an expected centre.

At the heart of *Hamlet* lie a number of riddling and important silences. The nature of the Ghost remains impenetrable. The Christian prohibition of revenge is never explicitly discussed. The Ghost's injunction 'Taint not thy mind' (I.5.85) resounds oddly, given that this, almost by definition, is what Elizabethan revengers always do. Arguably, Hamlet's mind was already tainted by melancholy and suspicion even before he met the Ghost and shouldered the burden of revenge. Ophelia's ideal Renaissance prince and courtier died with old Hamlet, and with Gertrude's remarriage. His subsequent destructiveness, however, is not that of the usual revenge hero obsessed and coarsened by his decision to kill. It derives, instead, from Hamlet's inability either to abandon the idea of revenge upon Claudius, or to carry it out. This dilemma is less easy to define than that of Aeschylus's Orestes, in part because the metaphysical structure of Shakespeare's play is so deliberately ambiguous, but it is as tragically irresolvable. For reasons which both Shakespeare and Hamlet himself refuse to make explicit, but about which they throw out a number of hints, the Prince cannot act in the brutal, uncomplicated way Amleth and Hamblet had acted in the older versions of the story. He is not that kind of person. But it is also impossible for him to ignore the Ghost's command and, like the exemplary but inhuman hero of Tourneur's *The Atheist's Tragedy, or the Honest Man's Revenge* (1609), simply sit still. He is not that kind of character either. Hamlet's problem is handed to the theatre audience shorn of any implied authorial solution, any intimation as to what the hero *ought* to have done.

Although critics have often pretended otherwise, the

Prince of Denmark is almost the only one of Shakespeare's tragic protagonists to whom it is impossible to give advice. The situation with the others is relatively clear-cut, or at least it appears to be so from the special vantage-point of the study or the theatre. Titus ought to have waited until Lucius returned to Rome with his army. Romeo ought not to have sought out the apothecary with such haste. Brutus and Macbeth ought not to have killed. Othello should not have listened to Iago, Lear should never have banished Cordelia, Coriolanus ought to have trusted his instincts and refused to stand for consul, and Timon would have been saved by heeding his steward. Only the Antony of *Antony and Cleopatra* resembles Hamlet, his fellow-humorist, in that no counsel given to this man so complexly torn between the rival worlds of Rome and Egypt could be other than an impertinence. Isolated actions may invite censure – Antony's flight from Actium, Hamlet's impulsive killing of Polonius – but even they are made difficult through their dependence upon a central situation in which there is no right course of action. Antony cannot opt for either Rome or Egypt without stifling a positive and vital half of himself. Even so, Hamlet can neither kill Claudius in cold blood nor decide to ignore his father's injunction without violating something in his innermost nature. The dilemma which torments both men is not really of their own making. Worse, it admits of no positive solution. To step either to the left or to the right is commit an act of culpable self-maiming. Under circumstances like these, attempts to temporize are not only understandable but inevitable. They are also doomed. Ultimately, the situation forbids compromise, either psychologically or in terms of external pressures.

Claudius has prevented Hamlet from succeeding to the throne of Denmark, contracted a scandalous marriage with Hamlet's mother, and accomplished both these things through the secret murder of the father Hamlet loved. By insisting that the Prince remain at court, rather than returning to university at Wittenberg, he forces him to confront these enormities daily. The situation is one that no realistically conceived human being, however pious and right-thinking, could possibly tolerate. Hamlet himself makes it plain throughout that he is baffled and exasperated by his inability to behave like the revenge heroes of the plays he has seen. He accuses himself of being a peasant, a coward, an unnatural and unfeeling son. In Act IV, he confesses despairingly that

> *I do not know*
> *Why yet I live to say 'This thing's to do',*
> *Sith I have cause, and will, and strength, and means*
> *To do't.*   IV.4.43–6

In the end, Hamlet goads himself into cutting Claudius down in a moment of fury, much as he killed Polonius, that intrusive but scarcely vicious meddler, two acts before. By this point in the play, Hamlet not only has multiple proof of the King's guilt, he knows that he himself is dying. But had Claudius not taken the initiative by arranging the treacherous fencing match, would Hamlet ever have accomplished his revenge? Although he asks Horatio at the beginning of Act V whether it would not be 'perfect conscience' to kill such a king, and damnation to spare him (V.2.67), he puts forward no plan of action. His references in this very scene to the 'divinity that shapes our ends', determining even the sparrow's fall, are strikingly fatalistic. They scarcely suggest that he has committed

39

himself now to the kind of active course embraced with such ease by Laertes, in which 'a man's life's no more than to say "one" ' (V.2.74).

Hamlet never says why it is that he should remain unable to do the obvious: collect his friends about him, confront Claudius, accuse him, and then draw his sword and run him through. It is true that, until Act IV, he lacks real evidence of his uncle's villainy. This fact matters more than some commentators on the play have allowed. But it cannot be the whole explanation for Hamlet's delay, if only because Hamlet's tortured self-accusations make it clear that it is not. His four major soliloquies after encountering the Ghost, complex and probing though they are, are much more evasive as delineations of his perplexity and state of mind than the equivalent speeches of an Othello or a Macbeth. Meditations generated by a central but mysteriously inexpressible problem, they seem to describe circles around that problem without ever confronting it head-on. There are areas in which Hamlet's reason either cannot or refuses to operate, inhibiting factors more potent than mere doubt of the Ghost's veracity. Because he never articulates them even to himself, the audience is impelled to draw conclusions – necessarily tentative – from his speech and behaviour, as though he were not a dramatic character but someone known in real life.

Acting on impulse, it seems, Hamlet can kill an invisible foe like Polonius. He can annihilate Rosencrantz and Guildenstern, at even greater distance, by signing a paper. This, as Hamlet himself recognizes, is the moment when his behaviour approximates most closely to that of the conventional stage revenger. (His judicious friend Horatio, significantly, is shaken when he learns how 'Guildenstern and Rosencrantz go to't': V.2.56.) What the Prince apparently cannot do is the thing Hieronymo, Titus, Antonio, Vindice, and the other revenge protagonists all manage before the end. He cannot look at the face of an individual human being, however criminal, and then deliberately take his life. At least two reasons for this redeeming inability are suggested in the play. It is clear that for Hamlet a man's life – even that of a 'satyr', a 'vice of kings' like Claudius – is something equivocal and strange, a riddling compound of the bestial and angelic. However dutifully he may try to work himself into a more primitive state of mind, as soon as he thinks about it, murder becomes much more 'than to say "one"'. Currents of intention turn awry and lose the name of action. Secondly, Hamlet is too intelligent to be able to deceive himself into Laertes's belief that revenge can constitute a real answer, a meaningful redress of the situation. Stabbing Claudius might relieve his feelings temporarily and gratify the Ghost. It cannot bring back the past: restore old Hamlet, the warrior king, to life, render Gertrude innocent again, or cancel out the effects of what the Prince describes bitterly as 'Excitements of my reason and my blood' (IV.4.58). Claudius has changed Hamlet's world irretrievably. Killing him can never reanimate what he has destroyed. Hamlet knows this, and the knowledge exposes the fundamental futility of the revenge code.

Experienced theatre-goer though he is, Hamlet finds that in real life he cannot reduce his own complexity and awareness to that of the conventional stage revenger. Nor can he make himself think that the world would be any less of an unweeded garden, stale, flat, and unprofitable, if he did. This is why he ends up killing Claudius almost accidentally. It is also why, unlike Hieronymo, Titus, Antonio, or Vindice, he never becomes an object of condescension, alienated from the theatre audience. Claudius interrupts *The Murder of Gonzago* in the middle of Act I, before the revenge for the Player-King – the action which must have occupied the bulk of the inset play – can begin. We are told, however, that like Gertrude and the old Hamlet, the Player-King and Queen have been married for some thirty years, long enough for them to have a son Hamlet's age. Hamlet himself indicates that he is familiar with the source for *The Murder of Gonzago*: 'The story is extant, and written in very choice Italian' (III.2.271–2). This may be one of Shakespeare's jokes. It is possible that he drew upon an account, now lost, of the murder of Francesco Maria della Rovere, Duke of Urbino. The Duke died in 1538. Poison had been poured into his ears, and suspicion fell upon his kinsman, Luigi Gonzaga. The avenger's task was taken up by Guidobaldo, the Duke's son. No one, however, has been able to discover either an account of this incident that Shakespeare might have read, or an original for the inset play.

Only the tragedians of the city and Hamlet himself, who already know the story, could provide a detailed description of how *The Murder of Gonzago* developed, and how it was meant to end. But the second dumb show must have introduced the Player-King's son as revenger. Judging from what happens in other revenge plays of the period, this mimic double of Hamlet would gradually have begun to doubt, suspect, and question. Finally, he would have killed Lucianus, avenging his father but condemning himself in the process. Because Claudius exits abruptly, calling for lights, the play within the play merely points towards, without delineating, this conventional revenge pattern. But the sense of the unrealized paradigm is strong: both in *The Mousetrap* itself, and at Elsinore. *The Murder of Gonzago* breaks off – with the King dead and the murderer in possession of his victim's estate and

Queen – precisely where the tragedy of *Hamlet* began. The Prince might finish the story in the traditional manner, allowing the fiction he has used to threaten Claudius to control the facts of his own situation. The pressure upon him is strong to do this, in effect to merge the inset play with its frame, continuing the action Claudius interrupted. Part of him desires nothing better. The rest repudiates the revenger's role, without understanding just why. Certainly it does not seem to be either God's prohibition or what might happen to his own personality that checks Hamlet. The situation is more vexed and disturbing than that. In exploring it, Shakespeare created a character of a complexity unknown in previous dramatic literature. He also extended to the limit the already considerable potentialities of the revenge play as a means of inquiring into the nature of the self, and into man's position in society.

*

In the soliloquy which constitutes the most vehement of his self-accusations, 'O, what a rogue and peasant slave am I' (II.2.547–603), Hamlet reviews his circumstances and finds that he is 'unpregnant of my cause, | And can say nothing'. He has just been contemplating the Player's over-reaction to the Hecuba speech, but his choice of the verb *say* as opposed to the expected *do* is still peculiar and revealing. The discrepancy between words and deeds is a familiar preoccupation of tragedy, indeed of drama generally. Laertes's caution to Ophelia to believe Hamlet's love-suit only so far as 'he in his particular act and place | May give his saying deed' (I.3.26–7), Claudius's despair over the relationship of 'my deed to my most painted word' (III.1.53), and Ophelia's suspicion that her brother may be a puritanical counsellor who 'recks not his own

43

rede' (I.3.51) are all well-tried versions of the antithesis. Hamlet's inactivity, however, an inactivity coupled with febrile and incessant verbalizing, gives the theme a special meaning and significance. Claudius asks Laertes what he would do to 'show yourself in deed your father's son | More than in words' (IV.7.124–5), and is assured that Laertes would willingly cut Hamlet's throat in a church. The attitude, brisk and unlovely, forms an obvious contrast with Hamlet's uncertainty. A convincing demonstration that he is his father's son in deed more than mere word is precisely what the Prince spends most of the play thinking he ought to accomplish and failing to achieve. The example of Fortinbras is especially humiliating. The Norwegian Prince, after all, has converted a mere word – the name of a profitless and insignificant patch of Polish ground – into a fact so tangible and consequential that soldiers are prepared to die for it. Hamlet, on the other hand, dissipates the accusing facts of 'a father killed, a mother stained' (IV.4.57) into a series of verbal inquiries. He becomes, in the process, a character far more interesting and sympathetic than either Fortinbras or Laertes, but the price he pays is heavy.

Whatever his deficiencies as a revenge hero, as a parodist Hamlet is unrivalled. He can imitate the windy circumlocutions of Polonius, the state rhetoric of Claudius, full of ponderous 'as' clauses and diplomatic excuses for murder, the ranting grief of Laertes at Ophelia's grave, or the preciosity of Osrick. His ventriloquism, an art he practises throughout the play, goes beyond simple mockery. It seems to be part of a private investigation into how other people structure their experience in words. At other moments, Hamlet displays a relentless literal-mindedness, an insistence upon using puns or irrelevant secondary meanings as a way of reducing language to its most basic and non-metaphoric level. In this mood he wilfully misinterprets single words – Claudius's 'clouds' or 'fares', Gertrude's 'seems', Polonius's 'matter', Guildenstern's 'distempered' – or deflects an inquiry as to what he is reading with the mock-innocent reply 'Words, words, words' (II.2.193). The technique itself is familiar from Shakespeare's comedies. The women of France, in *Love's Labour's Lost*, engaged in it habitually as a way of deflating their lovers, and it is part of the stock in trade of jesters and witty servants. When Hamlet employs it, often under cover of his antic disposition, he usually succeeds in his intention to baffle and disconcert. But there is one other character in the play who defeats the Prince at his own game.

Like the cobbler in the opening scene of *Julius Caesar*, the gravedigger in *Hamlet* has no proper name. He is identified in both the Quarto and the Folio texts simply as 'clown'. He shares with the anonymous cobbler of the preceding play what amounts to an occupational obsession. Just as the cobbler reduces all the variety of the world to a matter of shoes and shoe-making, so the gravedigger in a far more sinister fashion is interested only in death and burial. His riddles, his jokes, his small talk, and even his songs all end in the same place: a hole in the ground. Hamlet's first reaction to him is shock at the incongruous cheerfulness with which the gravedigger goes about his business. Time and habit, as Horatio points out, have rendered his employment quite matter-of-fact and impersonal. It is yet another example of something Hamlet has seen all too much of: the fragility and impermanence of all human feeling. Not only sympathy and a sense of the macabre, but friendship, fidelity, even the passions of love and hate, fall victim to time. After thirty years at his job, the gravedigger has become death's familiar, almost his spokesman. He took up his occupation on the day old Hamlet overcame King Fortinbras. This was also the day of young Hamlet's birth. He will, presumably, complete the circle by interring the Prince at the end of the play. Meanwhile he proceeds with devastating effectiveness to treat Hamlet linguistically as Hamlet himself has treated others.

As the gravedigger unearths the tongueless skulls of men who may once have been lawyers, politicians, and courtiers, Hamlet fantasizes, characteristically, about their vanished existences as epitomized by the language they used. These chop-fallen bones could once sing, as the sexton does now. The politician used words to circumvent religion, the courtier flattered his way into preferment, and the lawyer was a compound of verbal quiddities and quillets, cases, tenures, and tricks. Then they died, and the rest was silence. From these sombre reflections on the vanity of ambition, as embodied in the arts of language, Hamlet turns to address the gravedigger for the first time. And discovers that he has met his match.

HAMLET *Whose grave's this, sirrah?*
FIRST CLOWN *Mine, sir. . . .*
HAMLET *What man dost thou dig it for?*
FIRST CLOWN *For no man, sir.*
HAMLET *What woman then?*
FIRST CLOWN *For none neither.*
HAMLET *Who is to be buried in't?*
FIRST CLOWN *One that was a woman, sir. But, rest her soul, she's dead.*

V.1.115-34

Asked how Prince Hamlet came to be mad, the gravedigger retorts: 'Faith, e'en with losing his wits'. Per-

46

severance gets Hamlet nothing in the way of a more satisfactory reply. His further query, 'Upon what ground?' is wilfully misunderstood too, producing the non-answer 'Why, here in Denmark'.

There can be no arguing, nor even any dialogue, with a literal-mindedness so absolute and perverse. In the face of death, the wings of language are clipped. Hamlet's own verbal trick played back on him declares itself for what it is: a revelation of the essential meaninglessness, the non-sense of human existence beneath its metaphoric dress. Abruptly, the Prince abandons the contest in favour of the sort of question the gravedigger takes seriously, and to which he is willing to give a direct response: 'How long will a man lie i'th'earth ere he rot?' (V.1.161). Always delighted to expatiate on the history and secrets of his profession, the sexton obligingly produces one skull to which a name can still be attached. Yorick, the old King's jester, was a man defined twenty-three years before by his verbal inventiveness and wit. There is nothing to laugh at now. Hamlet, who lacks the gravedigger's familiarity with such metamorphoses, looks at what remains of his childhood friend and finds revulsion in his heart where once there was affection.

In the previous act, the Prince had confronted Claudius with a calculatedly malicious description of 'how a king may go a progress through the guts of a beggar' (IV.3.29–30). Now, as he traces the dust of Alexander stopping a bung-hole, or the earth which was once 'Imperious Caesar' plastering the chink in a cottage wall, he is attacking no one. These speculations, reproved gently by Horatio, have more of despair in them than wit. The gravedigger has brought Hamlet face to face with the ultimate reality. Before it, language fails and revenge becomes a bad joke. When Ophelia, the latest tenant of poor Yorick's grave, is brought in on her bier, the Prince may well feel that his whole world is slipping silently into the earth. His subsequent assault upon Laertes is complexly motivated: a mixture of shock, distaste for Laertes's futile rhetoric, and (surely) a sense of guilt engendered not only by remorse for his share in Ophelia's sufferings, but for the more basic human crime of having already forgotten about her.

Hamlet's physical grapple with Laertes in the graveyard, halted by Claudius, Gertrude, and the members of a shocked court, anticipates the ritualized combat of the final scene. By the time Shakespeare came to write *Hamlet*, the practice of ending revenge plays with some kind of play or show seems already to have become a convention. In *The Spanish Tragedy* Hieronymo and his accomplice Bel-Imperia stage *Soliman and Perseda* before the assembled court, and stab their fellow-actors in earnest, not in jest. Tamora and her sons in *Titus Andronicus* impersonate Revenge, Rapine, and Murder, only to find that Titus appropriates the entertainment for his own purposes, with lethal results. In *Antonio's Revenge* the conspirators kill Piero in a masque, a device also employed in *The Revenger's Tragedy* and in Middleton's *Women Beware Women* (1621) to bring about the final holocaust. A version of *The Murder of Gonzago* may or may not have appeared midway through the *Ur-Hamlet*. The evidence, however, of other revenge plays argues strongly for some equivalent at the end of the source play to the fencing match in Shakespeare's tragedy: a 'fictional' action, performed by selected characters before an unsuspecting on-stage audience, which explodes without warning into real, as opposed to mimic, destruction.

It is impossible to say how conscious sixteenth- and early-seventeenth-century dramatists were of their reasons for presenting the culminating revenge action in this particular form. Interestingly, Aeschylus seems to have felt the impulse too. His *Agamemnon*, the first play in the Oresteian trilogy, moves to its conclusion as Clytemnestra persuades her husband Agamemnon to enact his triumphal return as king of Argos by walking into the palace along a path strewn with rich, woven cloth. She, Cassandra, and the Chorus become an audience to this ceremonial action. Inside the palace, however, lie the shambles: the axe and the encircling net. Ritual collapses into chaos as Clytemnestra accomplishes her revenge. Classical scholars have often, on slender evidence, tried to explain Agamemnon's formalized entry into his ancestral house as an example of hubris, and almost a justification for his killing. It seems more likely that the episode represents an ancient version of the 'play' scenes favoured by so many Elizabethan and Jacobean revenge dramatists, and that it fulfils a similar theatrical and emotional purpose.

It is in the nature of revenge plots, whether Greek or Renaissance, to involve a significant amount of hypocrisy and dissembling. Both the avenger and his adversaries have usually indulged in a good deal of real-life playacting before they reach the final scene. When some of them agree openly to adopt roles, while others watch as passive members of an audience, all of this earlier duplicity takes on a new, and superficially less dangerous, aspect. It is out in the open, formalized, and apparently controlled. Masques and revels, amateur theatricals of various kinds, barriers at court, and fencing matches all show a society at play: relaxed, confident, and secure. The very staging of many of these play scenes constitutes a statement of social order, assembling a courtly audience according to rank and function. Often, as in the case of the

Agamemnon, the spectacle itself is intended as a glorification of that society, an image of its stability. When it disintegrates into violence, into something horrifying and wild, it is as though all the hidden corruption and ugliness masked by the unacknowledged play-acting of the preceding acts has suddenly erupted into view.

The fencing match at the end of *Hamlet* is a mimic action of this kind. For the third and last time in the tragedy the entire court of Denmark – now a little depleted – assembles at the King's command. The wager itself, which pits the Prince against Laertes, is supposedly a polite show: a playful and artificial version of the kind of mortal combat in which old Hamlet and the elder Fortinbras once engaged. Like *The Murder of Gonzago* earlier, it constitutes 'poison in jest. No offence i'th'world' (III.2.244–5). This time, however, the actors are not disengaged professionals adhering to a script. Any bout of swordplay involving Hamlet and Laertes is bound to be something more than a fiction, given what Hamlet has done to the family of Polonius. This would be true even if Laertes had not conspired with Claudius, and did not intend to play what Hamlet calls 'this brothers' wager' (V.2.247) with an unbated and envenomed rapier. Hamlet's phrase here is unfortunate. Laertes is really brother to only one person: the crazed Ophelia, now buried in earth; and her wrongs guide his sword. However well intended, Hamlet's attempt to create another and spurious fraternity rings hollow. So does his excuse to Laertes that madness was responsible for all the damage he had inflicted: a madness, he suggests, as ruinous to himself as it has proved to be for Polonius and Ophelia.

Hamlet's situation, of course, is impossible. The Prince cannot – in a complex and double sense – explain. He has to fabricate a fiction in order to gesture at something which is emotionally, although not literally, true. He never meant to hurt Laertes. The fiction Laertes counters him with is far more reprehensible: a calculated and treacherous lie, not a despairing evasion. There is nothing real at all in Laertes's assurance that, personally, he bears no grudge. His reference to lingering scruples about points of honour, to be settled by the adjudication of some elderly Osrick at a later day, is wholly dishonest. Both men are conscious performers in a staged ritual of reconciliation, to be followed by a 'show', but Hamlet characteristically seeks something genuine in the episode, even if it is only partial, where Laertes yields himself to the King's travesty of a punctilious and chivalric court – the drums, the trumpets, and the cannon, the mimic gallantry, the pearl in the cup, and the royal wager – and embroiders on it freely.

The end of *Hamlet*, with its four violent deaths tearing through what was meant to be an innocent entertainment, is something with which the tragedians of the city would have been perfectly familiar. That the revenge hero, his task accomplished at last, should be one of the four who dies would also have seemed natural. The extraordinary thing, however, about this conventional conclusion is its irrelevance to most of the central issues of the tragedy. The ending of *Hamlet* resolves nothing that really matters. The nature of the Ghost, the question of what Hamlet ought to have done, the enigma of his delay and his own inability to explain it, the validity of action in a world where all achievement, all relationships, are mocked by death: these issues, of far more consequence than the killing of Claudius, are left untouched by that killing. They are still there, confronting us, when the play is done. This is not true, to any comparable extent, of other revenge tragedies.

The cool and rational Horatio behaves surprisingly at the end. His passionate and unexpected impulse towards suicide is thwarted by a Hamlet eager that his friend should live to 'tell my story' (V.2.343). When Fortinbras arrives, after the Prince is dead, Horatio obediently sketches out his version of that story. The account itself, for anyone who has just read or watched *Hamlet*, is startling:

> *So shall you hear*
> *Of carnal, bloody, and unnatural acts,*
> *Of accidental judgements, casual slaughters,*
> *Of deaths put on by cunning and forced cause,*
> *And, in this upshot, purposes mistook*
> *Fallen on th'inventors' heads. All this can I*
> *Truly deliver.*   V.2.374–80

This sounds like the prologue to a conventional revenge tragedy. It means to whet the appetite of its potential audience by emphasizing intrigue and sensational event, Machiavellian scheming, and fatal miscalculation. It might be the world of Shakespeare's twice-removed source material, of Saxo Grammaticus and Belleforest. As an account of *The Spanish Tragedy*, *The Revenger's Tragedy*, Marlowe's *The Jew of Malta* – or *The Murder of Gonzago* – it is (just) acceptable. As a description of Shakespeare's *Hamlet*, it is not. Horatio astonishes us by leaving out everything that seems important, reducing all that is distinctive about this play to a plot stereotype. Although his tale is, on one level, accurate enough, it is certainly not Hamlet's 'story'.

Horatio speaks, of course, from a knowledge much inferior to that accorded the theatre audience. Equally important, he is addressing Fortinbras, the 'delicate and tender prince' of Hamlet's fourth-act panegyric. This dangerous young Norwegian, who seems over a long period to have been moving closer and closer to the kingdom he covets, is about to become ruler of Denmark. The ghost of old Fortinbras, if such a spirit exists, must be overwhelmed with joy. Young Fortinbras himself is clearly not the kind of man who would be tempted to speculate over-curiously in a graveyard. He seems to find the 'feast of Death' upon which he stumbles at Elsinore acceptable in itself, although inappropriate to the place: 'Such a sight as this | Becomes the field, but here shows much amiss' (V.2.395–6). A practical spirit, not much interested in moral dilemmas or elaborate explanations, he will doubtless regard Horatio's reductive narration as entirely satisfactory. Meanwhile he inaugurates his authority by decreeing for Hamlet precisely the kind of soldier's funeral he would want for himself.

When Hamlet caught sight of Ophelia's funeral procession, he was struck by the pathetic and 'maimèd rites' accorded her. The play as a whole has been characterized by maimed rites. Old Hamlet's funeral was truncated and derided by its juxtaposition with the festivities accompanying the precipitate second marriage of his widow. Claudius's all-night wassails trivialized and debased the outward signs of royal authority into a matter of drunken clamour. Like Ophelia, the murdered Polonius was shoved into the earth 'In hugger-mugger' (IV.5.85), and neither *The Murder of Gonzago* nor the fencing match was allowed to run its ceremonious course. Hamlet's funeral looks like being the first ritual seen in this court for a long time that will be conducted with dignity and without interruption.

Not knowing what else to do, Fortinbras treats the dead Prince as himself. He proposes to bury a Hamlet he has never met according to his own lights and understanding.

There is a certain rough grace and magnanimity in this, even though 'The soldiers' music and the rites of war' (V.2.393) constitute a painful simplification. They can speak only imperfectly for Hamlet, whatever they might do for Fortinbras himself. But then even Horatio, who has known and loved the Prince, seems unable to do anything more than 'Report' him and his 'cause aright' (V.2.333). He cannot tell his 'story'. That task was left to the tragedians of the city, the true custodians and interpreters of matter so complicated. And to their dramatist: a man well acquainted with the assumptions and conventions of revenge tragedy, who could see beyond them to a different kind of play. This play is the one Hamlet himself gestures towards in his last moments, when he addresses 'You that look pale and tremble at this chance, | That are but mutes or audience to this act' (V.2.328-9). It is part of the dizzying but creative self-consciousness of *Hamlet* that, as the Prince speaks these words, one should become aware that, in fact, the tragedy he wistfully perceives is the one Shakespeare has written.

Anne Barton
1979

FURTHER READING

It's hardly surprising that recent major editions of *Hamlet* should give so much attention in their introductory material to a proper understanding of the play's extraordinarily complicated textual situation where three quasi-independent editions – the first Quarto (1603), the second (1604–5), the Folio (1623) – vie for editorial consideration. Even the hitherto much despised Q1 has its advocates in Brian Loughrey and Graham Holderness in their treatment of it in the Shakespearean Originals series (1992) as an authentic and surprisingly powerful 'performance text' in which 'the problems of the play became less psychological, more circumstantial and contingent.' They argue with some justice that these first three editions of *Hamlet* are so different that they should be regarded 'not simply as variants of a single work, but as discrete textualisations independently framed within a complex and diversified product of cultural production'. The same year (1992) produced a differently focused view of Q1 in Thomas Clayton's volume, *The 'Hamlet' First Published (Q1, 1603): Origins, Form, Intertextualities.* Is the enigmatic Q1 an honest ghost or goblin damned? Defenders of Q1, Clayton argues, are motivated by political and/or theatrical reasons, not literary ones: 'perhaps another manifestation of the antiliterary decanonizing temper of our time'. The 'more literary' editors of the Arden *Hamlet* (1982), the New Cambridge Shakespeare (1985) and the Oxford Shakespeare (1987) continue to argue for the desperate inferiority of Q1. G. R. Hibbard, the Oxford editor, makes an impressive case for Q2 as Shakespeare's first draft, with the 1623 Folio a revision of this first draft and Q1 a reported version of an abridgement of this revised text. There are, it seems, as many indirections in the history of the play's printing career as in the play's plot. Paul Bertram and Bernice W. Kliman provide a means for the reader to understand what all the fuss is about with their *Three-Text 'Hamlet': Parallel Texts of the First and Second Quartos and First Folio* (1991). At all events it is important for students of the play to buttress their reading of this edition's 'An Account of the Text' with the above-mentioned works.

Before leaving them, a mention should also be made of their contributions to our understanding of the play in other important areas – its theatrical history, its sources, date, and its linguistic, theological, political and psychological cruxes. In particular, the three editions from the 80s shed much light on some old controversies. Even the 'To be' soliloquy gets a refurbishing from Harold Jenkins, the Arden editor, in one of his densely argued 'Longer Notes'. His dogmatic acuteness is apparent in his contention that in this, the most famous of all soliloquies, Hamlet cannot mean what so many readers have taken him to mean, namely that by opposing a sea of troubles he can overcome them – what Hamlet means is that the troubles will only end by the opposer's death (presumably by drowning) in his inevitably futile struggle against the overwhelming numbers implied in 'a sea of troubles'.

*

Given the mountains of commentary on *Hamlet*, Ossas piled on Pelions, a rewarding initial approach might well take advantage of the metacritical times we live in by looking at works that purport to explain just why so much has been written on the play. One such is Cedric Watts's fine Harvester New Critical Introduction (1988) which maintains that 'the play's pregnancy breeds midwives': 'it is the veering seismograph which registers the earth-tremors and landslides of ideology.' We should not shrink, he says, from acknowledging (and enjoying) in the play the 'fruitful friction between muddle and complexity, the improvised and the orchestrated, the traditional and the innovatory'. Another perspicacious combination of book about *Hamlet* and book about books about *Hamlet* is Michael Hattaway's in the Critics Debate Series (1987), while Paul Cantor's 'wide-angled approach' in the Landmarks of World Literature Series (1989) helps us to see *Hamlet* in the boundless reaches of the intertextuality of world literature. Cantor is particularly good on the importance for an understanding of *Hamlet* of the traditional ambivalence in world literature – especially Christian world literature – towards heroism. To change the angle of approach slightly, Martin Scofield's *The Ghosts of Hamlet: The Play and Modern Writers* (1980) looks at what modern writers like Eliot and Kafka have made of the play – modern not Romantic (no Yeats or Pasternak here) – and his own reading of *Hamlet* reflects their fascination with the play's indeterminacy. What Scofield does with modern writers, Michael Cohen attempts to do with nine modern productions in his '*Hamlet*' *in My Mind's Eye* (1989) which offers 'a kind of bedlam *Hamlet* with a multiple personality disorder'. James L. Calderwood's *To Be and Not To Be: Negation and Metadrama in 'Hamlet'* (1983) focuses on the pursuit of motes with Blakeian infinities in a play that 'seems dedicated to its own deconstruction'. These points of view owe a debt, I would say, to Harry Levin's masterly little book, *The Question of Hamlet* (1959), which examines the play in terms of its obsession with interrogation, doubt and irony. All these works celebrate rather than scold the play's intractability.

It was not always so (and often still isn't). T. S. Eliot's famous essay on the play (1919) – reprinted in David Bevington's *Twentieth-century Interpretations* (1968) along with other cavillers' and aspiring integrators' – found Hamlet's emotion about his parents excessive and disproportionate. G. W. Knight's equally famous essay in *The Wheel of Fire* (1930) judged Hamlet a villain. Ernest Jones in *Hamlet and Oedipus* (1949) pronounced Hamlet a victim of the Oedipus Complex. A. C. Bradley in his highly influential *Shakespearean Tragedy* (1904) diagnosed him as suffering from melancholy induced by the moral shock on a noble and idealistic nature of his mother's o'erhasty remarriage. Two very readable works by L. C. Knights are Bradleian in approach but far more censorious of the prince than he is: *An Approach to 'Hamlet'* (1961) and 'Prince Hamlet' (1940). These are some of the huge number of attempts to pluck out the heart of Hamlet's mystery in response to what Watts calls 'a quality of opacity in his nature'. The hectic pursuit continues. C. L. Barber and Richard P. Wheeler in *The Whole Journey: Shakespeare's Power of Development* (1986) see a connection between the play and Shakespeare's home life – John Shakespeare, for instance, as a possible alcoholic Claudius. Indeed, the 'whole tragic period can be seen as a reckoning with the problem of inheritance from one generation to the next.' This book might be read in conjunction with Janet Adelman's feminist *Suffocating Mothers: Fantasies of Maternal Origin in Shakespeare's Plays, 'Hamlet' to 'The Tempest'* (1992), in which the 'buried fantasy of *Hamlet*' is the subjection of the male to the female. The queen, the queen's to blame. An instructive contrast is Linda Bamber's equally feminist *Comic Women, Tragic Men: A Study of Gender and Genre in Shakespeare* (1982) which emphasizes – credibly I think – how *Hamlet* deflects our impulse to criticize Gertrude. Gertrude and Ophelia are, as it were, attendant lords, 'psychologically and morally neutral characters who take on the coloration of the play's mood'. H. R. Coursen concentrates on representations of Ophelia in *Shakespearean Performance as Interpretation* (1992).

Much was – and still is – made of the incompatibility of the play's, rather than the main character's, parents. That is, there are frequent attempts to explain the play's opacities in terms of a confluence in it of different and jarring dramatic and narrative traditions with Shakespeare's own complicating additions. A. J. A. Waldock's *Hamlet: A Study in Critical Method* (1931) follows Schücking and Stoll, among others, in this pursuit. Peter Mercer continues this tradition in *'Hamlet' and the Acting of Revenge* (1987) in which – in the context of Kyd's *Spanish Tragedy* (1587–9), Marston's *Antonio's Re-*

venge (1599?), and Middleton's *Revenger's Tragedy* (1607) – he argues that the peculiarity of *Hamlet* may come from the convergence of two different expressive modes: the dramatic mode of revenge tragedy and the rhetorical mode of satire and complaint. As we might imagine, such an enigmatic play as *Hamlet* is a frequent candidate for parabolically minded critics, particularly religious ones. Arthur McGee, for example, in *The Elizabethan Hamlet* (1987), in the rather strident tradition of Eleanor Prosser's *Hamlet and Revenge* (1967), argues for a Protestant Hamlet in a Catholic court possessed by the devil, whose emissary is Hamlet's father. Walter N. King's *Hamlet's Search for Meaning* (1982) finds its meaning – as do other works – in the notion that providence finally governs the play, though the carnage at the play's end might suggest otherwise. And Linda Kay Hoff's *Hamlet's Choice: A Reformation Allegory* (1988) thinks of the play as a '"typal" allegory of the Reformation itself'. The play, that is, as a king of infinite space.

Books on the play in the theatre are numerous and often helpful, given the succulent difficulties of its acting roles. Besides Coursen's and Michael Cohen's, John A. Mills in *Hamlet on Stage: The Great Tradition* (1985) deals with Hamlets from the Restoration to Albert Finney in 1975. Mary Maher's *Modern Hamlets and Their Soliloquies* (1992) interviews a number of recent Hamlets. Bernice W. Kliman's '*Hamlet': Film, Television and Audio Performance* (1988) looks at *Hamlet* on stage and television, in silent film and sound recordings. Maurice Charney's two books on the play – *Style in 'Hamlet'* (1969) and *Hamlet's Fictions* (1988) – are written with due awareness of the theatre and theatrical convention. And Marvin Rosenberg's *The Masks of 'Hamlet'* (1992) is a vast account of stage business associated with the play.

In his edition of Modern Critical Interpretations of *Hamlet* (1986) Harold Bloom maintains that these essays 'tell us again that Hamlet's consciousness remains the largest and most comprehensive of all Western representations of human

character and personality'. What also tells us this again –
and again – is the inexhaustibility of any of the topics of the
play that have been chewed over by critics for decades.
Despairing of these post-modern times, William Kerrigan in
Hamlet's Perfection (1994) responds to the 'shocking decadence'
of the *Hamlet* criticism of the 1980s by pleading for a return to
the Romantic Hamlet, even the Bradleian one. In *'Hamlet'
and the Concept of Character* (1992) Bert States obliges with a
stunning re-examination of Bradley's subject in the belief that
'old questions, like old soldiers and dead metaphors, never die
. . . it is only the answers that change or get expressed in
different language.' There is, he says, 'a combinatory logic in
character-formation' and his brilliant, quotable book persuades
us that he was right 'to give in to the seductive power of
mimesis' once again.

Michael Taylor, 1996

THE CHARACTERS IN THE PLAY

GHOST of Hamlet, lately King of Denmark
Claudius, his brother, now KING of Denmark
Gertrude, QUEEN of Denmark, widow of the late King
 and now wife of his brother Claudius
HAMLET, son of the late King Hamlet and of Gertrude

POLONIUS, counsellor to the King
LAERTES, son of Polonius
OPHELIA, daughter of Polonius
REYNALDO, servant of Polonius

HORATIO, friend of Prince Hamlet

VOLTEMAND ⎫
CORNELIUS ⎪
ROSENCRANTZ ⎪
GUILDENSTERN ⎬ members of the Danish court
OSRICK ⎪
A LORD ⎪
GENTLEMEN ⎭
FRANCISCO ⎫
BARNARDO ⎬ soldiers
MARCELLUS ⎭

Two MESSENGERS
A SAILOR
Two CLOWNS, a gravedigger and his companion
A PRIEST

THE CHARACTERS IN THE PLAY

FORTINBRAS, Prince of Norway
A CAPTAIN, a Norwegian

English AMBASSADORS

FIRST PLAYER, who leads the troupe and takes the part
of a king
SECOND PLAYER, who takes the part of a queen
THIRD PLAYER, who takes the part of Lucianus, nephew
of the king
FOURTH PLAYER, who speaks a Prologue

Lords, attendants, players, guards, soldiers, followers of
Laertes, sailors

Enter Francisco and Barnardo, two sentinels

BARNARDO Who's there?

FRANCISCO Nay, answer me. Stand and unfold yourself.

BARNARDO Long live the King!

FRANCISCO Barnardo?

BARNARDO He.

FRANCISCO
You come most carefully upon your hour.

BARNARDO
'Tis now struck twelve. Get thee to bed, Francisco.

FRANCISCO
For this relief much thanks. 'Tis bitter cold,
And I am sick at heart.

BARNARDO
Have you had quiet guard?

FRANCISCO   Not a mouse stirring.   10

BARNARDO
Well, good night.
If you do meet Horatio and Marcellus,
The rivals of my watch, bid them make haste.
       Enter Horatio and Marcellus

FRANCISCO
I think I hear them. Stand ho! Who is there?

HORATIO
Friends to this ground.

MARCELLUS   And liegemen to the Dane.

FRANCISCO
Give you good night.

MARCELLUS   O, farewell, honest soldier.
 Who hath relieved you?
FRANCISCO   Barnardo hath my place.
 Give you good night.   *Exit*
MARCELLUS   Holla, Barnardo!
BARNARDO   Say –
 What, is Horatio there?
HORATIO   A piece of him.
BARNARDO
20 Welcome, Horatio. Welcome, good Marcellus.
MARCELLUS
 What, has this thing appeared again tonight?
BARNARDO
 I have seen nothing.
MARCELLUS
 Horatio says 'tis but our fantasy,
 And will not let belief take hold of him
 Touching this dreaded sight twice seen of us.
 Therefore I have entreated him along
 With us to watch the minutes of this night,
 That, if again this apparition come,
 He may approve our eyes and speak to it.
HORATIO
 Tush, tush, 'twill not appear.
30 BARNARDO   Sit down awhile,
 And let us once again assail your ears,
 That are so fortified against our story,
 What we have two nights seen.
HORATIO   Well, sit we down,
 And let us hear Barnardo speak of this.
BARNARDO
 Last night of all,
 When yond same star that's westward from the pole

Had made his course t'illume that part of heaven
Where now it burns, Marcellus and myself,
The bell then beating one –
    Enter the Ghost

MARCELLUS

Peace, break thee off. Look where it comes again.   40

BARNARDO

In the same figure like the King that's dead.

MARCELLUS

Thou art a scholar. Speak to it, Horatio.

BARNARDO

Looks 'a not like the King? Mark it, Horatio.

HORATIO

Most like. It harrows me with fear and wonder.

BARNARDO

It would be spoke to.

MARCELLUS   Speak to it, Horatio.

HORATIO

What art thou that usurpest this time of night,
Together with that fair and warlike form
In which the majesty of buried Denmark
Did sometimes march? By heaven I charge thee, speak.

MARCELLUS

It is offended.

BARNARDO   See, it stalks away.   50

HORATIO

Stay. Speak, speak. I charge thee, speak.
        Exit the Ghost

MARCELLUS

'Tis gone and will not answer.

BARNARDO

How now, Horatio? You tremble and look pale.
Is not this something more than fantasy?

What think you on't?

HORATIO

Before my God, I might not this believe
Without the sensible and true avouch
Of mine own eyes.

MARCELLUS　　　　Is it not like the King?

HORATIO

As thou art to thyself.

60　Such was the very armour he had on
When he the ambitious Norway combated.
So frowned he once when, in an angry parle,
He smote the sledded poleaxe on the ice.
'Tis strange.

MARCELLUS

Thus twice before, and jump at this dead hour,
With martial stalk hath he gone by our watch.

HORATIO

In what particular thought to work I know not.
But, in the gross and scope of mine opinion,
This bodes some strange eruption to our state.

MARCELLUS

70　Good now, sit down, and tell me he that knows
Why this same strict and most observant watch
So nightly toils the subject of the land,
And why such daily cast of brazen cannon
And foreign mart for implements of war,
Why such impress of shipwrights, whose sore task
Does not divide the Sunday from the week.
What might be toward that this sweaty haste
Doth make the night joint-labourer with the day?
Who is't that can inform me?

HORATIO　　　　　　　　That can I.

80　At least the whisper goes so. Our last King,
Whose image even but now appeared to us,

Was, as you know, by Fortinbras of Norway,
Thereto pricked on by a most emulate pride,
Dared to the combat; in which our valiant Hamlet –
For so this side of our known world esteemed him –
Did slay this Fortinbras; who, by a sealed compact
Well ratified by law and heraldy,
Did forfeit, with his life, all these his lands
Which he stood seised of, to the conqueror;
Against the which a moiety competent   90
Was gagèd by our King, which had returned
To the inheritance of Fortinbras,
Had he been vanquisher, as, by the same covenant
And carriage of the article designed,
His fell to Hamlet. Now, sir, young Fortinbras,
Of unimprovèd mettle hot and full,
Hath in the skirts of Norway here and there
Sharked up a list of lawless resolutes
For food and diet to some enterprise
That hath a stomach in't; which is no other,   100
As it doth well appear unto our state,
But to recover of us by strong hand
And terms compulsatory those foresaid lands
So by his father lost. And this, I take it,
Is the main motive of our preparations,
The source of this our watch, and the chief head
Of this posthaste and romage in the land.

BARNARDO

I think it be no other but e'en so.
Well may it sort that this portentous figure
Comes armèd through our watch so like the King   110
That was and is the question of these wars.

HORATIO

A mote it is to trouble the mind's eye.
In the most high and palmy state of Rome,

67

A little ere the mightiest Julius fell,
The graves stood tenantless and the sheeted dead
Did squeak and gibber in the Roman streets –
As stars with trains of fire and dews of blood,
Disasters in the sun; and the moist star
Upon whose influence Neptune's empire stands
120 Was sick almost to Doomsday with eclipse.
And even the like precurse of feared events,
As harbingers preceding still the fates
And prologue to the omen coming on,
Have heaven and earth together demonstrated
Unto our climatures and countrymen.

    Enter the Ghost

But soft, behold, lo where it comes again!
I'll cross it, though it blast me.

    He spreads his arms

Stay, illusion.
If thou hast any sound or use of voice,
130 Speak to me.
If there be any good thing to be done
That may to thee do ease and grace to me,
Speak to me.
If thou art privy to thy country's fate,
Which happily foreknowing may avoid,
O, speak!
Or if thou hast uphoarded in thy life
Extorted treasure in the womb of earth,
For which, they say, you spirits oft walk in death,
Speak of it.

    The cock crows

140   Stay and speak. Stop it, Marcellus.

MARCELLUS
Shall I strike it with my partisan?

HORATIO
Do, if it will not stand.

BARNARDO   'Tis here.

HORATIO   'Tis here.

Exit the Ghost

MARCELLUS
'Tis gone.
We do it wrong, being so majestical,
To offer it the show of violence,
For it is as the air invulnerable,
And our vain blows malicious mockery.

BARNARDO
It was about to speak when the cock crew.

HORATIO
And then it started, like a guilty thing
Upon a fearful summons. I have heard   150
The cock, that is the trumpet to the morn,
Doth with his lofty and shrill-sounding throat
Awake the god of day, and at his warning,
Whether in sea or fire, in earth or air,
Th'extravagant and erring spirit hies
To his confine. And of the truth herein
This present object made probation.

MARCELLUS
It faded on the crowing of the cock.
Some say that ever 'gainst that season comes
Wherein our Saviour's birth is celebrated,   160
This bird of dawning singeth all night long.
And then, they say, no spirit dare stir abroad;
The nights are wholesome; then no planets strike;
No fairy takes; nor witch hath power to charm.
So hallowed and so gracious is that time.

HORATIO
So have I heard and do in part believe it.

But look, the morn in russet mantle clad
Walks o'er the dew of yon high eastward hill.
Break we our watch up. And by my advice
170 Let us impart what we have seen tonight
Unto young Hamlet. For, upon my life,
This spirit, dumb to us, will speak to him.
Do you consent we shall acquaint him with it,
As needful in our loves, fitting our duty?

MARCELLUS
Let's do't, I pray. And I this morning know
Where we shall find him most conveniently.   *Exeunt*

I.2   *Flourish*
             Enter Claudius, King of Denmark, Gertrude the
             Queen, and the Council, including Polonius with his
             son Laertes, Hamlet, Voltemand, Cornelius, and
             attendants

KING
Though yet of Hamlet our dear brother's death
The memory be green, and that it us befitted
To bear our hearts in grief, and our whole kingdom
To be contracted in one brow of woe,
Yet so far hath discretion fought with nature
That we with wisest sorrow think on him
Together with remembrance of ourselves.
Therefore our sometime sister, now our Queen,
Th'imperial jointress to this warlike state,
10 Have we, as 'twere with a defeated joy,
With an auspicious and a dropping eye,
With mirth in funeral and with dirge in marriage,
In equal scale weighing delight and dole,
Taken to wife. Nor have we herein barred

Your better wisdoms, which have freely gone
With this affair along. For all, our thanks.
Now follows that you know. Young Fortinbras,
Holding a weak supposal of our worth,
Or thinking by our late dear brother's death
Our state to be disjoint and out of frame,   20
Colleaguèd with this dream of his advantage,
He hath not failed to pester us with message
Importing the surrender of those lands
Lost by his father, with all bands of law,
To our most valiant brother. So much for him.
Now for ourself and for this time of meeting.
Thus much the business is: we have here writ
To Norway, uncle of young Fortinbras –
Who, impotent and bedrid, scarcely hears
Of this his nephew's purpose – to suppress   30
His further gait herein, in that the levies,
The lists, and full proportions are all made
Out of his subject. And we here dispatch
You, good Cornelius, and you, Voltemand,
For bearers of this greeting to old Norway,
Giving to you no further personal power
To business with the King, more than the scope
Of these delated articles allow.
Farewell; and let your haste commend your duty.

VOLTEMAND *and* CORNELIUS

In that, and all things, will we show our duty.   40

KING

We doubt it nothing. Heartily farewell.

                Exeunt Voltemand and Cornelius

And now, Laertes, what's the news with you?
You told us of some suit. What is't, Laertes?
You cannot speak of reason to the Dane
And lose your voice. What wouldst thou beg, Laertes,

71

That shall not be my offer, not thy asking?
The head is not more native to the heart,
The hand more instrumental to the mouth,
Than is the throne of Denmark to thy father.
What wouldst thou have, Laertes?

50 LAERTES   My dread lord,
Your leave and favour to return to France,
From whence though willingly I came to Denmark
To show my duty in your coronation,
Yet now I must confess, that duty done,
My thoughts and wishes bend again toward France
And bow them to your gracious leave and pardon.

KING

Have you your father's leave? What says Polonius?

POLONIUS

He hath, my lord, wrung from me my slow leave
By laboursome petition, and at last
60 Upon his will I sealed my hard consent.
I do beseech you give him leave to go.

KING

Take thy fair hour, Laertes. Time be thine;
And thy best graces spend it at thy will.
But now, my cousin Hamlet, and my son –

HAMLET (*aside*)

A little more than kin, and less than kind!

KING

How is it that the clouds still hang on you?

HAMLET

Not so, my lord. I am too much in the sun.

QUEEN

Good Hamlet, cast thy nighted colour off,
And let thine eye look like a friend on Denmark.
70 Do not for ever with thy vailèd lids
Seek for thy noble father in the dust.

Thou knowest 'tis common. All that lives must die,
Passing through nature to eternity.

HAMLET

Ay, madam, it is common.

QUEEN   If it be,
Why seems it so particular with thee?

HAMLET

'Seems', madam? Nay, it is. I know not 'seems'.
'Tis not alone my inky cloak, good mother,
Nor customary suits of solemn black,
Nor windy suspiration of forced breath,
No, nor the fruitful river in the eye,   80
Nor the dejected 'haviour of the visage,
Together with all forms, moods, shapes of grief,
That can denote me truly. These indeed 'seem';
For they are actions that a man might play.
But I have that within which passes show –
These but the trappings and the suits of woe.

KING

'Tis sweet and commendable in your nature, Hamlet,
To give these mourning duties to your father.
But you must know your father lost a father;
That father lost, lost his; and the survivor bound   90
In filial obligation for some term
To do obsequious sorrow. But to persever
In obstinate condolement is a course
Of impious stubbornness. 'Tis unmanly grief.
It shows a will most incorrect to heaven,
A heart unfortified, a mind impatient,
An understanding simple and unschooled.
For what we know must be, and is as common
As any the most vulgar thing to sense,
Why should we in our peevish opposition   100
Take it to heart? Fie, 'tis a fault to heaven,

73

A fault against the dead, a fault to nature,
To reason most absurd, whose common theme
Is death of fathers, and who still hath cried,
From the first corse till he that died today,
'This must be so'. We pray you throw to earth
This unprevailing woe, and think of us
As of a father. For, let the world take note,
You are the most immediate to our throne;
And with no less nobility of love
Than that which dearest father bears his son
Do I impart toward you. For your intent
In going back to school in Wittenberg,
It is most retrograde to our desire;
And, we beseech you, bend you to remain
Here in the cheer and comfort of our eye,
Our chiefest courtier, cousin, and our son.

QUEEN

Let not thy mother lose her prayers, Hamlet.
I pray thee stay with us. Go not to Wittenberg.

HAMLET

I shall in all my best obey you, madam.

KING

Why, 'tis a loving and a fair reply.
Be as ourself in Denmark. Madam, come.
This gentle and unforced accord of Hamlet
Sits smiling to my heart; in grace whereof
No jocund health that Denmark drinks today
But the great cannon to the clouds shall tell,
And the King's rouse the heaven shall bruit again,
Re-speaking earthly thunder. Come away.

    Flourish   *Exeunt all but Hamlet*

HAMLET

O that this too too sullied flesh would melt,

Thaw, and resolve itself into a dew; 130
Or that the Everlasting had not fixed
His canon 'gainst self-slaughter. O God, God,
How weary, stale, flat, and unprofitable
Seem to me all the uses of this world!
Fie on't, ah, fie, 'tis an unweeded garden
That grows to seed. Things rank and gross in nature
Possess it merely. That it should come to this –
But two months dead, nay, not so much, not two!
So excellent a king, that was to this
Hyperion to a satyr; so loving to my mother 140
That he might not beteem the winds of heaven
Visit her face too roughly. Heaven and earth,
Must I remember? Why, she would hang on him
As if increase of appetite had grown
By what it fed on. And yet within a month –
Let me not think on't. Frailty, thy name is woman.
A little month, or e'er those shoes were old
With which she followed my poor father's body
Like Niobe, all tears, why she, even she –
O God, a beast that wants discourse of reason 150
Would have mourned longer – married with my uncle,
My father's brother, but no more like my father
Than I to Hercules. Within a month,
Ere yet the salt of most unrighteous tears
Had left the flushing in her gallèd eyes,
She married. O, most wicked speed, to post
With such dexterity to incestuous sheets!
It is not, nor it cannot come to good.
But break, my heart, for I must hold my tongue.
        Enter Horatio, Marcellus, and Barnardo
HORATIO
Hail to your lordship!

160 HAMLET   I am glad to see you well.
Horatio – or I do forget myself.

HORATIO
The same, my lord, and your poor servant ever.

HAMLET
Sir, my good friend. I'll change that name with you.
And what make you from Wittenberg, Horatio?
Marcellus?

MARCELLUS
My good lord!

HAMLET
I am very glad to see you. (*To Barnardo*) Good even, sir.
(*To Horatio*)
But what, in faith, make you from Wittenberg?

HORATIO
A truant disposition, good my lord.

HAMLET
170 I would not hear your enemy say so,
Nor shall you do my ear that violence
To make it truster of your own report
Against yourself. I know you are no truant.
But what is your affair in Elsinore?
We'll teach you to drink deep ere you depart.

HORATIO
My lord, I came to see your father's funeral.

HAMLET
I prithee do not mock me, fellow-student.
I think it was to see my mother's wedding.

HORATIO
Indeed, my lord, it followed hard upon.

HAMLET
180 Thrift, thrift, Horatio. The funeral baked meats
Did coldly furnish forth the marriage tables.
Would I had met my dearest foe in heaven

Or ever I had seen that day, Horatio!
My father – methinks I see my father.

HORATIO

Where, my lord?

HAMLET   In my mind's eye, Horatio.

HORATIO

I saw him once. 'A was a goodly king.

HAMLET

'A was a man. Take him for all in all,
I shall not look upon his like again.

HORATIO

My lord, I think I saw him yesternight.

HAMLET

Saw? Who?   190

HORATIO

My lord, the King your father.

HAMLET   The King my father?

HORATIO

Season your admiration for a while
With an attent ear till I may deliver
Upon the witness of these gentlemen
This marvel to you.

HAMLET   For God's love, let me hear!

HORATIO

Two nights together had these gentlemen,
Marcellus and Barnardo, on their watch
In the dead waste and middle of the night
Been thus encountered: a figure like your father,
Armèd at point exactly, cap-a-pe,   200
Appears before them and with solemn march
Goes slow and stately by them. Thrice he walked
By their oppressed and fear-surprisèd eyes
Within his truncheon's length, whilst they, distilled
Almost to jelly with the act of fear,

Stand dumb and speak not to him. This to me
In dreadful secrecy impart they did,
And I with them the third night kept the watch,
Where, as they had delivered, both in time,

210   Form of the thing, each word made true and good,
The apparition comes. I knew your father.
These hands are not more like.

HAMLET   But where was this?

MARCELLUS
My lord, upon the platform where we watch.

HAMLET
Did you not speak to it?

HORATIO   My lord, I did,
But answer made it none. Yet once methought
It lifted up it head and did address
Itself to motion like as it would speak.
But even then the morning cock crew loud,
And at the sound it shrunk in haste away
And vanished from our sight.

220 HAMLET   'Tis very strange.

HORATIO
As I do live, my honoured lord, 'tis true.
And we did think it writ down in our duty
To let you know of it.

HAMLET
Indeed, indeed, sirs. But this troubles me.
Hold you the watch tonight?

ALL   We do, my lord.

HAMLET
Armed, say you?

ALL
Armed, my lord.

HAMLET
From top to toe?

ALL   My lord, from head to foot.

HAMLET

Then saw you not his face?

HORATIO

O, yes, my lord. He wore his beaver up.   230

HAMLET

What, looked he frowningly?

HORATIO

A countenance more in sorrow than in anger.

HAMLET

Pale or red?

HORATIO

Nay, very pale.

HAMLET   And fixed his eyes upon you?

HORATIO

Most constantly.

HAMLET   I would I had been there.

HORATIO

It would have much amazed you.

HAMLET

Very like, very like. Stayed it long?

HORATIO

While one with moderate haste might tell a hundred.

MARCELLUS *and* BARNARDO

Longer, longer.

HORATIO

Not when I saw't.

HAMLET   His beard was grizzled, no?   240

HORATIO

It was as I have seen it in his life,
A sable silvered.

HAMLET   I will watch tonight.

Perchance 'twill walk again.

HORATIO   I warrant it will.

HAMLET

If it assume my noble father's person,
I'll speak to it though hell itself should gape
And bid me hold my peace. I pray you all,
If you have hitherto concealed this sight,
Let it be tenable in your silence still.
And whatsomever else shall hap tonight,
250   Give it an understanding but no tongue.
I will requite your loves. So fare you well.
Upon the platform 'twixt eleven and twelve
I'll visit you.

ALL   Our duty to your honour.

HAMLET

Your loves, as mine to you. Farewell.

Exeunt all but Hamlet

My father's spirit! In arms! All is not well.
I doubt some foul play. Would the night were come!
Till then sit still, my soul. Foul deeds will rise,
Though all the earth o'erwhelm them, to men's eyes.

Exit

I.3   *Enter Laertes and Ophelia*

LAERTES

My necessaries are embarked. Farewell.
And, sister, as the winds give benefit
And convoy is assistant, do not sleep
But let me hear from you.

OPHELIA   Do you doubt that?

LAERTES

For Hamlet, and the trifling of his favour,
Hold it a fashion and a toy in blood,
A violet in the youth of primy nature,
Forward, not permanent, sweet, not lasting,

The perfume and suppliance of a minute,
No more.

OPHELIA No more but so?

LAERTES   Think it no more.   10
For nature crescent does not grow alone
In thews and bulk, but as this temple waxes
The inward service of the mind and soul
Grows wide withal. Perhaps he loves you now,
And now no soil nor cautel doth besmirch
The virtue of his will. But you must fear,
His greatness weighed, his will is not his own.
For he himself is subject to his birth.
He may not, as unvalued persons do,
Carve for himself. For on his choice depends   20
The safety and health of this whole state.
And therefore must his choice be circumscribed
Unto the voice and yielding of that body
Whereof he is the head. Then, if he says he loves you,
It fits your wisdom so far to believe it
As he in his particular act and place
May give his saying deed; which is no further
Than the main voice of Denmark goes withal.
Then weigh what loss your honour may sustain
If with too credent ear you list his songs,   30
Or lose your heart, or your chaste treasure open
To his unmastered importunity.
Fear it, Ophelia, fear it, my dear sister.
And keep you in the rear of your affection,
Out of the shot and danger of desire.
The chariest maid is prodigal enough
If she unmask her beauty to the moon.
Virtue itself 'scapes not calumnious strokes.
The canker galls the infants of the spring
Too oft before their buttons be disclosed;   40

And in the morn and liquid dew of youth
Contagious blastments are most imminent.
Be wary then. Best safety lies in fear.
Youth to itself rebels, though none else near.

OPHELIA

I shall the effect of this good lesson keep
As watchman to my heart. But, good my brother,
Do not, as some ungracious pastors do,
Show me the steep and thorny way to heaven
Whiles like a puffed and reckless libertine
50 Himself the primrose path of dalliance treads
And recks not his own rede.

LAERTES   O, fear me not.
I stay too long.

    Enter Polonius

           But here my father comes.
A double blessing is a double grace.
Occasion smiles upon a second leave.

POLONIUS

Yet here, Laertes? Aboard, aboard, for shame!
The wind sits in the shoulder of your sail,
And you are stayed for. There – my blessing with thee.
And these few precepts in thy memory
Look thou character. Give thy thoughts no tongue,
60 Nor any unproportioned thought his act.
Be thou familiar, but by no means vulgar.
Those friends thou hast, and their adoption tried,
Grapple them unto thy soul with hoops of steel.
But do not dull thy palm with entertainment
Of each new-hatched, unfledged courage. Beware
Of entrance to a quarrel. But, being in,
Bear't that th'opposèd may beware of thee.
Give every man thine ear, but few thy voice.
Take each man's censure, but reserve thy judgement.

Costly thy habit as thy purse can buy,
But not expressed in fancy; rich, not gaudy;
For the apparel oft proclaims the man,
And they in France of the best rank and station
Are of a most select and generous chief in that.
Neither a borrower nor a lender be,
For loan oft loses both itself and friend,
And borrowing dulleth edge of husbandry.
This above all: to thine own self be true,
And it must follow, as the night the day,
Thou canst not then be false to any man.   80
Farewell. My blessing season this in thee!

LAERTES

Most humbly do I take my leave, my lord.

POLONIUS

The time invites you. Go. Your servants tend.

LAERTES

Farewell, Ophelia; and remember well
What I have said to you.

OPHELIA   'Tis in my memory locked,
And you yourself shall keep the key of it.

LAERTES

Farewell.   *Exit*

POLONIUS

What is't, Ophelia, he hath said to you?

OPHELIA

So please you, something touching the Lord Hamlet.

POLONIUS

Marry, well bethought.   90
'Tis told me he hath very oft of late
Given private time to you, and you yourself
Have of your audience been most free and bounteous.
If it be so – as so 'tis put on me,
And that in way of caution – I must tell you

You do not understand yourself so clearly
As it behoves my daughter and your honour.
What is between you? Give me up the truth.

OPHELIA

He hath, my lord, of late made many tenders
Of his affection to me.

POLONIUS

Affection? Pooh! You speak like a green girl,
Unsifted in such perilous circumstance.
Do you believe his tenders, as you call them?

OPHELIA

I do not know, my lord, what I should think.

POLONIUS

Marry, I will teach you. Think yourself a baby
That you have ta'en these tenders for true pay
Which are not sterling. Tender yourself more dearly,
Or – not to crack the wind of the poor phrase,
Running it thus – you'll tender me a fool.

OPHELIA

My lord, he hath importuned me with love
In honourable fashion.

POLONIUS

Ay, 'fashion' you may call it. Go to, go to.

OPHELIA

And hath given countenance to his speech, my lord,
With almost all the holy vows of heaven.

POLONIUS

Ay, springes to catch woodcocks. I do know,
When the blood burns, how prodigal the soul
Lends the tongue vows. These blazes, daughter,
Giving more light than heat, extinct in both
Even in their promise, as it is a-making,
You must not take for fire. From this time
Be something scanter of your maiden presence.

Set your entreatments at a higher rate
Than a command to parle. For Lord Hamlet,
Believe so much in him that he is young,
And with a larger tether may he walk
Than may be given you. In few, Ophelia,
Do not believe his vows. For they are brokers,
Not of that dye which their investments show,
But mere implorators of unholy suits,
Breathing like sanctified and pious bawds,   130
The better to beguile. This is for all:
I would not, in plain terms, from this time forth
Have you so slander any moment leisure
As to give words or talk with the Lord Hamlet.
Look to't, I charge you. Come your ways.

OPHELIA
I shall obey, my lord.   *Exeunt*

Enter Hamlet, Horatio, and Marcellus   I.4
HAMLET
The air bites shrewdly. It is very cold.
HORATIO
It is a nipping and an eager air.
HAMLET
What hour now?
HORATIO   I think it lacks of twelve.
MARCELLUS
No, it is struck.
HORATIO
Indeed? I heard it not. It then draws near the season
Wherein the spirit held his wont to walk.
    *A flourish of trumpets, and two pieces of ordnance go
    off*

What does this mean, my lord?

HAMLET

The King doth wake tonight and takes his rouse,
Keeps wassail, and the swaggering upspring reels.
10   And as he drains his draughts of Rhenish down
The kettledrum and trumpet thus bray out
The triumph of his pledge.

HORATIO   Is it a custom?

HAMLET

Ay, marry, is't.
But to my mind, though I am native here
And to the manner born, it is a custom
More honoured in the breach than the observance.
This heavy-headed revel east and west
Makes us traduced and taxed of other nations.
They clepe us drunkards and with swinish phrase
20   Soil our addition; and indeed it takes
From our achievements, though performed at height,
The pith and marrow of our attribute.
So oft it chances in particular men
That – for some vicious mole of nature in them,
As in their birth, wherein they are not guilty,
Since nature cannot choose his origin –
By the o'ergrowth of some complexion,
Oft breaking down the pales and forts of reason,
Or by some habit that too much o'er-leavens
30   The form of plausive manners – that these men,
Carrying, I say, the stamp of one defect,
Being nature's livery or fortune's star,
His virtues else, be they as pure as grace,
As infinite as man may undergo,
Shall in the general censure take corruption
From that particular fault. The dram of evil

Doth all the noble substance of a doubt,
To his own scandal –
   Enter the Ghost

HORATIO   Look, my lord, it comes.

HAMLET

Angels and ministers of grace defend us!
Be thou a spirit of health or goblin damned,   40
Bring with thee airs from heaven or blasts from hell,
Be thy intents wicked or charitable,
Thou comest in such a questionable shape
That I will speak to thee. I'll call thee Hamlet,
King, father, royal Dane. O, answer me!
Let me not burst in ignorance. But tell
Why thy canonized bones, hearsèd in death,
Have burst their cerements; why the sepulchre
Wherein we saw thee quietly interred
Hath oped his ponderous and marble jaws   50
To cast thee up again. What may this mean
That thou, dead corse, again in complete steel,
Revisits thus the glimpses of the moon,
Making night hideous, and we fools of nature
So horridly to shake our disposition
With thoughts beyond the reaches of our souls?
Say, why is this? Wherefore? What should we do?
   The Ghost beckons him

HORATIO

It beckons you to go away with it,
As if it some impartment did desire
To you alone.

MARCELLUS   Look with what courteous action   60
It waves you to a more removèd ground.
But do not go with it.

HORATIO   No, by no means.

HAMLET

It will not speak. Then I will follow it.

HORATIO

Do not, my lord.

HAMLET   Why, what should be the fear?
I do not set my life at a pin's fee.
And for my soul, what can it do to that,
Being a thing immortal as itself?
It waves me forth again. I'll follow it.

HORATIO

What if it tempt you toward the flood, my lord,
70   Or to the dreadful summit of the cliff
That beetles o'er his base into the sea,
And there assume some other, horrible form,
Which might deprive your sovereignty of reason
And draw you into madness? Think of it.
The very place puts toys of desperation,
Without more motive, into every brain
That looks so many fathoms to the sea
And hears it roar beneath.

HAMLET   It waves me still. –
Go on. I'll follow thee.

MARCELLUS

You shall not go, my lord.

80 HAMLET   Hold off your hands.

HORATIO

Be ruled. You shall not go.

HAMLET   My fate cries out
And makes each petty artere in this body
As hardy as the Nemean lion's nerve.
Still am I called. Unhand me, gentlemen.
By heaven, I'll make a ghost of him that lets me!
I say, away! Go on. I'll follow thee.

Exeunt the Ghost and Hamlet

HORATIO
  He waxes desperate with imagination.
MARCELLUS
  Let's follow. 'Tis not fit thus to obey him.
HORATIO
  Have after. To what issue will this come?
MARCELLUS
  Something is rotten in the state of Denmark.   90
HORATIO
  Heaven will direct it.
MARCELLUS   Nay, let's follow him.

                                                   Exeunt

        Enter the Ghost and Hamlet   I.5
HAMLET
  Whither wilt thou lead me? Speak. I'll go no further.
GHOST
  Mark me.
HAMLET   I will.
GHOST   My hour is almost come,
  When I to sulphurous and tormenting flames
  Must render up myself.
HAMLET   Alas, poor ghost!
GHOST
  Pity me not, but lend thy serious hearing
  To what I shall unfold.
HAMLET   Speak. I am bound to hear.
GHOST
  So art thou to revenge, when thou shalt hear.
HAMLET
  What?
GHOST
  I am thy father's spirit,
  Doomed for a certain term to walk the night,   10

And for the day confined to fast in fires,
Till the foul crimes done in my days of nature
Are burnt and purged away. But that I am forbid
To tell the secrets of my prison house,
I could a tale unfold whose lightest word
Would harrow up thy soul, freeze thy young blood,
Make thy two eyes like stars start from their spheres,
Thy knotted and combinèd locks to part,
And each particular hair to stand an end
Like quills upon the fretful porpentine.
But this eternal blazon must not be
To ears of flesh and blood. List, list, O, list!
If thou didst ever thy dear father love –

HAMLET

O God!

GHOST

Revenge his foul and most unnatural murder.

HAMLET

Murder?

GHOST

Murder most foul, as in the best it is,
But this most foul, strange, and unnatural.

HAMLET

Haste me to know't, that I, with wings as swift
As meditation or the thoughts of love,
May sweep to my revenge.

GHOST   I find thee apt,
And duller shouldst thou be than the fat weed
That roots itself in ease on Lethe wharf,
Wouldst thou not stir in this. Now, Hamlet, hear.
'Tis given out that, sleeping in my orchard,
A serpent stung me. So the whole ear of Denmark
Is by a forgèd process of my death
Rankly abused. But know, thou noble youth,

The serpent that did sting thy father's life
Now wears his crown.

HAMLET   O my prophetic soul!   40
My uncle?

GHOST

Ay, that incestuous, that adulterate beast,
With witchcraft of his wit, with traitorous gifts –
O wicked wit and gifts, that have the power
So to seduce! – won to his shameful lust
The will of my most seeming-virtuous Queen.
O Hamlet, what a falling off was there,
From me, whose love was of that dignity
That it went hand in hand even with the vow
I made to her in marriage; and to decline   50
Upon a wretch whose natural gifts were poor
To those of mine!
But virtue as it never will be moved,
Though lewdness court it in a shape of heaven,
So lust, though to a radiant angel linked,
Will sate itself in a celestial bed
And prey on garbage.
But soft, methinks I scent the morning air.
Brief let me be. Sleeping within my orchard,
My custom always of the afternoon,   60
Upon my secure hour thy uncle stole
With juice of cursèd hebona in a vial,
And in the porches of my ears did pour
The leperous distilment; whose effect
Holds such an enmity with blood of man
That swift as quicksilver it courses through
The natural gates and alleys of the body,
And with a sudden vigour it doth posset
And curd, like eager droppings into milk,
The thin and wholesome blood. So did it mine.   70

And a most instant tetter barked about,
Most lazar-like, with vile and loathsome crust
All my smooth body.
Thus was I sleeping by a brother's hand
Of life, of crown, of queen at once dispatched,
Cut off even in the blossoms of my sin,
Unhouseled, disappointed, unaneled,
No reckoning made, but sent to my account
With all my imperfections on my head.
80 O, horrible! O, horrible! Most horrible!
If thou hast nature in thee, bear it not.
Let not the royal bed of Denmark be
A couch for luxury and damned incest.
But howsomever thou pursues this act,
Taint not thy mind, nor let thy soul contrive
Against thy mother aught. Leave her to heaven
And to those thorns that in her bosom lodge
To prick and sting her. Fare thee well at once.
The glow-worm shows the matin to be near
90 And 'gins to pale his uneffectual fire.
Adieu, adieu, adieu. Remember me.   *Exit*

HAMLET

O all you host of heaven! O earth! What else?
And shall I couple hell? O, fie! Hold, hold, my heart.
And you, my sinews, grow not instant old,
But bear me stiffly up. Remember thee?
Ay, thou poor ghost, whiles memory holds a seat
In this distracted globe. Remember thee?
Yea, from the table of my memory
I'll wipe away all trivial fond records,
100 All saws of books, all forms, all pressures past
That youth and observation copied there,
And thy commandment all alone shall live
Within the book and volume of my brain,

Unmixed with baser matter. Yes, by heaven!
O most pernicious woman!
O villain, villain, smiling, damnèd villain!
My tables – meet it is I set it down
That one may smile, and smile, and be a villain.
At least I am sure it may be so in Denmark.
       He writes
So, uncle, there you are. Now to my word: 110
It is 'Adieu, adieu, remember me'.
I have sworn't.
       Enter Horatio and Marcellus

HORATIO
My lord, my lord!
MARCELLUS   Lord Hamlet!
HORATIO   Heavens secure him!
HAMLET
So be it!
MARCELLUS
Illo, ho, ho, my lord!
HAMLET
Hillo, ho, ho, boy! Come, bird, come.
MARCELLUS
How is't, my noble lord?
HORATIO   What news, my lord?
HAMLET
O, wonderful!
HORATIO
Good my lord, tell it.
HAMLET   No, you will reveal it.
HORATIO
Not I, my lord, by heaven.
MARCELLUS   Nor I, my lord.   120
HAMLET
How say you then? Would heart of man once think it?

93

But you'll be secret?

HORATIO *and* MARCELLUS Ay, by heaven, my lord.

HAMLET

There's never a villain dwelling in all Denmark –
But he's an arrant knave.

HORATIO

There needs no ghost, my lord, come from the grave
To tell us this.

HAMLET   Why, right, you are in the right,
And so, without more circumstance at all,
I hold it fit that we shake hands and part:
You, as your business and desire shall point you,
130 For every man hath business and desire,
Such as it is; and for my own poor part
I will go pray.

HORATIO

These are but wild and whirling words, my lord.

HAMLET

I am sorry they offend you, heartily.
Yes, faith, heartily.

HORATIO   There's no offence, my lord.

HAMLET

Yes, by Saint Patrick, but there is, Horatio,
And much offence too. Touching this vision here,
It is an honest ghost, that let me tell you.
For your desire to know what is between us,
140 O'ermaster't as you may. And now, good friends,
As you are friends, scholars, and soldiers,
Give me one poor request.

HORATIO

What is't, my lord? We will.

HAMLET

Never make known what you have seen tonight.

HORATIO *and* MARCELLUS
  My lord, we will not.
HAMLET   Nay, but swear't.
HORATIO   In faith,
  My lord, not I.
MARCELLUS   Nor I, my lord – in faith.
HAMLET
  Upon my sword.
MARCELLUS   We have sworn, my lord, already.
HAMLET
  Indeed, upon my sword, indeed.
        The Ghost cries under the stage
GHOST
  Swear.
HAMLET
  Ha, ha, boy, sayst thou so? Art thou there, truepenny? 150
  Come on. You hear this fellow in the cellarage.
  Consent to swear.
HORATIO   Propose the oath, my lord.
HAMLET
  Never to speak of this that you have seen,
  Swear by my sword.
GHOST (*beneath*)
  Swear.
HAMLET
  Hic et ubique? Then we'll shift our ground.
  Come hither, gentlemen,
  And lay your hands again upon my sword.
  Swear by my sword
  Never to speak of this that you have heard. 160
GHOST (*beneath*)
  Swear by his sword.
HAMLET
  Well said, old mole! Canst work i'th'earth so fast?

A worthy pioneer! Once more remove, good friends.

HORATIO

O day and night, but this is wondrous strange!

HAMLET

And therefore as a stranger give it welcome.
There are more things in heaven and earth, Horatio,
Than are dreamt of in your philosophy.
But come.
Here as before, never, so help you mercy,
170   How strange or odd some'er I bear myself –
As I perchance hereafter shall think meet
To put an antic disposition on –
That you, at such times seeing me, never shall,
With arms encumbered thus, or this head-shake,
Or by pronouncing of some doubtful phrase,
As 'Well, well, we know', or 'We could, an if we
        would',
Or 'If we list to speak', or 'There be, an if they might',
Or such ambiguous giving out, to note
That you know aught of me – this do swear,
180   So grace and mercy at your most need help you.

GHOST (*beneath*)

Swear.

HAMLET

Rest, rest, perturbèd spirit! So, gentlemen,
With all my love I do commend me to you,
And what so poor a man as Hamlet is
May do t'express his love and friending to you,
God willing, shall not lack. Let us go in together,
And still your fingers on your lips, I pray.
The time is out of joint. O, cursèd spite,
That ever I was born to set it right!
190   Nay, come, let's go together.

Exeunt

POLONIUS

Give him this money and these notes, Reynaldo.

REYNALDO

I will, my lord.

POLONIUS

You shall do marvellous wisely, good Reynaldo,
Before you visit him, to make inquire
Of his behaviour.

REYNALDO   My lord, I did intend it.

POLONIUS

Marry, well said. Very well said. Look you, sir,
Inquire me first what Danskers are in Paris,
And how, and who, what means, and where they keep,
What company, at what expense; and finding
By this encompassment and drift of question   10
That they do know my son, come you more nearer
Than your particular demands will touch it.
Take you as 'twere some distant knowledge of him,
As thus, 'I know his father and his friends,
And in part him' – do you mark this, Reynaldo?

REYNALDO

Ay, very well, my lord.

POLONIUS

'And in part him, but', you may say, 'not well;
But if't be he I mean, he's very wild,
Addicted so and so'. And there put on him
What forgeries you please – marry, none so rank   20
As may dishonour him – take heed of that –
But, sir, such wanton, wild, and usual slips
As are companions noted and most known
To youth and liberty.

REYNALDO   As gaming, my lord.

POLONIUS

Ay, or drinking, fencing, swearing, quarrelling,
Drabbing. You may go so far.

REYNALDO

My lord, that would dishonour him.

POLONIUS

Faith, no, as you may season it in the charge.
You must not put another scandal on him,

30   That he is open to incontinency.
That's not my meaning. But breathe his faults so
        quaintly
That they may seem the taints of liberty,
The flash and outbreak of a fiery mind,
A savageness in unreclaimèd blood,
Of general assault.

REYNALDO   But, my good lord –

POLONIUS

Wherefore should you do this?

REYNALDO   Ay, my lord,
I would know that.

POLONIUS   Marry, sir, here's my drift,
And I believe it is a fetch of warrant.
You laying these slight sullies on my son,

40   As 'twere a thing a little soiled i'th'working,
Mark you,
Your party in converse, him you would sound,
Having ever seen in the prenominate crimes
The youth you breathe of guilty, be assured
He closes with you in this consequence:
'Good sir', or so, or 'friend', or 'gentleman' –
According to the phrase or the addition
Of man and country –

REYNALDO   Very good, my lord.

POLONIUS And then, sir, does 'a this – 'a does – What

was I about to say? By the mass, I was about to say 50
something! Where did I leave?

REYNALDO At 'closes in the consequence', at 'friend',
'or so', and 'gentleman'.

POLONIUS At 'closes in the consequence' – Ay, marry!
He closes thus: 'I know the gentleman.
I saw him yesterday, or th'other day,
Or then, or then, with such or such, and, as you say,
There was 'a gaming; there o'ertook in's rouse;
There falling out at tennis'; or perchance
'I saw him enter such a house of sale',   60
Videlicet, a brothel, or so forth.
See you now –
Your bait of falsehood takes this carp of truth,
And thus do we of wisdom and of reach,
With windlasses and with assays of bias,
By indirections find directions out.
So, by my former lecture and advice,
Shall you my son. You have me, have you not?

REYNALDO
My lord, I have.

POLONIUS   God bye ye, fare ye well.

REYNALDO
Good my lord.   70

POLONIUS
Observe his inclination in yourself.

REYNALDO
I shall, my lord.

POLONIUS
And let him ply his music.

REYNALDO   Well, my lord.

POLONIUS
Farewell.   *Exit Reynaldo*
    Enter Ophelia

99

How now, Ophelia, what's the matter?

OPHELIA

O my lord, my lord, I have been so affrighted!

POLONIUS

With what, i'th'name of God?

OPHELIA

My lord, as I was sewing in my closet,
Lord Hamlet, with his doublet all unbraced,
No hat upon his head, his stockings fouled,
80 Ungartered, and down-gyvèd to his ankle,
Pale as his shirt, his knees knocking each other,
And with a look so piteous in purport
As if he had been loosèd out of hell
To speak of horrors – he comes before me.

POLONIUS

Mad for thy love?

OPHELIA   My lord, I do not know,
But truly I do fear it.

POLONIUS   What said he?

OPHELIA

He took me by the wrist and held me hard.
Then goes he to the length of all his arm,
And with his other hand thus o'er his brow
90 He falls to such perusal of my face
As 'a would draw it. Long stayed he so.
At last, a little shaking of mine arm
And thrice his head thus waving up and down,
He raised a sigh so piteous and profound
As it did seem to shatter all his bulk
And end his being. That done, he lets me go;
And, with his head over his shoulder turned,
He seemed to find his way without his eyes;
For out o'doors he went without their helps
100 And to the last bended their light on me.

POLONIUS

Come, go with me. I will go seek the King.
This is the very ecstasy of love,
Whose violent property fordoes itself
And leads the will to desperate undertakings
As oft as any passion under heaven
That does afflict our natures. I am sorry.
What, have you given him any hard words of late?

OPHELIA

No, my good lord. But, as you did command,
I did repel his letters and denied
His access to me.

POLONIUS   That hath made him mad.   110
I am sorry that with better heed and judgement
I had not quoted him. I feared he did but trifle
And meant to wrack thee. But beshrew my jealousy.
By heaven, it is as proper to our age
To cast beyond ourselves in our opinions
As it is common for the younger sort
To lack discretion. Come, go we to the King.
This must be known, which, being kept close, might
          move
More grief to hide than hate to utter love.
Come.   *Exeunt* 120

Flourish   II.2
*Enter the King and Queen, Rosencrantz and Guilden-
stern, with attendants*

KING

Welcome, dear Rosencrantz and Guildenstern.
Moreover that we much did long to see you,
The need we have to use you did provoke

Our hasty sending. Something have you heard
Of Hamlet's transformation – so call it,
Sith nor th'exterior nor the inward man
Resembles that it was. What it should be,
More than his father's death, that thus hath put him
So much from th'understanding of himself
10 I cannot dream of. I entreat you both
That, being of so young days brought up with him,
And sith so neighboured to his youth and 'haviour,
That you vouchsafe your rest here in our court
Some little time, so by your companies
To draw him on to pleasures, and to gather
So much as from occasion you may glean,
Whether aught to us unknown afflicts him thus,
That, opened, lies within our remedy.

QUEEN
Good gentlemen, he hath much talked of you,
20 And sure I am two men there is not living
To whom he more adheres. If it will please you
To show us so much gentry and good will
As to expend your time with us awhile
For the supply and profit of our hope,
Your visitation shall receive such thanks
As fits a king's remembrance.

ROSENCRANTZ   Both your majesties
Might, by the sovereign power you have of us,
Put your dread pleasures more into command
Than to entreaty.

GUILDENSTERN   But we both obey,
30 And here give up ourselves in the full bent
To lay our service freely at your feet,
To be commanded.

KING
Thanks, Rosencrantz and gentle Guildenstern.

QUEEN

Thanks, Guildenstern and gentle Rosencrantz.
And I beseech you instantly to visit
My too much changèd son. – Go, some of you,
And bring these gentlemen where Hamlet is.

GUILDENSTERN

Heavens make our presence and our practices
Pleasant and helpful to him!

QUEEN   Ay, amen!

Exeunt Rosencrantz and
Guildenstern with attendants

Enter Polonius

POLONIUS

The ambassadors from Norway, my good lord,   40
Are joyfully returned.

KING

Thou still hast been the father of good news.

POLONIUS

Have I, my lord? Assure you, my good liege,
I hold my duty as I hold my soul,
Both to my God and to my gracious King.
And I do think – or else this brain of mine
Hunts not the trail of policy so sure
As it hath used to do – that I have found
The very cause of Hamlet's lunacy.

KING

O, speak of that! That do I long to hear.   50

POLONIUS

Give first admittance to th'ambassadors.
My news shall be the fruit to that great feast.

KING

Thyself do grace to them and bring them in.

Exit Polonius

He tells me, my dear Gertrude, he hath found

The head and source of all your son's distemper.

QUEEN

I doubt it is no other but the main,
His father's death and our o'erhasty marriage.

KING

Well, we shall sift him.

*Enter Voltemand and Cornelius, the ambassadors,
with Polonius*

Welcome, my good friends.
Say, Voltemand, what from our brother Norway?

VOLTEMAND

60 Most fair return of greetings and desires.
Upon our first, he sent out to suppress
His nephew's levies, which to him appeared
To be a preparation 'gainst the Polack,
But, better looked into, he truly found
It was against your highness; whereat grieved,
That so his sickness, age, and impotence
Was falsely borne in hand, sends out arrests
On Fortinbras; which he in brief obeys,
Receives rebuke from Norway, and in fine
70 Makes vow before his uncle never more
To give th'assay of arms against your majesty.
Whereon old Norway, overcome with joy,
Gives him three thousand crowns in annual fee
And his commission to employ those soldiers,
So levied as before, against the Polack,
With an entreaty, herein further shown,

(He gives a paper to the King)

That it might please you to give quiet pass
Through your dominions for this enterprise,
On such regards of safety and allowance
As therein are set down.

80 KING   It likes us well.

And at our more considered time we'll read,
Answer, and think upon this business.
Meantime we thank you for your well-took labour.
Go to your rest. At night we'll feast together.
Most welcome home!   *Exeunt the ambassadors*

POLONIUS   This business is well ended.
My liege and madam, to expostulate
What majesty should be, what duty is,
Why day is day, night night, and time is time,
Were nothing but to waste night, day, and time.
Therefore, since brevity is the soul of wit,   90
And tediousness the limbs and outward flourishes,
I will be brief. Your noble son is mad.
Mad call I it. For, to define true madness,
What is't but to be nothing else but mad?
But let that go.

QUEEN   More matter, with less art.

POLONIUS
Madam, I swear I use no art at all.
That he's mad, 'tis true. 'Tis true, 'tis pity,
And pity 'tis 'tis true – a foolish figure.
But farewell it; for I will use no art.
Mad let us grant him then. And now remains   100
That we find out the cause of this effect –
Or rather say, the cause of this defect,
For this effect defective comes by cause.
Thus it remains, and the remainder thus.
Perpend.
I have a daughter – have while she is mine –
Who in her duty and obedience, mark,
Hath given me this. Now gather, and surmise.
     (He reads the letter)
*To the celestial, and my soul's idol, the most beautified
Ophelia* – That's an ill phrase, a vile phrase; 'beautified'   110

is a vile phrase. But you shall hear. Thus:
    (*He reads*)
In her excellent white bosom, these, et cetera.

QUEEN

Came this from Hamlet to her?

POLONIUS

Good madam, stay awhile. I will be faithful.
    (*He reads*)
Doubt thou the stars are fire.
   Doubt that the sun doth move.
Doubt truth to be a liar.
   But never doubt I love.
O dear Ophelia, I am ill at these numbers. I have not art
to reckon my groans. But that I love thee best, O most best,
believe it. Adieu.

      Thine evermore, most dear lady, whilst
      this machine is to him,

                            Hamlet

This in obedience hath my daughter shown me,
And more above hath his solicitings,
As they fell out by time, by means, and place,
All given to mine ear.

KING   But how hath she

Received his love?

POLONIUS   What do you think of me?

KING

As of a man faithful and honourable.

POLONIUS

I would fain prove so. But what might you think
When I had seen this hot love on the wing –
As I perceived it, I must tell you that,
Before my daughter told me – what might you,
Or my dear majesty your Queen here, think

If I had played the desk or table-book,
Or given my heart a winking, mute and dumb,
Or looked upon this love with idle sight?
What might you think? No, I went round to work,
And my young mistress thus I did bespeak: 140
'Lord Hamlet is a prince, out of thy star.
This must not be.' And then I prescripts gave her,
That she should lock herself from his resort,
Admit no messengers, receive no tokens.
Which done, she took the fruits of my advice,
And he, repellèd, a short tale to make,
Fell into a sadness, then into a fast,
Thence to a watch, thence into a weakness,
Thence to a lightness, and, by this declension,
Into the madness wherein now he raves   150
And all we mourn for.

KING   Do you think 'tis this?
QUEEN
  It may be, very like.
POLONIUS
  Hath there been such a time – I would fain know that –
  That I have positively said ' 'Tis so'
  When it proved otherwise?
KING   Not that I know.
POLONIUS
  Take this from this, if this be otherwise.
  If circumstances lead me, I will find
  Where truth is hid, though it were hid indeed
  Within the centre.
KING   How may we try it further?
POLONIUS
  You know sometimes he walks four hours together   160
  Here in the lobby.

QUEEN   So he does indeed.

POLONIUS

At such a time I'll loose my daughter to him.

Be you and I behind an arras then.

Mark the encounter. If he love her not,

And be not from his reason fallen thereon,

Let me be no assistant for a state,

But keep a farm and carters.

KING   We will try it.

Enter Hamlet

QUEEN

But look where sadly the poor wretch comes reading.

POLONIUS

Away, I do beseech you both, away.

170 I'll board him presently. O, give me leave.

Exeunt the King and Queen

How does my good Lord Hamlet?

HAMLET Well, God-a-mercy.

POLONIUS Do you know me, my lord?

HAMLET Excellent well. You are a fishmonger.

POLONIUS Not I, my lord.

HAMLET Then I would you were so honest a man.

POLONIUS Honest, my lord?

HAMLET Ay, sir. To be honest, as this world goes, is to be
one man picked out of ten thousand.

180 POLONIUS That's very true, my lord.

HAMLET For if the sun breed maggots in a dead dog,
being a good kissing carrion – have you a daughter?

POLONIUS I have, my lord.

HAMLET Let her not walk i'th'sun. Conception is a blessing. But as your daughter may conceive, friend, look
to't.

POLONIUS (*aside*) How say you by that? Still harping on
my daughter. Yet he knew me not at first. 'A said I was

a fishmonger. 'A is far gone, far gone. And truly in my
youth I suffered much extremity for love, very near 190
this. I'll speak to him again. – What do you read, my
lord?

HAMLET Words, words, words.

POLONIUS What is the matter, my lord?

HAMLET Between who?

POLONIUS I mean the matter that you read, my lord.

HAMLET Slanders, sir. For the satirical rogue says here
that old men have grey beards, that their faces are
wrinkled, their eyes purging thick amber and plum-tree
gum, and that they have a plentiful lack of wit, together 200
with most weak hams; all which, sir, though I most
powerfully and potently believe, yet I hold it not
honesty to have it thus set down. For yourself, sir, shall
grow old as I am – if, like a crab, you could go backward.

POLONIUS (aside) Though this be madness, yet there
is method in't. – Will you walk out of the air, my
lord?

HAMLET Into my grave?

POLONIUS Indeed, that's out of the air. (Aside) How
pregnant sometimes his replies are! A happiness that
often madness hits on, which reason and sanity could 210
not so prosperously be delivered of. I will leave him
and suddenly contrive the means of meeting between
him and my daughter. – My honourable lord, I will
most humbly take my leave of you.

HAMLET You cannot, sir, take from me anything that I
will not more willingly part withal – except my life,
except my life, except my life.

POLONIUS Fare you well, my lord.

HAMLET These tedious old fools!

Enter Guildenstern and Rosencrantz

POLONIUS You go to seek the Lord Hamlet. There he is. 220

ROSENCRANTZ (*to Polonius*) God save you, sir!

                Exit Polonius

GUILDENSTERN My honoured lord!

ROSENCRANTZ My most dear lord!

HAMLET

My excellent good friends.
How dost thou, Guildenstern? Ah, Rosencrantz!
Good lads, how do you both?

ROSENCRANTZ

As the indifferent children of the earth.

GUILDENSTERN

Happy in that we are not over-happy.
On Fortune's cap we are not the very button.

HAMLET

Nor the soles of her shoe?

230 ROSENCRANTZ   Neither, my lord.

HAMLET Then you live about her waist, or in the middle
of her favours?

GUILDENSTERN Faith, her privates we.

HAMLET In the secret parts of Fortune? O, most true!
She is a strumpet. What news?

ROSENCRANTZ None, my lord, but that the world's
grown honest.

HAMLET Then is Doomsday near. But your news is not
true. Let me question more in particular. What have
240 you, my good friends, deserved at the hands of Fortune
that she sends you to prison hither?

GUILDENSTERN Prison, my lord?

HAMLET Denmark's a prison.

ROSENCRANTZ Then is the world one.

HAMLET A goodly one; in which there are many confines,
wards, and dungeons, Denmark being one o'th'worst.

ROSENCRANTZ We think not so, my lord.

HAMLET Why, then 'tis none to you. For there is nothing

either good or bad but thinking makes it so. To me it is
a prison. 250

ROSENCRANTZ Why, then your ambition makes it one.
'Tis too narrow for your mind.

HAMLET O God, I could be bounded in a nutshell and
count myself a king of infinite space, were it not that I
have bad dreams.

GUILDENSTERN Which dreams indeed are ambition.
For the very substance of the ambitious is merely the
shadow of a dream.

HAMLET A dream itself is but a shadow.

ROSENCRANTZ Truly; and I hold ambition of so airy and 260
light a quality that it is but a shadow's shadow.

HAMLET Then are our beggars bodies, and our monarchs
and outstretched heroes the beggars' shadows. Shall
we to th'court? For, by my fay, I cannot reason.

ROSENCRANTZ *and* GUILDENSTERN We'll wait upon
you.

HAMLET No such matter. I will not sort you with the rest
of my servants. For, to speak to you like an honest man,
I am most dreadfully attended. But in the beaten way
of friendship, what make you at Elsinore? 270

ROSENCRANTZ To visit you, my lord. No other occasion.

HAMLET Beggar that I am, I am even poor in thanks.
But I thank you. And sure, dear friends, my thanks are
too dear a halfpenny. Were you not sent for? Is it your
own inclining? Is it a free visitation? Come, come, deal
justly with me. Come, come. Nay, speak.

GUILDENSTERN What should we say, my lord?

HAMLET Why, anything but to th'purpose. You were
sent for. And there is a kind of confession in your looks,
which your modesties have not craft enough to colour. 280
I know the good King and Queen have sent for you.

ROSENCRANTZ To what end, my lord?

HAMLET That you must teach me. But let me conjure
you by the rights of our fellowship, by the consonancy
of our youth, by the obligation of our ever-preserved
love, and by what more dear a better proposer can charge
you withal, be even and direct with me whether you
were sent for or no.

ROSENCRANTZ (*aside to Guildenstern*) What say you?

290 HAMLET (*aside*) Nay then, I have an eye of you. – If you
love me, hold not off.

GUILDENSTERN My lord, we were sent for.

HAMLET I will tell you why. So shall my anticipation
prevent your discovery, and your secrecy to the King
and Queen moult no feather. I have of late – but wherefore I know not – lost all my mirth, forgone all custom
of exercises. And indeed it goes so heavily with my
disposition that this goodly frame the earth seems to
me a sterile promontory. This most excellent canopy,

300 the air, look you, this brave o'erhanging firmament,
this majestical roof fretted with golden fire – why, it
appeareth nothing to me but a foul and pestilent congregation of vapours. What a piece of work is a man,
how noble in reason, how infinite in faculties, in form
and moving how express and admirable, in action how
like an angel, in apprehension how like a god: the
beauty of the world, the paragon of animals! And yet
to me what is this quintessence of dust? Man delights
not me – nor woman neither, though by your smiling

310 you seem to say so.

ROSENCRANTZ My lord, there was no such stuff in my
thoughts.

HAMLET Why did ye laugh then, when I said 'Man
delights not me'?

ROSENCRANTZ To think, my lord, if you delight not in
man, what lenten entertainment the players shall

receive from you. We coted them on the way. And
hither are they coming to offer you service.

HAMLET He that plays the king shall be welcome – his
majesty shall have tribute of me; the adventurous 320
knight shall use his foil and target; the lover shall not
sigh gratis; the humorous man shall end his part in
peace; the clown shall make those laugh whose lungs
are tickle o'th'sere; and the lady shall say her mind
freely, or the blank verse shall halt for't. What players
are they?

ROSENCRANTZ Even those you were wont to take such
delight in, the tragedians of the city.

HAMLET How chances it they travel? Their residence,
both in reputation and profit, was better both ways. 330

ROSENCRANTZ I think their inhibition comes by the
means of the late innovation.

HAMLET Do they hold the same estimation they did when
I was in the city? Are they so followed?

ROSENCRANTZ No, indeed are they not.

HAMLET How comes it? Do they grow rusty?

ROSENCRANTZ Nay, their endeavour keeps in the wonted
pace. But there is, sir, an eyrie of children, little eyases,
that cry out on the top of question and are most tyrannically clapped for't. These are now the fashion, and so 340
berattle the common stages – so they call them – that
many wearing rapiers are afraid of goosequills and dare
scarce come thither.

HAMLET What, are they children? Who maintains 'em?
How are they escoted? Will they pursue the quality no
longer than they can sing? Will they not say afterwards,
if they should grow themselves to common players – as
it is most like, if their means are not better – their
writers do them wrong to make them exclaim against
their own succession? 350

ROSENCRANTZ Faith, there has been much to-do on both sides, and the nation holds it no sin to tarre them to controversy. There was, for a while, no money bid for argument unless the poet and the player went to cuffs in the question.

HAMLET Is't possible?

GUILDENSTERN O, there has been much throwing about of brains.

HAMLET Do the boys carry it away?

360 ROSENCRANTZ Ay, that they do, my lord – Hercules and his load too.

HAMLET It is not very strange. For my uncle is King of Denmark, and those that would make mows at him while my father lived give twenty, forty, fifty, a hundred ducats apiece for his picture in little. 'Sblood, there is something in this more than natural, if philosophy could find it out.

A flourish

GUILDENSTERN There are the players.

HAMLET Gentlemen, you are welcome to Elsinore. Your
370 hands. Come then. Th'appurtenance of welcome is fashion and ceremony. Let me comply with you in this garb, lest my extent to the players, which I tell you must show fairly outwards, should more appear like entertainment than yours. You are welcome. But my uncle-father and aunt-mother are deceived.

GUILDENSTERN In what, my dear lord?

HAMLET I am but mad north-north-west. When the wind is southerly, I know a hawk from a handsaw.

Enter Polonius

POLONIUS Well be with you, gentlemen.

380 HAMLET Hark you, Guildenstern – and you too – at each ear a hearer. That great baby you see there is not yet out of his swaddling clouts.

ROSENCRANTZ Happily he is the second time come to
them. For they say an old man is twice a child.

HAMLET I will prophesy he comes to tell me of the
players. Mark it. – You say right, sir. 'A Monday morning, 'twas then, indeed.

POLONIUS My lord, I have news to tell you.

HAMLET My lord, I have news to tell you. When Roscius
was an actor in Rome –   390

POLONIUS The actors are come hither, my lord.

HAMLET Buzz, buzz.

POLONIUS Upon my honour –

HAMLET Then came each actor on his ass –

POLONIUS The best actors in the world, either for
tragedy, comedy, history, pastoral, pastoral-comical,
historical-pastoral, tragical-historical, tragical-comical-
historical-pastoral, scene individable, or poem unlimited. Seneca cannot be too heavy, nor Plautus too
light. For the law of writ and the liberty, these are the   400
only men.

HAMLET O Jephthah, judge of Israel, what a treasure
hadst thou!

POLONIUS What a treasure had he, my lord?

HAMLET Why,

     'One fair daughter, and no more,
       The which he lovèd passing well.'

POLONIUS (aside) Still on my daughter.

HAMLET Am I not i'th'right, old Jephthah?

POLONIUS If you call me Jephthah, my lord, I have a   410
daughter that I love passing well.

HAMLET Nay, that follows not.

POLONIUS What follows then, my lord?

HAMLET Why,

      'As by lot, God wot,'
and then you know,

'It came to pass, as most like it was.'
The first row of the pious chanson will show you more.
For look where my abridgement comes.

Enter the Players

420 You are welcome, masters, welcome, all. – I am glad to
see thee well. – Welcome, good friends. – O old friend,
why, thy face is valanced since I saw thee last. Comest
thou to beard me in Denmark? – What, my young lady
and mistress? By'r Lady, your ladyship is nearer to
heaven than when I saw you last by the altitude of a
chopine. Pray God your voice, like a piece of uncurrent
gold, be not cracked within the ring. – Masters, you are
all welcome. We'll e'en to't like French falconers: fly
at anything we see. We'll have a speech straight. Come,
430 give us a taste of your quality. Come, a passionate
speech.

FIRST PLAYER What speech, my good lord?

HAMLET I heard thee speak me a speech once, but it was
never acted, or if it was, not above once. For the play, I
remember, pleased not the million. 'Twas caviary to the
general. But it was – as I received it, and others, whose
judgements in such matters cried in the top of mine –
an excellent play, well digested in the scenes, set down
with as much modesty as cunning. I remember one said
440 there were no sallets in the lines to make the matter
savoury, nor no matter in the phrase that might indict
the author of affectation, but called it an honest method,
as wholesome as sweet, and by very much more handsome than fine. One speech in't I chiefly loved. 'Twas
Aeneas' tale to Dido; and thereabout of it especially
when he speaks of Priam's slaughter. If it live in your
memory, begin at this line – let me see, let me see.

'The rugged Pyrrhus, like th'Hyrcanian beast –'
'Tis not so. It begins with Pyrrhus.

116

'The rugged Pyrrhus, he whose sable arms,   450
Black as his purpose, did the night resemble
When he lay couchèd in th'ominous horse,
Hath now this dread and black complexion smeared
With heraldy more dismal. Head to foot
Now is he total gules, horridly tricked
With blood of fathers, mothers, daughters, sons,
Baked and impasted with the parching streets,
That lend a tyrannous and a damnèd light
To their lord's murder; roasted in wrath and fire,
And thus o'er-sizèd with coagulate gore,   460
With eyes like carbuncles, the hellish Pyrrhus
Old grandsire Priam seeks.'
  So, proceed you.

POLONIUS 'Fore God, my lord, well spoken, with good
  accent and good discretion.

FIRST PLAYER   'Anon he finds him,
Striking too short at Greeks. His antique sword,
Rebellious to his arm, lies where it falls,
Repugnant to command. Unequal matched,
Pyrrhus at Priam drives, in rage strikes wide,   470
But with the whiff and wind of his fell sword
Th'unnervèd father falls. Then senseless Ilium,
Seeming to feel this blow, with flaming top
Stoops to his base, and with a hideous crash
Takes prisoner Pyrrhus' ear. For lo! his sword,
Which was declining on the milky head
Of reverend Priam, seemed i'th'air to stick.
So as a painted tyrant Pyrrhus stood,
And like a neutral to his will and matter
Did nothing.   480
But as we often see, against some storm,
A silence in the heavens, the rack stand still,
The bold winds speechless, and the orb below

As hush as death; anon the dreadful thunder
Doth rend the region; so after Pyrrhus' pause,
A rousèd vengeance sets him new a-work,
And never did the Cyclops' hammers fall
On Mars's armour, forged for proof eterne,
With less remorse than Pyrrhus' bleeding sword
490 Now falls on Priam.
Out, out, thou strumpet Fortune! All you gods,
In general synod, take away her power!
Break all the spokes and fellies from her wheel,
And bowl the round nave down the hill of heaven,
As low as to the fiends!'

POLONIUS This is too long.

HAMLET It shall to the barber's, with your beard. –
Prithee say on. He's for a jig or a tale of bawdry, or he
sleeps. Say on. Come to Hecuba.

FIRST PLAYER
500 'But who, ah woe!, had seen the mobled Queen –'

HAMLET 'The mobled Queen'?

POLONIUS That's good. 'Mobled Queen' is good.

FIRST PLAYER
'Run barefoot up and down, threatening the flames
With bisson rheum; a clout upon that head
Where late the diadem stood; and for a robe,
About her lank and all o'er-teemèd loins,
A blanket in the alarm of fear caught up –
Who this had seen, with tongue in venom steeped
'Gainst Fortune's state would treason have
                    pronounced.
510 But if the gods themselves did see her then,
When she saw Pyrrhus make malicious sport
In mincing with his sword her husband's limbs,
The instant burst of clamour that she made,
Unless things mortal move them not at all,

Would have made milch the burning eyes of heaven
And passion in the gods.'

POLONIUS Look whe'er he has not turned his colour,
and has tears in's eyes. Prithee no more.

HAMLET 'Tis well. I'll have thee speak out the rest of this
soon. – Good my lord, will you see the players well 520
bestowed? Do you hear? Let them be well used, for
they are the abstract and brief chronicles of the time.
After your death you were better have a bad epitaph
than their ill report while you live.

POLONIUS My lord, I will use them according to their
desert.

HAMLET God's bodkin, man, much better! Use every
man after his desert, and who shall 'scape whipping?
Use them after your own honour and dignity. The less
they deserve, the more merit is in your bounty. Take 530
them in.

POLONIUS Come, sirs.

HAMLET Follow him, friends. We'll hear a play tomorrow. (*Aside to First Player*) Dost thou hear me, old
friend? Can you play *The Murder of Gonzago*?

FIRST PLAYER Ay, my lord.

HAMLET We'll ha't tomorrow night. You could for a
need study a speech of some dozen lines or sixteen lines,
which I would set down and insert in't, could you not?

FIRST PLAYER Ay, my lord. 540

HAMLET Very well. – Follow that lord, and look you mock
him not.

Exeunt Polonius and Players

My good friends, I'll leave you till night. You are welcome to Elsinore.

ROSENCRANTZ Good my lord.

HAMLET Ay, so, God bye to you.

Exeunt Rosencrantz and Guildenstern

Now I am alone.

O, what a rogue and peasant slave am I!
Is it not monstrous that this player here,
But in a fiction, in a dream of passion,
Could force his soul so to his own conceit
That from her working all his visage wanned,
Tears in his eyes, distraction in his aspect,
A broken voice, and his whole function suiting
With forms to his conceit? And all for nothing.
For Hecuba!
What's Hecuba to him, or he to her,
That he should weep for her? What would he do
Had he the motive and the cue for passion
That I have? He would drown the stage with tears
And cleave the general ear with horrid speech,
Make mad the guilty and appal the free,
Confound the ignorant, and amaze indeed
The very faculties of eyes and ears. Yet I,
A dull and muddy-mettled rascal, peak
Like John-a-dreams, unpregnant of my cause,
And can say nothing, no, not for a king
Upon whose property and most dear life
A damned defeat was made. Am I a coward?
Who calls me villain? Breaks my pate across?
Plucks off my beard and blows it in my face?
Tweaks me by the nose? Gives me the lie i'th'throat
As deep as to the lungs? Who does me this?
Ha, 'swounds, I should take it. For it cannot be
But I am pigeon-livered and lack gall
To make oppression bitter, or ere this
I should ha' fatted all the region kites
With this slave's offal. Bloody, bawdy villain!
Remorseless, treacherous, lecherous, kindless villain!
O, vengeance!

Why, what an ass am I! This is most brave,   580
That I, the son of a dear father murdered,
Prompted to my revenge by heaven and hell,
Must like a whore unpack my heart with words
And fall a-cursing like a very drab,
A stallion! Fie upon't, foh!
About, my brains. Hum – I have heard
That guilty creatures sitting at a play
Have by the very cunning of the scene
Been struck so to the soul that presently
They have proclaimed their malefactions.   590
For murder, though it have no tongue, will speak
With most miraculous organ. I'll have these players
Play something like the murder of my father
Before mine uncle. I'll observe his looks.
I'll tent him to the quick. If 'a do blench,
I know my course. The spirit that I have seen
May be a devil, and the devil hath power
T'assume a pleasing shape, yea, and perhaps
Out of my weakness and my melancholy,
As he is very potent with such spirits,   600
Abuses me to damn me. I'll have grounds
More relative than this. The play's the thing
Wherein I'll catch the conscience of the King.

Exit

Enter the King and Queen, Polonius, Ophelia, Rosen- III.1
crantz, Guildenstern, and lords

KING

And can you by no drift of conference
Get from him why he puts on this confusion,
Grating so harshly all his days of quiet

With turbulent and dangerous lunacy?

ROSENCRANTZ

He does confess he feels himself distracted,
But from what cause 'a will by no means speak.

GUILDENSTERN

Nor do we find him forward to be sounded,
But with a crafty madness keeps aloof
When we would bring him on to some confession
Of his true state.

10 QUEEN　　　　　　Did he receive you well?

ROSENCRANTZ

Most like a gentleman.

GUILDENSTERN

But with much forcing of his disposition.

ROSENCRANTZ

Niggard of question, but of our demands
Most free in his reply.

QUEEN　　　　　　　Did you assay him
To any pastime?

ROSENCRANTZ

Madam, it so fell out that certain players
We o'er-raught on the way. Of these we told him,
And there did seem in him a kind of joy
To hear of it. They are here about the court,
20 And, as I think, they have already order
This night to play before him.

POLONIUS　　　　　　　　'Tis most true,
And he beseeched me to entreat your majesties
To hear and see the matter.

KING

With all my heart, and it doth much content me
To hear him so inclined.
Good gentlemen, give him a further edge
And drive his purpose into these delights.

ROSENCRANTZ
  We shall, my lord.
                  Exeunt Rosencrantz, Guildenstern, and lords
KING   Sweet Gertrude, leave us too.
  For we have closely sent for Hamlet hither,
  That he, as 'twere by accident, may here   30
  Affront Ophelia.
  Her father and myself, lawful espials,
  We'll so bestow ourselves that, seeing unseen,
  We may of their encounter frankly judge,
  And gather by him, as he is behaved,
  If't be th'affliction of his love or no
  That thus he suffers for.
QUEEN   I shall obey you. –
  And for your part, Ophelia, I do wish
  That your good beauties be the happy cause
  Of Hamlet's wildness. So shall I hope your virtues   40
  Will bring him to his wonted way again,
  To both your honours.
OPHELIA   Madam, I wish it may.
                                          Exit the Queen
POLONIUS
  Ophelia, walk you here. – Gracious, so please you,
  We will bestow ourselves. (*To Ophelia*) Read on this
            book,
  That show of such an exercise may colour
  Your loneliness. We are oft to blame in this,
  'Tis too much proved, that with devotion's visage
  And pious action we do sugar o'er
  The devil himself.
KING   O, 'tis too true.
  (*Aside*) How smart a lash that speech doth give my
            conscience!   50
  The harlot's cheek, beautied with plastering art,

123

III.1

Is not more ugly to the thing that helps it
Than is my deed to my most painted word.
O, heavy burden!

POLONIUS

I hear him coming. Let's withdraw, my lord.

Exeunt the King and Polonius

Enter Hamlet

HAMLET

To be, or not to be – that is the question;
Whether 'tis nobler in the mind to suffer
The slings and arrows of outrageous fortune
Or to take arms against a sea of troubles
60 And by opposing end them. To die, to sleep –
No more – and by a sleep to say we end
The heartache and the thousand natural shocks
That flesh is heir to. 'Tis a consummation
Devoutly to be wished. To die, to sleep –
To sleep – perchance to dream. Ay, there's the rub.
For in that sleep of death what dreams may come
When we have shuffled off this mortal coil
Must give us pause. There's the respect
That makes calamity of so long life.
70 For who would bear the whips and scorns of time,
Th'oppressor's wrong, the proud man's contumely,
The pangs of despised love, the law's delay,
The insolence of office, and the spurns
That patient merit of th'unworthy takes,
When he himself might his quietus make
With a bare bodkin? Who would fardels bear,
To grunt and sweat under a weary life,
But that the dread of something after death,
The undiscovered country, from whose bourn
80 No traveller returns, puzzles the will,
And makes us rather bear those ills we have

Than fly to others that we know not of?
Thus conscience does make cowards of us all;
And thus the native hue of resolution
Is sicklied o'er with the pale cast of thought,
And enterprises of great pitch and moment
With this regard their currents turn awry
And lose the name of action. Soft you now,
The fair Ophelia! – Nymph, in thy orisons
Be all my sins remembered.

OPHELIA   Good my lord,   90
How does your honour for this many a day?

HAMLET
I humbly thank you, well, well, well.

OPHELIA
My lord, I have remembrances of yours
That I have longèd long to re-deliver.
I pray you now receive them.

HAMLET   No, not I.
I never gave you aught.

OPHELIA
My honoured lord, you know right well you did,
And with them words of so sweet breath composed
As made the things more rich. Their perfume lost,
Take these again. For to the noble mind   100
Rich gifts wax poor when givers prove unkind.
There, my lord.

HAMLET Ha, ha! Are you honest?

OPHELIA My lord?

HAMLET Are you fair?

OPHELIA What means your lordship?

HAMLET That if you be honest and fair, your honesty
should admit no discourse to your beauty.

OPHELIA Could beauty, my lord, have better commerce
than with honesty?   110

HAMLET Ay, truly. For the power of beauty will sooner transform honesty from what it is to a bawd than the force of honesty can translate beauty into his likeness. This was sometime a paradox, but now the time gives it proof. I did love you once.

OPHELIA Indeed, my lord, you made me believe so.

HAMLET You should not have believed me. For virtue cannot so inoculate our old stock but we shall relish of it. I loved you not.

120 OPHELIA I was the more deceived.

HAMLET Get thee to a nunnery. Why wouldst thou be a breeder of sinners? I am myself indifferent honest, but yet I could accuse me of such things that it were better my mother had not borne me. I am very proud, revengeful, ambitious, with more offences at my beck than I have thoughts to put them in, imagination to give them shape, or time to act them in. What should such fellows as I do crawling between earth and heaven? We are arrant knaves all. Believe none of us. Go thy ways to a
130 nunnery. Where's your father?

OPHELIA At home, my lord.

HAMLET Let the doors be shut upon him, that he may play the fool nowhere but in's own house. Farewell.

OPHELIA O, help him, you sweet heavens!

HAMLET If thou dost marry, I'll give thee this plague for thy dowry: be thou as chaste as ice, as pure as snow, thou shalt not escape calumny. Get thee to a nunnery. Go, farewell. Or if thou wilt needs marry, marry a fool. For wise men know well enough what monsters you
140 make of them. To a nunnery, go, and quickly too. Farewell.

OPHELIA O heavenly powers, restore him!

HAMLET I have heard of your paintings too, well enough. God hath given you one face, and you make yourselves

another. You jig and amble, and you lisp. You nickname God's creatures and make your wantonness your
ignorance. Go to, I'll no more on't. It hath made me
mad. I say we will have no more marriage. Those that
are married already – all but one – shall live. The rest
shall keep as they are. To a nunnery, go. *Exit* 150

OPHELIA

O, what a noble mind is here o'erthrown!
The courtier's, soldier's, scholar's, eye, tongue, sword,
Th'expectancy and rose of the fair state,
The glass of fashion and the mould of form,
Th'observed of all observers, quite, quite down!
And I, of ladies most deject and wretched,
That sucked the honey of his music vows,
Now see that noble and most sovereign reason
Like sweet bells jangled, out of time and harsh,
That unmatched form and feature of blown youth 160
Blasted with ecstasy. O, woe is me
T'have seen what I have seen, see what I see!
Enter the King and Polonius

KING

Love? His affections do not that way tend;
Nor what he spake, though it lacked form a little,
Was not like madness. There's something in his soul
O'er which his melancholy sits on brood,
And I do doubt the hatch and the disclose
Will be some danger; which for to prevent,
I have in quick determination
Thus set it down: he shall with speed to England 170
For the demand of our neglected tribute.
Haply the seas, and countries different,
With variable objects, shall expel
This something-settled matter in his heart,
Whereon his brains still beating puts him thus

From fashion of himself. What think you on't?

POLONIUS

It shall do well. But yet do I believe
The origin and commencement of his grief
Sprung from neglected love. – How now, Ophelia?
180 You need not tell us what Lord Hamlet said.
We heard it all. – My lord, do as you please,
But if you hold it fit, after the play
Let his Queen mother all alone entreat him
To show his grief. Let her be round with him,
And I'll be placed, so please you, in the ear
Of all their conference. If she find him not,
To England send him, or confine him where
Your wisdom best shall think.

KING   It shall be so.
Madness in great ones must not unwatched go.

Exeunt

III.2   *Enter Hamlet and the Players*

HAMLET Speak the speech, I pray you, as I pronounced
it to you, trippingly on the tongue. But if you mouth it
as many of our players do, I had as lief the town crier
spoke my lines. Nor do not saw the air too much with
your hand, thus. But use all gently. For in the very tor-
rent, tempest, and, as I may say, whirlwind of your
passion, you must acquire and beget a temperance that
may give it smoothness. O, it offends me to the soul to
hear a robustious periwig-pated fellow tear a passion to
10 tatters, to very rags, to split the ears of the groundlings,
who for the most part are capable of nothing but inexplicable dumb shows and noise. I would have such a
fellow whipped for o'erdoing Termagant. It out-Herods
Herod. Pray you avoid it.

FIRST PLAYER I warrant your honour.

HAMLET Be not too tame neither. But let your own discretion be your tutor. Suit the action to the word, the word to the action, with this special observance, that you o'erstep not the modesty of nature. For anything so o'erdone is from the purpose of playing, whose end, both at the first and now, was and is to hold, as 'twere, the mirror up to nature, to show virtue her own feature, scorn her own image, and the very age and body of the time his form and pressure. Now this overdone, or come tardy off, though it make the unskilful laugh, cannot but make the judicious grieve; the censure of the which one must in your allowance o'erweigh a whole theatre of others. O, there be players that I have seen play, and heard others praise, and that highly, not to speak it profanely, that, neither having th'accent of Christians nor the gait of Christian, pagan, nor man, have so strutted and bellowed that I have thought some of Nature's journeymen had made men, and not made them well, they imitated humanity so abominably.

FIRST PLAYER I hope we have reformed that indifferently with us, sir.

HAMLET O, reform it altogether! And let those that play your clowns speak no more than is set down for them. For there be of them that will themselves laugh to set on some quantity of barren spectators to laugh too, though in the meantime some necessary question of the play be then to be considered. That's villainous, and shows a most pitiful ambition in the fool that uses it. And then you have some again that keeps one suit of jests, as a man is known by one suit of apparel; and gentlemen quote his jests down in their tables before they come to the play; as thus, 'Cannot you stay till I eat my porridge?', and 'You owe me a quarter's wages', and 'My coat

wants a cullison', and 'Your beer is sour', and blabber-
50 ing with his lips, and thus keeping in his cinquepace of
jests, when, God knows, the warm clown cannot make a
jest unless by chance, as the blind man catcheth a hare.
Masters, tell him of it.

FIRST PLAYER We will, my lord.

HAMLET Well, go make you ready.   *Exeunt Players*
          Enter Polonius, Rosencrantz, and Guildenstern
How now, my lord? Will the King hear this piece of
work?

POLONIUS And the Queen too, and that presently.

HAMLET Bid the players make haste.   *Exit Polonius*
60 Will you two help to hasten them?

ROSENCRANTZ Ay, my lord.
                    Exeunt Rosencrantz and Guildenstern

HAMLET What, ho, Horatio!
          Enter Horatio

HORATIO
Here, sweet lord, at your service.

HAMLET
Horatio, thou art e'en as just a man
As e'er my conversation coped withal.

HORATIO
O my dear lord –

HAMLET   Nay, do not think I flatter.
For what advancement may I hope from thee,
That no revenue hast but thy good spirits
To feed and clothe thee? Why should the poor be
          flattered?
70 No, let the candied tongue lick absurd pomp,
And crook the pregnant hinges of the knee
Where thrift may follow fawning. Dost thou hear?
Since my dear soul was mistress of her choice
And could of men distinguish her election,

Sh'hath sealed thee for herself. For thou hast been
As one, in suffering all, that suffers nothing,
A man that Fortune's buffets and rewards
Hast ta'en with equal thanks. And blest are those
Whose blood and judgement are so well commeddled
That they are not a pipe for Fortune's finger   80
To sound what stop she please. Give me that man
That is not passion's slave, and I will wear him
In my heart's core, ay, in my heart of heart,
As I do thee. Something too much of this.
There is a play tonight before the King.
One scene of it comes near the circumstance,
Which I have told thee, of my father's death.
I prithee, when thou seest that act afoot,
Even with the very comment of thy soul
Observe my uncle. If his occulted guilt   90
Do not itself unkennel in one speech,
It is a damnèd ghost that we have seen,
And my imaginations are as foul
As Vulcan's stithy. Give him heedful note.
For I mine eyes will rivet to his face,
And after we will both our judgements join
In censure of his seeming.

HORATIO   Well, my lord.
If 'a steal aught the whilst this play is playing,
And 'scape detecting, I will pay the theft.

HAMLET They are coming to the play. I must be idle. Get   100
you a place.

> *Danish march. Flourish*
> *Trumpets and kettledrums*
> *Enter the King and Queen, Polonius, Ophelia, Rosen-*
> *crantz, Guildenstern, and other lords attendant, with*
> *the guard carrying torches*

KING How fares our cousin Hamlet?

He is drunk

HAMLET Excellent, i'faith; of the chameleon's dish. I eat the air, promise-crammed. You cannot feed capons so.

KING I have nothing with this answer, Hamlet. These words are not mine.

HAMLET No, nor mine now. (*To Polonius*) My lord, you played once i'th'university, you say?

POLONIUS That did I, my lord, and was accounted a good actor.

HAMLET What did you enact?

POLONIUS I did enact Julius Caesar. I was killed i'th'Capitol. Brutus killed me.

HAMLET It was a brute part of him to kill so capital a calf there. Be the players ready?

ROSENCRANTZ Ay, my lord. They stay upon your patience.

QUEEN Come hither, my dear Hamlet, sit by me.

HAMLET No, good mother. Here's metal more attractive.

POLONIUS (*to the King*) O ho! Do you mark that?

HAMLET Lady, shall I lie in your lap?

OPHELIA No, my lord.

HAMLET I mean, my head upon your lap?

OPHELIA Ay, my lord.

HAMLET Do you think I meant country matters?

OPHELIA I think nothing, my lord.

HAMLET That's a fair thought – to lie between maids' legs.

OPHELIA What is, my lord?

HAMLET Nothing.

OPHELIA You are merry, my lord.

HAMLET Who, I?

OPHELIA Ay, my lord.

HAMLET O God, your only jig-maker! What should a man do but be merry? For look you how cheerfully my mother looks, and my father died within's two hours.

OPHELIA Nay, 'tis twice two months, my lord.

HAMLET So long? Nay then, let the devil wear black, for
I'll have a suit of sables. O heavens! Die two months
ago, and not forgotten yet? Then there's hope a great 140
man's memory may outlive his life half a year. But, by'r
Lady, 'a must build churches then, or else shall 'a suffer
not thinking on, with the hobby-horse, whose epitaph
is 'For O, for O, the hobby-horse is forgot!'

The trumpets sound

*Dumb show follows: Enter a King and a Queen very
lovingly, the Queen embracing him, and he her. She
kneels, and makes show of protestation unto him. He
takes her up, and declines his head upon her neck. He
lies him down upon a bank of flowers. She, seeing him
asleep, leaves him. Anon come in another man; takes
off his crown, kisses it, pours poison in the sleeper's
ears, and leaves him. The Queen returns, finds the
King dead, makes passionate action. The poisoner,
with some three or four, come in again, seem to con-
dole with her. The dead body is carried away. The
poisoner woos the Queen with gifts. She seems harsh
awhile, but in the end accepts love*

Exeunt dumb show

OPHELIA What means this, my lord?

HAMLET Marry, this is miching mallecho. It means mischief.

OPHELIA Belike this show imports the argument of the
play.

Enter the Fourth Player as Prologue

HAMLET We shall know by this fellow. The players can- 150
not keep counsel. They'll tell all.

OPHELIA Will 'a tell us what this show meant?

HAMLET Ay, or any show that you will show him. Be not
you ashamed to show, he'll not shame to tell you what
it means.

OPHELIA You are naught, you are naught. I'll mark the
play.

FOURTH PLAYER (*as Prologue*)
    For us and for our tragedy,
    Here stooping to your clemency,
160   We beg your hearing patiently.

Exit

HAMLET Is this a prologue, or the posy of a ring?
OPHELIA 'Tis brief, my lord.
HAMLET As woman's love.
    Enter two Players as King and Queen
FIRST PLAYER (*as King*)
    Full thirty times hath Phoebus' cart gone round
    Neptune's salt wash and Tellus' orbèd ground,
    And thirty dozen moons with borrowed sheen
    About the world have times twelve thirties been
    Since love our hearts, and Hymen did our hands,
    Unite commutual in most sacred bands.

SECOND PLAYER (*as Queen*)
170   So many journeys may the sun and moon
    Make us again count o'er ere love be done!
    But woe is me, you are so sick of late,
    So far from cheer and from your former state
    That I distrust you. Yet, though I distrust,
    Discomfort you, my lord, it nothing must.
    For women fear too much, even as they love,
    And women's fear and love hold quantity,
    In neither aught, or in extremity.
    Now what my love is, proof hath made you know,
180   And as my love is sized, my fear is so.
    Where love is great, the littlest doubts are fear.

Where little fears grow great, great love grows there.

FIRST PLAYER (as *King*)

Faith, I must leave thee, love, and shortly too.
My operant powers their functions leave to do.
And thou shalt live in this fair world behind,
Honoured, beloved; and haply one as kind
For husband shalt thou –

SECOND PLAYER (as *Queen*)

                O, confound the rest!
Such love must needs be treason in my breast.
In second husband let me be accurst!
None wed the second but who killed the first. 190

HAMLET (*aside*)

That's wormwood.

SECOND PLAYER (as *Queen*)

The instances that second marriage move
Are base respects of thrift, but none of love.
A second time I kill my husband dead
When second husband kisses me in bed.

FIRST PLAYER (as *King*)

I do believe you think what now you speak,
But what we do determine oft we break.
Purpose is but the slave to memory,
Of violent birth, but poor validity,
Which now, like fruit unripe, sticks on the tree, 200
But fall unshaken when they mellow be.
Most necessary 'tis that we forget
To pay ourselves what to ourselves is debt.
What to ourselves in passion we propose,
The passion ending, doth the purpose lose.
The violence of either grief or joy
Their own enactures with themselves destroy.
Where joy most revels, grief doth most lament.
Grief joys, joy grieves, on slender accident.

210   This world is not for aye, nor 'tis not strange
That even our loves should with our fortunes change.
For 'tis a question left us yet to prove,
Whether love lead fortune, or else fortune love.
The great man down, you mark his favourite flies.
The poor advanced makes friends of enemies.
And hitherto doth love on fortune tend,
For who not needs shall never lack a friend,
And who in want a hollow friend doth try
Directly seasons him his enemy.

220   But, orderly to end where I begun,
Our wills and fates do so contrary run
That our devices still are overthrown.
Our thoughts are ours, their ends none of our own.
So think thou wilt no second husband wed,
But die thy thoughts when thy first lord is dead.

SECOND PLAYER (*as Queen*)
Nor earth to me give food, nor heaven light,
Sport and repose lock from me day and night,
To desperation turn my trust and hope,
An anchor's cheer in prison be my scope,

230   Each opposite that blanks the face of joy
Meet what I would have well, and it destroy,
Both here and hence pursue me lasting strife,
If, once a widow, ever I be wife!

HAMLET (*aside*)
If she should break it now!

FIRST PLAYER (*as King*)
'Tis deeply sworn. Sweet, leave me here awhile.
My spirits grow dull, and fain I would beguile
The tedious day with sleep.

SECOND PLAYER (*as Queen*)
                Sleep rock thy brain,
And never come mischance between us twain!

          The Player-King sleeps. Exit the Player-Queen

HAMLET

Madam, how like you this play?

QUEEN

The lady doth protest too much, methinks.   240

HAMLET

O, but she'll keep her word.

KING Have you heard the argument? Is there no offence in't?

HAMLET No, no, they do but jest, poison in jest. No offence i'th'world.

KING What do you call the play?

HAMLET *The Mousetrap.* Marry, how? Tropically. This play is the image of a murder done in Vienna. Gonzago is the duke's name; his wife, Baptista. You shall see anon. 'Tis a knavish piece of work. But what of that?   250 Your majesty, and we that have free souls, it touches us not. Let the galled jade wince. Our withers are unwrung.

Enter the Third Player, as Lucianus

This is one Lucianus, nephew to the King.

OPHELIA You are as good as a chorus, my lord.

HAMLET I could interpret between you and your love, i I could see the puppets dallying.

OPHELIA You are keen, my lord, you are keen.

HAMLET It would cost you a groaning to take off mine edge.

OPHELIA Still better, and worse.   260

HAMLET So you must take your husbands. – Begin, murderer. Pox, leave thy damnable faces and begin. Come; the croaking raven doth bellow for revenge.

THIRD PLAYER (*as Lucianus*)

Thoughts black, hands apt, drugs fit, and time agreeing,
Confederate season, else no creature seeing,
Thou mixture rank, of midnight weeds collected,
With Hecat's ban thrice blasted, thrice infected,

Thy natural magic and dire property
On wholesome life usurps immediately.

He pours the poison in the King's ears

270 HAMLET 'A poisons him i'th'garden for his estate. His name's Gonzago. The story is extant, and written in very choice Italian. You shall see anon how the murderer gets the love of Gonzago's wife.

OPHELIA The King rises.

HAMLET What, frighted with false fire?

QUEEN How fares my lord?

POLONIUS Give o'er the play.

KING Give me some light. Away!

POLONIUS Lights, lights, lights!

Exeunt all but Hamlet and Horatio

HAMLET

280 Why, let the strucken deer go weep,
　　The hart ungallèd play.
For some must watch, while some must sleep.
　　Thus runs the world away.
Would not this, sir, and a forest of feathers – if the rest of my fortunes turn Turk with me – with two Provincial roses on my razed shoes, get me a fellowship in a cry of players, sir?

HORATIO Half a share.

HAMLET A whole one, I.

290 For thou dost know, O Damon dear
　　This realm dismantled was
Of Jove himself; and now reigns here
　　A very, very – peacock.

HORATIO You might have rhymed.

HAMLET O good Horatio, I'll take the ghost's word for a thousand pound. Didst perceive?

HORATIO Very well, my lord.

HAMLET Upon the talk of the poisoning?

HORATIO I did very well note him.

HAMLET Aha! Come, some music! Come, the recorders! 300
   For if the King like not the comedy,
   Why then, belike he likes it not, perdy.
   Come, some music!

   Enter Rosencrantz and Guildenstern

GUILDENSTERN Good my lord, vouchsafe me a word
   with you.

HAMLET Sir, a whole history.

GUILDENSTERN The King, sir –

HAMLET Ay, sir, what of him?

GUILDENSTERN Is in his retirement marvellous distempered. 310

HAMLET With drink, sir?

GUILDENSTERN No, my lord, with choler.

HAMLET Your wisdom should show itself more richer to
   signify this to the doctor. For for me to put him to his
   purgation would perhaps plunge him into more choler.

GUILDENSTERN Good my lord, put your discourse into
   some frame, and start not so wildly from my affair.

HAMLET I am tame, sir. Pronounce.

GUILDENSTERN The Queen your mother in most great
   affliction of spirit hath sent me tò you. 320

HAMLET You are welcomè.

GUILDENSTERN Nay, good my lord, this courtesy is not
   of the right breed. If it shall please you to make me a
   wholesome answer, I will do your mother's commandment. If not, your pardon and my return shall be the
   end of my business.

HAMLET Sir, I cannot.

ROSENCRANTZ What, my lord?

HAMLET Make you a wholesome answer. My wit's
   diseased. But, sir, such answer as I can make, you shall 330
   command; or rather, as you say, my mother. Therefore

no more, but to the matter. My mother, you say –

ROSENCRANTZ Then thus she says: your behaviour hath struck her into amazement and admiration.

HAMLET O wonderful son, that can so 'stonish a mother! But is there no sequel at the heels of this mother's admiration? Impart.

ROSENCRANTZ She desires to speak with you in her closet ere you go to bed.

340 HAMLET We shall obey, were she ten times our mother. Have you any further trade with us?

ROSENCRANTZ My lord, you once did love me.

HAMLET And do still, by these pickers and stealers.

ROSENCRANTZ Good my lord, what is your cause of distemper? You do surely bar the door upon your own liberty if you deny your griefs to your friend.

HAMLET Sir, I lack advancement.

ROSENCRANTZ How can that be, when you have the voice of the King himself for your succession in Den-
350 mark?

HAMLET Ay, sir, but 'while the grass grows' – the proverb is something musty.

Enter a Player with recorders

O, the recorders. Let me see one. – To withdraw with you – why do you go about to recover the wind of me, as if you would drive me into a toil?

GUILDENSTERN O my lord, if my duty be too bold, my love is too unmannerly.

HAMLET I do not well understand that. Will you play upon this pipe?

360 GUILDENSTERN My lord, I cannot.

HAMLET I pray you.

GUILDENSTERN Believe me, I cannot.

HAMLET I do beseech you.

GUILDENSTERN I know no touch of it, my lord.

HAMLET It is as easy as lying. Govern these ventages with your fingers and thumb; give it breath with your mouth; and it will discourse most eloquent music. Look you, these are the stops.

GUILDENSTERN But these cannot I command to any utterance of harmony. I have not the skill. 370

HAMLET Why, look you now, how unworthy a thing you make of me! You would play upon me. You would seem to know my stops. You would pluck out the heart of my mystery. You would sound me from my lowest note to the top of my compass. And there is much music, ex-cellent voice, in this little organ. Yet cannot you make it speak. 'Sblood, do you think I am easier to be played on than a pipe? Call me what instrument you will, though you can fret me, you cannot play upon me.

Enter Polonius

God bless you, sir! 380

POLONIUS My lord, the Queen would speak with you, and presently.

HAMLET Do you see yonder cloud that's almost in shape of a camel?

POLONIUS By th'mass, and 'tis like a camel indeed.

HAMLET Methinks it is like a weasel.

POLONIUS It is backed like a weasel.

HAMLET Or like a whale.

POLONIUS Very like a whale.

HAMLET Then I will come to my mother by and by. 390 (*Aside*) They fool me to the top of my bent. – I will come by and by.

POLONIUS I will say so.

HAMLET

'By and by' is easily said. *Exit Polonius*

Leave me, friends.

Exeunt all but Hamlet

141

'Tis now the very witching time of night,
When churchyards yawn, and hell itself breathes out
Contagion to this world. Now could I drink hot blood
And do such bitter business as the day
Would quake to look on. Soft, now to my mother.
400 O heart, lose not thy nature. Let not ever
The soul of Nero enter this firm bosom.
Let me be cruel, not unnatural.
I will speak daggers to her, but use none.
My tongue and soul in this be hypocrites.
How in my words somever she be shent,
To give them seals never, my soul, consent!   *Exit*

III.3   *Enter the King, Rosencrantz, and Guildenstern*

KING

I like him not; nor stands it safe with us
To let his madness range. Therefore prepare you.
I your commission will forthwith dispatch,
And he to England shall along with you.
The terms of our estate may not endure
Hazard so near us as doth hourly grow
Out of his brows.

GUILDENSTERN   We will ourselves provide.
Most holy and religious fear it is
To keep those many many bodies safe
10   That live and feed upon your majesty.

ROSENCRANTZ

The single and peculiar life is bound
With all the strength and armour of the mind
To keep itself from noyance; but much more
That spirit upon whose weal depends and rests
The lives of many. The cess of majesty
Dies not alone, but like a gulf doth draw

What's near it with it; or 'tis a massy wheel
Fixed on the summit of the highest mount,
To whose huge spokes ten thousand lesser things
Are mortised and adjoined; which when it falls,   20
Each small annexment, petty consequence,
Attends the boisterous ruin. Never alone
Did the king sigh, but with a general groan.

KING

Arm you, I pray you, to this speedy voyage.
For we will fetters put about this fear,
Which now goes too free-footed.

ROSENCRANTZ   We will haste us.

Exeunt Rosencrantz and Guildenstern

    Enter Polonius

POLONIUS

My lord, he's going to his mother's closet.
Behind the arras I'll convey myself
To hear the process. I'll warrant she'll tax him home.
And, as you said, and wisely was it said,   30
'Tis meet that some more audience than a mother,
Since nature makes them partial, should o'erhear
The speech, of vantage. Fare you well, my liege.
I'll call upon you ere you go to bed
And tell you what I know.

KING   Thanks, dear my lord.

Exit Polonius

O, my offence is rank. It smells to heaven.
It hath the primal eldest curse upon't,
A brother's murder. Pray can I not,
Though inclination be as sharp as will.
My stronger guilt defeats my strong intent,   40
And like a man to double business bound
I stand in pause where I shall first begin,
And both neglect. What if this cursèd hand

Were thicker than itself with brother's blood,
Is there not rain enough in the sweet heavens
To wash it white as snow? Whereto serves mercy
But to confront the visage of offence?
And what's in prayer but this twofold force,
To be forestallèd ere we come to fall
50 Or pardoned being down? Then I'll look up.
My fault is past. But, O, what form of prayer
Can serve my turn? 'Forgive me my foul murder'?
That cannot be, since I am still possessed
Of those effects for which I did the murder,
My crown, mine own ambition, and my Queen.
May one be pardoned and retain th'offence?
In the corrupted currents of this world
Offence's gilded hand may shove by justice;
And oft 'tis seen the wicked prize itself
60 Buys out the law. But 'tis not so above.
There is no shuffling. There the action lies
In his true nature, and we ourselves compelled,
Even to the teeth and forehead of our faults,
To give in evidence. What then? What rests?
Try what repentance can. What can it not?
Yet what can it when one cannot repent?
O, wretched state! O, bosom black as death!
O limèd soul, that struggling to be free
Art more engaged! Help, angels! Make assay.
70 Bow, stubborn knees, and, heart with strings of steel,
Be soft as sinews of the new-born babe.
All may be well.
          The King kneels. Enter Hamlet
HAMLET
  Now might I do it pat, now 'a is a-praying.
  And now I'll do't. And so 'a goes to heaven.
  And so am I revenged. That would be scanned.

A villain kills my father, and for that
I, his sole son, do this same villain send
To heaven.
Why, this is hire and salary, not revenge.
'A took my father grossly, full of bread,   80
With all his crimes broad blown, as flush as May;
And how his audit stands, who knows save heaven?
But in our circumstance and course of thought,
'Tis heavy with him. And am I then revenged,
To take him in the purging of his soul,
When he is fit and seasoned for his passage?
No.
Up, sword, and know thou a more horrid hent.
When he is drunk asleep, or in his rage,
Or in th'incestuous pleasure of his bed,   90
At game, a-swearing, or about some act
That has no relish of salvation in't –
Then trip him, that his heels may kick at heaven,
And that his soul may be as damned and black
As hell, whereto it goes. My mother stays.
This physic but prolongs thy sickly days.   *Exit*
KING (*rising*)
My words fly up, my thoughts remain below.
Words without thoughts never to heaven go.   *Exit*

Enter the Queen and Polonius   III.4
POLONIUS
'A will come straight. Look you lay home to him.
Tell him his pranks have been too broad to bear with,
And that your grace hath screened and stood between
Much heat and him. I'll silence me even here.
Pray you be round with him.

145

III.4

HAMLET (*within*) Mother, mother, mother!

QUEEN I'll warrant you. Fear me not. Withdraw. I hear
him coming.

Polonius hides behind the arras
Enter Hamlet

HAMLET

Now, mother, what's the matter?

QUEEN

10 Hamlet, thou hast thy father much offended.

HAMLET

Mother, you have my father much offended.

QUEEN

Come, come, you answer with an idle tongue.

HAMLET

Go, go, you question with a wicked tongue.

QUEEN

Why, how now, Hamlet?

HAMLET   What's the matter now?

QUEEN

Have you forgot me?

HAMLET   No, by the Rood, not so!
You are the Queen, your husband's brother's wife,
And, would it were not so, you are my mother.

QUEEN

Nay, then I'll set those to you that can speak.

HAMLET

Come, come, and sit you down. You shall not budge.

20 You go not till I set you up a glass
Where you may see the inmost part of you.

QUEEN

What wilt thou do? Thou wilt not murder me?
Help, ho!

POLONIUS (*behind*)

What, ho! Help!

HAMLET (*drawing his sword*)

  How now? A rat? Dead for a ducat, dead!

    He makes a thrust through the arras and kills Polonius

POLONIUS

  O, I am slain!

QUEEN   O me, what hast thou done?

HAMLET

  Nay, I know not. Is it the King?

QUEEN

  O, what a rash and bloody deed is this!

HAMLET

  A bloody deed – almost as bad, good mother,

  As kill a king and marry with his brother.   30

QUEEN

  As kill a king!

HAMLET   Ay, lady, it was my word.

    He sees Polonius

  Thou wretched, rash, intruding fool, farewell!

  I took thee for thy better. Take thy fortune.

  Thou findest to be too busy is some danger. –

  Leave wringing of your hands. Peace, sit you down,

  And let me wring your heart. For so I shall,

  If it be made of penetrable stuff,

  If damnèd custom have not brassed it so

  That it be proof and bulwark against sense.

QUEEN

  What have I done that thou darest wag thy tongue   40

  In noise so rude against me?

HAMLET   Such an act

  That blurs the grace and blush of modesty;

  Calls virtue hypocrite; takes off the rose

  From the fair forehead of an innocent love

  And sets a blister there; makes marriage vows

  As false as dicers' oaths; O, such a deed

III.4

As from the body of contraction plucks
The very soul, and sweet religion makes
A rhapsody of words! Heaven's face does glow,
50   Yea, this solidity and compound mass,
With heated visage, as against the Doom,
Is thought-sick at the act.

QUEEN   Ay me, what act,
That roars so loud and thunders in the index?

HAMLET

Look here upon this picture, and on this,
The counterfeit presentment of two brothers.
See what a grace was seated on this brow:
Hyperion's curls, the front of Jove himself,
An eye like Mars, to threaten and command,
A station like the herald Mercury
60   New lighted on a heaven-kissing hill –
A combination and a form indeed
Where every god did seem to set his seal
To give the world assurance of a man.
This was your husband. Look you now what follows.
Here is your husband; like a mildewed ear,
Blasting his wholesome brother. Have you eyes?
Could you on this fair mountain leave to feed,
And batten on this moor? Ha! Have you eyes?
You cannot call it love. For at your age
70   The heyday in the blood is tame; it's humble,
And waits upon the judgement; and what judgement
Would step from this to this? Sense sure you have,
Else could you not have motion. But sure that sense
Is apoplexed. For madness would not err,
Nor sense to ecstasy was ne'er so thralled
But it reserved some quantity of choice
To serve in such a difference. What devil was't

148

That thus hath cozened you at hoodman-blind?
Eyes without feeling, feeling without sight,
Ears without hands or eyes, smelling sans all,   80
Or but a sickly part of one true sense
Could not so mope.
O shame, where is thy blush? Rebellious hell,
If thou canst mutine in a matron's bones,
To flaming youth let virtue be as wax
And melt in her own fire. Proclaim no shame
When the compulsive ardour gives the charge,
Since frost itself as actively doth burn,
And reason panders will.

QUEEN   O Hamlet, speak no more.
Thou turnest mine eyes into my very soul,   90
And there I see such black and grainèd spots
As will not leave their tinct.

HAMLET   Nay, but to live
In the rank sweat of an enseamèd bed,
Stewed in corruption, honeying and making love
Over the nasty sty –

QUEEN   O, speak to me no more.
These words like daggers enter in mine ears.
No more, sweet Hamlet.

HAMLET   A murderer and a villain,
A slave that is not twentieth part the tithe
Of your precedent lord, a vice of kings,
A cutpurse of the empire and the rule,   100
That from a shelf the precious diadem stole
And put it in his pocket –

QUEEN   No more.

HAMLET
A king of shreds and patches –
      (*Enter the Ghost*)

Save me and hover o'er me with your wings,
You heavenly guards! – What would your gracious
    figure?

QUEEN

Alas, he's mad.

HAMLET

Do you not come your tardy son to chide,
That, lapsed in time and passion, lets go by
Th'important acting of your dread command?
110 O, say!

GHOST

Do not forget. This visitation
Is but to whet thy almost blunted purpose.
But look, amazement on thy mother sits.
O, step between her and her fighting soul!
Conceit in weakest bodies strongest works.
Speak to her, Hamlet.

HAMLET   How is it with you, lady?

QUEEN

Alas, how is't with you,
That you do bend your eye on vacancy,
And with th'incorporal air do hold discourse?
120 Forth at your eyes your spirits wildly peep,
And, as the sleeping soldiers in th'alarm,
Your bedded hair like life in excrements
Start up and stand an end. O gentle son,
Upon the heat and flame of thy distemper
Sprinkle cool patience. Whereon do you look?

HAMLET

On him, on him! Look you, how pale he glares!
His form and cause conjoined, preaching to stones,
Would make them capable. – Do not look upon me,
Lest with this piteous action you convert
130 My stern effects. Then what I have to do

Will want true colour – tears perchance for blood.

QUEEN

  To whom do you speak this?

HAMLET   Do you see nothing there?

QUEEN

  Nothing at all. Yet all that is I see.

HAMLET

  Nor did you nothing hear?

QUEEN   No, nothing but ourselves.

HAMLET

  Why, look you there! Look how it steals away!
  My father, in his habit as he lived!
  Look where he goes, even now, out at the portal!

                                        Exit the Ghost

QUEEN

  This is the very coinage of your brain.
  This bodiless creation ecstasy
  Is very cunning in.

HAMLET   Ecstasy?   140
  My pulse as yours doth temperately keep time
  And makes as healthful music. It is not madness
  That I have uttered. Bring me to the test,
  And I the matter will re-word, which madness
  Would gambol from. Mother, for love of grace,
  Lay not that flattering unction to your soul,
  That not your trespass but my madness speaks.
  It will but skin and film the ulcerous place
  Whiles rank corruption, mining all within,
  Infects unseen. Confess yourself to heaven.   150
  Repent what's past. Avoid what is to come;
  And do not spread the compost on the weeds
  To make them ranker. Forgive me this my virtue.
  For in the fatness of these pursy times
  Virtue itself of vice must pardon beg,

Yea, curb and woo for leave to do him good.

QUEEN

O Hamlet, thou hast cleft my heart in twain.

HAMLET

O, throw away the worser part of it,
And live the purer with the other half.
160 Good night. But go not to my uncle's bed.
Assume a virtue, if you have it not.
That monster custom, who all sense doth eat,
Of habits devil, is angel yet in this,
That to the use of actions fair and good
He likewise gives a frock or livery
That aptly is put on. Refrain tonight,
And that shall lend a kind of easiness
To the next abstinence; the next more easy;
For use almost can change the stamp of nature,
170 And either master the devil or throw him out
With wondrous potency. Once more, good night.
And when you are desirous to be blest,
I'll blessing beg of you. For this same lord,
I do repent. But heaven hath pleased it so,
To punish me with this, and this with me,
That I must be their scourge and minister.
I will bestow him and will answer well
The death I gave him. So again good night.
I must be cruel only to be kind.
180 This bad begins, and worse remains behind.
One word more, good lady.

QUEEN   What shall I do?

HAMLET

Not this, by no means, that I bid you do:
Let the bloat King tempt you again to bed,
Pinch wanton on your cheek, call you his mouse,
And let him, for a pair of reechy kisses,

Or paddling in your neck with his damned fingers,
Make you to ravel all this matter out,
That I essentially am not in madness,
But mad in craft. 'Twere good you let him know.
For who that's but a queen, fair, sober, wise,   190
Would from a paddock, from a bat, a gib,
Such dear concernings hide? Who would do so?
No, in despite of sense and secrecy,
Unpeg the basket on the house's top.
Let the birds fly, and like the famous ape,
To try conclusions, in the basket creep
And break your own neck down.

QUEEN
Be thou assured, if words be made of breath,
And breath of life, I have no life to breathe
What thou hast said to me.   200

HAMLET
I must to England. You know that?

QUEEN   Alack,
I had forgot. 'Tis so concluded on.

HAMLET
There's letters sealed, and my two schoolfellows,
Whom I will trust as I will adders fanged,
They bear the mandate. They must sweep my way
And marshal me to knavery. Let it work.
For 'tis the sport to have the enginer
Hoist with his own petar; and't shall go hard
But I will delve one yard below their mines
And blow them at the moon. O, 'tis most sweet   210
When in one line two crafts directly meet.
This man shall set me packing.
I'll lug the guts into the neighbour room.
Mother, good night. Indeed, this counsellor
Is now most still, most secret, and most grave,

Who was in life a foolish prating knave.
Come, sir, to draw toward an end with you.
Good night, mother.

> *Exeunt Hamlet, tugging in Polonius, and the Queen*

IV.1 *Enter the King and Queen, with Rosencrantz and Guildenstern*

KING
There's matter in these sighs. These profound heaves
You must translate. 'Tis fit we understand them.
Where is your son?

QUEEN
Bestow this place on us a little while.

> *Exeunt Rosencrantz and Guildenstern*

Ah, mine own lord, what have I seen tonight!

KING
What, Gertrude? How does Hamlet?

QUEEN
Mad as the sea and wind when both contend
Which is the mightier. In his lawless fit,
Behind the arras hearing something stir,
10 Whips out his rapier, cries 'A rat, a rat!'
And in this brainish apprehension kills
The unseen good old man.

KING   O, heavy deed!
It had been so with us, had we been there.
His liberty is full of threats to all,
To you yourself, to us, to everyone.
Alas, how shall this bloody deed be answered?
It will be laid to us, whose providence
Should have kept short, restrained, and out of haunt
This mad young man. But so much was our love,
20 We would not understand what was most fit,
But, like the owner of a foul disease,
To keep it from divulging let it feed

154

Even on the pith of life. Where is he gone?

QUEEN

To draw apart the body he hath killed;
O'er whom his very madness, like some ore
Among a mineral of metals base,
Shows itself pure. 'A weeps for what is done.

KING

O Gertrude, come away!
The sun no sooner shall the mountains touch
But we will ship him hence; and this vile deed   30
We must with all our majesty and skill
Both countenance and excuse. Ho, Guildenstern!

    Enter Rosencrantz and Guildenstern

Friends both, go join you with some further aid.
Hamlet in madness hath Polonius slain,
And from his mother's closet hath he dragged him.
Go seek him out. Speak fair. And bring the body
Into the chapel. I pray you haste in this.

         Exeunt Rosencrantz and Guildenstern

Come, Gertrude, we'll call up our wisest friends
And let them know both what we mean to do
And what's untimely done. So haply slander,   40
Whose whisper o'er the world's diameter
As level as the cannon to his blank
Transports his poisoned shot, may miss our name
And hit the woundless air. O, come away!
My soul is full of discord and dismay.   *Exeunt*

    Enter Hamlet   IV.2

HAMLET Safely stowed.

GENTLEMEN (*within*) Hamlet! Lord Hamlet!

HAMLET

But soft, what noise? Who calls on Hamlet?
O, here they come.

    Enter Rosencrantz, Guildenstern, and attendants

ROSENCRANTZ

What have you done, my lord, with the dead body?

HAMLET

Compounded it with dust, whereto 'tis kin.

ROSENCRANTZ

Tell us where 'tis, that we may take it thence
And bear it to the chapel.

HAMLET Do not believe it.

10 ROSENCRANTZ Believe what?

HAMLET That I can keep your counsel and not mine own.
Besides, to be demanded of a sponge, what replication
should be made by the son of a king?

ROSENCRANTZ Take you me for a sponge, my lord?

HAMLET Ay, sir, that soaks up the King's countenance,
his rewards, his authorities. But such officers do the
King best service in the end. He keeps them, like an ape
an apple, in the corner of his jaw, first mouthed, to be
last swallowed. When he needs what you have gleaned,

20 it is but squeezing you and, sponge, you shall be dry
again.

ROSENCRANTZ I understand you not, my lord.

HAMLET I am glad of it. A knavish speech sleeps in a
foolish ear.

ROSENCRANTZ My lord, you must tell us where the body
is, and go with us to the King.

HAMLET The body is with the King, but the King is not
with the body. The King is a thing –

GUILDENSTERN A thing, my lord?

30 HAMLET Of nothing. Bring me to him. Hide fox, and all
after.   *Exeunt*

KING

    I have sent to seek him and to find the body.

    How dangerous is it that this man goes loose!

    Yet must not we put the strong law on him.

    He's loved of the distracted multitude,

    Who like not in their judgement but their eyes;

    And where 'tis so, th'offender's scourge is weighed,

    But never the offence. To bear all smooth and even,

    This sudden sending him away must seem

    Deliberate pause. Diseases desperate grown

    By desperate appliance are relieved,   10

    Or not at all.

        Enter Rosencrantz, Guildenstern, and all the rest

            How now? What hath befallen?

ROSENCRANTZ

    Where the dead body is bestowed, my lord,

    We cannot get from him.

KING   But where is he?

ROSENCRANTZ

    Without, my lord; guarded, to know your pleasure.

KING

    Bring him before us.

ROSENCRANTZ   Ho! Bring in the lord.

    Enter attendants with Hamlet

KING Now, Hamlet, where's Polonius?

HAMLET At supper.

KING At supper? Where?

HAMLET Not where he eats, but where 'a is eaten. A certain convocation of politic worms are e'en at him. Your 20 worm is your only emperor for diet. We fat all creatures else to fat us, and we fat ourselves for maggots. Your fat king and your lean beggar is but variable service – two dishes, but to one table. That's the end.

KING Alas, alas!

HAMLET A man may fish with the worm that hath eat of a king, and eat of the fish that hath fed of that worm.

KING What dost thou mean by this?

HAMLET Nothing but to show you how a king may go a
30 progress through the guts of a beggar.

KING Where is Polonius?

HAMLET In heaven. Send thither to see. If your messenger find him not there, seek him i'th'other place yourself. But if indeed you find him not within this month, you shall nose him as you go up the stairs into the lobby.

KING (*to attendants*) Go seek him there.

HAMLET 'A will stay till you come.   *Exeunt attendants*

KING
Hamlet, this deed, for thine especial safety,
40 Which we do tender as we dearly grieve
For that which thou hast done, must send thee hence
With fiery quickness. Therefore prepare thyself.
The bark is ready and the wind at help,
Th'associates tend, and everything is bent
For England.

HAMLET For England?

KING Ay, Hamlet.

HAMLET Good.

KING
So is it, if thou knewest our purposes.

50 HAMLET I see a cherub that sees them. But come, for England! Farewell, dear mother.

KING Thy loving father, Hamlet.

HAMLET My mother. Father and mother is man and wife; man and wife is one flesh; and so, my mother. Come, for England!   *Exit*

KING

    Follow him at foot. Tempt him with speed aboard.
    Delay it not. I'll have him hence tonight.
    Away! For everything is sealed and done
    That else leans on the affair. Pray you make haste.
                    Exeunt all but the King
    And, England, if my love thou holdest at aught –   60
    As my great power thereof may give thee sense,
    Since yet thy cicatrice looks raw and red
    After the Danish sword, and thy free awe
    Pays homage to us – thou mayst not coldly set
    Our sovereign process, which imports at full,
    By letters congruing to that effect,
    The present death of Hamlet. Do it, England.
    For like the hectic in my blood he rages,
    And thou must cure me. Till I know 'tis done,
    Howe'er my haps, my joys were ne'er begun.   *Exit* 70

       Enter Fortinbras with his army over the stage   IV.4

FORTINBRAS

    Go, captain, from me greet the Danish King.
    Tell him that by his licence Fortinbras
    Craves the conveyance of a promised march
    Over his kingdom. You know the rendezvous.
    If that his majesty would aught with us,
    We shall express our duty in his eye.
    And let him know so.

CAPTAIN   I will do't, my lord.

FORTINBRAS Go softly on.   *Exeunt all but the Captain*
       Enter Hamlet, Rosencrantz, Guildenstern, and at-
       tendants

HAMLET Good sir, whose powers are these?

CAPTAIN They are of Norway, sir.   10

HAMLET How purposed, sir, I pray you?

CAPTAIN Against some part of Poland.

HAMLET Who commands them, sir?

CAPTAIN

The nephew to old Norway, Fortinbras.

HAMLET

Goes it against the main of Poland, sir,
Or for some frontier?

CAPTAIN

Truly to speak, and with no addition,
We go to gain a little patch of ground
That hath in it no profit but the name.
20 To pay five ducats, five, I would not farm it;
Nor will it yield to Norway or the Pole
A ranker rate, should it be sold in fee.

HAMLET

Why, then the Polack never will defend it.

CAPTAIN

Yes, it is already garrisoned.

HAMLET

Two thousand souls and twenty thousand ducats
Will not debate the question of this straw.
This is th'imposthume of much wealth and peace,
That inward breaks, and shows no cause without
Why the man dies. I humbly thank you, sir.

CAPTAIN

God bye you, sir.   *Exit*

30 ROSENCRANTZ   Will't please you go, my lord?

HAMLET

I'll be with you straight. Go a little before.

Exeunt all but Hamlet

How all occasions do inform against me
And spur my dull revenge! What is a man,
If his chief good and market of his time

Be but to sleep and feed? A beast, no more.
Sure He that made us with such large discourse,
Looking before and after, gave us not
That capability and godlike reason
To fust in us unused. Now, whether it be
Bestial oblivion, or some craven scruple   40
Of thinking too precisely on th'event –
A thought which, quartered, hath but one part wisdom
And ever three parts coward – I do not know
Why yet I live to say 'This thing's to do',
Sith I have cause, and will, and strength, and means
To do't. Examples gross as earth exhort me.
Witness this army of such mass and charge,
Led by a delicate and tender prince,
Whose spirit, with divine ambition puffed,
Makes mouths at the invisible event,   50
Exposing what is mortal and unsure
To all that fortune, death, and danger dare,
Even for an eggshell. Rightly to be great
Is not to stir without great argument,
But greatly to find quarrel in a straw
When honour's at the stake. How stand I then,
That have a father killed, a mother stained,
Excitements of my reason and my blood,
And let all sleep, while to my shame I see
The imminent death of twenty thousand men   60
That for a fantasy and trick of fame
Go to their graves like beds, fight for a plot
Whereon the numbers cannot try the cause,
Which is not tomb enough and continent
To hide the slain? O, from this time forth,
My thoughts be bloody, or be nothing worth!   *Exit*

Enter the Queen, Horatio, and a Gentleman

QUEEN

    I will not speak with her.

GENTLEMAN

    She is importunate, indeed distract.

    Her mood will needs be pitied.

QUEEN   What would she have?

GENTLEMAN

    She speaks much of her father; says she hears

    There's tricks i'th'world, and hems, and beats her heart,

    Spurns enviously at straws, speaks things in doubt

    That carry but half sense. Her speech is nothing.

    Yet the unshapèd use of it doth move

    The hearers to collection. They aim at it,

10   And botch the words up fit to their own thoughts,

    Which, as her winks and nods and gestures yield them,

    Indeed would make one think there might be thought,

    Though nothing sure, yet much unhappily.

HORATIO

    'Twere good she were spoken with, for she may strew

    Dangerous conjectures in ill-breeding minds.

QUEEN

    Let her come in.   *Exit the Gentleman*

    (*Aside*) To my sick soul, as sin's true nature is,

    Each toy seems prologue to some great amiss.

    So full of artless jealousy is guilt

10   It spills itself in fearing to be spilt.

        Enter Ophelia

OPHELIA

    Where is the beauteous majesty of Denmark?

QUEEN How now, Ophelia?

OPHELIA (*sings*)

           How should I your true-love know

              From another one?

> By his cockle hat and staff
> And his sandal shoon.

QUEEN
Alas, sweet lady, what imports this song?

OPHELIA Say you? Nay, pray you, mark.
> (*sings*) He is dead and gone, lady.
> He is dead and gone. 30
> At his head a grass-green turf,
> At his heels a stone.

O, ho!

QUEEN Nay, but, Ophelia –

OPHELIA Pray you, mark.
> (*sings*) White his shroud as the mountain snow –
> *Enter the King*

QUEEN Alas, look here, my lord.

OPHELIA (*sings*)
> Larded all with sweet flowers,
> Which bewept to the ground did not go
> With true-love showers. 40

KING How do you, pretty lady?

OPHELIA Well, God dild you! They say the owl was a baker's daughter. Lord, we know what we are, but know not what we may be. God be at your table!

KING Conceit upon her father –

OPHELIA Pray let's have no words of this, but when they ask you what it means, say you this:
> (*sings*) Tomorrow is Saint Valentine's day,
> All in the morning betime,
> And I a maid at your window 50
> To be your Valentine.

> Then up he rose and donned his clothes,
> And dupped the chamber door;

    Let in the maid, that out a maid
      Never departed more.

KING Pretty Ophelia!

OPHELIA Indeed, la, without an oath, I'll make an end
on't.

    (*sings*) By Gis and by Saint Charity,
60   Alack, and fie for shame!
    Young men will do't if they come to't.
      By Cock, they are to blame.

    Quoth she, 'Before you tumbled me,
      You promised me to wed.'
He answers:
    'So would I ha' done, by yonder sun,
      An thou hadst not come to my bed.'

KING How long hath she been thus?

OPHELIA I hope all will be well. We must be patient. But
I cannot choose but weep to think they would lay him
70 i'th'cold ground. My brother shall know of it. And so I
thank you for your good counsel. Come, my coach!
Good night, ladies, good night. Sweet ladies, good
night, good night.   *Exit*

KING
Follow her close. Give her good watch, I pray you.
                    Exit Horatio
O, this is the poison of deep grief. It springs
All from her father's death – and now behold!
O Gertrude, Gertrude,
When sorrows come, they come not single spies,
80 But in battalions: first, her father slain;
Next, your son gone, and he most violent author
Of his own just remove; the people muddied,
Thick and unwholesome in their thoughts and whispers

For good Polonius' death, and we have done but greenly
In hugger-mugger to inter him; poor Ophelia
Divided from herself and her fair judgement,
Without the which we are pictures or mere beasts;
Last, and as much containing as all these,
Her brother is in secret come from France,
Feeds on his wonder, keeps himself in clouds,   90
And wants not buzzers to infect his ear
With pestilent speeches of his father's death,
Wherein necessity, of matter beggared,
Will nothing stick our person to arraign
In ear and ear. O my dear Gertrude, this,
Like to a murdering-piece, in many places
Gives me superfluous death.

    A noise within

QUEEN

    Alack, what noise is this?

KING

    Attend. Where is my Switzers? Let them guard the
        door.

    Enter a Messenger

    What is the matter?

MESSENGER   Save yourself, my lord.   100
The ocean, overpeering of his list,
Eats not the flats with more impiteous haste
Than your Laertes, in a riotous head,
O'erbears your officers. The rabble call him lord,
And, as the world were now but to begin,
Antiquity forgot, custom not known,
The ratifiers and props of every word,
They cry 'Choose we! Laertes shall be king!'
Caps, hands, and tongues applaud it to the clouds:
'Laertes shall be king! Laertes king!'   110

    A noise within

IV.5

QUEEN

How cheerfully on the false trail they cry!
O, this is counter, you false Danish dogs!

KING

The doors are broke.

Enter Laertes with his followers

LAERTES

Where is this King? – Sirs, stand you all without.

HIS FOLLOWERS

No, let's come in.

LAERTES   I pray you give me leave.

HIS FOLLOWERS

We will, we will.

LAERTES

I thank you. Keep the door.   *Exeunt his followers*
                                   O thou vile King,
Give me my father.

QUEEN   Calmly, good Laertes.

LAERTES

That drop of blood that's calm proclaims me bastard,
120   Cries cuckold to my father, brands the harlot
Even here between the chaste unsmirchèd brows
Of my true mother.

KING   What is the cause, Laertes,
That thy rebellion looks so giant-like?
Let him go, Gertrude. Do not fear our person.
There's such divinity doth hedge a king
That treason can but peep to what it would,
Acts little of his will. Tell me, Laertes,
Why thou art thus incensed. Let him go, Gertrude.
Speak, man.

LAERTES

Where is my father?

KING   Dead.

QUEEN   But not by him.   130

KING

Let him demand his fill.

LAERTES

How came he dead? I'll not be juggled with.
To hell allegiance! Vows to the blackest devil!
Conscience and grace to the profoundest pit!
I dare damnation. To this point I stand,
That both the worlds I give to negligence,
Let come what comes, only I'll be revenged
Most throughly for my father.

KING   Who shall stay you?

LAERTES

My will, not all the world's.
And for my means, I'll husband them so well   140
They shall go far with little.

KING   Good Laertes,

If you desire to know the certainty
Of your dear father, is't writ in your revenge
That, swoopstake, you will draw both friend and foe,
Winner and loser?

LAERTES

None but his enemies.

KING   Will you know them then?

LAERTES

To his good friends thus wide I'll ope my arms
And like the kind life-rendering pelican
Repast them with my blood.

KING   Why, now you speak

Like a good child and a true gentleman.   150
That I am guiltless of your father's death,
And am most sensibly in grief for it,

It shall as level to your judgement 'pear
As day does to your eye.
   A noise within

VOICES (*within*)   Let her come in.

LAERTES

How now? What noise is that?
   Enter Ophelia

O heat, dry up my brains! Tears seven times salt
Burn out the sense and virtue of mine eye!
By heaven, thy madness shall be paid with weight
Till our scale turn the beam. O rose of May,
160 Dear maid, kind sister, sweet Ophelia!
O heavens, is't possible a young maid's wits
Should be as mortal as an old man's life?
Nature is fine in love, and where 'tis fine,
It sends some precious instance of itself
After the thing it loves.

OPHELIA (*sings*)

     They bore him barefaced on the bier,
       Hey non nony, nony, hey nony,
      And in his grave rained many a tear –
Fare you well, my dove!

LAERTES

170 Hadst thou thy wits, and didst persuade revenge,
It could not move thus.

OPHELIA You must sing 'A-down a-down, and you call
him a-down-a.' O, how the wheel becomes it! It is the
false steward, that stole his master's daughter.

LAERTES This nothing's more than matter.

OPHELIA There's rosemary, that's for remembrance.
Pray you, love, remember. And there is pansies, that's
for thoughts.

LAERTES A document in madness: thoughts and re-
180 membrance fitted.

OPHELIA There's fennel for you, and columbines. There's
rue for you, and here's some for me. We may call it
herb of grace o'Sundays. O, you must wear your rue
with a difference. There's a daisy. I would give you some
violets, but they withered all when my father died. They
say 'a made a good end.

> (*sings*) For bonny sweet Robin is all my joy.

LAERTES
Thought and afflictions, passion, hell itself,
She turns to favour and to prettiness.

OPHELIA (*sings*)

> And will 'a not come again? 190
> And will 'a not come again?
> No, no, he is dead.
> Go to thy deathbed.
> He never will come again.
>
> His beard was as white as snow,
> All flaxen was his poll.
> He is gone, he is gone,
> And we cast away moan.
> God 'a' mercy on his soul!

And of all Christian souls, I pray God. God bye you. 200

> *Exit*

LAERTES
Do you see this? O God!

KING
Laertes, I must commune with your grief,
Or you deny me right. Go but apart,
Make choice of whom your wisest friends you will,
And they shall hear and judge 'twixt you and me.
If by direct or by collateral hand
They find us touched, we will our kingdom give,
Our crown, our life, and all that we call ours,

To you in satisfaction. But if not,
210 Be you content to lend your patience to us,
And we shall jointly labour with your soul
To give it due content.

LAERTES   Let this be so.
His means of death, his obscure funeral –
No trophy, sword, nor hatchment o'er his bones,
No noble rite nor formal ostentation –
Cry to be heard, as 'twere from heaven to earth,
That I must call't in question.

KING   So you shall.
And where th'offence is, let the great axe fall.
I pray you go with me.   *Exeunt*

IV.6   *Enter Horatio and a Gentleman*

HORATIO
What are they that would speak with me?

GENTLEMAN Seafaring men, sir. They say they have
letters for you.

HORATIO
Let them come in.   *Exit the Gentleman*
I do not know from what part of the world
I should be greeted if not from Lord Hamlet.
      Enter Sailors

SAILOR God bless you, sir.

HORATIO Let him bless thee, too.

SAILOR 'A shall, sir, an't please him. There's a letter for
10 you, sir – it came from th'ambassador that was bound
for England – if your name be Horatio, as I am let to
know it is.

HORATIO (*reads the letter*) *Horatio, when thou shalt have
overlooked this, give these fellows some means to the King.
They have letters for him. Ere we were two days old at sea,*

a pirate of very warlike appointment gave us chase. Find-
ing ourselves too slow of sail, we put on a compelled valour,
and in the grapple I boarded them. On the instant they got
clear of our ship. So I alone became their prisoner. They
have dealt with me like thieves of mercy. But they knew 20
what they did. I am to do a good turn for them. Let the
King have the letters I have sent, and repair thou to me
with as much speed as thou wouldst fly death. I have words
to speak in thine ear will make thee dumb. Yet are they
much too light for the bore of the matter. These good fel-
lows will bring thee where I am. Rosencrantz and Guilden-
stern hold their course for England. Of them I have much
to tell thee. Farewell.

> *He that thou knowest thine,*

Hamlet 30

Come, I will give you way for these your letters,
And do't the speedier that you may direct me
To him from whom you brought them.   *Exeunt*

Enter the King and Laertes   IV.7

KING

Now must your conscience my acquittance seal,
And you must put me in your heart for friend,
Sith you have heard, and with a knowing ear,
That he which hath your noble father slain
Pursued my life.

LAERTES   It well appears. But tell me
Why you proceeded not against these feats
So criminal and so capital in nature,
As by your safety, greatness, wisdom, all things else,
You mainly were stirred up.

KING   O, for two special reasons,

171

10 Which may to you perhaps seem much unsinewed,
But yet to me they're strong. The Queen his mother
Lives almost by his looks, and for myself –
My virtue or my plague, be it either which –
She is so conjunctive to my life and soul
That, as the star moves not but in his sphere,
I could not but by her. The other motive
Why to a public count I might not go
Is the great love the general gender bear him,
Who, dipping all his faults in their affection,
20 Work like the spring that turneth wood to stone,
Convert his gyves to graces; so that my arrows,
Too slightly timbered for so loud a wind,
Would have reverted to my bow again,
And not where I had aimed them.

LAERTES
And so have I a noble father lost,
A sister driven into desperate terms,
Whose worth, if praises may go back again,
Stood challenger, on mount, of all the age
For her perfections. But my revenge will come.

KING
30 Break not your sleeps for that. You must not think
That we are made of stuff so flat and dull
That we can let our beard be shook with danger,
And think it pastime. You shortly shall hear more.
I loved your father, and we love ourself,
And that, I hope, will teach you to imagine –
        Enter a Messenger with letters
How now? What news?

MESSENGER   Letters, my lord, from Hamlet.
These to your majesty. This to the Queen.

KING
From Hamlet? Who brought them?

MESSENGER

    Sailors, my lord, they say. I saw them not.

    They were given me by Claudio. He received them   40

    Of him that brought them.

KING   Laertes, you shall hear them. –

    Leave us.   *Exit the Messenger*

      (*He reads*)

High and mighty, you shall know I am set naked on your
kingdom. Tomorrow shall I beg leave to see your kingly
eyes; when I shall, first asking your pardon thereunto,
recount the occasion of my sudden and more strange return.

                          Hamlet

    What should this mean? Are all the rest come back?

    Or is it some abuse, and no such thing?

LAERTES

    Know you the hand?

KING   'Tis Hamlet's character. 'Naked'!   50

    And in a postscript here, he says 'alone'.

    Can you devise me?

LAERTES

    I am lost in it, my lord. But let him come.

    It warms the very sickness in my heart

    That I shall live and tell him to his teeth

    'Thus didest thou'.

KING   If it be so, Laertes –

    As how should it be so? How otherwise? –

    Will you be ruled by me?

LAERTES   Ay, my lord,

    So you will not o'errule me to a peace.

KING

    To thine own peace. If he be now returned,   60

    As checking at his voyage, and that he means

    No more to undertake it, I will work him

    To an exploit now ripe in my device,

Under the which he shall not choose but fall;
And for his death no wind of blame shall breathe,
But even his mother shall uncharge the practice
And call it accident.

LAERTES   My lord, I will be ruled;
The rather if you could devise it so
That I might be the organ.

KING   It falls right.
70 You have been talked of since your travel much,
And that in Hamlet's hearing, for a quality
Wherein they say you shine. Your sum of parts
Did not together pluck such envy from him
As did that one, and that, in my regard,
Of the unworthiest siege.

LAERTES   What part is that, my lord?

KING
A very riband in the cap of youth,
Yet needful too, for youth no less becomes
The light and careless livery that it wears
Than settled age his sables and his weeds,
80 Importing health and graveness. Two months since,
Here was a gentleman of Normandy.
I have seen myself, and served against, the French,
And they can well on horseback. But this gallant
Had witchcraft in't. He grew unto his seat,
And to such wondrous doing brought his horse
As had he been incorpsed and demi-natured
With the brave beast. So far he topped my thought
That I, in forgery of shapes and tricks,
Come short of what he did.

LAERTES   A Norman was't?

KING
90 A Norman.

LAERTES

  Upon my life, Lamord.

KING   The very same.

LAERTES

  I know him well. He is the brooch indeed
  And gem of all the nation.

KING

  He made confession of you,
  And gave you such a masterly report
  For art and exercise in your defence,
  And for your rapier most especial,
  That he cried out 'twould be a sight indeed
  If one could match you; the scrimers of their nation
  He swore had neither motion, guard, nor eye,   100
  If you opposed them. Sir, this report of his
  Did Hamlet so envenom with his envy
  That he could nothing do but wish and beg
  Your sudden coming o'er to play with you.
  Now, out of this –

LAERTES   What out of this, my lord?

KING

  Laertes, was your father dear to you?
  Or are you like the painting of a sorrow,
  A face without a heart?

LAERTES   Why ask you this?

KING

  Not that I think you did not love your father,
  But that I know love is begun by time,   110
  And that I see, in passages of proof,
  Time qualifies the spark and fire of it.
  There lives within the very flame of love
  A kind of wick or snuff that will abate it,
  And nothing is at a like goodness still;

For goodness, growing to a pleurisy,
Dies in his own too-much. That we would do
We should do when we would. For this 'would' changes,
And hath abatements and delays as many
120   As there are tongues, are hands, are accidents.
And then this 'should' is like a spendthrift sigh,
That hurts by easing. But to the quick o'th'ulcer –
Hamlet comes back. What would you undertake
To show yourself in deed your father's son
More than in words?

LAERTES   To cut his throat i'th'church!
KING

No place, indeed, should murder sanctuarize.
Revenge should have no bounds. But, good Laertes,
Will you do this: keep close within your chamber?
Hamlet returned shall know you are come home.
130   We'll put on those shall praise your excellence
And set a double varnish on the fame
The Frenchman gave you; bring you in fine together,
And wager on your heads. He, being remiss,
Most generous, and free from all contriving,
Will not peruse the foils, so that with ease,
Or with a little shuffling, you may choose
A sword unbated, and, in a pass of practice,
Requite him for your father.

LAERTES   I will do't,
And for that purpose I'll anoint my sword.
140   I bought an unction of a mountebank,
So mortal that, but dip a knife in it,
Where it draws blood no cataplasm so rare,
Collected from all simples that have virtue
Under the moon, can save the thing from death
That is but scratched withal. I'll touch my point
With this contagion, that, if I gall him slightly,

It may be death.

KING   Let's further think of this,
Weigh what convenience both of time and means
May fit us to our shape. If this should fail,
And that our drift look through our bad performance,   150
'Twere better not assayed. Therefore this project
Should have a back or second, that might hold
If this did blast in proof. Soft, let me see.
We'll make a solemn wager on your cunnings –
I ha't!
When in your motion you are hot and dry –
As make your bouts more violent to that end –
And that he calls for drink, I'll have preferred him
A chalice for the nonce, whereon but sipping,
If he by chance escape your venomed stuck,   160
Our purpose may hold there. – But stay, what noise?
    Enter the Queen
How, sweet Queen!

QUEEN

One woe doth tread upon another's heel,
So fast they follow. Your sister's drowned, Laertes.

LAERTES

Drowned! O, where?

QUEEN

There is a willow grows askant the brook,
That shows his hoar leaves in the glassy stream.
Therewith fantastic garlands did she make
Of crowflowers, nettles, daisies, and long purples,
That liberal shepherds give a grosser name,   170
But our cold maids do dead-men's-fingers call them.
There on the pendent boughs her crownet weeds
Clambering to hang, an envious sliver broke,
When down her weedy trophies and herself
Fell in the weeping brook. Her clothes spread wide,

And mermaid-like awhile they bore her up;
Which time she chanted snatches of old tunes,
As one incapable of her own distress,
Or like a creature native and indued
180 Unto that element. But long it could not be
Till that her garments, heavy with their drink,
Pulled the poor wretch from her melodious lay
To muddy death.

LAERTES   Alas, then she is drowned?

QUEEN
Drowned, drowned.

LAERTES
Too much of water hast thou, poor Ophelia,
And therefore I forbid my tears. But yet
It is our trick. Nature her custom holds,
Let shame say what it will. When these are gone,
The woman will be out. Adieu, my lord.
190 I have a speech o'fire that fain would blaze,
But that this folly drowns it.   *Exit*

KING   Let's follow, Gertrude.
How much I had to do to calm his rage!
Now fear I this will give it start again.
Therefore let's follow.   *Exeunt*

V.1   *Enter two Clowns*

FIRST CLOWN Is she to be buried in Christian burial
when she wilfully seeks her own salvation?

SECOND CLOWN I tell thee she is. Therefore make her
grave straight. The crowner hath sat on her, and finds
it Christian burial.

FIRST CLOWN How can that be, unless she drowned
herself in her own defence?

SECOND CLOWN Why, 'tis found so.

FIRST CLOWN It must be *se offendendo*. It cannot be else. For here lies the point: if I drown myself wittingly, it argues an act, and an act hath three branches – it is to act, to do, and to perform. Argal, she drowned herself wittingly.

SECOND CLOWN Nay, but hear you, Goodman Delver.

FIRST CLOWN Give me leave. Here lies the water – good. Here stands the man – good. If the man go to this water and drown himself, it is, will he nill he, he goes, mark you that. But if the water come to him and drown him, he drowns not himself. Argal, he that is not guilty of his own death shortens not his own life.

SECOND CLOWN But is this law?

FIRST CLOWN Ay, marry, is't – crowner's quest law.

SECOND CLOWN Will you ha' the truth on't? If this had not been a gentlewoman, she should have been buried out o'Christian burial.

FIRST CLOWN Why, there thou sayst. And the more pity that great folk should have countenance in this world to drown or hang themselves more than their even-Christian. Come, my spade. There is no ancient gentlemen but gardeners, ditchers, and grave-makers. They hold up Adam's profession.

SECOND CLOWN Was he a gentleman?

FIRST CLOWN 'A was the first that ever bore arms.

SECOND CLOWN Why, he had none.

FIRST CLOWN What, art a heathen? How dost thou understand the Scripture? The Scripture says Adam digged. Could he dig without arms? I'll put another question to thee. If thou answerest me not to the purpose, confess thyself –

SECOND CLOWN Go to!

FIRST CLOWN What is he that builds stronger than

either the mason, the shipwright, or the carpenter?

SECOND CLOWN The gallows-maker, for that frame outlives a thousand tenants.

FIRST CLOWN I like thy wit well, in good faith. The gallows does well. But how does it well? It does well to those that do ill. Now thou dost ill to say the gallows is built stronger than the church. Argal, the gallows may do well to thee. To't again, come.

50 SECOND CLOWN Who builds stronger than a mason, a shipwright, or a carpenter?

FIRST CLOWN Ay, tell me that, and unyoke.

SECOND CLOWN Marry, now I can tell.

FIRST CLOWN To't.

SECOND CLOWN Mass, I cannot tell.

FIRST CLOWN Cudgel thy brains no more about it, for your dull ass will not mend his pace with beating. And when you are asked this question next, say 'a grave-maker'. The houses he makes lasts till Doomsday. Go,
60 get thee in, and fetch me a stoup of liquor.

Exit Second Clown

(*sings*) In youth when I did love, did love,
   Methought it was very sweet
  To contract – O – the time for – a – my behove,
   O, methought there – a – was nothing – a – meet.
Enter Hamlet and Horatio

HAMLET Has this fellow no feeling of his business? 'A sings in grave-making.

HORATIO Custom hath made it in him a property of easiness.

HAMLET 'Tis e'en so. The hand of little employment
70 hath the daintier sense.

FIRST CLOWN (*sings*)
   But age with his stealing steps
    Hath clawed me in his clutch,

> And hath shipped me into the land,
> As if I had never been such.
>
> *He throws up a skull*

HAMLET That skull had a tongue in it, and could sing
once. How the knave jowls it to the ground, as if 'twere
Cain's jawbone, that did the first murder! This might be
the pate of a politician, which this ass now o'erreaches;
one that would circumvent God, might it not?

HORATIO It might, my lord. 80

HAMLET Or of a courtier, which could say 'Good morrow, sweet lord! How dost thou, sweet lord?' This
might be my Lord Such-a-one, that praised my Lord
Such-a-one's horse when 'a meant to beg it, might it
not?

HORATIO Ay, my lord.

HAMLET Why, e'en so, and now my Lady Worm's, chopless, and knocked about the mazzard with a sexton's
spade. Here's fine revolution, an we had the trick to
see't. Did these bones cost no more the breeding but 90
to play at loggats with them? Mine ache to think on't.

FIRST CLOWN (*sings*)
> A pickaxe and a spade, a spade,
> For and a shrouding sheet.
> O, a pit of clay for to be made
> For such a guest is meet.
>
> *He throws up another skull*

HAMLET There's another. Why may not that be the skull
of a lawyer? Where be his quiddities now, his quillets,
his cases, his tenures, and his tricks? Why does he
suffer this mad knave now to knock him about the
sconce with a dirty shovel, and will not tell him of his 100
action of battery? Hum! This fellow might be in's
time a great buyer of land, with his statutes, his recognizances, his fines, his double vouchers, his recoveries.

Is this the fine of his fines, and the recovery of his recoveries, to have his fine pate full of fine dirt? Will his vouchers vouch him no more of his purchases, and double ones too, than the length and breadth of a pair of indentures? The very conveyances of his lands will scarcely lie in this box, and must th'inheritor himself
110 have no more, ha?

HORATIO Not a jot more, my lord.

HAMLET Is not parchment made of sheep-skins?

HORATIO Ay, my lord, and of calves' skins too.

HAMLET They are sheep and calves which seek out assurance in that. I will speak to this fellow. – Whose grave's this, sirrah?

FIRST CLOWN Mine, sir.

    (sings) O, a pit of clay for to be made
          For such a guest is meet.

120 HAMLET I think it be thine indeed, for thou liest in't.

FIRST CLOWN You lie out on't, sir, and therefore 'tis not yours. For my part, I do not lie in't, yet it is mine.

HAMLET Thou dost lie in't, to be in't and say it is thine. 'Tis for the dead, not for the quick. Therefore thou liest.

FIRST CLOWN 'Tis a quick lie, sir. 'Twill away again from me to you.

HAMLET What man dost thou dig it for?

FIRST CLOWN For no man, sir.

130 HAMLET What woman then?

FIRST CLOWN For none neither.

HAMLET Who is to be buried in't?

FIRST CLOWN One that was a woman, sir. But, rest her soul, she's dead.

HAMLET How absolute the knave is! We must speak by the card, or equivocation will undo us. By the Lord, Horatio, this three years I have took note of it, the age

is grown so picked that the toe of the peasant comes so
near the heel of the courtier he galls his kibe. – How
long hast thou been grave-maker? 140

FIRST CLOWN Of all the days i'th'year, I came to't that
day that our last King Hamlet overcame Fortinbras.

HAMLET How long is that since?

FIRST CLOWN Cannot you tell that? Every fool can tell
that. It was that very day that young Hamlet was born –
he that is mad, and sent into England.

HAMLET Ay, marry, why was he sent into England?

FIRST CLOWN Why, because 'a was mad. 'A shall recover his wits there. Or, if 'a do not, 'tis no great matter
there. 150

HAMLET Why?

FIRST CLOWN 'Twill not be seen in him there. There
the men are as mad as he.

HAMLET How came he mad?

FIRST CLOWN Very strangely, they say.

HAMLET How strangely?

FIRST CLOWN Faith, e'en with losing his wits.

HAMLET Upon what ground?

FIRST CLOWN Why, here in Denmark. I have been
sexton here, man and boy, thirty years. 160

HAMLET How long will a man lie i'th'earth ere he rot?

FIRST CLOWN Faith, if 'a be not rotten before 'a die, as
we have many pocky corses nowadays that will scarce
hold the laying in, 'a will last you some eight year or
nine year. A tanner will last you nine year.

HAMLET Why he more than another?

FIRST CLOWN Why, sir, his hide is so tanned with his
trade that 'a will keep out water a great while, and your
water is a sore decayer of your whoreson dead body.
Here's a skull now hath lien you i'th'earth three-and- 170
twenty years.

HAMLET Whose was it?

FIRST CLOWN A whoreson mad fellow's it was. Whose do you think it was?

HAMLET Nay, I know not.

FIRST CLOWN A pestilence on him for a mad rogue! 'A poured a flagon of Rhenish on my head once. This same skull, sir, was, sir, Yorick's skull, the King's jester.

HAMLET This?

180 FIRST CLOWN E'en that.

HAMLET Let me see. Alas, poor Yorick! I knew him, Horatio. A fellow of infinite jest, of most excellent fancy. He hath bore me on his back a thousand times. And now how abhorred in my imagination it is! My gorge rises at it. Here hung those lips that I have kissed I know not how oft. Where be your gibes now? Your gambols, your songs, your flashes of merriment that were wont to set the table on a roar? Not one now to mock your own grinning? Quite chop-fallen? Now get
190 you to my lady's table and tell her, let her paint an inch thick, to this favour she must come. Make her laugh at that. Prithee, Horatio, tell me one thing.

HORATIO What's that, my lord?

HAMLET Dost thou think Alexander looked o'this fashion i'th'earth?

HORATIO E'en so.

HAMLET And smelt so? Pah!

HORATIO E'en so, my lord.

HAMLET To what base uses we may return, Horatio! Why
200 may not imagination trace the noble dust of Alexander till 'a find it stopping a bunghole?

HORATIO 'Twere to consider too curiously to consider so.

HAMLET No, faith, not a jot. But to follow him thither with modesty enough, and likelihood to lead it; as thus:

Alexander died, Alexander was buried, Alexander returneth to dust; the dust is earth; of earth we make loam; and why of that loam whereto he was converted might they not stop a beer barrel?

Imperious Caesar, dead and turned to clay,
Might stop a hole to keep the wind away.   210
O, that that earth which kept the world in awe
Should patch a wall t'expel the winter's flaw!
But soft, but soft awhile!

Enter the King and Queen, Laertes, and the corpse of
Ophelia, with lords attendant and a Priest

                            Here comes the King,
The Queen, the courtiers. Who is this they follow?
And with such maimèd rites? This doth betoken
The corse they follow did with desperate hand
Fordo it own life. 'Twas of some estate.
Couch we awhile, and mark.

He withdraws with Horatio

LAERTES
What ceremony else?

HAMLET
That is Laertes, a very noble youth. Mark.   220

LAERTES
What ceremony else?

PRIEST
Her obsequies have been as far enlarged
As we have warranty. Her death was doubtful,
And, but that great command o'ersways the order,
She should in ground unsanctified have lodged
Till the last trumpet. For charitable prayers,
Shards, flints, and pebbles should be thrown on her.
Yet here she is allowed her virgin crants,
Her maiden strewments, and the bringing home
Of bell and burial.   230

185

LAERTES

Must there no more be done?

PRIEST   No more be done.

We should profane the service of the dead

To sing a requiem and such rest to her

As to peace-parted souls.

LAERTES   Lay her i'th'earth,

And from her fair and unpolluted flesh

May violets spring! I tell thee, churlish priest,

A ministering angel shall my sister be

When thou liest howling.

HAMLET   What, the fair Ophelia?

QUEEN

Sweets to the sweet! Farewell.

    She scatters flowers

240 I hoped thou shouldst have been my Hamlet's wife.

I thought thy bride-bed to have decked, sweet maid,

And not have strewed thy grave.

LAERTES   O, treble woe

Fall ten times double on that cursèd head

Whose wicked deed thy most ingenious sense

Deprived thee of! Hold off the earth awhile,

Till I have caught her once more in mine arms.

    He leaps in the grave

Now pile your dust upon the quick and dead

Till of this flat a mountain you have made

T'o'ertop old Pelion or the skyish head

Of blue Olympus.

HAMLET (*coming forward*)

250   What is he whose grief

Bears such an emphasis, whose phrase of sorrow

Conjures the wandering stars, and makes them stand

Like wonder-wounded hearers? This is I,

Hamlet the Dane.

LAERTES   The devil take thy soul!

HAMLET

Thou prayest not well.

I prithee take thy fingers from my throat.

For, though I am not splenitive and rash,

Yet have I in me something dangerous,

Which let thy wisdom fear. Hold off thy hand.

KING

Pluck them asunder.

QUEEN   Hamlet, Hamlet!   260

ALL

Gentlemen!

HORATIO   Good my lord, be quiet.

HAMLET

Why, I will fight with him upon this theme

Until my eyelids will no longer wag.

QUEEN

O my son, what theme?

HAMLET

I loved Ophelia. Forty thousand brothers

Could not with all their quantity of love

Make up my sum. What wilt thou do for her?

KING

O, he is mad, Laertes.

QUEEN

For love of God, forbear him.

HAMLET

'Swounds, show me what thou't do.   270

Woo't weep? Woo't fight? Woo't fast? Woo't tear
          thyself?

Woo't drink up eisel? Eat a crocodile?

I'll do't. Dost thou come here to whine?

To outface me with leaping in her grave?

Be buried quick with her, and so will I.

And if thou prate of mountains, let them throw
Millions of acres on us, till our ground,
Singeing his pate against the burning zone,
Make Ossa like a wart! Nay, an thou'lt mouth,
I'll rant as well as thou.

280 QUEEN   This is mere madness.
And thus a while the fit will work on him.
Anon, as patient as the female dove
When that her golden couplets are disclosed,
His silence will sit drooping.

HAMLET   Hear you, sir.
What is the reason that you use me thus?
I loved you ever. But it is no matter.
Let Hercules himself do what he may,
The cat will mew, and dog will have his day.

KING
I pray thee, good Horatio, wait upon him.

                    Exeunt Hamlet and Horatio
(To Laertes)
290 Strengthen your patience in our last night's speech.
We'll put the matter to the present push.
Good Gertrude, set some watch over your son.
This grave shall have a living monument.
An hour of quiet shortly shall we see.
Till then in patience our proceeding be.   *Exeunt*

V.2   *Enter Hamlet and Horatio*
HAMLET
So much for this, sir. Now shall you see the other.
You do remember all the circumstance?
HORATIO
Remember it, my lord!
HAMLET
Sir, in my heart there was a kind of fighting

188

That would not let me sleep. Methought I lay
Worse than the mutines in the bilboes. Rashly,
And praised be rashness for it – let us know
Our indiscretion sometime serves us well
When our deep plots do pall, and that should learn us
There's a divinity that shapes our ends,   10
Rough-hew them how we will –

HORATIO   That is most certain.

HAMLET
Up from my cabin,
My sea-gown scarfed about me, in the dark
Groped I to find out them, had my desire,
Fingered their packet, and in fine withdrew
To mine own room again, making so bold,
My fears forgetting manners, to unseal
Their grand commission; where I found, Horatio –
Ah, royal knavery! – an exact command,
Larded with many several sorts of reasons,   20
Importing Denmark's health, and England's too,
With, ho! such bugs and goblins in my life,
That on the supervise, no leisure bated,
No, not to stay the grinding of the axe,
My head should be struck off.

HORATIO   Is't possible?

HAMLET
Here's the commission. Read it at more leisure.
But wilt thou hear now how I did proceed?

HORATIO
I beseech you.

HAMLET
Being thus be-netted round with villainies,
Or I could make a prologue to my brains   30
They had begun the play. I sat me down,
Devised a new commission, wrote it fair.

I once did hold it, as our statists do,
A baseness to write fair, and laboured much
How to forget that learning. But, sir, now
It did me yeoman's service. Wilt thou know
Th'effect of what I wrote?

HORATIO   Ay, good my lord.

HAMLET

An earnest conjuration from the King,
As England was his faithful tributary,
40 As love between them like the palm might flourish,
As peace should still her wheaten garland wear
And stand a comma 'tween their amities,
And many such-like as's of great charge,
That on the view and knowing of these contents,
Without debatement further, more or less,
He should those bearers put to sudden death,
Not shriving time allowed.

HORATIO   How was this sealed?

HAMLET

Why, even in that was heaven ordinant.
I had my father's signet in my purse,
50 Which was the model of that Danish seal,
Folded the writ up in the form of th'other,
Subscribed it, gave't th'impression, placed it safely,
The changeling never known. Now, the next day
Was our sea-fight, and what to this was sequent
Thou knowest already.

HORATIO

So Guildenstern and Rosencrantz go to't.

HAMLET

Why, man, they did make love to this employment.
They are not near my conscience. Their defeat
Does by their own insinuation grow.
60 'Tis dangerous when the baser nature comes

Between the pass and fell incensèd points
Of mighty opposites.

HORATIO   Why, what a king is this!

HAMLET

Does it not, think thee, stand me now upon –
He that hath killed my King and whored my mother,
Popped in between th'election and my hopes,
Thrown out his angle for my proper life,
And with such cozenage – is't not perfect conscience
To quit him with this arm? And is't not to be damned
To let this canker of our nature come
In further evil?   70

HORATIO

It must be shortly known to him from England
What is the issue of the business there.

HAMLET

It will be short. The interim is mine;
And a man's life's no more than to say 'one'.
But I am very sorry, good Horatio,
That to Laertes I forgot myself.
For by the image of my cause I see
The portraiture of his. I'll court his favours.
But sure the bravery of his grief did put me
Into a towering passion.

HORATIO   Peace, who comes here? 80

Enter Osrick

OSRICK Your lordship is right welcome back to Denmark.

HAMLET I humbly thank you, sir. (*Aside to Horatio*) Dost
know this waterfly?

HORATIO (*aside to Hamlet*) No, my good lord.

HAMLET (*aside to Horatio*) Thy state is the more gracious,
for 'tis a vice to know him. He hath much land, and
fertile. Let a beast be lord of beasts, and his crib shall
stand at the king's mess. 'Tis a chough, but, as I say,

spacious in the possession of dirt.

90 OSRICK Sweet lord, if your lordship were at leisure, I should impart a thing to you from his majesty.

HAMLET I will receive it, sir, with all diligence of spirit. Put your bonnet to his right use. 'Tis for the head.

OSRICK I thank your lordship, it is very hot.

HAMLET No, believe me, 'tis very cold. The wind is northerly.

OSRICK It is indifferent cold, my lord, indeed.

HAMLET But yet methinks it is very sultry and hot for my complexion.

100 OSRICK Exceedingly, my lord. It is very sultry, as 'twere – I cannot tell how. But, my lord, his majesty bade me signify to you that 'a has laid a great wager on your head. Sir, this is the matter –

HAMLET I beseech you remember.

He invites Osrick to put on his hat

OSRICK Nay, good my lord. For my ease, in good faith. Sir, here is newly come to court Laertes; believe me, an absolute gentleman, full of most excellent differences, of very soft society and great showing. Indeed, to speak feelingly of him, he is the card or calendar of gentry.

110 For you shall find in him the continent of what part a gentleman would see.

HAMLET Sir, his definement suffers no perdition in you, though, I know, to divide him inventorially would dizzy th'arithmetic of memory, and yet but yaw neither in respect of his quick sail. But, in the verity of extolment, I take him to be a soul of great article, and his infusion of such dearth and rareness as, to make true diction of him, his semblable is his mirror, and who else would trace him, his umbrage, nothing more.

120 OSRICK Your lordship speaks most infallibly of him.

HAMLET The concernancy, sir? Why do we wrap the

gentleman in our more rawer breath?

OSRICK Sir?

HORATIO Is't not possible to understand in another tongue? You will to't, sir, really.

HAMLET What imports the nomination of this gentleman?

OSRICK Of Laertes?

HORATIO (aside to Hamlet) His purse is empty already. All's golden words are spent.   130

HAMLET Of him, sir.

OSRICK I know you are not ignorant –

HAMLET I would you did, sir. Yet, in faith, if you did, it would not much approve me. Well, sir?

OSRICK You are not ignorant of what excellence Laertes is –

HAMLET I dare not confess that, lest I should compare with him in excellence. But to know a man well were to know himself.

OSRICK I mean, sir, for his weapon. But in the imputation laid on him by them, in his meed he's unfellowed.   140

HAMLET What's his weapon?

OSRICK Rapier and dagger.

HAMLET That's two of his weapons. But well!

OSRICK The King, sir, hath wagered with him six Barbary horses, against the which he has impawned, as I take it, six French rapiers and poniards, with their assigns, as girdle, hangers, and so. Three of the carriages, in faith, are very dear to fancy, very responsive to the hilts, most delicate carriages, and of very liberal conceit.   150

HAMLET What call you the carriages?

HORATIO (aside to Hamlet) I knew you must be edified by the margent ere you had done.

OSRICK The carriages, sir, are the hangers.

HAMLET The phrase would be more germane to the

matter if we could carry a cannon by our sides. I would it might be 'hangers' till then. But on! Six Barbary horses against six French swords, their assigns, and three liberal-conceited carriages. That's the French bet

160 against the Danish. Why is this all impawned, as you call it?

OSRICK The King, sir, hath laid, sir, that in a dozen passes between yourself and him he shall not exceed you three hits. He hath laid on twelve for nine; and it would come to immediate trial if your lordship would vouch-safe the answer.

HAMLET How if I answer no?

OSRICK I mean, my lord, the opposition of your person in trial.

170 HAMLET Sir, I will walk here in the hall. If it please his majesty, it is the breathing time of day with me. Let the foils be brought, the gentleman willing, and the King hold his purpose, I will win for him an I can. If not, I will gain nothing but my shame and the odd hits.

OSRICK Shall I re-deliver you e'en so?

HAMLET To this effect, sir, after what flourish your nature will.

OSRICK I commend my duty to your lordship.

HAMLET Yours, yours. *Exit Osrick*

180 He does well to commend it himself. There are no tongues else for's turn.

HORATIO This lapwing runs away with the shell on his head.

HAMLET 'A did comply, sir, with his dug before 'a sucked it. Thus has he, and many more of the same bevy that I know the drossy age dotes on, only got the tune of the time and, out of an habit of encounter, a kind of yeasty collection, which carries them through and through the most fanned and winnowed opinions; and do but blow them to their trial, the bubbles are out.

Enter a Lord

LORD My lord, his majesty commended him to you by
young Osrick, who brings back to him that you attend
him in the hall. He sends to know if your pleasure hold
to play with Laertes, or that you will take longer time.

HAMLET I am constant to my purposes. They follow the
King's pleasure. If his fitness speaks, mine is ready,
now or whensoever, provided I be so able as now.

LORD The King and Queen and all are coming down.

HAMLET In happy time.

LORD The Queen desires you to use some gentle entertainment to Laertes before you fall to play.

HAMLET She well instructs me.   *Exit the Lord*

HORATIO You will lose this wager, my lord.

HAMLET I do not think so. Since he went into France I
have been in continual practice. I shall win at the odds.
But thou wouldst not think how ill all's here about my
heart. But it is no matter.

HORATIO Nay, good my lord –

HAMLET It is but foolery. But it is such a kind of gaingiving as would perhaps trouble a woman.

HORATIO If your mind dislike anything, obey it. I will
forestall their repair hither and say you are not fit.

HAMLET Not a whit. We defy augury. There is special
providence in the fall of a sparrow. If it be now, 'tis not
to come. If it be not to come, it will be now. If it be not
now, yet it will come. The readiness is all. Since no man
knows of aught he leaves, what is't to leave betimes?
Let be.

Trumpets and drums
A table prepared, with flagons of wine on it
Enter officers with cushions, and other attendants with
foils, daggers, and gauntlets

V.2

Enter the King and Queen, Osrick, Laertes, and all the state

KING

Come, Hamlet, come, and take this hand from me.
He puts Laertes's hand into Hamlet's

HAMLET

220   Give me your pardon, sir. I have done you wrong.
But pardon't, as you are a gentleman.
This presence knows, and you must needs have heard,
How I am punished with a sore distraction.
What I have done
That might your nature, honour, and exception
Roughly awake, I here proclaim was madness.
Was't Hamlet wronged Laertes? Never Hamlet.
If Hamlet from himself be ta'en away,
And when he's not himself does wrong Laertes,

230   Then Hamlet does it not. Hamlet denies it.
Who does it then? His madness. If't be so,
Hamlet is of the faction that is wronged.
His madness is poor Hamlet's enemy.
Sir, in this audience,
Let my disclaiming from a purposed evil
Free me so far in your most generous thoughts
That I have shot my arrow o'er the house
And hurt my brother.

LAERTES   I am satisfied in nature,
Whose motive in this case should stir me most

240   To my revenge. But in my terms of honour
I stand aloof, and will no reconcilement
Till by some elder masters of known honour
I have a voice and precedent of peace
To keep my name ungored. But till that time
I do receive your offered love like love,
And will not wrong it.

HAMLET   I embrace it freely,
  And will this brothers' wager frankly play.
  Give us the foils. Come on.

LAERTES   Come, one for me.

HAMLET
  I'll be your foil, Laertes. In mine ignorance
  Your skill shall, like a star i'th'darkest night,   250
  Stick fiery off indeed.

LAERTES   You mock me, sir.

HAMLET
  No, by this hand.

KING
  Give them the foils, young Osrick. Cousin Hamlet,
  You know the wager?

HAMLET   Very well, my lord.
  Your grace has laid the odds o'th'weaker side.

KING
  I do not fear it. I have seen you both.
  But since he is bettered, we have therefore odds.

LAERTES
  This is too heavy. Let me see another.

HAMLET
  This likes me well. These foils have all a length?

OSRICK
  Ay, my good lord.   260
      They prepare to play

KING
  Set me the stoups of wine upon that table.
  If Hamlet give the first or second hit,
  Or quit in answer of the third exchange,
  Let all the battlements their ordnance fire.
  The King shall drink to Hamlet's better breath,
  And in the cup an union shall he throw
  Richer than that which four successive kings

In Denmark's crown have worn. Give me the cups,
And let the kettle to the trumpet speak,
270   The trumpet to the cannoneer without,
The cannons to the heavens, the heaven to earth,
'Now the King drinks to Hamlet.' Come, begin.
        (*Trumpets the while*)
And you, the judges, bear a wary eye.

HAMLET
Come on, sir.

LAERTES   Come, my lord.
        They play

HAMLET   One.

LAERTES   No.

HAMLET   Judgement?

OSRICK
A hit, a very palpable hit.

        Drum, trumpets, and shot. Flourish. A piece goes off

LAERTES   Well, again.

KING
Stay, give me drink. Hamlet, this pearl is thine.
Here's to thy health. Give him the cup.

HAMLET
I'll play this bout first; set it by awhile.
Come.

        They play

        Another hit. What say you?

LAERTES
280   A touch, a touch. I do confess't.

KING
Our son shall win.

QUEEN   He's fat and scant of breath.
Here, Hamlet, take my napkin. Rub thy brows.
The Queen carouses to thy fortune, Hamlet.

HAMLET
  Good madam!

KING   Gertrude, do not drink.

QUEEN
  I will, my lord. I pray you, pardon me.
    She drinks

KING (*aside*)
  It is the poisoned cup. It is too late.

HAMLET
  I dare not drink yet, madam. By and by.

QUEEN
  Come, let me wipe thy face.

LAERTES (*aside to the King*)
  My lord, I'll hit him now.

KING (*aside to Laertes*)   I do not think't.

LAERTES (*aside*)
  And yet it is almost against my conscience.   290

HAMLET
  Come for the third, Laertes. You do but dally.
  I pray you, pass with your best violence.
  I am afeard you make a wanton of me.

LAERTES
  Say you so? Come on.
    They play

OSRICK
  Nothing neither way.

LAERTES
  Have at you now!
    In scuffling they change rapiers, and both are wounded
    with the poisoned weapon

KING   Part them. They are incensed.

HAMLET
  Nay, come. Again!
    The Queen falls

199

OSRICK   Look to the Queen there. Ho!

HORATIO
They bleed on both sides. How is it, my lord?

OSRICK
How is't, Laertes?

LAERTES
300   Why, as a woodcock to mine own springe, Osrick.
I am justly killed with mine own treachery.

HAMLET
How does the Queen?

KING   She swounds to see them bleed.

QUEEN
No, no, the drink, the drink! O my dear Hamlet!
The drink, the drink! I am poisoned.
      She dies

HAMLET
O, villainy! Ho! Let the door be locked.
Treachery! Seek it out.

LAERTES
It is here, Hamlet. Hamlet, thou art slain.
No medicine in the world can do thee good.
In thee there is not half an hour's life.
310   The treacherous instrument is in thy hand,
Unbated and envenomed. The foul practice
Hath turned itself on me. Lo, here I lie,
Never to rise again. Thy mother's poisoned.
I can no more. The King, the King's to blame.

HAMLET
The point envenomed too?
Then, venom, to thy work.
      He wounds the King

ALL
Treason! Treason!

KING

 O, yet defend me, friends. I am but hurt.

HAMLET

 Here, thou incestuous, murderous, damnèd Dane,
 Drink off this potion.

  He forces the King to drink

      Is thy union here?   320

 Follow my mother.

  The King dies

LAERTES   He is justly served.

 It is a poison tempered by himself.
 Exchange forgiveness with me, noble Hamlet.
 Mine and my father's death come not upon thee,
 Nor thine on me!

  He dies

HAMLET

 Heaven make thee free of it! I follow thee.
 I am dead, Horatio. Wretched Queen, adieu!
 You that look pale and tremble at this chance,
 That are but mutes or audience to this act,
 Had I but time – as this fell sergeant, Death,   330
 Is strict in his arrest – O, I could tell you –
 But let it be. Horatio, I am dead.
 Thou livest. Report me and my cause aright
 To the unsatisfied.

HORATIO   Never believe it.

 I am more an antique Roman than a Dane.
 Here's yet some liquor left.

HAMLET   As th' art a man,

 Give me the cup. Let go. By heaven, I'll ha't!
 O God, Horatio, what a wounded name,
 Things standing thus unknown, shall I leave behind me!
 If thou didst ever hold me in thy heart,   340

Absent thee from felicity awhile,
And in this harsh world draw thy breath in pain,
To tell my story.
    A march afar off, and shout within
          What warlike noise is this?

OSRICK

Young Fortinbras, with conquest come from Poland,
To the ambassadors of England gives
This warlike volley.

HAMLET   O, I die, Horatio!
The potent poison quite o'er-crows my spirit.
I cannot live to hear the news from England.
But I do prophesy th'election lights
350 On Fortinbras. He has my dying voice.
So tell him, with th'occurrents, more and less,
Which have solicited – the rest is silence.
    He dies

HORATIO

Now cracks a noble heart. Good night, sweet Prince,
And flights of angels sing thee to thy rest!
    (*March within*)
Why does the drum come hither?
    Enter Fortinbras, with the Ambassadors and with his
    train of drum, colours, and attendants

FORTINBRAS

Where is this sight?

HORATIO   What is it you would see?
If aught of woe or wonder, cease your search.

FORTINBRAS

This quarry cries on havoc. O proud Death,
What feast is toward in thine eternal cell
360 That thou so many princes at a shot
So bloodily hast struck?

AMBASSADOR   The sight is dismal,

And our affairs from England come too late.
The ears are senseless that should give us hearing,
To tell him his commandment is fulfilled,
That Rosencrantz and Guildenstern are dead.
Where should we have our thanks?

HORATIO   Not from his mouth,
Had it th'ability of life to thank you.
He never gave commandment for their death.
But since, so jump upon this bloody question,
You from the Polack wars, and you from England,   370
Are here arrived, give order that these bodies
High on a stage be placèd to the view.
And let me speak to th'yet unknowing world
How these things came about. So shall you hear
Of carnal, bloody, and unnatural acts,
Of accidental judgements, casual slaughters,
Of deaths put on by cunning and forced cause,
And, in this upshot, purposes mistook
Fallen on th'inventors' heads. All this can I
Truly deliver.

FORTINBRAS   Let us haste to hear it,   380
And call the noblest to the audience.
For me, with sorrow I embrace my fortune.
I have some rights of memory in this kingdom,
Which now to claim my vantage doth invite me.

HORATIO
Of that I shall have also cause to speak,
And from his mouth whose voice will draw on more.
But let this same be presently performed,
Even while men's minds are wild, lest more mischance
On plots and errors happen.

FORTINBRAS   Let four captains
Bear Hamlet like a soldier to the stage.   390
For he was likely, had he been put on,

To have proved most royal. And for his passage
The soldiers' music and the rites of war
Speak loudly for him.
Take up the bodies. Such a sight as this
Becomes the field, but here shows much amiss.
Go, bid the soldiers shoot.

*Exeunt marching; after the which a peal of
ordnance is shot off*

COMMENTARY

In the Commentary and the Account of the Text the abbreviation 'Q1' is used for the first ('bad') quarto (1603), 'Q2' for the second ('good') quarto (1604) and 'F' for the first Folio (1623). Biblical quotations are given, with modernized spelling and punctuation, from the Bishops' Bible (1568 etc.), the version probably most familiar to Shakespeare.

I.1   The action of the scene takes place on a *platform* (I.2.213) – a level place for mounting guns – of the Danish royal castle at Elsinore. Historically, the castle included a gun-platform where batteries commanded the narrow entrance to the Baltic Sea between Denmark and (modern) Sweden, exacting tolls from ships passing through. It was well known to British voyagers.

(stage direction) *Enter Francisco and Barnardo, two sentinels*. Francisco is on duty, presumably pacing up and down. Barnardo enters to relieve him.

1   *Who's there?* Perhaps he fancies he sees the Ghost.

2   *Nay, answer me. Stand and unfold yourself*. The emphasis is on *me* and (perhaps) *yourself*. Francisco is the sentinel at his post, and it is his duty, not Barnardo's, to challenge anyone who approaches. By putting the challenge in the mouth of the new arrival, Shakespeare creates a feeling of tension.

unfold identify

6   *carefully upon your hour* considerately on time

7   *twelve* (when ghosts begin to walk; this prepares for I.4.3–6: compare III.2.395–7)

8   *'Tis bitter cold*. Shakespeare carefully establishes the winter night, of which we are reminded at I.4.1–2.

9   *I am sick at heart*. This, from an unimportant soldier,

contributes to the emotional atmosphere and prepares for the Prince's heart-sickness at I.2.129–59. It oddly contrasts with the disciplined military scene.

10   *Have you had quiet guard?* Francisco's *I am sick at heart* prompts Barnardo to think of the apparition and so to ask his vague question.

       Not a mouse stirring. The ordinary image gives a sense of reality to the soldiers' language, preparing us to accept the supernatural happenings. It also implies the silence and acuteness of perception which anticipate the coming awareness of the Ghost.

13   *rivals* partners

       bid them make haste. Barnardo does not want to be left alone now that it is time for the feared appearance of the Ghost.

15   *this ground* (the land of Denmark)

       liegemen. The soldiers in this scene seem to be nationals, not like the *Switzers* (IV.5.99), who are the King's personal bodyguard and imply a tyrant's reliance on foreign mercenaries.

       the Dane the King of Denmark

16, 18   *Give you good night* may God give you good night. The repetition suggests Francisco's effort to get away as soon as he can.

19   *What, is Horatio there?* This adds to the impression that we are witnessing a night scene.

21   *What . . . tonight?* Marcellus at once asks the question which is uppermost in their minds. The phrase *this thing* indicates his puzzled awe. The line is attributed to Horatio in Q2, but to Marcellus in Q1 (a good authority in this scene) and in F. It seems to come more naturally from Marcellus in view of Barnardo's promptly understanding reply and of Horatio's disbelief.

29   *approve our eyes* corroborate the existence of what we have seen

       speak to it. See the note to line 42.

30, 33   *Sit . . . sit* (referring to Horatio and Marcellus, not Barnardo, who is at his post)

31   *assail your ears* try to overcome your incredulity by narrating to you. The military imagery is appropriate in a soldier's speech.

34   *let us hear Barnardo*. He has already heard the story from Marcellus.

36   *yond same star*. Barnardo presumably points to the sky at one side of the stage, guiding the eyes of the audience away from where the Ghost will enter. A soldier on night duty notices the stars and their changing positions as the hours pass; and Shakespeare throughout the scene gives an impression of a clear, frosty, starlit sky.

the pole (the point where the Pole Star shines)

37   *Had made his course*. This, together with the strong words *illume* and *burns*, seems to imply that the *star* is a planet.

39   (stage direction) *Enter the Ghost*. It passes close to them (*Within his truncheon's length* (I.2.204), that is, only a few feet), and so can be imagined as seen clearly in the dim light. It is in full armour, carries a truncheon, and walks in military fashion, as is frequently iterated (lines 47, 60, and 110; I.2.200–204, 226–30, and 255; I.4.52). Further visual details are given at I.2.231–4 and 242. On the Elizabethan stage it would almost certainly have emerged from a trap-door and have descended by the same means. This is appropriate, for it later *cries under the stage* (I.5.148) and is called *this fellow in the cellarage* (I.5.151).

41   *like the King that's dead*. The likeness, insisted on (lines 43–4, 47–9, and 58–63), helps the watchers to believe that it is really King Hamlet's spirit, not a demon.

42   *Thou art a scholar. Speak to it*. Horatio was a fellow-student of Hamlet, and would therefore know Latin, in which language ghosts were conventionally addressed

(though theatrical convention permitted English), and the correct form of words for exorcism. Hamlet in fact uses a Latin phrase in addressing the Ghost at I.5.156.

42, 45   *Speak to it . . . . It would be spoke to.* Ghosts could not initiate conversation. See lines 128–39 and III.4.105–10.

43   *'a* (the weakened, unstressed form of 'he')

44   *harrows* distresses

45   *would be* wants to be

46   *usurpest* (because this is not a time when human beings are expected to be out walking, and because you are bearing the form of one we know to be dead and buried)

48   *buried Denmark* the dead King of Denmark

49   *sometimes* formerly

50   *It is offended* (presumably by Horatio's *usurpest*)

54   *fantasy.* See line 23.

57   *sensible* affecting my senses
    avouch assurance

61   *he the ambitious Norway combated.* The episode is described later (lines 80–95). Horatio seems to speak from personal observation of the occasion, which we learn at V.1.141–60 was thirty years ago. But such details are not to be pressed as evidence for a time-scheme or as indications of Horatio's age.
    ambitious. The word was generally derogatory; Hamlet describes himself as *very proud, revengeful, ambitious* (III.1.124–5). At I.1.83 this King of Norway is described as *pricked on by a most emulate pride.*
    Norway the King of Norway

62   *So frowned he.* Presumably this connects with Marcellus's *It is offended,* and refers only to that moment; when Hamlet later asks *looked he frowningly?*, Horatio replies *A countenance more in sorrow than in anger* (I.2.231–2), apparently describing the Ghost's usual expression.
    parle (one syllable) parley

63   *sledded poleaxe* long military axe, weighted with lead
      (like a 'sledge-hammer'): a favourite Scandinavian
      weapon. Q2 (and Q1) reads 'sleaded pollax', and F
      'sledded Pollax'. Later in the play an inhabitant of
      Poland is called a *Polack* (II.2.63 etc.), as well as *Pole*
      (IV.4.21). It has therefore often been supposed that the
      phrase should be 'sledded Polacks', that is, 'Poles on
      their sleighs', referring to a different military episode
      from the quarrel with the King of Norway. But the
      King is said to have been frowning during heated verbal
      negotiations (*angry parle*), and this does not seem an
      appropriate moment for his raining blows upon the
      enemy Poles, mounted on their sledges, during a
      battle on a frozen lake or river. In *Love's Labour's
      Lost*, V.2.571, the word 'poleaxe' is spelt 'Polax' by Q1
      (1598) and 'Pollax' by F and by Q2 (1631).

65   *jump* exactly

67   *thought to work* train of thinking to act upon

68   *in the gross and scope of mine opinion* so far as I can make
      a general surmise without going into details

69   *strange eruption to our state* startling disturbance in
      the affairs of our country

70   *Good now* if you please

71   *watch* (literally, keeping awake; both the military night-
      watch and the night labours of the citizens in manu-
      facturing armaments and building ships)

72   *toils* causes to toil
      subject subjects

73   *cast* casting in a foundry

74   *foreign mart for implements of war* seeking foreign trade
      in armaments

75   *impress* conscription, forced enrolment

75-6, *whose sore task | Does not divide the Sunday from the*
  78   *week | ... the night joint-labourer with the day.* They
      are working on Sundays and night shifts.

77   *toward* impending

79   *That can I.* Horatio provides the information needed by

209

the audience to understand the situation. But in the next scene (I.2.164–9) he has recently arrived from Wittenberg, ignorant of events, and I.4.12 he has to be informed about a local Danish custom. Later he becomes Hamlet's confidant and often receives from him the information the audience requires. He is clearly *a Dane* at V.2.335. There is consistency in his character, but not in his role in the play.

80   *whisper* rumour

80–95   The account of the Danish successes against Norway emphasizes the strength of Denmark under the late King Hamlet and, potentially, under his successor. This impression is increased by the success of the diplomatic pressure put on the King of Norway at I.2.17–39 and II.2.60–80, and the reference to Danish power in England at IV.3.60–64.

81   *even but* only just

83   *emulate* (a strong word) emulous, full of jealous rivalry

84   *our valiant Hamlet.* This is the first mention of the family name, identifying *the majesty of buried Denmark* (line 48) and *Our last King* (line 80). Throughout, old Hamlet's virtue, dignity, valour, physical prowess, and personal beauty are strongly emphasized. It is in the shadow of his worth that Hamlet has to reveal himself to us, and to act.

85   *so* (that is, *valiant*)
      this side of our known world (all Europe, or the western hemisphere)

86–7   This personal combat between King Hamlet and King Fortinbras, authorized by *heraldy* and so on, seems to belong to a different and older world from that of King Claudius, who is a modern politician and works through his ambassadors.

86   *sealed compact* certified agreement

87   *heraldy* (an alternative form of 'heraldry') chivalric formalities

89   *stood seised* was possessed (*stood* is an emphatic auxili-

ary). The pronunciation of *seised* is the same as 'seized'. What Fortinbras offered as a wager was his personal possessions of land. The fate of the two kingdoms was, of course, not involved in this personal wager.

90   *moiety competent* equivalent portion of land

91   *gagèd* wagered

     returned passed (not necessarily 'passed back again')

92   *inheritance* subsequent possession (not necessarily with the notion of heirship)

93   *covenant.* This is F's reading (spelt 'Cou'nant'). It is intelligible, but metrically clumsy. Q2 has 'comart', which is a possible word ('co-mart', presumably meaning 'mutual bargain'), but there is no adequate evidence of its existence.

94   *carriage of the article designed* fulfilment of the article or clause in the prearranged compact

95   *sir.* Horatio seems to be addressing only Marcellus here, though it is Barnardo who next comments.

     young Fortinbras. The parallel between the fathers and sons, Fortinbras and Hamlet, is deliberate. It becomes clear from I.2.30 and II.2.62 and 70 that in Norway, as in Denmark, a brother has succeeded to the throne in preference to the late monarch's son. Just as a remarkable contrast between old and young Hamlet is given us (see the note to line 84), so a difference of personality between old and young Fortinbras is implied. Old Fortinbras was a worthy opponent of old Hamlet. They met in personal combat. But young Fortinbras acts by a different code of conduct: he seeks by *terms compulsatory*, with *a list of lawless resolutes*, to wrest back what his father had honourably lost.

96   *unimprovèd mettle* vigour of mind and body uncultivated and unchastened by experience

97   *skirts* outskirts or borders (less in the control of the King's government)

98   *Sharked up* (presumably) recruited indiscriminately, like a shark seizing its prey at haphazard

98   *list* (perhaps disparagingly) collection, mere catalogue
       (but compare I.2.32)

       lawless resolutes determined and desperate characters,
       with nothing to lose because they have rejected the
       obligations and protection of the law. But when Fortin-
       bras and his army appear in IV.4, they do not corres-
       pond to this derogatory description. The reading
       lawless comes from Q2 and is supported by Q1. But F's
       'Landlesse' might be preferred on the grounds that
       Fortinbras was himself one who had lost his inheritance
       of lands.

99   *For* (acting) in return for
       diet daily pay

100   *stomach* exercise of stubborn courage (with a quibble on
       food). The *lawless resolutes* appreciate an enterprise with
       the excitement of danger.

101   *our state* (the government of Denmark)

102   *of* from

103   *compulsatory* (accented on the second syllable, and with
       a weakened fourth syllable) involving compulsion

106   *head* fountain-head

107   *romage* commotion

109–11 There is no hint in this scene of suspicion that the late
       King has met his death by foul play. See the note to
       lines 128–40.

109   *sort* be appropriate

111   *question* cause

112   *A mote it is to trouble the mind's eye.* (The apparition is,
       after all, a trifle. Yet a speck of dust can be troublesome
       in the eye, and so this apparition troubles our mental
       vision.)

113–20 This passage on the portents which preceded Caesar's
       murder recalls I.3 and II.2 of *Julius Caesar*, probably
       written shortly before *Hamlet*. Both derive from
       Plutarch's *Life of Julius Caesar* in Sir Thomas North's
       translation (1579 etc.). Horatio, a *scholar* (line 42),
       discourses impressively to the two soldiers from his

reading of Roman history. Perhaps he also shows an unexpectedly superstitious side.

113   *the most high and palmy state of Rome.* Julius Caesar was regarded as the first Roman emperor and his rule as the high point of Roman prosperity (ordained by Divine Providence to produce a world at peace in readiness for the birth of Christ). But Horatio means simply 'in ancient Rome, whose glories we all know about'.

palmy flourishing

state government

115   *sheeted* wearing their shrouds

116   *gibber* (pronounced with hard 'g' as in 'give'). The shrill, weak, piping cries of the souls of the dead are a detail from classical poetry.

117   The syntax here is much broken; probably a line or two have been lost between 116 and 117, to the effect that 'there were prodigies visible in the heavens as well as on earth, for example. . .'. An alternative explanation is that some lines have been misplaced: to insert 121–5 between 116 and 117 makes good sense.

stars with trains of fire comets (rather than shooting stars)

dews of blood. The phenomenon of 'red dews' is now known to be caused by insects.

118   *Disasters* (an astrological word) unfavourable appearances: here probably eclipses or sun-spots

the moist star the moon (*moist* because of its relation to the tides). The *influence* of its movements upon marine tides was well known and accurately calculated in Shakespeare's time; but the cause of the relation between the moon and the oceans was not known.

119   *Neptune's empire* the sea

120   *sick almost to Doomsday.* On the Day of Judgement, it was prophesied, the second coming of Christ would be accompanied by eclipses of the sun and moon. Scriptural language colours this whole passage; see especially Matthew 24.29, Luke 21.25–6, and Revelation 6.12–13.

121   *precurse* forerunner
        feared. Q2 reads 'feare', which could easily be a mis-
        reading of 'feard'.

122   *still* always

123   *prologue*. This is the first instance of the theatrical
        language which becomes prominent in the play.
        omen ominous event, calamity

125   *our*. The word is emphasized: such prodigies have
        occurred not only in ancient Roman times but also in
        the history of our own people. English history, as read
        by the Elizabethans, contained a good many super-
        natural warnings, and in recent years several eclipses
        had occurred, which superstitious persons (like
        Gloucester in *King Lear*, I.2.103–4) regarded with
        anxiety.
        climatures regions of the earth

127   *cross it* stand in its path and so attempt to halt it. This
        was a dangerous action.
        (stage direction) *He spreads his arms*. Q2 has the
        direction '*It spreads his armes.*' This would seem to
        refer to an action by the Ghost. But the stage business
        required is that Horatio, with arms outstretched,
        should *cross* the Ghost, and '*It*' is usually regarded as
        an error for '*He*'. Horatio thus also resembles the
        Cross, which would repel the spirit if it were of dia-
        bolical origin.

128   *illusion*. Presumably Horatio retains his scepticism
        about the Ghost's true nature.

128–40 Horatio interrogates the Ghost and suggests, one by
        one, the usual explanations for its walking: (a) it needs
        something to be done (for example, burial of its body)
        to give it rest; (b) it is a warning spirit (a *harbinger* of
        feared events, such as was discussed in lines 122–5);
        (c) it has buried treasure on its conscience. Horatio
        does not reach, before the cock crows, the fourth
        possible explanation – the true one: (d) a demand of
        revenge for murder.

130, 133, *Speak to me . . . . O, speak!* The short lines no doubt
136   indicate pauses while Horatio awaits an answer.

135   *happily* haply (and perhaps also 'fortunately')

138   *Extorted* ill-gotten

141   *partisan* a pike with a broad head and (sometimes) a
side projection

142   *stand* stop

144   *being* since it is

145–6   *offer it the show of violence,* | *For* offer it violence –
which is only a show of violence, because

151   *trumpet* trumpeter

152   *his* its
shrill-sounding high-pitched (not necessarily un-
pleasant)

153   *god of day* (sun-god, Phoebus Apollo)
his (the cock's)

155   *extravagant* vagrant outside its legitimate boundaries
erring wandering
hies hastens

156   *confine* place of confinement

157   *This present object made probation* the Ghost that has
just appeared affords a proof

158–76   From the spectral terrors of this night, the mood of the
scene now changes to the contemplation of the health
and grace of Christmas nights, and then to the dawn of
the new day with a revival of courage and determination.

159–65   This belief is not recorded elsewhere. Perhaps Shakespeare invented it for his theatrical purpose. Brilliantly
written, it is also made plausible by Horatio's response
(line 166).

159   *'gainst that season comes* in expectation of that season

162   *sir.* This is the Q2 reading; but 'walk' in Q1 and F is
the more appropriate word for a ghost.

163   *The nights are wholesome.* The night air was proverbially bad for the health at ordinary times.
strike exert their malign influence (presumably upon
night travellers)

164 *takes* bewitches (not 'takes away')
  charm work magic

165 *gracious* full of divine grace

167–8 *the morn . . . hill*. The rising sun is personified as a countryman appearing on the horizon at the break of day.

167 *the morn*. The period of time between midnight (line 7) and dawn has been shortened for dramatic purposes.
  russet. The word can mean either 'grey' or 'reddish'. Either meaning would be suitable here; perhaps Shakespeare intended both. The light and colour replace the darkness and shadow of the early part of this episode.

171 *young Hamlet*. The first reference to the hero. The epithet, doubtless intended to differentiate him from the late King Hamlet, is the first indication of his youthfulness, emphasized in the early part of the play. Towards the end, he is felt to be older than the university student he was at the beginning. This does not mean that the time-scheme need include the passage of an equivalent amount of time. Shakespeare gives clear indications that Hamlet has matured, knowing that we shall not notice or protest that time has been inadequate.

I.2 It is not stated when exactly the marriage of Claudius and Gertrude, and their coronation, took place. This scene seems to be the first formal gathering after these events. We are perhaps given the impression that the Ghost began to walk three nights before, at the same time as the festivities commenced.
 (stage direction) *Flourish*. This royal trumpet call would have been very prominent in production.

1 *our*. The King uses the 'royal plural', but sometimes in this speech *we*, *us*, and *our* refer to the Danish nation.

2   *that* (a substitute for *Though* in the previous line)

4   *contracted* drawn together (like the *brow* in a frown)

      in one brow of woe with unanimous sorrow

5   *so far hath discretion fought with nature* to such an extent has our prudence struggled against our natural affection. This is also the theme of the King's speech to Hamlet at lines 87–106.

7   *Together with remembrance of ourselves.* This goes closely with *think on him* and explains *wisest.*

8   *our sometime sister, now our Queen.* The reprehensible nature of the relation between the King and his Queen (his former sister-in-law) is at once emphasized. Such a marriage was explicitly forbidden by the 'Table of Kindred and Affinity, wherein whosoever are related are forbidden in scripture and our laws to marry together', first printed in 1563 and incorporated into the Book of Common Prayer.

      sometime former

9   *jointress* joint heretrix. No explanation is given of how Claudius's claim to the throne could be strengthened by his marriage to the late King's widow. It is not mentioned again.

      this warlike state. This reminds us of the condition of vigorous military preparedness initiated by King Claudius, already described at I.1.71–8.

10   *defeated* overcome (by its enemy, sorrow)

11   *With an auspicious and a dropping eye.* The comic or repulsive image (one eye smiling, the other weeping) is stronger in the F reading: 'With one Auspicious, and one Dropping eye'.

13   *In equal scale weighing* weighing out an equal quantity of

      dole grief

14   *barred* kept out (of the discussion and the decision)

15–16   *Your better wisdoms . . . this affair along.* Claudius is shown as prudently consulting his Council of State and not as acting tyrannically; compare IV.1.38–40.

17   *Now follows that you know* the next matter for us to consider is something you know about already

18   *weak supposal* low estimate

20   *Our state to be disjoint and out of frame* (a curious anticipation (and refutation) of Hamlet's later *The time is out of joint*, I.5.188)
    frame order

21   *Colleaguèd with* having as an (imaginary) ally and supporter. But perhaps this is the main verb (*Young Fortinbras* being the subject), with a full stop after *advantage*.
    dream of his advantage fanciful estimate of his superiority

23   *Importing* concerning

25   *our most valiant brother*. Claudius tactfully praises the late King, in the same way as he had shown his affection for *our dear brother* (lines 1 and 19). Compare Horatio's *our valiant Hamlet* (I.1.84).
    F gives the entry of Voltemand and Cornelius at this point. It probably means that they come forward, to kneel and to receive the King's letter and their commission (line 38) from his hands.

28   *Norway* the King of Norway

29   *impotent* helpless

31   *gait* proceedings
    in that because

32   *lists* enlistments
    full proportions supporting forces and supplies

33   *his subject* those subject to him

35   *greeting* (perhaps to be spoken ironically)

36–8   *no further . . . allow*. They are not plenipotentiaries but are to negotiate only in accordance with the limits laid down in Claudius's instructions.

38   *delated* set out in detail
    allow. The plural form is used after *scope* because influenced by *articles*.

39 *let your haste commend your duty* show by your haste your high sense of duty

42 *Laertes* (accented on the second syllable: lay-ér-tees)

43 *suit* formal request

44 *speak of reason* make any reasonable request
    Dane King of Denmark

45 *lose your voice* ask to no purpose
    thou. The King shifts to the singular form and further softens to *my* (not 'our') *offer* in line 46.

46 *That shall not be my offer, not thy asking* ('Whenever they call, I will answer them; while they are yet but thinking how to speak, I will hear them', Isaiah 65.24)

47 *native* by its very nature closely related

48 *instrumental* serviceable

49 *the throne of Denmark.* The King tactfully generalizes Polonius's personal services to him into a devotion to the whole royal family.

50 *dread* revered

51 *leave and favour* kind permission
    return to France (to Paris: II.1.7). Shakespeare carefully builds up Laertes as a *foil* (V.2.249) to Hamlet, by sending one to Paris, the other to Wittenberg.

53 *To show my duty in your coronation.* Laertes, as a loyal subject and the son of the principal minister, returned to swear fealty to the new King. Horatio says (line 176) that he has returned to see King Hamlet's funeral.

56 *bow* (as in entreaty)
    pardon permission to depart

57 *Polonius* (pronounced with the first 'o' short and the second 'o' (accented) long). This is Latin for 'of Poland': a surprising choice for the name of the principal minister of Denmark in a play which involves the conquest of part of the adjacent kingdom of Poland. In real life, there is no reason why someone who happened to be named Mr Britain should not be President of the United States, or a M. Langlais Minister of Defence in

France. But in fiction we expect things to be more carefully arranged.

58-61 *He hath . . . go.* Polonius's first speech is characterful: he takes thirty-three words to say 'yes'.

58 *slow* reluctantly given

60 *will* (perhaps punning on the sense 'testament', which needs to have a *seal* impressed upon it)
hard obtained with difficulty

62 *Take thy fair hour* enjoy your time of youth
Time be thine (presumably) stay away as long as you please. The King grants Laertes's request and dismisses him. But it would presumably be a violation of court etiquette to insert an exit for Laertes: he withdraws to the side, and can watch Hamlet, in preparation for his talk to Ophelia in the next scene.

64 *my cousin Hamlet, and my son.* Perhaps Claudius keeps his stepson (*son*) waiting while he dispatches other business; thus Hamlet is kept in his place. Certainly Claudius's refusal to permit Hamlet's return to Wittenberg contrasts with his treatment of Laertes.

65 *A little more than kin, and less than kind!* This must be spoken aside, as it interrupts Claudius's sentence. Hamlet's first words are, characteristically, a sardonic and cryptic pun. As Claudius's nephew he is more than a *cousin*, but he resents being called *son*, for any natural relationship (*kind*), such as a father and son feel, is impossible between them. Perhaps *kind* also means 'kindly' but we see no action of the King towards Hamlet which is not, at least on the surface, affectionate.

66 *the clouds still hang on you.* Hamlet's disaffection and melancholy, evident in his costume, are stressed after we have seen the King deal efficiently with state business.

67 *too much in the sun.* Another cryptic pun: presumably Hamlet refers to Claudius's *my son* (line 64) as well as to his being in the sunshine of court favour. He

insinuates his resentment at having been deprived of
the succession and at his new position of Claudius's
stepson.

68	*nighted colour* (his black mourning garments and his melancholy)
69	*Denmark* the King of Denmark
70	*vailèd lids* downcast eyelids
75	*particular* personal
78	*customary* (either 'following the conventions of society in wearing mourning for several months' or 'having now become usual with me')
79	*windy suspiration of forced breath* (an elaborate phrase for 'uncontrollable sighs')
80	*fruitful* flowing copiously
82	*moods* modes, appearances
	shapes (in theatrical language, 'assumed roles')
83	*denote* portray
84	*play* (like an actor)
85	*passes* surpasses, goes beyond
86	*These* (both his clothes and his general behaviour)
87	*commendable* (accented on the first syllable)
90	*That father* (your grandfather)
	bound was bound
92	*obsequious* dutifully mourning in a way appropriate to his obsequies
	persever (accented on the second syllable)
93	*condolement* sorrowing
95	*incorrect to heaven* behaving contrary to piety
96	*unfortified* (against the inevitable misfortunes of life)
	impatient lacking in the important Christian virtue of patience
99	*any the most vulgar thing to sense* (death is as common as) the most familiar experience we could have through our senses
100	*peevish* obstinate, foolish
103–4	*whose . . . who* (reason)
104	*still* always

105   *the first corse*. Actually the first *corse* ('corpse') in the world's history was a son and brother (Abel), not a father (Genesis 4.8). Further allusions to the biblical fratricide are at III.3.37–8 and V.1.77.

107   *unprevailing* unavailing

109   *the most immediate* closest in succession. Hamlet's position as heir under a quasi-elective system is strong. Ophelia testifies to his courtly qualities (III.1.151–5) and Claudius to his being loved by the people (IV.3.4 and IV.7.18). Claudius seeks to placate Hamlet with the expectation that his succession to the throne has been merely postponed. But with this public declaration he loses some of his power: by taking a secret revenge, Hamlet could now easily achieve the throne. It is only when Hamlet's disaffection shows him to be apparently irresponsible and dangerous and (eventually) to know about the fratricide that Claudius changes his intention about the succession. Shakespeare shows Claudius not as a usurper, but as duly elected. Later, facing death, Hamlet himself supports the election of Fortinbras, and Horatio thinks that this recommendation will win Fortinbras more votes (V.2.349–50 and 382–6).

112   *I*. Claudius adopts the singular pronoun when he addresses Hamlet as a *father* to a *son*.
   impart toward bestow (my affection) upon. The syntax seems awkward; *with* in line 110 expects a different verb.
   For as for

113   *school* university. Wittenberg was famous as Luther's university (founded in 1502), where in 1517 he nailed up his ninety-five theses. Elizabethan audiences also knew it as Dr Faustus's university, from Marlowe's play.

114   *retrograde* contrary

115   *bend you* incline yourself (imperative)

117   *cousin* (probably a vocative)

120 *I shall ... obey you, madam.* Hamlet pointedly accedes
to his mother's appeal to his affection, not to the King's
ingratiating plea. But the King, with skilful tact,
appropriates Hamlet's compliance as *a loving and a fair
reply.*

in all my best in so far as I can

127 *rouse* bumper of wine

bruit echo

129–59 The importance of this soliloquy lies in its establishing
Hamlet's personality and revealing his mental condition. The syntax is abrupt; the sentences progress by
increments and interruptions; exclamations are followed by clarifications, questions, and imperatives.

129 *sullied.* Q2 reads 'sallied' (which could be a spelling of
sullied). F reads 'solid', which contrasts well with *melt,* |
Thaw, and resolve itself ... and until the twentieth
century was generally preferred by editors. But it may
have an unpleasantly comic effect, especially if Richard
Burbage, the actor who first played Hamlet, were
putting on weight (compare *He's fat and scant of
breath,* V.2.281). *Sullied* fits well into the feeling of
contamination expressed by Hamlet; and for *sullies*
(F 'sulleyes') at II.1.39 Q2 has the spelling 'sallies'.

130 *resolve* dissolve

132 *His canon 'gainst self-slaughter.* The sixth commandment, 'Thou shalt not kill' (Exodus 20.13), was generally regarded as a sufficient condemnation of suicide.

canon religious law

134 *all the uses* the whole routine of affairs

136 *rank* coarsely luxuriant

137 *merely* completely

139, *to this ... to a satyr* compared to this ... compared
140 to a satyr

140 *Hyperion to a satyr.* Hamlet's insistence (here and at
III.4.65–103) on Claudius's unworthiness for the
kingship is not corroborated by what Claudius does
before the eyes of the audience, at any rate in the first

223

half of the play. We are doubtless expected to feel that Hamlet is exaggerating Claudius's incompetence, while we share his moral indignation at the homicide and incest.

140 *Hyperion* (the sun-god). See also III.4.57. From his scansion here and in other plays it is clear that Shakespeare thought the accent was on the second syllable. Owing to the influence of these two famous passages in *Hamlet* and to false analogy with such names as Tiberius and Valerius, the customary pronunciation has become 'high-peer-i-on', and more 'correct' pronunciations – 'hipper-eye-on' or 'highper-eye-on' – would be intolerable.

satyr (pronounced 'satter'). In classical mythology, a satyr had a goat's legs, tail, ears, and budding horns, the rest of his form being human.

141 *beteem* permit

146 *Frailty, thy name is woman.* Shakespeare early establishes Hamlet's generalizing frame of mind.

147 *or e'er* before. Compare line 183 below. Probably Shakespeare and his contemporaries supposed the second word to be 'ever'. In fact both *or* and *e'er* (or *ere*) are forms of the same word, meaning 'before'.

149 *Niobe*. She was the type of the grieving mother – her seven sons and seven daughters were slain by Apollo and Diana – who shed so many tears that she was turned into stone.

150 *wants discourse of reason* lacks the (human) faculty of reason

153 *Hercules*. The amount of classical allusion (*Hyperion*, *satyr*, *Niobe*, *Hercules*) by the university-educated Hamlet is doubtless intended to be a character-indication.

154 *unrighteous* impiously insincere

155 *Had left the flushing in her gallèd eyes* had had time to cause redness in her eyes, that her salt tears had made sore; or, perhaps, 'had left off causing redness . . .'.

Here *flushing* means 'reddening', not 'filling with water'.

156   *post* hasten

157   *dexterity* facility

159   *break, my heart*. A powerful phrase which derived its currency from its use in the Bible: 'The Lord is nigh unto them that are of a broken heart', Psalm 34.17 (also 51.17, 69.21, and 147.3; Isaiah 61.1; Luke 4.16–21). Compare *Now cracks a noble heart* (V.2.353). The modern use of the phrase as referring sentimentally to amorous disappointment came much later.

160   *I am glad to see you well*. At first, Hamlet merely gives a polite reply; then he recognizes Horatio.

163   *I'll change that name with you* I will be your *servant*, instead of your being mine

164   *make you from* are you doing away from

165   *Marcellus?* Presumably Hamlet recognizes Marcellus. He greets Barnardo formally as if not previously known to him, though Barnardo seems to be of the same military rank as Marcellus. Horatio refers to them as *gentlemen* (lines 194 and 196).

169   *A truant disposition* a disposition to play truant (from his university studies)

175   *teach you to drink deep* (probably ironical, perhaps prompted by a piece of stage business such as the passing of a drink-laden servant or a burst of drunken hilarity off stage)

180   *Thrift, thrift*. The repetition of words is soon felt to be characteristic of Hamlet. Compare lines 224 and 237 below. But these are more common in F than in Q2; so they may be due to an actor's affectation of a trick of speech.

180–81   *The funeral baked meats | Did coldly furnish forth the marriage tables*. Hamlet's bitter jest seems to derive from the King's remark about *mirth in funeral* and *dirge in marriage* (line 12). There was of course *A little month* (line 147) between the ceremonies.

180   *baked meats* pies

181   *coldly* as cold dishes

182   *dearest* (closest, and therefore deadliest)

185   *Where, my lord?* Horatio, who has come to give the news of the Ghost, is momentarily startled by the thought that Hamlet is himself seeing an apparition.

186   *once.* This seems inconsistent with I.1.59–63 (which implies that Horatio was thoroughly familiar with King Hamlet's appearance) and with lines 211–12 and 241 below.

187   *'A was a man.* Hamlet has a view of moral worth largely based on stoical ideals. This is elaborated in his description of Horatio in III.2.75–81.

192   *Season your admiration* control your amazement

193   *attent* attentive
        deliver report

198   *dead waste* desolate time (of night), as still as death. Q1 reads 'dead vast', which many editors have found attractive.

200   *at point* (as if) in readiness
        cap-a-pe from head to foot

203   *oppressed* distressed, troubled

204   *truncheon* military baton
        distilled melted

205   *act* effect

207   *dreadful* full of dread

212   *These hands are not more like* (each other than the Ghost was like your father). An expressive gesture for the actor.

216   *it* its

216–17 *address . . . would* begin to move as if it were about to

222   *writ down* prescribed

229   *Then saw you not his face?* Hamlet is testing his informants. This may be a question, or a statement of inference which throws doubt upon their story of recognizing the late King Hamlet.

230   *beaver* visor of a helmet (the movable upper part which

could be drawn down over the face for protection but was normally kept in the lifted position except when fighting)

235 *constantly* unchangingly, fixedly

236 *amazed* (a strong word) confounded

238 *tell* count

240 *grizzled* grey

242 *A sable silvered* black streaked with white
watch keep the watch (with you). But the everyday meaning of *watch* was 'stay awake'.

243 *warrant* guarantee

248 *tenable in your silence* kept secret

249 *whatsomever* whatsoever

251 *requite your loves* reward your affectionate behaviour

254 *loves* (not merely *duty*)

256 *doubt* suspect. Hamlet is already suspicious of the cause of his father's death, and the Ghost's revelations confirm his *prophetic soul* (I.5.40).

257–8 *Foul deeds . . . men's eyes.* Compare II.2.591–2.

I.3   This scene informs the audience of the strong family feeling in Polonius's family. Laertes's love for his sister Ophelia, whom we see for the first time, and their regard for their father, in spite of his foibles, prepare for the violence of Laertes's impulses to revenge later. There is nothing to show that Laertes and Ophelia are contemptuous of Polonius's long-windedness.

1 *necessaries* personal baggage for the journey

2–3 *as the winds give benefit | And convoy is assistant* whenever the wind is favourable for the sailing of a ship to France and whenever any other means of sending a letter is available

5 *For Hamlet, and the trifling of his favour.* This remark introduces the love affair between Hamlet and Ophelia. Both Polonius and Laertes suppose that Hamlet has only a passing interest in the girl and that, since they

see no hope of a royal marriage for their family, she will be either jilted or seduced. Yet she is the second lady in the land and might seem eligible.

6   *fashion* modish way of behaving

       a toy in blood mere whim of amorous passion

7   *violet*. It was proverbial for transient existence, as well as being associated with love.

       the youth of primy nature its spring-like prime

8   *Forward* blossoming precociously early

9   *suppliance* pastime

11   *crescent* increasing by the passage of time

       alone only

12   *thews* muscles, bodily strength

       this temple the human body that each of us possesses (a biblical phrase: 'ye are the temple of God', 1 Corinthians 3.16 etc.)

13   *inward service* faculties which are not visible in our physical exterior

14   *withal* also. Laertes is suggesting that Hamlet will soon grow out of his shallow love for Ophelia. These lines suggest Hamlet's youth.

15   *soil* blemish

       cautel deceitfulness

16   *will* (sexual impulse, as well as 'intentions'; and Laertes continues the complex meanings of *will* by using it in line 17 as 'faculty of making decisions')

       fear be anxious about the fact that

17   *His greatness weighed* if you take into account his high rank

18   *he himself is subject to his birth* he may be a member of the royal family and we his subjects, but he too is *subject* to the princely rank into which he was born. This line was omitted from Q2, presumably by accident.

19   *unvalued persons* those whose social and political position is of no importance

20   *Carve for himself* make his own choice of a royal consort

(like one who chooses to take his own slice of meat at the dinner table)

choice (of a wife)

23 *voice* declared opinion (or approval)

yielding compliance

body nation (the 'body politic')

26 *he in his particular act and place* one who is in his personal position (as a prince). But the text may be wrong, for F reads the even more difficult phrase 'he in his peculiar Sect and force'.

27 *give his saying deed* fulfil by his actions what his words promise

28 *main voice* majority opinion

withal along with

30 *credent* trustful

list listen to

songs seductive avowals of love

32 *unmastered* uncontrolled

34 *keep you in the rear of your affection* do not go as far as your feelings would lead you

35 *shot*. Feelings of love were often imagined as provoked by Cupid's arrows. But here perhaps the image is from gunshot.

36 *chariest* most cautious

prodigal enough quite sufficiently prodigal (if she does no more than *unmask her beauty* merely *to the* chaste *moon*, whose pale light will show little of it)

39 *canker* canker-worm or caterpillar

galls injures

infants of the spring young spring-time plants

40 *buttons* flower-buds

disclosed opened out

41-2 *in the morn . . . most imminent*. It is in the moist air of the morning that infectious diseases are most likely to strike. Similarly, it is young people who are especially vulnerable.

42 *blastments* blights

43   *Best safety lies in fear* to be afraid of doing something
      dangerous is the best way of keeping safe

44   *Youth to itself rebels, though none else near.* Young
      people are both frightened and adventurous. Their
      fearfulness is in conflict with their adventurousness,
      and may keep them safe when no other help is avail-
      able. Or perhaps: the passions of youth lead to instinc-
      tive rebellion against self-restraint, even though no
      temptation is near.

47   *ungracious* without grace
      pastors. The word is carefully chosen. The 'good
      shepherd', unlike the *ungracious pastor*, will 'put forth
      his own sheep; he goeth before them, and the sheep
      follow him' (John 10.4).

48   *the steep and thorny way to heaven.* This, and *the
      primrose path of dalliance* (line 50), seem to derive from
      Matthew 7.13–14: 'Wide is the gate and broad is the
      way that leadeth to destruction . . . . Strait is the gate
      and narrow is the way which leadeth unto life.'

49   *puffed* swollen with pride (or excess)

50   *primrose path of dalliance.* Similar phrases are used in
      All's Well That Ends Well, IV.5.51–3: 'the flowery way
      that leads to the broad gate and the great fire', and by
      the Porter in *Macbeth*, II.3.18: 'the primrose way to
      the everlasting bonfire'.

51   *recks not his own rede* disregards his own advice
      fear me not don't worry about me

53   *A double blessing.* Laertes has already once said good-
      bye to his father and received his blessing.

54   *Occasion smiles upon a second leave* it is a lucky chance
      when there is a second leave-taking

56   *sits in the shoulder of your sail* (an elaborate way of say-
      ing 'is favourable')

57   *There.* Polonius places his hand on the head of the
      kneeling Laertes.

59   *Look* be sure that
      character (accented on the second syllable) inscribe

60   *unproportioned* inappropriate to the circumstances (or perhaps 'badly calculated' and so 'reckless')
       his its

61   *Be thou familiar, but by no means vulgar* be affable in dealing with others, but don't make yourself cheap among the common people

62   *and their adoption tried* once their association in friendship with you has been tested

64   *do not dull thy palm* (so that your handshake becomes meaningless, or so that you lose your power of discrimination among true friends)

65   *courage* young man of bravado. F reads 'Comrade'.

67   *Bear't* sustain it, carry it through

68   *voice* spoken opinion, support

69   *Take each man's censure* take notice of the opinions expressed by other people (on any matter)

71   *expressed in fancy* designed in some peculiar and fanciful way

74   *Are of a most select and generous* (perhaps) show their refined and well-bred taste. But the line is difficult to interpret, and its twelve syllables suggest an error in the text.
       chief in that especially in that respect (of good taste in clothes)

77   *husbandry* thrift

81   *season this in thee* in due season bring my good advice to fruition in you (or 'make it palatable')

83   *invites you* requests your presence
       tend attend you

90   *Marry* (a mild oath: 'by the Virgin Mary')
       well bethought well remembered ('I am glad you reminded me'; or perhaps 'That was a good idea of his')

93   *audience* attention (to what Hamlet has said)

94   *put on me* impressed upon me

101   *green* inexperienced

102   *Unsifted* untried

107   *Tender.* Polonius puns on *tenders* meaning 'offers' (lines

231

103 and 106, and line 99) and to *Tender* (line 107) meaning 'look after' or 'have a proper esteem for'.

108   *crack the wind*. The image is from the excessive galloping of a horse or over-exertion of a hound, which will get the stitch.

109   *tender me a fool* (as the father of a girl who is intriguing with the heir to the throne, or who has been seduced; or perhaps 'exhibit yourself to me as a fool, a girl who has been seduced'. Ophelia's reply shows that she understands her father to think she might be seduced.

111   *fashion*. Ophelia uses the word simply as 'manner', but Polonius interprets it like Laertes in line 6 above.

112   *Go to* (an interjection of impatience)

113   *countenance* support, favourable appearance

115   *springes to catch woodcocks*. Proverbially the woodcock was a foolish bird which easily fell into snares (*springes*, pronounced to rhyme with 'hinges'). Compare *as a woodcock to mine own springe* (V.2.300).

116   *prodigal* prodigally

118   *extinct in both* both the light and heat of which are extinguished

121   *something* somewhat

122   *your entreatments* his solicitations of your favour

123   *a command to parle* an invitation to carry on a love conversation with him. Polonius sees the relationship between Hamlet and Ophelia as a siege of her chastity.

125   *with a larger tether* with a longer tethering-rope (and so with less control)

126   *In few* in brief

127   *brokers* go-betweens

128   *investments* garments (especially of a religious or otherwise imposing kind)

129   *implorators* solicitors

130   *Breathing* speaking persuasively

        bawds. This is an emendation of 'bonds' (Q2 and F), which has been defended as meaning 'marriage bonds'.

131   *beguile* cheat
        This is for all to sum up

133   *slander* misuse
        moment moment's

135   *Come your ways* come away

I.4   (stage direction) Barnardo is not now included in the group, though from I.2.225 and 253 we are led to expect him. As a sentinel, he could not abandon his post; and it would be awkward to leave him on stage when Horatio and Marcellus rush off after Hamlet.

1   *shrewdly* 'wickedly', sharply

2   *eager* biting

3   *lacks of* is a little before

5   *season* time of day

6   (stage direction) *pieces of ordnance.* The gun-salutes honour Hamlet's *gentle and unforced accord* (I.2.123), so celebrate a kind of triumph of the King over Hamlet.

8   *The King doth wake tonight ....* Compare I.2.124-8.
        doth wake stays awake, holds a late-night revel
        rouse bumper of wine

9   *Keeps wassail* gives a drinking-party
        swaggering upspring reels. Probably the rare noun *upspring* indicates some kind of Teutonic dance which Shakespeare introduces as local colour.

10   *Rhenish* Rhineland wine (imported in large quantities into England in Shakespeare's time)

12   *The triumph of his pledge* his glorious achievement as a drinker of toasts (usually that of drinking a vessel of wine down at one draught)

15   *to the manner born* habituated to it from my birth

16   *More honoured in the breach than the observance* which it is more honourable to disregard than to keep

17-38   *This heavy-headed ... scandal.* This passage about the drunkenness of the Danes is not in F. Probably it

233

seemed tactless after the accession of James VI of Scotland to the English throne, with his Danish consort, Anne.

17 *heavy-headed*. Presumably the *revel* causes heavy heads, rather than being characterized by them.

east and west (presumably) throughout the length and breadth of Denmark (but perhaps the phrase goes with *Makes us traduced* and means 'throughout Europe')

18 *Makes us traduced and taxed of* causes us to be calumniated and to have faults imputed to us by

19 *clepe us* describe us as

with swinish phrase in comparing us to pigs

20 *Soil* blemish

addition honorary title (and so 'good name')

it (the Danish custom of drunkenness)

21 *though performed at height* though they are the summit of our endeavour

22 *our attribute* the reputation attributed to us by others

23 *particular men* individuals

24 *vicious mole of nature* natural blemish

25 *As* for instance

26 *his* its

27 *o'ergrowth of some complexion* overdevelopment of some natural trait

28 *pales* fences

29 *habit* acquired habit

too much o'er-leavens has too strong an effect upon (like something damaged by excessive fermentation)

30 *form of plausive* behaviour resulting from pleasing

32 *Being nature's livery or fortune's star* which is due either to their subservience to nature or to the influence of ill fortune (the *defect* is either natural or accidental)

33 *His*. So Q2, and probably the shift from plural to singular is Shakespeare's; but some editors emend to 'Their'.

virtues else other qualities

34 *may undergo* can support

35   *general censure* overall opinion of him

35-6 *take corruption | From* be falsely esteemed because of. Hamlet means that a man may have many virtues and one fault, but this one fault will so damage his reputation that his virtues will be misjudged.

36-8 *The dram of evil ... scandal.* These words do not make grammatical sense. It seems best to take the rather complicated sentence as broken off in the middle by the Ghost's appearance.

36   *dram* tiny quantity

      evil. Q2 prints 'eale' (Q1 and F omit this passage), perhaps a misreading of 'evil'.

37   *of a doubt.* Plausible emendations are 'oft adulter' ('often adulterate or corrupt') and 'often dout' ('often efface')

38   *his* that man's

      scandal shame

39   *ministers of grace* messengers from God

40-41 *Be thou ... from hell.* Hamlet has initial doubts about the Ghost, but these are soon displaced by his (and the audience's) conviction that it is a veritable vision of his father. On two later occasions Hamlet suspects that *The spirit that I have seen | May be a devil*, which *Abuses me to damn me* (II.2.596-601 and III.2.92).

40   *Be thou* whether you are

      spirit of health benevolent spirit (or possibly 'saved soul')

      goblin damned evil spirit that has suffered damnation

41   *Bring* whether you bring

42   *Be thy intents* whether your intentions are

43   *questionable* inviting interrogation by me (since you appear like my father)

44   *call thee* invoke you by the name of

47   *thy canonized bones, hersèd in death.* Hamlet's father had been properly buried with all due religious rites (see the note to I.1.128-40).

      canonized (accented on the second syllable) consecrated by Christian burial

235

47   *hearsèd* coffined

48   *cerements* (two syllables, pronounced 'seer-') waxed shroud

49   *interred*. F's reading, 'enurn'd', is attractive, although the Roman-style obsequies of placing ashes in an urn would be inconsistent with the Christian burial of the shrouded body (the *canonized bones* in their *cerements*). Possibly 'enurn'd' merely means 'put into a coffin'.

52   *complete steel* full armour
      complete (accented on the first syllable)

53   *the glimpses of the moon* the earth illuminated by the uncertain light of the moon

54   *fools of nature* weak creatures limited by nature (but now having to face experience of the supernatural)

55   *horridly* (probably with the notion of 'making our hair stand on end')
      disposition composure of feelings

56   *reaches* capacity

59   *impartment* communication

65   *a pin's fee* the value of a trifle

69   *flood* sea

71   *beetles* projects

73   *your sovereignty of reason* your reason of its control over you

75   *toys of desperation* fanciful impulses leading to despair (and suicide)

82   *petty* (relatively) weak
      artere (two syllables: an alternative form of 'artery') channel through which flowed the 'vital spirits' (not the blood)

83   *Nemean lion*. The killing of the terrible lion of Nemea was one of the twelve labours of Hercules.
      Nemean (accented on the first syllable, which is short: 'nemm-ee-an')

85   *lets* hinders

87   *waxes* becomes increasingly

89   *Have after* I will follow

91 *Nay* (a mild contradiction to *Heaven will direct it*, implying that they themselves can do something)

I.5. 3 *sulphurous and tormenting flames.* This sounds more like hell than the purgatory referred to in lines 9–13 below.

6 *bound* ready (but the Ghost takes it to mean 'obliged')

11 *fast* do penance

12 *foul crimes.* The Ghost does not necessarily imply that he has been particularly wicked, but refers to the common situation of a sinner in this mortal life.

my days of nature this mortal life

17 *spheres* (in which the heavenly bodies normally moved: see the note to IV.7.15)

19 *an* on

20 *fretful porpentine* porcupine when it has become angry. Q2 has 'fearefull' ('timid') for F's 'fretfull'.

21 *eternal blazon* revelation about what has been appointed for all eternity

25, 28 *unnatural* (because contrary to family feeling)

27 *in the best* even at best

30 *meditation* thought

32 *shouldst thou be* you would have to be

32–3 *the fat weed | That roots itself in ease on Lethe wharf.* Lethe is a river of Hades: according to the classical poets, it caused oblivion in those who drank it. The word *wharf* is used because the spirits were supposed to embark on Charon's boat in order to cross the river. As *the fat weed* Shakespeare may have had in mind asphodel, which grew in the fields of Hades.

33 *roots.* F reads 'rots', which perhaps gives a more expressive meaning and is supported by *Antony and Cleopatra*, I.4.45–7.

35 *orchard* garden (as at III.2.270)

36–8 *the whole ear of Denmark . . . abused.* Old Hamlet's anticipation of his account of his own poisoned ear (lines 63–4; see also III.2.144, stage direction) is almost like one of his son's characteristic puns. The many allusions in the play to ears (especially damaged ones) – e.g. I.1.31, I.2.171, II.2.475 and 560, III.2.10, III.4.65 and 96, and IV.5.91 – produce a half-conscious reminder of the circumstances of the murder.

37   *forgèd process* fabricated official report

38   *abused* deceived

40   *prophetic soul*. See I.2.255–8.

42   *adulterate*. This word, and the whole passage 42–57, seem to imply that Claudius had seduced Gertrude before her husband's death. But nothing in the rest of the play supports this, except perhaps Hamlet's *whored my mother* (V.2.64) and, conceivably, Horatio's words *carnal . . . acts* (V.2.375). In the play of *The Murder of Gonzago* the wooing definitely takes place after the poisoning (III.2.144, stage direction, and 270–73).

47   *falling off* (both 'decline in moral standards' and 'desertion')

50–51   *decline | Upon* sink to the level of

52   *To* in comparison with

53   *virtue as it* as virtue

54   *lewdness* lust
      a shape of heaven a physical appearance of angelic attractiveness

56   *sate itself in a celestial bed* grow weary of sexual union with a lawful and virtuous partner. The F and Q1 reading *sate* seems to be required, against Q2's 'sort' ('separate'), which gives only a strained meaning.

57   *garbage* (originally) the offal and entrails of animals

61   *secure* (accented on the first syllable) thoughtlessly unguarded

62   *juice of cursèd hebona*. It is doubtful what precisely Shakespeare and his contemporaries meant by this poison. F uses the form 'Hebenon'. The word is related to 'ebony', but here it seems to be combined with some of the qualities of henbane.

63 *porches of mine ears.* Poisoning through the ears was a legendary Italian method; but according to medical authority it could not be effective.

64 *leperous distilment* distillation causing a disease like leprosy (still fairly common in Shakespeare's England)

67 *gates and alleys.* The body is represented under the image of a city.

68 *sudden* rapid in action
    vigour power, efficacy
    posset curdle (so that the blood is clotted). A posset was a drink made from milk curdled with wine or ale.

69 *eager* sharp, sour (and so curdling the milk)

70 *thin* (not curdled into clots)

71 *tetter* scurf
    barked about (coated with a *crust*)

72 *lazar-like* like leprosy (the disease usually attributed to the beggar Lazarus in Luke 16.20)

75 *dispatched* deprived

76-9 *Cut off . . . With all my imperfections on my head.* Hamlet remembers this at III.3.80-81.

76 *in the blossoms of my sin* when my sins were at their height

77 *Unhouseled* without having received the sacrament
    disappointed unprepared (for death, as having had no opportunity for repentance, confession, and absolution)
    unaneled (rhyming with 'healed') without having been given extreme unction

78 *reckoning* assessing and settling of my debts (his sins) to God
    my account (at God's judgement seat)

80 *O . . . Most horrible!* On the stage, from Garrick's time, this line has often been transferred to Prince Hamlet. The interruption serves to break up the Ghost's long speech.

81 *nature* natural feelings of a son for a father

83 *luxury* lechery

86 *Leave her to heaven* entrust her to God's judgement.

According to usual religious teaching, revenge upon Claudius should also be left *to heaven*.

89   *matin* morning

90   *uneffectual* (becoming feeble as day dawns). The glow-worm's *fire* contrasts imaginatively with the purgatorial fires to which the Ghost is about to return (lines 11–13).

92   *host of heaven* (angels)

93   *couple hell* include hell in my invocation

     O, fie! (presumably a rejection of the powers of hell)

     Hold hold together, remain unbroken

94   *instant* immediately

95   *stiffly* strongly. This is F's reading; Q2 has 'swiftly', which, though awkward, perhaps has some support from lines 29–30.

97   *this distracted globe* (probably his head, which he holds, rather than the world itself or 'the little world of man')

98   *the table of my memory* my memory, which is now like a memorandum tablet on which experience writes. The *table* was generally made of thin leaves of ivory or slate, from which one could *wipe away* previous *records* or notes. The customary contents of such notebooks are listed in lines 99–101.

99   *fond* foolish

     records (accented on the second syllable)

100   *saws* (usually somewhat derogatory) wise sayings, platitudes

     forms general ideas

     pressures past impressions previously received

110   *there you are* (I have set down my comment on you, accordingly, in my notebook)

     word watchword, motto (or perhaps 'promise given')

113   *secure him* keep him safe

114   *So be it* (either a continuation of his own thought, *I have sworn't*, or a response to Horatio's *Heavens secure him!*)

115   *Illo, ho, ho* (originally the falconer's cry in calling a hawk down)

116   *Come, bird, come*. In his excited mood, Hamlet mocks his friends' cries as if they were bird-calls.

121   *once think it* ever believe what the Ghost has told me

124   *But he's an arrant knave*. Probably Hamlet intends to say 'who is worse than King Claudius', or something similar, but checks himself, deciding not to tell anyone what the Ghost has revealed to him.

127   *without more circumstance* cutting the matter short

136   *Saint Patrick*. Hamlet swears by him because Saint Patrick was a keeper of purgatory (whence the Ghost comes), having found an entrance to it in Donegal; or perhaps because he banished serpents from Ireland (see *Richard II*, II.1.157–8), and Hamlet's task is to get rid of a *serpent* (line 39).

137   *much offence*. Hamlet deliberately mistakes Horatio's word *offence* and takes it as concerning the revelation of the Ghost, which has told him of the terrible *offence* of Claudius.

138   *honest ghost*. Hamlet assures them that the Ghost is a *spirit of health*, not a *goblin damned* (I.4.40).

141   *scholars, and soldiers* (probably generic, including Horatio in the one category and Marcellus in the other)

142   *Give* grant

146   *not I* I will never make known what I have seen. (Horatio is not refusing to take the oath.)

147   *Upon my sword*. The handle of a sword forms a cross upon which an oath can be administered. Hamlet is not content with oaths *in faith*.

149   *Swear*. The Ghost's insistence on, or approval of, the oath upon the hilt of the sword as a Cross and its response to the appeals to God's mercy in lines 169 and 180 are further evidence that it is not a diabolical tempter. Presumably Hamlet's mockery of the Ghost is intended to conceal from Horatio and Marcellus how seriously he takes it and its revelations.

150   *truepenny* honest fellow

151   *You hear this fellow*. It is not certain that they do hear the

Ghost any more than the Queen does in III.4.103–40.

151   *cellarage* (not a particularly appropriate word for a *platform* (I.2.252). But the space under the stage in the Elizabethan theatre was known as the cellarage.)

153   *Never to speak of this that you have seen.* The first oath concerns what they have *seen*, the second, what they have *heard* (from each other, not the Ghost), the third, Hamlet's subsequent behaviour (lines 170–79). So it seems that they swear three times, though no words are given to them. But the scene is usually played as if their words were interrupted by the Ghost at lines 155 and 161, and only at line 181 do they silently complete their oaths (see the note).

156   *Hic et ubique?* (Latin) here and everywhere?

      Then we'll shift our ground. Hamlet seems to move his companions around inexplicably. But Horatio and Marcellus perhaps flee in terror from the spot whence the Ghost's voice comes, and Hamlet follows them to different parts of the stage.

163   *pioneer* miner

165   *stranger* (punningly, alluding to the proverb that a guest (*stranger*) should be received hospitably, with no questions asked)

167   *your philosophy.* The exact meaning of *your* is difficult to decide. It may refer to Horatio's rationalist philosophy (he was established as a sceptic at I.1.23–32); or *your philosophy* may express a general disdain for rationalizing explanations, not Horatio's modes of thought particularly.

169   *help you mercy* may God's mercy save you at his judgement seat

170   *How strange or odd some'er I bear myself.* Hamlet's assumption of madness in order to lull suspicion seems to have been an essential element in the Hamlet story, and would be expected by an audience familiar with the earlier play on the stage.

172   *antic* fantastically disguised

174   *encumbered* folded

176   *an if* if

177   *list* wished

        There be, an if they might (there *are* persons – meaning themselves – who could explain things if only they were at liberty to do so)

178   *giving out* intimation

        to note to draw attention to the fact

179   *know aught* have confidential knowledge

181   *Swear.* But Horatio and Marcellus are not given any words of an oath as they place their hands on the sword.

185   *friending* friendliness

186   *lack* be lacking

187   *still* always

188–9   *cursèd spite, | That ever I was born to set it right.* Hamlet seems to be following Job (3.1–3) in cursing the day of his nativity. He laments, not merely his task, but that he was ever born.

188   *spite* (of Fortune)

190   *together* (without an order of precedence. Hamlet's friendliness and avoidance of formality seem to be emphasized.)

I.1   Some time has elapsed: Laertes has arrived in Paris and is settling down there; Ophelia has repelled Hamlet's letters and *denied | His access* (lines 109–10); the King already knows of *Hamlet's transformation* (II.2.5) and has summoned Rosencrantz and Guildenstern. This scene reveals that the King's chief minister is skilful at organizing spying – in this case, upon his own son. So Hamlet's danger, and the justification of his putting on an *antic disposition*, are understandable.

1   *Reynaldo* (a suitable name for a 'foxy' character)

3   *marvellous* very

7   *me* (the indefinite indirect object (the 'ethic dative'), used so as to give an air of ingratiating ease)

7   *Danskers* Danes (his fellow-countrymen). The unusually correct form of the word seems to imply Shakespeare's interest in giving local colour.

8   *what means* what their financial position is
keep maintain an establishment

10   *encompassment and drift of question* roundabout and gradual inquiry

11   *more nearer*. The 'double comparative' is common in Shakespeare's grammar.

12   *particular demands will touch it* detailed questions would achieve
it (the scheme for finding out how Laertes is behaving)

13   *Take you* assume

19   *put on* attribute to

20   *forgeries* fictions (invented accounts of wrong-doing)
rank gross

26   *Drabbing* pursuing loose women

28   *season it in the charge* modify (or soften) the accusation

30   *incontinency* habitual sexual indulgence

31   *breathe . . . quaintly* allude to, hint at . . . subtly

32   *taints of liberty* faults resulting from freedom

34-5 *A savageness . . . | Of general assault* a wildness . . . that attacks all indiscriminately

34   *unreclaimèd* unreformed (like an untamed hawk)

38   *fetch of warrant* justifiable device. For F's 'warrant', Q2 reads 'wit'.

39   *sullies*. See the note to I.2.129.

40   *a little soiled i'th' working* somewhat blemished as a result of contact with the world

42   *converse* conversation

43   *Having* if he has
prenominate before-mentioned

45   *closes with you in this consequence* will end by becoming confidential with you and speak as follows

47   *addition* polite form of address

49   *does 'a* he does

50   *By the mass* (an oath)

58   *o'ertook in's rouse* overcome by drunkenness when carousing

61   *Videlicet* that is to say

64   *we of wisdom and of reach* those of us characterized by (or 'we who by means of') wisdom and penetration

65   *windlasses and . . . assays of bias* roundabout methods and indirect attacks. A *windlass* in this sense was a circuit made by a portion of a hunting party to intercept and head back the game. In the game of bowls, the *bias* is the curved course of a bowl which reaches its aim (the jack) by not going in a straight line.

66   *indirections* indirect approaches
       directions ways of proceeding

68   *have* understand

69   *God bye ye* God be with you

71   *in yourself* for yourself (as well as by report)

73   *let him ply his music* (perhaps with a literal meaning, or perhaps 'let him go his own way')

77   *closet* small private room

78–80   *his doublet . . . ankle.* Hamlet's disordered clothing, presumably deliberately assumed, and the rest of his behaviour here, resemble the usual symptoms of love-sickness as described in *As You Like It*, III.2.363–6.

78   *doublet* close-fitting jacket with short skirt
       unbraced not laced up or fastened

79   *No hat upon his head.* Elizabethans normally wore hats indoors, even in church and at meals. Compare V.2.93.

80   *down-gyvèd to his ankle* fallen down like fetters ('gyves') around the ankles

82   *purport* expression

89   *his other hand thus o'er his brow.* Ophelia places her open hand palm downwards shading her eyes.

91   *As* as if

95   *bulk* body from neck to waist

102   *ecstasy* madness

103   *violent property* quality of being violent
       fordoes damages

105   *passion* violent state of feeling

112   *quoted* made my observation of

113   *wrack* dishonour (by seducing)

       beshrew my jealousy a curse upon my suspiciousness

114   *proper to* characteristic of

       our age (that is, old age)

115   *cast beyond ourselves* over-estimate in our calculations

117   *go we to the King.* But Q2 and F give no indication of
Ophelia's being present in the next scene, and there
are strong reasons for not introducing her there.

118   *This must be known* we must make this known to the
King (probably, rather than 'whatever we may do to
conceal it, the story of this will soon become common
knowledge')

       close secret

118-19   *move | More grief to hide than hate to utter love* cause
more ill-feeling if I conceal this love (by leading to
further derangement of Hamlet's mind) than will be
the indignation provoked in the King if I reveal (*utter*)
it. Polonius feels that his daughter is no match for
Hamlet; but later the Queen approves, discreetly at
III.1.38-42 and (after Ophelia's death) plainly at
V.1.240-41.

II.2   (stage direction) *attendants* (an interpretation of F's
'*Cum alijs*' ('with others'); not in Q2. *Go, some of you*
(line 36) implies that attendants are on stage, or easily
summoned.)

1   *Rosencrantz and Guildenstern.* They seem to be young
noblemen, chosen as the childhood companions of the
Prince.

2   *Moreover that* in addition to the fact that

5   *transformation* metamorphosis, involving both the
exterior (his appearance) and *the inward man* (his mental
qualities)

6   *Sith nor* since neither

11   *of so young days* from such an early age

12   *sith* since that time (probably, rather than 'because' as in line 6)

13   *vouchsafe* be pleased to agree to
       rest residence

14   *your companies* the company of each of you

16   *occasion* opportunity

18   *opened* when it is revealed (perhaps a medical image: 'lanced')

20   *is.* F amends Q2's 'is' to 'are', but such lack of concord, often in emphatic speech, is not uncommon in Shakespeare.

21   *adheres* feels united

22   *gentry* courtesy

24   *For the supply and profit of our hope* in order to feed our hopes and cause them to progress successfully

26   *fits a king's remembrance* would be fitting to be paid by a king who takes note of the services rendered him

27   *of us* over us

28   *dread pleasures* revered wishes

30   *in the full bent* completely (like a bow in archery)

38   *practices* conduct of this affair (but perhaps implying 'sharp practices')

40–41   *The ambassadors . . . returned.* This indicates the passage of time since I.2, where Cornelius and Voltemand were dispatched on their embassy.

42   *still* always

47   *Hunts . . . the trail* (like a dog following the scent)
       policy investigation

52   *fruit* (at the end of the *feast*)

53   *do grace to them* conduct them into the royal presence (as if he were saying grace before a *feast*). This gives Claudius an opportunity for a private word with Gertrude.

55   *distemper* malady

57   *His father's death and our o'erhasty marriage.* Gertrude shrewdly enough interprets Hamlet's original state of

mind, but she is ignorant of the murder, knowledge of which has transformed Hamlet.

58   *sift him* question Polonius carefully

59   *brother.* Monarchs of different countries were 'brothers'.

60   *desires* good wishes

61   *Upon our first* immediately upon our making our representations

62   *His nephew's levies* (described at I.1.95–104)

63   *the Polack* the inhabitants of Poland

66   *impotence* helplessness

67   *falsely borne in hand* deluded
       arrests summons to desist

69   *fine* conclusion

71   *give th'assay of arms* make trial of a military engagement

73   *three thousand.* Q2 reads 'threescore thousand', but this is unmetrical, and 60,000 crowns is rather a large *annual* sum for a comparatively small expedition; moreover, F's reading, adopted here, is supported by Q1.

76, 80   *herein . . . therein* (in the document which they have brought. The change from *herein* to *therein* seems to justify the addition of the stage direction.)

77   *quiet pass* peaceful passage

79   *regards of safety* conditions concerning safety (or 'conditions that may be safely granted')
       allowance the permission granted

80   *likes* pleases

81   *considered* fit for considering

86   *expostulate* expound

90   *wit* intelligence, wisdom

93–4   *to define . . . mad?* Polonius probably means 'it would be madness to try to define madness, for everyone knows what it is', rather than 'the definition of madness is to be mad'. It may be an intentional bathos: Polonius embarks on a definition and breaks down.

95   *art* rhetorical art

97	*'Tis true, 'tis pity* of course it is a pity
98	*figure* (of speech)
102	*defect* (weakness of Hamlet's mind)
103	*this effect defective* the effect we have been aware of, which is a mental deficiency
104	*Thus it remains, and the remainder thus* this is the situation; and now here is the solution (in so far as one can paraphrase Polonius's verbal tangles)
105	*Perpend* consider carefully (probably a comic pomposity)
106	*while she is mine* (until she is married)
109, 110	*beautified.* Probably an affected word for 'beautiful' (Robert Greene in 1592 described Shakespeare as an 'upstart crow, beautified with our feathers'). Presumably Polonius objects to the word as being a past participle of the verb 'to beautify' and therefore an incorrect usage for 'beautiful'.
112	*these* this letter (a common phrase)
	et cetera (sometimes interpreted as if Polonius were omitting indecorous allusions suggested by *bosom*; but probably he is merely indicating that he is glancing at, and omitting, some superfluous comments)
114	*faithful* (to the contents of the letter)
115–18	*Doubt thou . . . I love.* This little poem is a clever epitome of some of the poetical tendencies of the 1590s: cosmological imagery, the Copernican revolution, moral paradoxes, all illustrating amorous responses.
117	*Doubt truth.* In this line *Doubt* means 'suspect' (as at I.2.256).
119	*ill at* unskilful in making
	numbers verses
123	*this machine* (his body)
	to him his
126–8	*more above hath . . . given* she has in addition given
126	*solicitings* (not necessarily deceitful or immoral importunings)

127   *fell out* took place
      by according to

131   *would fain* should very much wish to

136   *played the desk or table-book* served as a mute and useful means of communication (between the lovers; or possibly 'noted the matter privately for myself')
      table-book notebook (like *table*, I.5.98)

137   *given my heart a winking* shut my eyes (to what was going on). For F's 'winking', Q2 reads 'working', a word Shakespeare often uses of the heart and of mental activities (compare line 551 and I.1.67); but it seems to have the contrary meaning to what is required here.

138   *idle sight* careless observation

139   *round* roundly, straightforwardly

140   *bespeak* summon to address her

141   *star* sphere

142   *prescripts* orders. F's reading, 'Precepts', seems a simplification.

143   *resort* visits

148   *watch* sleeplessness

149   *lightness* lightheadedness
      declension downward course

151   *all* (into) everything that

152   *like* likely

156   *Take this from this* (generally interpreted as 'Cut my head off'; but Polonius might more decorously point to his staff or chain of office – 'Remove me from my office as your chief minister'; compare lines 166–7)

159   *centre* (of the earth, which, according to medieval cosmology, was the centre of the universe)
      try judge

162   *loose* release (like an animal in a stud)

163   *arras* (a tapestry hanging, such as covered the full height of the walls of rooms in great Elizabethan houses)

165   *thereon* on account of this (disappointed love)

166   *assistant for a state* government minister

167   (stage direction) *Enter Hamlet.* It has been suggested
that Hamlet should enter a little earlier and overhear
something of the plot in lines 159–67. This would
provide a justification for his bitterness to Polonius in
lines 171–219 and his treatment of Ophelia at III.1.89–
150.

168   *sadly* seriously (not 'sorrowfully')
reading. The symbol of his detachment from revenge is
striking.

170   *board him presently* accost him immediately (drawing
alongside like a sea-vessel)
give me leave excuse me (as he hurries the King and
Queen off stage)
In Q1 the soliloquy *To be, or not to be* is placed here;
see the note to III.1.56–88.

172   *God-a-mercy* thank you

174   *fishmonger.* Probably the primary allusion is to the
smell of corruption that seems to emanate from
Polonius, though the word is sometimes thought to
imply 'bawd'. This is the first occasion on which the
audience sees Hamlet assume his *antic disposition*
(I.5.170–72). He deceives Polonius, who has been
boasting of his own shrewdness.

181–2   *For if. . . carrion* (possibly spoken from the book Hamlet
is carrying)

182   *a good kissing carrion.* The phrase is difficult: the carrion is good for kissing, as the sun shines on a dead dog
and breeds maggots in it. Hamlet is deliberately
indulging in mad-talk; but there is generally *method
in't* (line 206), and it is not easy to see the point here.
Eighteenth-century editors emended *good* to 'god'
(the sun-god Apollo), with great probability. Perhaps
Hamlet is obscurely saying 'Honesty is rare in this
world, which is so corrupt that even the sun produces
nothing but maggots in shining upon carrion'.

184   *walk i'th'sun.* Spenser in *The Faerie Queene* (III.vi)

had told how Amoret and Belphoebe were begotten by the impregnating rays of the sun.

187   *harping on* (like a harper playing on one string)

194   *matter* subject-matter

199   *purging* exuding

199–200   *plum-tree gum* (sap from the bark of a plum-tree)

201   *hams* thighs and buttocks

203   *honesty* decent
   set down (in print)

204   *backward* (actually, of course, crabs move sideways)

206   *method* logical organization of thought. Polonius does not mean that Hamlet is using his apparent madness as a device for certain ends.
   out of the air (probably) out of the fresh air into a confined room (since the open air was regarded as dangerous to the sick)

209   *pregnant* full of meaning. The image is continued in *be delivered of* (line 211).

209–   *A happiness that often madness hits on.* This was the
10   doctrine of 'poetic fury' (*furor poeticus*), to which Theseus also refers in linking 'The lunatic, the lover, and the poet' (*A Midsummer Night's Dream*, V.1.7).

209   *happiness* felicity of expression

212   *suddenly* immediately

216   *not more.* F makes the sentence more rational by omitting *not*. But Q2 is probably correct, as confusing Polonius's wits still further by the double negatives – which the audience will take as emphatic.
   withal with

227   *indifferent* average
   children of the earth ordinary fellows

229   *button* (summit)

230   *soles of her shoe* (so as to be trodden underfoot by Fortune)

232   *favours.* Hamlet alludes bawdily to her sexual *favours*; Guildenstern follows this by *her privates* ('intimates', and so 'sexual organs'), and Hamlet again by her

secret parts. The progress then is to the commonplace notion of *Fortune* as a *strumpet* who bestows her favours in a fickle and indiscriminate manner (see line 491).

245   *confines* places of confinement

254   *count* (nevertheless) account

255   *bad.* As nothing develops from *bad* in the subsequent dialogue, emendation to 'had' is attractive.

257–8 *the very substance . . . a dream* what an ambitious man actually achieves is only a pale shadow of what he had set out to achieve

262–3 *Then are our beggars bodies, and our monarchs and out-stretched heroes the beggars' shadows* if this is so, the beggars have substance, because they have no ambition, whereas great people are unreal (*shadows*) because they are filled with ambition. Therefore, as it is *bodies* that cast *shadows*, the great people may be regarded as the *shadows* of *beggars*. Or perhaps Hamlet means that *beggars* too have ambitions and long to be *monarchs* and *heroes*; since ambitions are *shadows*, *monarchs* and *heroes* are therefore *beggars' shadows*. Presumably this cryptic utterance baffles Rosencrantz and Guildenstern, for Hamlet promptly breaks off.

263   *outstretched heroes* great men whose ambitions stretch them. But *outstretched* also suggests their strutting gait and the length of their shadows.

264   *fay* faith

       reason carry on an intellectual conversation at this level

265–6 *wait upon you* accompany you (but Hamlet takes it to mean 'act as your servants')

267   *sort you with* put you in the category of

269   *dreadfully attended* incompetently waited upon

269–70 *in the beaten way of friendship* as the course of our friendship has been well-tried and reliable

274   *too dear a halfpenny* cost a little too much. Presumably Hamlet is being cryptically insulting: his friends' visit

253

is not worth his thanks because it is not a voluntary kindness on their part. Or, if *a halfpenny* means 'at a halfpenny' rather than 'by a halfpenny', he may mean: 'the thanks of a beggar such as I am are worthless'.

275   *free* voluntary

278   *but to th'purpose* except a straightforward answer

280   *modesties* sense of shame
        colour disguise

283   *conjure* solemnly ask

284   *consonancy* harmony

286-7   *what more dear a better proposer can charge you withal* whatever motive a more skilful speaker than I am might propose in order to appeal to you (that you should be frank with me)

287   *even* straightforward

290   *of* on

291   *hold not off* do not remain aloof

293-4   *my anticipation prevent your discovery* my own statement about the matter be made before you have any opportunity of revealing the truth to me

294   *discovery* disclosure

295   *moult no feather* be quite unimpaired

296   *forgone* done without

296-7   *custom of exercises* practice of manly sports

298   *frame* ordered arrangement

299   *sterile promontory.* Presumably this striking image is that of a barren headland jutting out into the sea, contrasted with the fertile cultivated countryside inland.

299,   *canopy . . . roof.* The roof overhanging the stage in an
301   Elizabethan public playhouse was known as the 'heavens' and seems to have been painted with stars. This may have given special point to Hamlet's imagery here.

300   *brave* fine

301   *fretted with golden fire* adorned with the heavenly bodies, as a chamber roof is decorated (*fretted*) with bosses

302-3 *pestilent congregation of vapours*. It was widely believed that diseases were borne upon the air and spread by winds.

congregation mass

303 *piece of work* masterpiece

305 *express* (probably) direct. This seems to go with *moving* rather than with *form*.

306 *apprehension* powers of comprehension

307 *paragon* pattern of supreme excellence

308 *quintessence of dust*. The reference is to Genesis 3.19: 'For dust thou art, and into dust shalt thou be turned again'.

309 *woman*. Q2 reads 'women', which may well be right.

316 *lenten entertainment* (the kind of meagre reception one would expect in Lent, not in a season of festivity when theatrical activities would be welcomed)

317 *coted* caught up with and passed

320 *tribute*. The Prince will pay money to *the king*.

321 *foil and target* sword (blunted for fencing or for stage use) and light shield

322 *gratis* without payment

humorous man (not the comic, but the eccentric, capricious, or carping character, whose state of mind, according to Elizabethan physiology, was due to some excess of one of the humours)

324 *tickle o'th' sere* easily provoked. The image is of a gun whose trigger-catch (*sere*) was sensitive or unstable (*tickle*) and easily went off.

325 *freely* (perhaps 'with a certain amount of ad-libbing' because the boy actor might not know his part very well; or perhaps 'with complete freedom of speech' (without feeling a need to omit indecent words or allusions). There is not much evidence for either explanation.)

halt limp (scan badly)

328 *tragedians* actors (not necessarily performing only tragedies)

the city. In spite of the dramatic situation, London is in

Shakespeare's mind, as the following dialogue makes clear.

329   *travel* are on tour
      residence normal place of performance

331   *inhibition.* The word was used of the official indictment of stage plays by the authorities, but here seems to refer metaphorically to the players' inability to continue acting in the city.

332   *late* recent
      innovation fashion (the popularity of the boy actors in 1600–1601)

336–61   This passage, giving the reason for the decline in *estimation* of *the tragedians of the city*, is not in Q2. The discussion of the success of the child actors is somewhat intrusive into the play and the tone is more personal and acerb than we like to associate with Shakespeare. Its inclusion in F is surprising, because the episode must have become more obscure with the passage of years.

337   *keeps* continues

338   *eyrie* nestful
      eyases hawk nestlings

339   *on the top of question.* This probably means that their voices are heard above all others in the argument.

339–40 *tyrannically* outrageously

341   *berattle* clamour abusively against
      common stages (that is, public theatres, as distinct from the 'private' playhouses, occupied by the boys' companies)

342   *rapiers* (the sign of a gentleman and man of quality)
      are afraid of goosequills fear the satire and ridicule they would hear in the plays written for the boys' companies
      goosequills (the usual writing implement in Shakespeare's time)

345   *escoted* paid for

345–6   *pursue the quality no longer than they can sing* follow their profession as actors only until their voices break

348   *their means are not better* they have no other resources for earning their livelihood

349–50   *exclaim against their own succession* speak disdainfully about the profession to which they will themselves belong (as actors in adult companies)

351   *to-do* (an Elizabethan usage as well as a modern colloquialism) bustle, turmoil

352   *nation* people in general (that is, the audiences)
      tarre (pronounced like 'tar') incite

353–4   *money bid for argument* payment offered (to an author) for the plot of a play (or perhaps 'money paid (by the audience) unless this particular controversy formed part of the entertainment')

354   *went to cuffs* (metaphorically) came to blows

355   *in the question* about the controversy

357–8   *much throwing about of brains* a great battle of wits

359   *carry it away* win the day

360–61   *Hercules and his load too*. The sign of the Globe Theatre was Hercules bearing up the globe (relieving Atlas). This passage implies, perhaps ironically, that the success of the boys' companies had had its effect on Shakespeare's company too.

363   *make mows* put on a mocking expression of face

365   *ducats*. The ducat was a gold coin, worth about nine shillings, so Hamlet is speaking of considerable sums.
      picture in little miniature painting
      'Sblood by God's blood (in the eucharist)

366   *philosophy* 'natural philosophy' or (as we now call it) science

370   *appurtenance* proper or usual accompaniment

371   *fashion and ceremony* conventional ceremonious behaviour

371–2   *comply with you in this garb* show you polite conduct in this manner (shaking your hands)

257

372   *my extent to* the politeness that I intend to extend towards

373   *show fairly outwards* give every evidence of cordiality

373-4   *entertainment* a good reception

375   *deceived* mistaken (in thinking him to be mad)

377   *I am but mad north-north-west.* In the very assertion of his sanity Hamlet makes such a cryptic remark that they must regard him as having lost his senses: 'I am only a very little off compass – one point ($22\frac{1}{2}°$) out of sixteen (360°)'.

378   *handsaw.* This is usually interpreted as a variant of 'hernshaw', heron. Hamlet seems to be warning his companions that, though he may seem a bit mad, he usually has his wits about him and can distinguish between true and false friends.

383   *Happily* perhaps

384   *twice* for the second time

386-7   *You say . . . indeed.* As Polonius comes on stage, Hamlet pretends to be engaged in conversation.

386   *'A* on

389   *Roscius* (the most famous actor in ancient Rome)

392   *Buzz* (a contemptuous exclamation on hearing stale news)

396-9   *tragedy, comedy . . . unlimited.* This is a jest at the expense of the Renaissance theories of the specific 'kinds' of drama, with their special rules or principles.

397-8   *tragical-comical-historical-pastoral.* This mixture may seem absurd until one remembers that Shakespeare later wrote *Cymbeline.*

398   *scene individable* (plays in which the scene is not changed, so that the so-called 'unity of place' is preserved)

398-9   *poem unlimited* (more imaginative plays in which the classicizing unities of place and time are not preserved – like nearly all of Shakespeare's)

399   *Seneca.* The ten tragedies attributed to him were well-known in Shakespeare's time and represented the

classical type of tragedy more than did those of
Aeschylus, Sophocles, and Euripides. They were performed in academic circles in Latin and in English
translation.

Plautus. The two Latin comic playwrights Plautus and
Terence had a considerable influence on Elizabethan
drama. Shakespeare's *The Comedy of Errors* is based on
Plautus's *Menaechmi* and *Amphitruo.*

400   *the law of writ and the liberty* plays (like those of Ben
Jonson) in which the classical principles are followed,
and plays (like those of Shakespeare) with greater
freedom of structure

402   *Jephthah, judge of Israel.* Jephthah made a vow to
Jehovah that, if he were successful over the Ammonites,
he would sacrifice the first living thing that came to
meet him (Judges 11.9–40). This was his daughter.

406–7   *One fair daughter . . . well.* In 1567–8 the printing of
'A ballad entitled the song of Jephthah's daughter at
her death' was authorized. No copy of this is known,
but it is probably the same as a ballad authorized in
1624 with the title 'Jephthah Judge of Israel', which
begins:

> I read that many year ago
> When Jephthah, Judge of Israel,
> Had one fair daughter and no more,
>   Whom he loved passing well,
> And as by lot, God wot,
> It came to pass most like it was
> Great wars there should be,
>   And who should be the chief but he.

407   *passing well* very well indeed
412   *that follows not* what you have just said is not the next
line of the ballad I was quoting
415   *lot* chance
417   *as most like it was* as was very probable
418   *row* stanza

418   *pious* (because it has a biblical subject)
       chanson song

419   *abridgement* (1) interruption; (2) entertainment

422   *valanced* fringed (with a beard). A valance is a draped edging of cloth.

423   *beard* defy (punningly)

423–4   *my young lady and mistress*. Hamlet is addressing the boy (probably in his early teens) who takes the female roles in the plays.

424–5   *is nearer to heaven* has grown taller

426   *chopine*. The high bases on the fashionable Venetian-styled women's shoes ('chopines') raised them several inches. Hamlet continues to jest with the boy by allusions to women's roles.

426–7   *a piece of uncurrent gold*. A gold coin was regarded as no longer legally current at its full value if it had been 'clipped' or *cracked* within the ring surrounding the monarch's head.

428–9   *like French falconers: fly at anything we see*. This was the British opinion of French sportsmen, who allegedly did not select the prey for their falcons with sufficient care. Hamlet asks for a speech at once, without worrying much what it is to be. (In fact, however, he chooses one carefully.)

429   *straight* straightaway

430   *taste of your quality* specimen of what your profession (acting) can provide

435   *caviary*. Caviare, introduced into England in Shakespeare's time, was an expensive delicacy, unpalatable to those without an acquired taste for it.

436   *general* ordinary people
       received considered

437   *cried in the top of* were spoken more loudly and with more authority than

438   *digested* arranged

439   *modesty* moderation in writing
       cunning skill

440   *sallets* tasty bits (probably he means 'bawdy')

441   *indict* convict

442   *affectation.* Q2 reads 'affection', perhaps a variant form.

443-4   *more handsome than fine* not showy in decoration, but genuinely beautiful in proportions

444   *One speech in't I chiefly loved.* It concerns a revenge taken by a son and a vigorous homicide. At certain points – *blood of fathers* (line 456), *Did nothing* (line 480) – Hamlet probably responds with personal feeling.

445   *Aeneas' tale to Dido.* This is given in Books 2 and 3 of Virgil's *Aeneid.* The murder of King Priam by Pyrrhus, son of Achilles, during the night of the fall of Troy is in 2.526–88. In writing the speech, Shakespeare derived many hints from Virgil.

448–   The old-fashioned style of this speech marks it off from
516   the rest of the play as 'theatrical'. It is a serious performance, and the First Player is a distinguished actor.

448   *Hyrcanian beast.* The tigers of Hyrcania (a province in Asia Minor near the Caspian Sea) were a commonplace image of ferocity. In the *Aeneid* (4.367) Dido says of Aeneas that Hyrcanian tigresses must have suckled him.

450   *rugged* hairy
       sable black

452   *ominous* fateful
       horse (the wooden horse used by the Greeks to intrude men secretly inside the walls of Troy)

454   *dismal* (a strong word) disastrous

455   *total* entirely
       gules (a heraldic term; pronounced with a hard 'g') red
       tricked (a heraldic term) spotted

457   *Baked and impasted with the parching streets.* The hot air (from the burning city of Troy) has congealed the blood smeared upon Pyrrhus as he went through the streets killing Trojans.
       impasted made into a paste

458   *tyrannous* cruel

458   *damnèd* (because resembling the flames of hell)

459   *their lord's murder*. Pyrrhus will soon be the murderer of Priam, the rightful *lord* of Troy and its *streets*.

460   *o'er-sizèd* covered with something like size, painted over

461   *carbuncles* (red and fiery precious stones)

466   *Anon* soon afterwards

467   *too short* with blows which fall short

468   *Rebellious to* not obeying

469   *Repugnant to command* offering resistance to its orders. The old man misses his blow and his arm is so jarred by this that he is unable to raise the sword again.

471   *fell* cruel

472   *unnervèd* without energy
        senseless although lacking the senses of a human being
        Ilium (pronounced '*eye*-li-um') Troy

475   *Takes prisoner* captures (so that he cannot act)

476   *declining* falling
        milky white-haired

478   *as a painted tyrant* like a tyrant represented in a painting (in which his sword is shown as held up in the act of descending but never descends)

479   *a neutral to his will and matter* one who is inactive despite both his will and his duty. For a moment Pyrrhus becomes like Hamlet.

481   *against* just before

482   *rack* cloud-formation

485   *region* sky

487   *the Cyclops' hammers*. The Cyclops assisted Vulcan in forging armour for the gods.

488   *Mars's armour*. In the *Iliad* it is Achilles' armour, in the *Aeneid* Aeneas's, that is forged by Vulcan and the Cyclops. Neither hero is suitable for mention in this context. So Mars is reasonably supposed as having a suit of Cyclopean armour too.
        for proof eterne to remain strong and impenetrable for ever

489   *remorse* pity

491   *strumpet Fortune.* See the note to line 232.

492   *synod* assembly

493   *fellies* (the curved wooden pieces which, when joined together, make the rim of a wheel)

       wheel. Fortune was generally imagined as standing on a wheel which revolved (compare III.3.17–22).

494   *nave* hub of the wheel

497   *shall to* will have to go to

498   *jig.* In some theatres, but probably not at Shakespeare's Globe, performances concluded with a farcical playlet, called a *jig*, including singing and lively dancing.

499   *Hecuba.* Hamlet is interested in the effect of her husband's murder upon the wife.

500   *who . . . had* anyone who had

       mobled (a rare and homely word, rhyming with 'cobbled') muffled up, veiled

503–4 *threatening the flames | With bisson rheum* (her profuse tears seem likely to put out the fires which are burning Troy)

504   *bisson* blinding

       clout piece of cloth

505   *late* recently

506   *all o'er-teemèd loins.* According to Homer and Virgil, Priam's wives and concubines bore him fifty sons. Perhaps this gave an impression that his chief wife, Hecuba, was worn-out with bearing children.

508   *tongue in venom steeped* extremely bitter words

515   *milch* moist (literally 'milky')

       burning eyes of heaven heavenly bodies

516   *passion* (would have made) sympathetic sorrow

521   *bestowed* accommodated

522   *abstract* summary. F has 'Abstracts', an easier reading.

523   *you were better* it would be better for you to

527   *God's bodkin* (one of the nails of Christ on the Cross; or *bodkin* may be a form of 'bodykin', a diminutive of

'body' referring originally to the unconsecrated wafer in the mass)

528   *after* according to

537–8   *for a need* if necessary

538   *study* learn by heart

541   *mock* make fun by mimicking (not merely 'deride')

547   *rogue and peasant slave* (on the one hand a cheat, and on the other a spiritless coward)
    peasant (usually derogatory in Shakespeare) base

549   *But* merely

550   *force his soul so to his own conceit* make his imagination so control the workings of his mind and body

551   *from her working* as a result of this activity of his soul (commonly thought of as feminine)
    wanned grew pale

553–4   *his whole function suiting | With forms to his conceit* all his bodily powers responding with physical expressiveness appropriate to these fictitious imaginings

560   *the general ear* the ears of people generally
    horrid horrifying

561   *appal* turn pale (and so 'dismay')
    the free the innocent

562   *ignorant* (of the crime that has been committed)
    amaze bewilder, stun

564   *muddy-mettled* sluggish
    peak mope

565   *John-a-dreams* (apparently a byword for 'a dreamer')
    unpregnant of my cause not stirred to action by my just cause

568   *defeat* destruction

570   *beard*. Presumably Hamlet must be imagined as bearded in the fashion of a young man of the early seventeenth century.

571   *Gives me the lie i'th'throat* calls me a downright liar

572   *to the lungs* (making him swallow the insult)

573   *'swounds* by God's wounds
    take it accept the insult

574   *pigeon-livered and lack gall.* Pigeons were believed not to secrete gall (the reputed cause of anger).

575   *To make oppression bitter* which would make me resent the oppression

576   *region kites* kites in the sky

578   *kindless* inhuman

. 580   *brave* fine (ironically)

582   *heaven and hell* (that is, a sense of natural justice and the fury of his anger)

585   *stallion* a prostitute (like *drab*). F reads 'Scullion', an acceptable reading sometimes preferred by editors. But *whore* and *drab* perhaps lead naturally to *stallion*.

586   *About* to work

588   *by the very cunning of the scene* simply by the skill in presentation of the play

589   *presently* at once

591–2   *murder . . . organ.* Compare I.2.257–8.

595   *tent him to the quick* probe him until he feels the pain
        blench flinch (not 'turn pale')

596–   *The spirit . . . damn me.* Hamlet now explains or
601   excuses his inactivity by distrusting the Ghost's statements. Though he and his friends had already envisaged the possibility that the Ghost might be an evil spirit (*a spirit of health or goblin damned*, I.4.40–42, and Horatio's warning at I.4.69–74), Hamlet had concluded *It is an honest ghost* (I.5.138).

599–   *my melancholy, | As he is very potent with such spirits.*
600   According to Elizabethan physiology, persons suffering from an excess of black bile (*melancholy*) were prone to exercising strong imaginations, and were therefore subject to mental instability and hallucinations. So they were an easy prey to the devil.

601   *Abuses* deceives

602   *relative* closely related to fact
        this (the narrative and promptings of the Ghost)

III.1   (stage direction) Unlike I.2 and II.2, here the royal entry is not marked with a '*Flourish*' in Q2 or F. This may indicate a more private interview than the formal, though genial, reception of Rosencrantz and Guildenstern in II.2.

1   *drift of conference* directing of your conversations with him

2   *puts on.* This indicates suspicion that Hamlet's *antic disposition* is a pose.
    confusion mental distraction

3   *Grating* harassing

7   *forward* readily disposed
    sounded questioned

8   *crafty* cunning

12   *forcing of his disposition* constraint, forcing himself to be in an accommodating mood

14   *assay him* try to win him

17   *o'er-raught* overtook

26   *give him a further edge* stimulate him to a keener desire

29   *closely* privately

31   *Affront* come face to face with

32   *lawful espials* spies made excusable by the circumstances

38–42   *for your part ... honours.* This probably shows that Ophelia hears the plotting against Hamlet, so that she must take responsibility for deceiving him. But it cannot be regarded as certain, for the Elizabethan stage was large, and she could have been so placed that (by convention) she did not hear lines 32–7. Nothing in what she says in lines 90–162 implies that she knows she is being spied upon.

40   *wildness.* This is a mild word for Hamlet's *confusion*, *lunacy*, *affliction*. To Ophelia the Queen tactfully avoids the word 'madness'.

42   *To both your honours* to the credit of you both

43   *Gracious* (to the King)

44   *bestow* conceal
    book (clearly a prayer book: lines 45, 47–8, 89–90)

266

45   *exercise* religious exercise
        colour provide plausible explanation of

46   *loneliness* being alone (without a chaperon)

47   *proved* found by experience
        devotion's visage an outward appearance of religious devotion

48   *pious action* performance of religious acts

49   *O, 'tis too true.* Probably this is spoken aloud, for the King is a self-controlled character. The '*Aside*' direction in line 50 is added by editors.

50–54   *How smart . . . burden!* This is the first sign that the King has a bad conscience. From now on, the audience has no reason to doubt the Ghost's veracity. It is just at this point that Hamlet has begun to have doubts (II.2.596–601).

52   *to the thing* in comparison with the cosmetic. But the meaning is strained. Possibly *the thing that helps it* is the harlot's servant who arranges her toilet and so knows how ugly she really is.

53   *painted* hypocritically disguised

55   (stage direction) *Enter Hamlet.* It is possible that Hamlet enters reading a book and speaks his soliloquy while ruminating upon it. For Q1 has the introductory line spoken by the King: 'see where hee comes poring vpon a booke', which probably indicates what the actor who reported the text had seen upon the stage. If, as seems probable, the soliloquy was originally spoken at II.2.170 (where Q1 places it), the Queen's *But look where sadly . . .* is a vestige of this 'business'.

56–88   *To be, or not to be . . . action.* Q1 prints this soliloquy, and the meeting with Ophelia, after II.2.170, which may well indicate stage practice in early productions. Some modern directors have found that placing the soliloquy there, at a low point in Hamlet's despair, is more effective than it is here, just after his vigorous decision to test Claudius. The placing of the soliloquy here may indicate an afterthought – not altogether successful – influenced by the fact that including it in II.2 gives the actor a very long period on stage.

56   *To be, or not to be* whether or not to continue this mortal existence (the choice is between continuing to live and committing suicide). An alternative explanation is: 'is there an afterlife, or not?' This, though congruous with the line of thought later in the soliloquy, is more difficult to communicate on the stage.

57–60   *Whether 'tis nobler ... end them* it does not matter (in discussing *the question* of the advantages and disadvantages of suicide) whether we think a stoical attitude to misfortune or an active fighting back against the blows of fate is the more honourable course for a man to take. An alternative explanation is that lines 57–8 expand *To be* and lines 59–60 expand *not to be*: Hamlet can either endure his misfortunes (and so continue to live) or follow an active plan of attacking the King (and so expose himself to an inevitable avenger's death or suicide). At II.2.547 Hamlet had supposed that such an endurance of wrongs was fit only for a *rogue and peasant slave*.

57   *in the mind* (probably goes with *to suffer* rather than with *nobler*)

58   *outrageous.* Hamlet seems to be emphasizing the unbearable irrationality of Fortune.

60   *by opposing* (as distinct from using other methods of ending one's troubles, such as stoical endurance or suicide)

61   *No more* (than to sleep)

63   *consummation* final completion (of life)

65   *rub* obstacle (in the game of bowls)

67   *shuffled off this mortal coil* (like a snake shedding its slough, or perhaps a butterfly – a symbol of the soul – emerging from its chrysalis)
       this mortal coil the turmoil of this mortal life

68   *give us pause* cause us to hesitate
       respect consideration

69   *makes calamity of so long life* makes those afflicted by calamity willing to endure it for so long

70   *time* the world in which one lives, 'the times'

72   *despised* (not necessarily by the lady). F has 'dispriz'd' ('unvalued'), which also makes good sense.

      the law's delay (a typically Elizabethan misfortune)

73   *office* those who hold official positions

74   *patient merit of th'unworthy takes* the deserving have to endure patiently from the unworthy

75   *quietus* release from a debt (*quietus est*, 'it is discharged') and so from the troubles of life

76   *a bare* merely a

      bodkin dagger (but *bodkin* had come also to mean 'a large pin', and possibly that is the vivid image here)

      fardels burdens

79-80 *from whose bourn | No traveller returns.* The inconsistency between this statement and Hamlet's experience of his father's ghost is obvious. It might be intended to indicate his waning faith in the authenticity of the Ghost (see II.2.596–601). But it is more likely to be an imaginative intensification of his thoughts on death, not to be related too literally to the action in other parts of the play. Moreover, the image is that of a *traveller* returning to his home from a sojourn elsewhere – which is quite unlike the transitory visitation of a ghost.

79   *bourn* region, boundary

80   *puzzles* (a strong word) bewilders

83   *conscience* introspection, reflection on the contents of the consciousness

84   *native hue* (complexion characteristic of a state of natural health)

85   *cast* tinge

      thought anxiety

86   *pitch* (the height of a soaring falcon's flight) high aspiration

      moment importance

87   *With this regard* owing to this consideration (because this is thought about)

88   *Soft you now* (an interjection expressing moderate surprise)

89–150 The interview between Hamlet and Ophelia is difficult to interpret. We do not know whether Hamlet is talking with the knowledge that there are eavesdroppers; whether he thinks Ophelia is in the plot and is acting as a decoy; whether he becomes suspicious of her halfway through and thereupon turns nasty. The scene is usually played as if Hamlet were merely suspicious up to line 130, when he asks *Where's your father?* From that point, realizing that the King and Polonius are listening, he puts on a vicious act intended for their ears.

    The first part of the interview can be spoken by Hamlet in his typical cryptic ironic manner. At line 130, it seems, he wonders what Ophelia is doing alone and unchaperoned after having been kept immured from him so long, and learns that her father is not with her. It is an easy step to suppose that she was brought here by the Queen and that, if anyone, it is the Queen who is listening to their conversation. Hamlet therefore begins an attack on womanhood intended for her ears. The irony is that it is not his mother but the King, with Polonius, who overhears his bitter words, and so he unknowingly betrays himself (*all but one – shall live*, line 149) and prepares the King for the trick in the play scene (III.2).

    There is no exit for the Queen at line 42 in either Q2 or F. If the audience can be made aware of the Queen's curiosity in observing what goes on between Hamlet and Ophelia, then the revelation at line 162 that Hamlet has been mistaken, and the eavesdropper is, not the Queen, but – more importantly and more dangerously – the King, can be an exciting moment.

89   *orisons* prayers (because Ophelia carries a book of devotions, and is perhaps visibly at prayer)

93   *remembrances* gifts as souvenirs of affection

99   *perfume* (given by the *words of so sweet breath composed*)

103, 107   *honest* (of a woman) chaste

108   *admit no discourse to* permit no parleying with

109–13   *Could beauty . . . likeness.* Ophelia supposes Hamlet to have said that *beauty* and chastity should not go together, and he accepts the misinterpretation as interesting and develops it.

109   *commerce* intercourse

111–13   *the power of beauty . . . likeness.* This is very like the typical paradox on which academic wits exercised themselves in Shakespeare's time. In the second element, Hamlet is presumably referring obscurely to the failure of his *honest* father to keep his beautiful mother in the path of virtue.

113   *translate* transform (probably with some implication of 'elevate')

    his likeness the likeness of *honesty*

114   *sometime* formerly (before his mother's disillusioning behaviour)

    the time 'the times' (but, in particular, his experience of his mother's behaviour)

118   *inoculate our old stock* be grafted (by the insertion of a bud) into the human inheritance of original sin (occasioned by an apple tree; and no doubt Hamlet is thinking of his family inheritance from his mother)

118–19   *relish of it* have a flavour of the original *stock*, with its inheritance of original sin

121   *Get thee to a nunnery* (so avoiding sexual temptation, marriage, and the begetting of children). *Hamlet* is a play of long ago, set in a foreign country but in Christian times; and it is given a vaguely Catholic setting. The withdrawal of a noble young lady to a convent to avoid the wickedness of the world is a not unreasonable

suggestion. After Shakespeare's time, 'nunnery' was used facetiously to mean 'brothel', but in this context (*Why wouldst thou be a breeder of sinners?*) that meaning seems impossible.

122   *indifferent honest* of average honourableness

124-5   *I am very proud, revengeful, ambitious.* This, although it bitterly misrepresents Hamlet himself, is not unlike the character of a hero-villain in a revenge story, such as that derived from Belleforest in *The History of Hamlet*.

131   *At home.* Ophelia's lie (if it is a lie and she knows Polonius is listening) is the beginning of the calamity that falls upon her, though she thinks she is only humouring a madman.

133   *play the fool* ('I have sinned . . . behold, I have played the fool, and have erred exceedingly', 1 Samuel 26.21)

139   *monsters* (probably) cuckolds (who traditionally wear horns and so look like monstrous animals. The actor can make the gesture of horns with his fingers on his head.)
    you (women in general, not Ophelia in particular)

143   *paintings* use of cosmetics

145   *jig* dance, move jerkily
    amble walk affectedly
    lisp talk affectedly

145-6   *nickname God's creatures* use foolish (or indecent) invented names for creatures which were given their proper names by Adam at God's direction (Genesis 2.19)

146-7   *make your wantonness your ignorance* affect ignorance and use this as an excuse for your foolishness or wanton speech

148   *marriage.* So Q2; in F (as often happens) the meaning is simplified by reading 'Marriages', the concrete for the abstract word.

149   *all but one.* This clearly refers to the King. It is an uncharacteristically and dangerously open warning if Hamlet suspects that the King is listening. Perhaps it is

his first mistake, putting the King on his guard (as is expressed in lines 163–76). But if he supposes that his mother is listening (see the note to lines 89–150), then it is a warning to *her* about what is going to happen. Or the phrase may be spoken aside, rather than shouted as a threat.

152   *The courtier's, soldier's, scholar's, eye, tongue, sword.* The *eye*, *tongue*, and *sword* do not seem to apply independently to the three types of a man, though *tongue* and *sword* would go with the *scholar* and *soldier*. Rather, Ophelia seems to be insisting on the unity of qualities in Hamlet in his various capacities.

153   *expectancy* hope for the future
       rose 'the very flower'
       fair (perhaps 'made fair by Hamlet's presence and participation', rather than vaguely approving of the state of Denmark)

154   *glass* mirror
       mould of form pattern of behaviour (as distinct from garments and physical appearance)

155   *of* by

157   *music*. This is the F reading. Q2 has 'musickt'.

159   *out of time*. F has 'tune' for Q2's *time*. The image of the harmony of the human faculties under the government of reason is common in Shakespeare.

160   *feature* general physical appearance (not only the face)
       blown youth youth in its bloom

161   *Blasted* withered
       ecstasy madness

162   *have seen what I have seen, see what I see* see now such a great change from what I have seen

163   *affections* emotions

164–5   *Nor ... Was not* (the emphatic negative, not uncommon in Shakespeare)

166   *sits on brood* (like a bird on its eggs, leading to *hatch* in line 167)

167   *doubt* feel anxious that

273

167   *disclose*. This also means 'hatching', as at V.1.283.

170   *he shall with speed to England*. Similarly in *The History of Hamblet* the prince is sent to England. The King has now changed his mind from I.2.112–17, where he was intent on keeping Hamlet at home. At this point the King still claims to hope that Hamlet may be cured of his melancholy. But after he and Hamlet have confronted each other in the play scene he resolves to use the expedition to England as a means of sending Hamlet to his death (IV.3.60–70).

171   *tribute*. Shakespeare has a sense of the historical background of the play; this is the famous Danegelt.

173   *variable objects* variety of surroundings for him to observe

174   *something-settled matter* somewhat settled matter (*idée fixe*)

175   *still beating* for ever hammering in his head

176   *From fashion of himself* out of his ordinary way of conducting himself

178   *grief* grievance

180–81 *You need not . . . all*. This could be taken to mean that Ophelia had not known that their conversation was being overheard. See the note to lines 38–42.

184   *be round with* speak bluntly to

185   *in the ear* within earshot

186   *find him not* fails to discover what is the matter with him

187   *confine him* lock him up (as a madman rather than as a political danger)

189   *great ones* highly-placed persons

III.2. 1–53 *Speak the speech . . . of it*. Hamlet begins by referring only to the elocution of *my lines*, the inserted *speech of some dozen lines or sixteen lines* (II.2.538) which he had himself written. But he soon moves to a consideration of the principles of acting generally.

5   *use all* treat everything

9   *robustious* boisterous

       periwig-pated with his head covered with a wig

       passion passionate speech

10   *groundlings* (the part of the audience who stood on the ground in the open yard of the theatre, paying only a penny for entrance)

11   *capable of* capable of understanding

13   *o'erdoing* outdoing

       Termagant. This imaginary deity believed to be worshipped by Mohammedans appears in the medieval religious plays as violent and overbearing.

13–14 *out-Herods Herod* gives a performance which is even more violent than that of Herod (represented in medieval religious plays as a wild tyrant)

19   *modesty* moderation

20   *from* contrary to

22   *the mirror up to nature.* This image of art as a mirror of reality had had a long history before Shakespeare used it.

22–3   *show virtue her own feature, scorn her own image.* The virtues and vices, by being represented in a lifelike way, are to be immediately recognizable for what they are, without confusing the spectator.

23   *scorn* folly (the object of scorn)

23–4   *very age and body of the time* (that is, present state of things)

24   *his* its (grammatically, their)

       pressure impression (as in wax)

24–5   *come tardy off* imperfectly achieved

25   *unskilful* uneducated part of the audience (contrasted with *the judicious*)

26–7   *censure of the which one* judgement of one of *the judicious*

27   *must in your allowance* you should allow to

29–30 *not to speak it profanely* (by suggesting impiously that they were made not by God but by *some of Nature's journeymen*)

33   *journeymen* (that is, indifferent workmen)

34   *abominably*. This word was generally (but incorrectly) supposed to derive from the Latin *ab homine*, interpreted as 'inhuman'; and both Q2 and F here spell it 'abhominably'. So Hamlet is punning on *humanity*.

35-6   *indifferently* to some extent. The First Player seems to give only a half-hearted assurance of reformation.

39   *there be of them that* there are some of those (clowns) who

43-55   *And then you . . . Well*. This passage is found only in Q1. This is generally unreliable, but there are good reasons for regarding this expansion of Hamlet's speech as a fairly accurate report of a passage later cut. It gives examples of the silly 'character' jests of the comic actors. This part of the scene is quite well remembered by the actor who betrayed the play to a piratical printer – he was obviously interested in this discussion of acting and appreciated the satirical comments on bad actors. Moreover, it is just the kind of passage which would soon become out-of-date and would therefore be cut in later performances. Since, however, we are dependent upon the actor's memory, we cannot trust the exact wording.

45   *quote* note

46   *tables* notebooks

49   *cullison* (a corruption of 'cognizance', a badge)

49-50   *blabbering* babbling

50   *keeping in* (perhaps 'accompanying', that is, the *gentlemen* speak the catch-phrases along with the clown)

       cinquepace (a lively dance)

51   *warm* (presumably as the result of his strenuous efforts to amuse)

56-7   *piece of work* masterpiece (ironically). Compare II.2.303.

58   *presently* immediately

64   *e'en* indeed

       just honourable

65   *conversation coped withal* dealings with people brought me into contact with

70-71 *let the candied tongue . . . hinges of the knee.* Hamlet is describing an allegorical scene in which a figure of Flattery first licks another figure (Pomp), and then kneels down before him, expecting to be flattered. Hamlet is thinking of Rosencrantz and Guildenstern, whom he has just now dismissed.

70 *absurd* ridiculously unreasonable

71 *crook the pregnant hinges of the knee* curtsy or kneel (as a gesture of respect)
  pregnant productive of profit

72 *thrift may follow fawning* personal profit may derive from sycophantic behaviour

74 *of men distinguish her election* make discriminating choice among men

75 *sealed* marked as a possession (like a legal document)

76 *one, in suffering all, that suffers nothing* one who, however great his sufferings may be, shows none of the effects of suffering

79 *blood and judgement* passion and reason
  commeddled mixed. F has 'co-mingled', a more usual word.

81 *stop* finger-hole (and the note produced by 'stopping' it)

83 *core . . . heart* (probably a pun, on the supposition that 'core' is related to Latin *cor*, 'heart')

89 *the very comment of thy soul* your closest observation

90 *occulted* hidden

91 *unkennel* reveal (like a dog emerging from its lair)
  in one speech at one speech. It is natural to suppose that this is the speech that Hamlet proposed to insert. This is not certain. He has chosen the play, *The Murder of Gonzago*, because of the resemblance of its plot to the actual situation in Denmark, and it may already contain a speech which will strike Claudius *to the soul* and make him *blench* (II.2.589, 595). Hamlet may from the first have intended his speech to be directed at his mother. See the note to lines 196–225.

94 *Vulcan's stithy* the anvil of Vulcan, the blacksmith god,

whose forge was supposed to be under Mount Etna, and so came to be connected with the idea of hell (therefore *foul*). Compare *the Cyclops' hammers* (II.2.487).

96   *after* afterwards

96–7   *we will both our judgements join | In censure of his seeming.* It is noteworthy that Hamlet has no plan for action if Claudius reveals his guilt, and he ignores the consequences of his revealing to Claudius that he is aware of the crime.

97   *censure of his seeming* assessment of the way he behaves outwardly

98   *steal* hide by stealth (any emotion)

100   *be idle* seem to have nothing on my mind

101   (stage direction) *Danish march. Flourish. Trumpets and kettledrums ... guard carrying torches.* The *Trumpets and kettledrums* are in the Q2 direction, the *Flourish*, the *guard carrying torches*, and the *Danish march* in F. They indicate stage business for a formal entry with royal and national music. Probably early productions were content with trumpets and drums. The F direction suggests later elaboration. The phrase *Danish march* is interesting. The fact that King James I's consort was Anne of Denmark and that Christian IV of Denmark visited him in 1606 and 1614 may have meant that a *Danish march* had come to be recognizable to some of Shakespeare's audiences and was appropriately inserted into the play.

Trumpets ... kettledrums (probably to be heard off stage)

torches. Perhaps some of these are extinguished when the play begins (line 144), to give point to the King's and Polonius's demands for *light* (lines 278–9).

102   *cousin* (used of any close relative)

103   *chameleon's dish.* The chameleon was alleged to live on air alone. Hamlet takes up Claudius's *fares* as if it were an inquiry about his food.

104   *air* (doubtless punning on 'heir')

        promise-crammed. This alludes to Claudius's promise of the succession to the throne (I.2.108–9 and lines 348–52 below).

105   *have nothing with* understand nothing of

105–6   *These words are not mine* what you have said is irrelevant to my remark

107   *nor mine now* (because he has spoken them and they have left him)

113   *Capitol*. In fact Caesar was not killed in the Capitol at Rome, but the error (found also in *Julius Caesar* and *Antony and Cleopatra*) was common.

        Brutus killed me. Hamlet encourages references to the murder of a tyrant.

114   *brute . . . capital*. Hamlet's jeering puns have an extra irony in that he will soon kill Polonius (III.4.24–34).

        calf fool

116–17   *stay upon your patience* await your permission to begin

119   *metal more attractive* (of Ophelia) more magnetic metal. By his behaviour Hamlet encourages Polonius's belief that distracted love is the cause of his trouble. But his other reason for sitting near Ophelia is that it is a position from which he can watch the King closely.

121   *shall I lie in your lap?* Hamlet's sexual innuendos in this scene are quite unlike any other lover's speech to his beloved in Shakespeare, but it must be admitted that several of Shakespeare's pure heroines listen to and tolerate ribald raillery from a man (e.g. Helena from Parolles, *All's Well That Ends Well*, I.1.109–61, and Desdemona from Iago, *Othello*, II.1.100–161).

122   *No, my lord*. Ophelia keeps Hamlet at a distance by addressing him in almost every speech as *my lord*, emphasizing her inferior position.

124   *Ay*. Probably she is accepting his interpretation of what he had said, rather than consenting to his suggestion.

125   *meant country matters* was referring to sexual intercourse

130   *Nothing* (the figure nought). Presumably the actor makes the point about *country matters* by some such gesture as putting his thumb and first finger together to make a circle, representing the female organ, the *fair thought ... between maids' legs*. Ophelia understands the obscenity: *You are merry, my lord*.

134   *your only jig-maker* the very representative of mindless jesting. Compare II.2.498.

136   *within's* within these

137   *twice two months*. As the Ghost appeared when he was *But two months dead, nay, not so much, not two* (I.2.138), the information is thus given us that it is now more than two months since the apparition, during which time Hamlet has done nothing.

138-9   *let the devil wear black, for I'll have a suit of sables* (that is, to hell with mourning! I'll wear a rich garment). 'Sables' could mean both 'black mourning garments' and 'expensive furs'.

139-40 *Die two months ago*. Hamlet seems to ignore the *twice two months* of Ophelia and to revert to *But two months dead*.

142   *build churches* (that is, endow chapels where prayers may be said for his soul)

142-3 *else shall 'a suffer not thinking on* otherwise he will have to endure being forgotten

143   *with* like

       the hobby-horse (in morris dancing, a man with a figure of a horse strapped around his waist. The word could also mean 'unchaste woman', and some association of thought may be intended here.)

144   *For O ... forgot!* This *epitaph* is apparently from some ballad not extant.

       (stage direction) *The trumpets sound*. This is the direction in Q2. F has 'Hoboyes play', which may represent later theatrical practice. Perhaps the oboe was felt to be more suitable than the trumpet to accompany the following love scenes.

Dumb show a mime, common in Elizabethan drama, usually foreshadowing part or all of a play, or summarizing part of the action. Claudius can sit through this dumb show with an outward appearance of calm because he is a practised hypocrite. It is only on the second telling of the story, where it is made a more intense experience, that he breaks down.

makes show of protestation gives a performance of one affirming strongly her love. There is no question of insincerity; the boy player is performing a role.

declines leans

146   *miching mallecho* (an obscure phrase; *mallecho* may be related to the Spanish *malhecho*, 'mischief'. It is usually pronounced to rhyme with 'calico' or 'pal echo'.)

148   *Belike* probably
      show dumb show
      imports represents
      argument story

149   (stage direction) *Prologue* (that is, speaker of the Prologue, a chorus-figure)

151   *keep counsel* keep a secret

153-4   *Be not you* provided that you are not

156   *naught* improper

161   *the posy of a ring* a motto inscribed in a ring (therefore short, and often in rhyme)

163   *As woman's love.* The injustice of this statement to Ophelia would be shocking were it not obvious that Hamlet is observing his mother and thinking of her. It also anticipates the situation in the playlet, where the Queen succumbs to the seductions of the poisoner.

164   *Phoebus' cart* the chariot of Apollo, the sun-god

165   *Neptune's salt wash and Tellus' orbèd ground* the sea and the earth
      Tellus (goddess of the earth)
      orbèd rounded (the earth being a sphere)

166   *borrowed sheen* (because the light of the moon is only the reflection of the sun's)

168   *Hymen* (the pagan god of marriage)

169   *commutual* mutually

173   *cheer* cheerfulness

174   *distrust you* am anxious about you

175   *Discomfort* trouble

176   As there is no rhyme, a line may have been accidentally omitted.

       love (love too much)

177   *hold quantity* are of equivalent amount

178   *In neither aught, or in extremity* either there is nothing of either of them (*fear and love*) or both are present to the utmost limit

179   *proof* your experience

180   *as my love is sized* according to the amount of my love for you

182   *Where little fears grow great, great love grows there* where great anxiety develops from only small causes, that is evidence of great love. The meaning is close to that of line 176.

184   *operant powers* vital faculties

       leave to do cease to perform

185   *behind* after I have gone

190   *None wed the second but who* let no woman marry a second husband except the one who

191   *wormwood* (a plant of bitter taste, and so 'something bitter to a person's feelings')

192   *instances that . . . move* motives that lead to

193   *base respects of thrift* a dishonourable concern for personal advantage

194   *A second time I killed my husband dead* I give offence to the memory of my first husband and trouble his spirit

196–   *I do believe . . . dead.* This is sometimes believed to
225   be the speech which Hamlet said (II.2.538–9) he would insert into *The Murder of Gonzago*. It would be an ingenious device of Shakespeare to have Hamlet write a speech about his own vacillations and his mother's misconduct when he was expected to be writing one

about his uncle's guilt. But probably the promised lines do not appear at all: it is enough for Hamlet to declare that the playlet will contain something that will frighten the King and then to keep us in suspense. Be that as it may, this is an important speech, echoed by Hamlet and the Ghost at III.4.107–12, by Hamlet at IV.4.32–66, by Claudius at IV.7.110–22, and by Hamlet to Horatio at V.2.10–11.

196   *you think* your real opinion is

198   *Purpose is but the slave 10 memory* our decisions about what we are going to do depend entirely upon our being able to remember them afterwards

199   *Of violent birth, but poor validity* (our initial declarations of our intentions may be emphatic, but they have little stamina)

200   *Which* (*Purpose*, line 198)

202   *Most necessary 'tis* it is inevitable

203   *pay ourselves what to ourselves is debt* fulfil the promises we have made about actions which we ourselves have to perform

204   *passion* the heat of the moment

207   *Their own enactures with themselves destroy* destroys them even by putting them into action

209   *joys . . . grieves* turns to joy . . . turns to grief
         on slender accident for trivial causes

210   *is not for aye* will not last for ever
         nor and so

212   *prove* decide by experience

213   *lead* determine the direction of

214   *down* being displaced

215   *The poor advanced makes friends of enemies* when a humble man is promoted to a position of importance, his enemies become his friends

216   *hitherto* to this extent

217   *who not needs* the rich and important, who do not need friends

218   *try* test (by making an appeal for help)

219   *seasons him* confirms him as, converts him into

221   *Our wills and fates* what we want to happen and what is fated to happen to us

         contrary in contrary directions

222   *devices* plans for the future

         still always

223   *their ends* what happens as a result of our *thoughts*

         none of our own outside our control

224   *think* you may think now

225   *die thy thoughts* what you think will come to nothing

226   *Nor* let neither

227   *Sport* recreation

         lock from me deprive me of (*Sport and repose*)

229   *An anchor's cheer* the food of an anchorite (hermit). The Q2 reading 'cheere' is sometimes interpreted as 'chair'. But both this spelling and the meaning are difficult.

         my scope what I have in prospect

230   *Each opposite* whatever is in opposition

         blanks the face of joy changes a happy face to a miserable one

232   *here and hence* in the present and in the future (or possibly 'in this world and the next')

240   *protest* promise publicly

242–3   *Have you heard . . . in't?* The King presumably speaks to Polonius, though Hamlet replies to him.

244   *poison in jest.* Poison has not been mentioned so far in the playlet; and Hamlet again anticipates the action by referring to *murder* in line 248. Apparently the King begins to reveal his distress or anger *Upon the talk of the poisoning* (line 298).

245   *offence.* Hamlet's meaning is different from Claudius's in line 242: this is only a play; there is no reality in it, so no actual injury is done by this pretence of poisoning.

247   *The Mousetrap.* The new name for the play seems to derive from Hamlet's belief that he could *catch* the King's *conscience* (II.2.603).

Tropically figuratively (like a 'trope', a rhetorical figure). There may be a pun on 'trap'.

248   *image* imitation of the reality

250   *knavish* wicked

251   *free* innocent

252   *galled* made sore

      jade ill-conditioned horse (also a contemptuous term for a woman, possibly glancing at the Queen)

      withers shoulder-bones (of a horse)

      unwrung not chafed

253   *nephew*. Although the circumstances of the murder in the playlet correspond to the murder of King Hamlet by his brother Claudius, the agent is the murdered man's *nephew*, not his brother. So the playlet could reasonably be interpreted as a threat against Claudius by his nephew Hamlet. Only Claudius knows that it is also an accusation of murder.

      the King (the King in the playlet)

255   *interpret* provide dialogue (that is, act as a pander). Hamlet imagines Ophelia and a supposed lover (*love*) as puppets, and himself as presenter speaking the words of their play.

256   *dallying* indulging in dalliance (that is love-play)

257   *keen* bitter, quick-witted. Hamlet seems to take the word as meaning 'eager for sexual intercourse'.

258–9 *It would cost you a groaning to take off mine edge* you would have to pay for it if you were to satisfy my sexual appetite, because it would cause you the pangs of childbirth

260   *Still better, and worse* your words are getting both more witty and more disgraceful

261   *So you must take your husbands* ('for better, for worse . . .': the marriage service)

      must take. This reading comes from Q1. Both Q2 and F read 'mistake', from which it is difficult to get any satisfactory meaning (unless it is another sneer at his

285

mother, who had 'mis-taken' her husbands by going from a good to a bad one).

262   *Pox* a pox on you, may (venereal) disease afflict you. The oath is inserted in F.

263   *the croaking raven doth bellow for revenge.* These words seem irrelevant to the situation portrayed. They sound like a fragment of an 'old play', and something like them occurs in the anonymous *True Tragedy of Richard III* (printed in 1594). They also seem to be a cue for Lucianus, but they do not begin his speech. The word *bellow* applied to the sound of a raven reduces the line to burlesque.

264   *apt* skilful (perhaps in preparing the poison or in pouring it into his victim's ear)

265   *Confederate season* a helpful opportunity being provided which acts as an ally
    else no creature seeing no other living creature observing me

266   *rank* evil-smelling
    midnight weeds collected. It was supposed that poisonous or magical herbs were especially potent when gathered at midnight.

267   *Hecat* (two syllables: 'hekkett'; goddess of the underworld and hence supposed to be the ruler of witchcraft)
    ban curse

268   *natural magic* inherent magic power
    dire property terribly dangerous power

270   *estate* high rank (as king)

275   *false fire* blank cartridges

280–83 This and lines 290–93 are probably fragments of an old, lost ballad. Hamlet is contrasting those who are wounded in some way (*the strucken deer*) with those who are in a more fortunate position (*The hart ungallèd*): that is, the King and himself.

280   *the strucken deer.* It was believed that a deer would shed tears when wounded to death (see *As You Like It*, II.1.33–40).

282   *watch* remain awake (with pain or sorrow)

283   *Thus runs the world away* it's the way of the world

284   *this.* Perhaps this refers to Hamlet's skill in play-revision, or to his managerial ability in selecting a play and bringing about its intended effect on its audience (King Claudius). Characteristically Hamlet, while excitedly triumphing in his theatrical success, has no thought of any action to deal with the new situation.

       feathers (as worn by actors)

285   *turn Turk* make a complete change for the worse (like a Christian becoming a renegade to the Turks, the great non-Christian power in the seventeenth century)

285–6 *Provincial roses* (double rose patterns, made of ribbons, worn on shoes, and named from Provins, a town in northern France famous for its roses)

286   *razed* (with 'open work', sometimes showing inside cloth of another colour)

       fellowship partnership (in a company of actors)

       cry company. The word is normally used of a pack of hounds; so Hamlet is thinking of the way they *mouth* their lines (line 2).

290   *O Damon dear.* Perhaps Hamlet is thinking of Horatio and himself as like Damon and Pythias, the legendary friends.

291–2 *This realm dismantled was | Of Jove himself.* Presumably he is still thinking of his father (who had *the front of Jove himself*, III.4.57), whose kingdom was usurped by a *peacock* (Claudius) or (as the rhyme suggests) an 'ass'.

292   *dismantled* deprived, stripped

301   *comedy.* The word could be used generally of a play.

302   *perdy* by God (*par Dieu*)

309   *retirement* withdrawal (from the play to his private apartments)

309–10 *distempered* sick (in mind or body)

312   *choler* anger (supposed to be caused by bile in the stomach)

314   *signify* report

315   *purgation* (of the *choler*; one cure was by bleeding)

317   *frame* order

        start jump away (like a horse that is startled, or not tame)

323   *breed* sort

324   *wholesome* reasonable

325   *pardon* permission to leave your presence

328   *What, my lord?* Q2 attributes this to Rosencrantz, but F to Guildenstern (perhaps rightly), waiting until line 333 for Rosencrantz to take over the dialogue.

331   *command* have for the asking

332   *to the matter* come to the point

334   *admiration* bewilderment

338–9   *She desires . . . bed.* Rosencrantz and Guildenstern are the messengers of the plot devised by Polonius (III.1. 182–6).

339   *closet* small private room. It is not a bedroom, though modern directors sometimes turn it into one in order to communicate Hamlet's Oedipal condition.

341   *trade* (an insulting word) business

343   *these pickers and stealers* (his hands, or perhaps those of Rosencrantz who is holding them out in protestation). The allusion is to the Catechism in the Prayer Book: 'My duty towards my neighbour is to . . . keep my hands from picking and stealing'. Instead of the usual oath 'by this hand', Hamlet swears one that is not valid, as if the only purpose of hands was theft.

346   *liberty* liberation (from your *distemper*). But perhaps this contains a threat, preparing for the dialogue with the King in III.3.1–26.

        deny refuse to speak about

349   *voice* vote, support

351–2   *the proverb* ('While the grass grows the starving horse dies')

353–4   *To withdraw with you.* Presumably he takes Guildenstern aside, so that the Player does not hear. Perhaps he gets him at a disadvantage by separating him from Rosencrantz.

354   *recover the wind* get to windward (like a huntsman trying to get the quarry to run with the wind, so that the scent of the nets and of the men who have prepared them is not perceived)

355   *toil* net

356-7   *if my duty be too bold, my love is too unmannerly.* This is an evasive response to Hamlet's accusation. It is difficult to work out any exact meaning: perhaps 'if my manner of behaving to you (in lines 316-26) seemed rather insolent, it was only the strength of my love for you which made me discourteous.' But the antithesis is merely verbal, and it produces Hamlet's tart rejoinder.

365   *ventages* finger-holes

368   *stops.* Hamlet shows how the finger-holes can be covered with his *fingers and thumb.*

374   *sound* fathom (with a quibble on 'produce sound from a musical instrument')

375   *top of my compass* uppermost range of my notes

376   *organ* (the recorder)

377   *'Sblood* by God's blood (on the Cross)

379   *fret* (punning on the meanings 'a mark on the fingerboard of a stringed instrument' and 'irritate')

383   *yonder cloud.* In an Elizabethan theatre open to the sky, Hamlet's pointing to a cloud would not seem incongruous.

390   *by and by* at once

391   *to the top of my bent* till I can put up with it no longer (like a bow *bent* to the full)

396   *yawn* open wide

400   *nature* (natural feelings)

401   *Nero* (the emperor who slew his mother, Agrippina)

404   *be hypocrites* (deceive her by a show of bitter censure without meaning actually to harm her)

405   *shent* shamed

406   *give them seals* confirm my words by actions

III.3. 1   *like him not* am nervous about his actions and intentions

2   *range* roam at liberty

3   *your commission* (the *letters sealed* and the *mandate* (III.4.203–5). It is nowhere made clear that Rosencrantz and Guildenstern are aware of the murderous instructions given in the letters.)

   dispatch quickly prepare (for you to take)

5   *The terms of our estate* my position as ruler of the state

7   *brows*. This Q2 reading is difficult. Perhaps the King is thinking of the intensely attentive face, with knitted brows, watching him during the play scene; and so the meaning is something like 'bold opposition'. The compiler of the F text found the word unreasonable, and substituted 'Lunacies', regardless of metre, perhaps an echo of *turbulent and dangerous lunacy* (III.1.4). Emendations proposed include 'blows', 'brains', 'braves', 'brawls', 'frowns', and 'lunes'.

   provide act with careful foresight

8–23   This view of kingship, although put into the mouths of the ingratiating Guildenstern and Rosencrantz, was the orthodox Elizabethan one. Its expression here shows the dangerous position into which Hamlet has got himself: his enemies now have political morality on their side and he has offended against it.

8   *religious fear* sacred duty

10   *upon* (that is, at the expense of (like parasites))

11   *single and peculiar life* private individual (contrasted with a king)

13   *noyance* harm

14   *That spirit* (the life of a king)

   weal welfare

15   *cess of majesty* cessation of royal rule (by the death or deposition of the king). In F the more familiar word 'cease' has replaced the unusual *cess*.

16   *Dies not alone* is not a single death

   gulf whirlpool

17–20 *a massy wheel . . . adjoined.* The king is described as resembling the wheel of Fortune.

20 *mortised and adjoined* fitted together (like joints of wood)

21 *annexment* appendage

petty consequence unimportant follower

22 *Attends* accompanies

boisterous ruin tumultuous downfall

23 *a general groan* (the people share in the misery)

24 *Arm you* prepare

25 *about this fear* upon this cause of our fear

28 *arras.* Again Polonius enjoys spying on Hamlet from a hiding-place.

convey surreptitiously place

29 *the process* what happens

tax him home reproach him unsparingly

30 *as you said.* In fact the suggestion came from Polonius himself (III.1.185–6).

32 *them* (mothers)

33 *of vantage* (perhaps 'in addition', or 'from the vantage-ground of concealment')

36–72 This is the first time we see the King alone and the only occasion we have a full confession from him (but see III.1.50–54). The conscience-stricken King, unlike Hamlet, knows his theological position exactly, and argues about his situation with clarity of mind. Ironically, only after Hamlet's departure (with the same erroneous belief as ourselves) do we learn that the King has not achieved a state of grace.

37 *the primal eldest curse* (the oldest curse upon mankind)

39 *Though inclination be as sharp as will* (he sincerely desires to pray; he is not merely forcing himself to do so by an act of will)

41 *like a man to double business bound* (he wishes to repent and wishes to persist in his guilty situation)

43 *both neglect* fail to deal with either

44 *thicker* deeply covered (made more than double its usual thickness)

291

45   *Is there not rain enough in the sweet heavens* ('How fair a thing is mercy in the time of anguish and trouble? It is like a cloud of rain that cometh in the time of drought', Ecclesiasticus 35.19)

46   *wash it white as snow* ('thou shalt wash me, and I shall be whiter than snow', Psalm 51.7)
    Whereto serves what is the use of

47   *confront the visage of offence* meet sin face to face

48   *twofold force* double efficacy, in preventing us from sinning and in helping us to win pardon when we have sinned ('lead us not into temptation, but deliver us from evil', Matthew 6.13)

49   *forestallèd* prevented

51   *My fault is past* once I have appealed to God for mercy, my sin will have been forgiven. (But he knows that appealing to God brings with it certain conditions.)

54   *effects* resulting benefits

55   *mine own ambition* (that is, the fulfilment of my ambition)

56   *retain th'offence* continue to enjoy what has been gained by the wicked deed

57   *corrupted currents* corrupt ways of behaviour

58   *Offence's gilded hand* the hand of an offender bearing gold as bribes to the judges
    shove by thrust aside

59–60   *the wicked prize itself | Buys out the law* what has been gained by wicked actions – such as power and riches – is used to obtain exemption from the laws against those very actions

60   *above* in heaven

61   *There . . . There* (emphasized) in heaven
    shuffling trickery

61–2   *the action lies | In* (probably 'legal action can be brought against us according to', as well as 'the wicked deed is revealed in')

62   *his* its

62–4   *we ourselves . . . evidence.* In the law courts a man may

not be constrained to give evidence that will incrimin-
ate himself; but before God's seat of judgement it is
different.

62   *compelled* are compelled

63   *to the teeth and forehead* in the very face

64   *give in* provide

      What rests? what remains for me to do?

65   *can* can do

68   *limèd soul.* The soul is like a bird which has been
caught by the laying of 'lime', a glue-like substance.

69   *engaged* entangled

      Make assay make a vigorous attempt (probably ad-
dressed to himself rather than to the angels or to his
knees)

70   *strings of steel.* He imagines his heart-strings have
hardened to steel as a result of his crime.

73   *pat* neatly, opportunely

74   *'a goes to heaven.* At first Hamlet uses the conventional
phrase, meaning 'he dies'. Then he begins to analyse
it literally. He supposes that the King is in a state of
contrition, and so his death at this moment will,
quite literally, enable him to go *to heaven.*

75   *would be scanned* needs to be subjected to scrutiny

77   *sole son* only son (and therefore the only person upon
whom the duty of revenge lies)

79   *hire and salary* (like a payment for services, instead of
punishment for crimes)

80   *took* (took at a disadvantage and killed)

      grossly, full of bread (in a condition of gross unpre-
paredness, without having had an opportunity of a
penitential fast)

81   *crimes* sins. See the first note to I.5.12.

      broad blown, as flush as May in full bloom, like the
vigorous vegetation in the month of May. Hamlet is
recalling that the Ghost said he was *Cut off even in the
blossoms of my sin* (I.5.76).

82   *audit* account (with God)

83   *our circumstance and course of thought.* The exact mean-
      ing is difficult to decide, but, roughly interpreted,
      Hamlet is saying 'so far as we, here on earth, can judge'
      or 'according to our evidence and speculation'.

86   *seasoned* prepared
      passage (to the next world)

88   *Up* (that is, come out of your sheath)
      a more horrid hent a grasp causing more horror (that is,
      when he is about to execute a more terrible deed of
      vengeance upon Claudius)

89   *drunk asleep* dead drunk

91   *game* gambling

91-2 *some act | That has no relish of salvation in't.* This is
      what Hamlet ultimately achieves in V.2.316–21, stab-
      bing the King when he is engaged in acts of murderous
      treachery.

92   *relish* savour

93   *trip him* (still addressing his sword) take him by a
      quick act of treachery
      his heels may kick at heaven. Hamlet imagines his
      enemy as receiving a deadly blow and sprawling for-
      wards, so that in his death throes his legs bend upwards
      from his knees.

95   *stays* awaits me

96   *This physic but prolongs thy sickly days* the spiritual
      medicine you (the King) are now taking (by praying to
      God, and in *the purging of his soul*, line 85) only gives
      you a respite; you are like a sick man who takes medi-
      cine, but thereby only postpones the inevitable approach
      of death

97   *My words fly up, my thoughts remain below.* The King
      has been uttering the *words* of prayers, but has not been
      thinking about them. His mind has been busy with
      thoughts of his worldly affairs. So he has not been in a
      state of contrition.

III.4   This scene takes place in Gertrude's *closet* (III.2.339).

1   *lay home* talk severely

2   *broad* unrestrained

4   *heat* anger (of the court, and of the King in particular)

       silence. This is the reading of both Q2 and F. Editors often accept the emendation 'sconce' (hide). But *silence* may be right, as a stroke of irony against the *foolish prating knave* who can only be *still* when dead (lines 215–16).

5   *round with* plain-spoken to

7   *Fear me not* do not doubt that I will do what you have suggested

9   *Now, mother. . . .* Q1 makes Hamlet say 'but first weele make all safe.' This may be a genuine memory of a piece of stage business by which Hamlet bolts the door.

10   *thy father* your stepfather

12   *idle* foolish

15   *forgot me* forgotten that I am your mother

       the Rood Christ's Cross

18   *I'll set those to you that can speak.* Presumably she rises, resentful of Hamlet's insult.

21   *see the inmost part of you.* The Queen interprets this as a threat of personal violence. But Hamlet means merely 'see the bottom of your soul'.

23   *Help, ho!* That Hamlet behaves in a way that genuinely frightens his mother is suggested by the absurd lines which the reporter of Q1 based on his memory of the action: 'I first bespake him faire, | But then he throwes and tosses me about, | As one forgetting that I was his mother' (to the King at IV.1.8).

25   *Dead for a ducat* I would wager a ducat that I have killed it

31   *As kill a king!* The Queen's amazement and horror both remind the audience of the terrible nature of the King's crime and confirm our impression of her innocence of any knowledge of it.

34   *busy* interfering (like a busy-body)

38 *damnèd custom* vice that has become habitual. See Hamlet's lines on *that monster custom* (162–71).

brassed. Q2 reads 'brasd', which probably indicates *brassed*, 'hardened like brass'. But F reads 'braz'd', which makes it possible that 'brazed' ('made brazen') is correct.

39 *proof* impenetrable
sense feeling

40 *wag* (not a ludicrous word) move

41 *act* (presumably incest; the accusation of adultery is scarcely evidenced: see the note to I.5.42)

43 *Calls virtue hypocrite* makes all virtue seem a mere pretence

43–4 *takes off the rose . . . innocent love.* Presumably he is thinking of his love for Ophelia, and is summarizing his interview with her at III.1.89–150. Compare Laertes's language at IV.5.120–22: *brands the harlot | . . . between the chaste unsmirchèd brows | Of my true mother.*

45 *blister* mark made by the branding iron. Criminals, including harlots, were branded on the forehead.

47 *contraction* witnessed ceremony and contract of marriage

48–9 *sweet religion makes | A rhapsody of words* (probably referring to the marriage service; but Hamlet's attitude is scarcely justified, for the vows undertaken are to last 'so long as ye both shall live')

49 *rhapsody* medley of items strung together without meaningful order
words (merely, and nothing more)
glow blush

50 *this solidity and compound mass* (the earth)
compound composed of the various elements

51 *heated*. F has 'tristfull' ('sad'), which many editors adopt.
as against the Doom as if the Day of Judgement were at hand

52   *thought-sick* sick with horror

53   *index* table of contents (as in a book – the index was formerly at the beginning, not at the end – and so 'prelude to what you are going to say')

54   *upon this picture, and on this.* It is uncertain whether these are miniatures or large pictures hanging on the wall. Miniatures have generally been preferred; Hamlet wears one and his mother another, and he can force her to gaze upon them as he puts them together. Moreover, two large pictures would be inconvenient stage properties, quite apart from the indecorum of the Queen's having portraits of both her husbands in her closet. Nevertheless, the pose described in lines 55–63 would best suit a full-length portrait; and in the first illustration of this scene (in Rowe's edition, 1709) wall portraits (but half-lengths) are shown. Some actors have preferred to suppose the pictures to be in the mind's eye only, but *counterfeit presentment* (line 55) is strongly against this.

55   *counterfeit presentment* presentation by artistic portraiture

57   *Hyperion.* See the second note to I.2.140.
       front forehead

59   *station* stance
       Mercury (the winged messenger of the gods, and so an image of graceful movement and poise)

60   *New lighted* newly alighted

61   *combination* (of the elements)

62   *every god did seem to set his seal.* This seems to be a reminiscence of the classical story of the creation of man, in which each of the gods gave something.

63   *assurance* confirmation

65   *ear* (of wheat)

66   *Blasting* blighting

67–8   *this fair mountain leave to feed, | And batten on this moor.* The contrast is difficult to explain. Presumably it is suggested by *hill* (line 60) and *mildewed ear* (line 65).

Neither mountains nor moors (uncultivated highlands) are especially attractive for sheep-fattening. We should expect the contrast to be between the healthful pasturage on the hillsides and the unhealthful pasturage in the rank lower ground.

68	*batten* fatten (like sheep)
70	*heyday* time of wildness in youth
	blood passion, sexual urge
71	*waits upon* obeys
72	*Sense*. The exact meaning is uncertain; perhaps 'control of the senses', or 'ability to apprehend and distinguish', or 'sexual desire'.
74	*apoplexed* paralysed (as by a stroke)
75	*ecstasy* madness
	thralled enslaved
76	*reserved some quantity* preserved some small element
78	*cozened you at hoodman-blind* tricked you in playing blind-man's buff (into choosing the very worst)
80	*sans all* without using any of the other senses
82	*so mope* behave so aimlessly
84	*mutine* make a mutiny
85–6	*be as wax	And melt in her own fire*. The image is probably of a stick of sealing-wax, which is ignited and then nearly inverted so that drops of the melting wax fall from it.
87	*charge* command (to go forward)
88	*frost* (of middle age)
89	*reason panders will* reason (the powers of judgement appropriate to middle age) acts as a pander to lust
91	*grainèd* deeply ingrained
92	*will not leave their tinct* cannot have the stain washed out of them
93	*enseamèd* greasy
94	*Stewed* soaked. ('Stews' were brothels.)
95	*sty* (place like a pig-sty)
98	*tithe* tenth part

99   *precedent lord* previous husband

vice of kings king who behaves like a buffoon (like the Vice in the Morality plays of the sixteenth century)

103   *of shreds and patches* (as if he were wearing the clown's motley)

(stage direction) Q1 has '*Enter the ghost in his night gowne*' (i.e. dressing-gown), probably reflecting stage practice. It appears at the climax of Hamlet's tirade, presumably as he is about to tell his mother the circumstances of the murder.

106   *he's mad*. It is clear from this and lines 125 and 133 that the Queen cannot see the Ghost.

108   *lapsed in time and passion* having allowed time to slip by and his passionate commitment to his task of revenge to cool (also sometimes interpreted as 'deteriorated into mere emotion')

109   *important* urgent

113·   *amazement* distraction (at Hamlet's behaviour, not at the Ghost)

114   *fighting soul* mind in agony

115   *Conceit* imagination

118   *bend* aim

vacancy space, thin air

119   *incorporal* incorporeal

120   *Forth . . . peep* (that is, you look astonished)

121   *in th'alarm* when an alarm is sounded

122   *bedded* normally lying flat (like *soldiers* on their beds)

hair. This is sometimes emended to 'hairs', but the plural forms *Start* and *stand* may be influenced by *excrements*.

excrements outgrowths (hair grows out of the body, but has no independent *life*)

123   *an* on

127   *form and cause* physical appearance (which inspires pity) and the reason he has for appealing to us

conjoined united

128 *capable* (of responding to what he said)

129 *this piteous action* these gestures (like an actor's) stirring pity

129–30 *convert | My stern effects* transform the results of my stern intentions

131 *want true colour* lack its proper appearance (look pale and bloodless; with a quibble on *colour* meaning 'motive')

  tears . . . for blood shedding tears instead of blood

136 *his habit as he lived* his familiar everyday clothing

138 *very coinage* complete invention

139 *This bodiless creation* this kind of hallucination

139–40 *ecstasy | Is very cunning in* madness is very skilful in creating

141 *temperately keep time* beat steadily

144 *re-word* repeat word for word

145 *gambol* capriciously lead me astray

146 *that flattering unction* the soothing balm of that flattery

149 *mining* undermining

151 *what is to come* further opportunities of sinful behaviour

154 *fatness* grossness

  pursy short-winded (and so in bad condition morally)

156 *curb* bow

  him (vice)

161 *Assume* acquire

162 *who all sense doth eat* which destroys all sensibility

163 *Of habits devil* being the evil genius of our habits. For *devil* many editors prefer the emendation 'evil'; the meaning is then 'custom, which deprives one of all feeling for the evil nature of habits'.

  angel yet nevertheless our good genius

164 *use* habitual practice

165 *frock or livery* (new) dress or uniform

166 *aptly* easily

169 *stamp of nature* inborn characteristics of personality

170   *And either master the devil.* Q2 omits the verb, doubtless accidentally. (The passage is not in F.) The fourth quarto edition (1611) has 'And maister the devil'; and, although this quarto's changes have no known authority, the choice of this word to fill the gap could be due to stage practice. Other plausible suggestions are 'curb', 'lay', 'oust', 'quell', 'shame', or 'tame', or to replace *either* by 'exorcize'. Perhaps, however, the use of *either ... or* demands a word contrasting with *throw ... out*, such as 'aid', 'house', or 'speed'.

172–3   *when you are desirous to be blest,| I'll blessing beg of you* that is, I shall not ask for your blessing (as a son would normally do on departure) until you are repentant and seek God's blessing)

174   *heaven hath pleased it so* such has been the will of heaven. Hamlet seems to transfer the responsibility for Polonius's death to Providence.

175   *this* (Polonius's corpse)

176   *scourge and minister* both the lash which inflicts punishment and the officer who administers it

177   *bestow* put away somewhere
    answer account for

179   *only to be kind* (purely to fulfil my filial love for my father and to effect a reformation of character in you)

180   *This bad begins* this calamity (the killing of Polonius) is a beginning of trouble

183   *bloat* bloated

184   *wanton* wantonly
    mouse (a common term of endearment)

185   *reechy* dirty (literally, 'smoky')

186   *paddling* playing wantonly

187   *ravel ... out* disentangle, make clear

188   *essentially* in my essential nature

189   *in craft* by cunning
    'Twere good (sarcastic)

191   *paddock* toad
    gib tom-cat

192   *Such dear concernings* matters that concern him so closely

193   *sense and secrecy* instinct and your impulse towards secrecy

194-7   *Unpeg the basket . . . down.* This story is not known from any other source. It can be reconstructed as follows: an ape steals a wickerwork cage (*basket*) of birds and carries it to the top of a house. Out of curiosity, or by accident, he releases the pegs of the cage, and the birds fly out. The ape is prompted to imitate them; he creeps into the basket and then leaps out, supposing that he will be able to fly like the birds. But, of course, he falls to the ground and breaks his neck.

     Hamlet's application of the fable is as follows: if you reveal my secrets to the King, you will be like this ape. You will gain nothing by it; and if you imagine you can act with the King as cleverly as I can, independently of me, you will be like the ape trying to fly, and so will come to grief.

196   *try conclusions* see what will happen

197   *down* in the fall

205   *mandate* command

       sweep my way prepare the way for me (literally, sweep a path before me)

206   *marshal me to knavery* conduct me into some trap. Hamlet guesses that the King is plotting some treachery.

       work go forward

207   *enginer* maker of military 'engines'

208   *Hoist* hoisted (here, 'blown up')

       petar bomb

208-9   *'t shall go hard | But I will delve* it will be unlucky if I don't succeed in delving

209-10 *delve one yard . . . moon.* Hamlet imagines that, like the garrison of a besieged town whose walls have been mined, he will dig a counter-mine below the attackers' mine and so blow them up.

211   *in one line two crafts directly meet* (like mining and

counter-mining). Perhaps Hamlet is quibbling on *crafts* meaning 'ships'.

212   *set me packing* make me start plotting (with a quibble on the other meaning, 'cause me to be sent away quickly')

217   *draw toward an end with you* conclude my conversation with you (who were such a *prating* fellow)

V.1   As there is clearly no real lapse of time between this and the previous scene, the traditional act division is unreasonable; but it is preserved here for readers' convenience.

1   *matter* significance
     heaves heavy sighs

2   *translate* explain

10   *Whips* he whips

11   *brainish apprehension* headstrong illusion

12   *heavy* grievous

13   *us ... we* (the royal plural. Claudius knows that the blow was intended for him.)

16   *answered* explained

17   *laid to* blamed upon
     providence foresight

18   *short* under control
     out of haunt away from public places

22   *divulging* becoming known in public

25   *O'er whom his very madness* over which his madness itself
     ore vein of gold

26   *mineral of metals base* mine of non-precious metals

27   *'A weeps* (probably an invention of Gertrude's to palliate Hamlet's conduct)

29   *The sun ... touch* (a reminder that it is still the middle of the night)

32   *countenance* assume responsibility for

40   *So haply slander*. There is a gap in the Q2 text here

(F omits the whole sentence). Some extra words are needed for both metre and sense. Those printed here, proposed by eighteenth-century editors, seem more satisfactory than other suggestions.

41   *the world's diameter* the extent of the world from side to side

42   *level* straight
his blank its point of aim (the 'white' in the middle of the target)

44   *woundless* invulnerable

IV.2   Again, no time elapses between this and the previous scene.

1   *Safely stowed.* By hiding the body, Hamlet makes his murder of Polonius seem to be an act of madness.

6   *Compounded it with dust* (hardly true; Hamlet has only stowed it in a cupboard on the stairs: IV.3.35–6)
Compounded. Shakespeare normally accents this word on the first syllable, so Q2's 'Compound' may be correct.

11   *I can keep your counsel and not mine own.* Hamlet's riddling speech is as baffling to us as to Rosencrantz. Perhaps *counsel* means 'secret', and Hamlet is referring to his not betraying their confession at II.2.292 that they had been *sent for*. His own *counsel* (or 'secret') is the whereabouts of the body.

12   *to be demanded of* on being questioned by
replication (a legal term) reply

15   *countenance* favour

16   *his authorities* the exercise of his powers. Doubtless Hamlet is speaking scornfully of their position of new authority over him.

17–18 *like an ape an apple.* F's reading is 'like an Ape'; Q2 has 'like an apple'. Each gives only a very strained meaning. Q1 transfers this conversation to follow III.2.379 and reads 'hee doth keep you as an Ape doth nuttes, | In the corner of his Iaw, first mouthes you, |

Then swallowes you.' It is tempting to adopt the clear
reading of Q1 ('as an ape doth nuts'). But it seems most
likely that the Q2 and F readings are each a confusion
of *like an ape an apple.*

18   *first* at first
    mouthed taken into the mouth

19   *last* at last

23–4   *A knavish speech sleeps in a foolish ear* a sarcastic remark
is wasted upon an unintelligent hearer

27–8   *The body is . . . body.* Hamlet may mean 'the body is
now in the next world with the King (my father Hamlet), but King Claudius has not yet been killed.' Or he
may be talking deliberate, sinister nonsense.

28–30   *The King is a thing . . . Of nothing.* Again Hamlet is
using suggestive threatening language, echoing the
passage in the Psalms about the transitoriness of mortal
life: 'Man is like a thing of nought. His time passeth
away like a shadow' (144.4; Prayer Book version).
Claudius is doomed to death.

30–31   *Hide fox, and all after.* These words in F are not in Q2,
and may be an interpolation to introduce a bit of exit
business, such as Hamlet's eluding his captors and
running off stage. This has become common theatrical
practice, but is not justified by Hamlet's entry at
IV.3.15. The words probably refer to some children's
game of hide-and-seek.

IV.3   (stage direction) *attendants* (presumably a group of
counsellors or supporters, perhaps the *wisest friends* of
IV.1.38)

4   *of* by
    distracted unreasonable, unstable

5   *like not in* choose not by

6   *scourge* punishment. Claudius supposes that the people
will not allow Hamlet to be punished for murdering
Polonius.

7   *bear all smooth and even* conduct the affair so as not to give offence or seem high-handed

9   *Deliberate pause* the result of deliberately and unhurriedly considering the matter

9–11   *Diseases desperate grown . . . at all* (a proverbial idiom, which occurs in the form 'A desperate disease must have a desperate cure')

10   *appliance* remedies

11   (stage direction) *all the rest* (probably, in Shakespeare's theatre, any extras who could be spared to stand in as courtiers)

20   *convocation of politic worms.* There is doubtless a punning allusion to the Diet of Worms (a city on the Rhine), opened by the Emperor (see line 21) Charles V in 1521, which brought together the dignitaries of the Roman Empire.
    convocation parliament
    politic crafty
    e'en even now

21   *fat* fatten

23   *but variable service* just different courses of a meal

30   *progress* (the usual word for a monarch's official journeys through his kingdom)

35   *nose* smell

39   *thine especial safety.* Claudius is presumably referring to possible retribution upon Hamlet by Polonius's son or friends rather than to Hamlet's judicial prosecution for murder.

40   *tender* feel concern for
    dearly keenly

42   *With fiery quickness* as quickly as spreading flames

43   *at help* ready to help

44   *associates* companions (Rosencrantz and Guildenstern)
    tend await you
    bent prepared (like a drawn bow)

50   *cherub* (a heavenly spirit with exceptional powers of vision: Ezekiel 1.18 and 10.12)

54   *man and wife is one flesh*. Hamlet ironically uses the language of the marriage service.

56   *at foot* close behind him

58   *everything is sealed and done*. Claudius is here referring ostensibly to *the demand of our neglected tribute* (III.1.171) but, in his thoughts, to the letters ordering *The present death of Hamlet* (lines 66–7). There is an emphasis on the secrecy of these instructions. Hamlet has to *unseal | Their grand commission* at V.2.17–18 and seal the new one with his *father's signet* (V.2.49).

59   *leans* depends

60   *England* (probably) King of England

61   *As* for so

       thereof may give thee sense may well give you a just appreciation of the importance of that love

62   *cicatrice* scar

63   *free awe* awe of us which is still felt though without military occupation

64   *coldly set* set a low value upon

65   *sovereign process* royal instructions

       imports at full calls in detail for

66   *congruing* agreeing. Claudius seems to be referring to a second letter with more explicit instructions. Nothing further is made of this. F reads 'coniuring' ('earnestly requesting'), which would correspond to *earnest conjuration* (V.2.38).

67   *present* immediate

68   *hectic* persistent fever

70   *Howe'er my haps* whatever my fortunes may be

       were ne'er begun. This is the F reading. Q2 reads 'will nere begin', which is perhaps better grammar, but fails to rhyme.

V.4   (stage direction) *Fortinbras*. We have not heard about old Norway and Fortinbras since II.2.60–80. The vigour of Fortinbras, like that of Laertes, is an adverse reflection upon Hamlet's inactivity, as he himself recognizes (lines 46–53).

3 *the conveyance of* escort during

  promised previously agreed (II.2.80–82, where a favourable answer to the Norwegian request is implied)

5–6 *If that his majesty . . . eye.* Fortinbras expresses his respect for the King of Denmark and accepts his authority, in accordance with the vow (shown now to be sincere) he had given to his uncle (II.2.70–71).

5 *would aught* wishes to have any communication

6 *in his eye* by presenting myself (*us*, the royal plural) personally before him

8 *Go softly on.* This is probably addressed to his troops, not to the Captain.

  softly slowly, leisurely (perhaps; but the word seems to imply the respectful march of the army through the Danish territory)

9 *powers* troops

15 *main* central part

16 *frontier* frontier-fortress

17 *addition* fine words to exaggerate the matter

19 *name* (reputation for having conquered it)

20 *five ducats, five.* The repeated numeral emphasizes its smallness: it would not be worth paying an annual rent of a mere five ducats (a coin worth about nine shillings) for the lease of the land as a farm.

22 *ranker rate* higher rate of interest (on the purchase money)

  in fee as a freehold property

25–6 *Two thousand souls . . . straw.* It has been plausibly suggested that these two lines belong to the Captain, who is in a better position to speak of *Two thousand* and *twenty thousand* than is Hamlet. Perhaps the repetition of *straw* in line 55 supports this.

25 *Two thousand souls* (his estimate of the size of the armies involved)

308

twenty thousand ducats (his estimate of the expenditure on the war)

26   *Will not debate the question* are not enough to settle the dispute

      straw trivial matter

27   *imposthume* abscess. The consequences of the luxury of society and its vices accumulate unperceived during peace, like the pus in a swollen abscess.

28   *inward . . . without* internally . . . externally (of the body)

32–66   *How all occasions . . . worth.* The importance of this soliloquy is that it enables Hamlet to make a strong impression on the audience before his long absence, and gives a reassurance that he is still true to his oath of vengeance. It is the most 'reasonable' of his soliloquies, and is probably intended to reveal his developing maturity.

32   *occasions* (such dissimilar chance meetings as with the players and with this Norwegian army)

      inform against me denounce me, provide evidence to my discredit (as in a law-suit)

34   *market* profitable employment

36   *large discourse* wide-ranging faculty of understanding

37   *Looking before and after* able to review the past and to use experience as a guide in facing the future

38   *capability* capacity of mind

      godlike (because shared with the Creator Himself)

39   *fust* go mouldy

40   *Bestial oblivion* animal-like inability to retain past impressions

      craven scruple cowardly scrupulousness

41–3   *thinking . . . coward.* Anxiety about the precise consequences of one's actions is due to cowardice much more than to prudence (a remarkably unillusioned analysis by Hamlet of his own feelings and motives).

41   *event* outcome

44   *to do* still to be done

45   *Sith* since

46   *gross* weighty

47   *mass and charge* size and expense

49   *puffed* (not necessarily derogatory) swollen

50   *Makes mouths at* scorns

52   *dare* could inflict upon him

53-6   *Rightly to be . . . stake* true greatness does not consist in rushing into action on account of any trivial cause; but when the cause is one involving honour, it is noble to act, however trivial the subject of dispute may be

54   *argument* cause

55   *greatly* nobly

58   *Excitements* incentives
       blood passions

60   *twenty thousand men.* Hamlet has confusedly transferred the number of ducats in line 25 to the men (who were then only *Two thousand*).

61   *trick of fame* whim of seeking fame. Probably *of fame* goes with both *fantasy* and *trick*.

62   *plot* (of ground)

63   *Whereon the numbers cannot try the cause* where there is not enough space for the two armies to fight out the dispute

64   *continent* receptacle (that is, earth to cover the bodies of those who are killed in battle)

66   *thoughts.* He speaks only of *thoughts*, not of deeds.

IV.5   There is clearly a considerable lapse of time between the previous scene and the opening of this.

1   *I will not speak with her.* The Queen is reluctant to see her son's beloved, the daughter of the man he has murdered.

2   *distract* distracted

3   *mood will needs be* mental condition cannot fail to be

5   *hems.* She makes a noise like 'hmm', confirming her knowledge that *There's tricks i'th'world*.

6   *Spurns* (with her foot)
    enviously spitefully
    straws trifles
    in doubt ambiguous

7   *Her speech is nothing* she talks nonsense

8   *unshapèd* uncontrolled

9   *to collection* to gather something of a meaning
    aim at it make a guess at its meaning. This is the F
    reading ('ayme'). Q2 has 'yawne', which can hardly be
    right, though in an appropriate context 'yawn' can
    mean 'let the mouth gape open with surprise'.

10   *botch* patch clumsily
    fit to their own thoughts to suit their own inferences
    (about her state of mind and the meaning she is trying
    to convey)

11   *Which* (her words)
    yield them deliver (interpret) her words

13   *nothing* not at all
    much unhappily very unskilfully

15   *Dangerous conjectures* (about the murder of Polonius and
    ill-treatment of herself)

16   *Let her come in.* Q2 attributes these words to Horatio.
    If this were retained, the Queen must give some silent
    assent to Horatio's request.

17   *as sin's true nature is* (that is, as is characteristic of
    someone in a state of sin)

18   *toy* trifling event. Apparently she does not yet take
    Ophelia's madness as a serious thing.
    amiss misfortune

19   *artless jealousy* uncontrolled suspicion

20   *spills* reveals and destroys
    (stage direction) Q1 has '*Enter Ofelia playing on a Lute,
    and her haire downe singing*'. This doubtless is a memory
    of a performance.

21   *Where is the beauteous majesty of Denmark?* This may
    mean merely 'Where is the Queen?', or possibly 'Where
    has your queenly beauty gone?' (addressed to the

Queen, who, now conscience-ridden, may be looking very different from the happy woman of the scenes up to III.4).

23-40 *How should I . . . showers.* In these snatches of ballads Ophelia seems to be confusing recollections of her lost lover with her dead father. They hint that the cause of her madness is not only her father's death but her estrangement from Hamlet and his banishment. Shakespeare does not reveal whether she knows that Hamlet killed her father. Her song to the Queen about *your true-love* and *another one* may seem to hint at the difference between her first and second husbands. The next two stanzas remind the Queen of the death of King Hamlet as well as of Polonius. For the music of Ophelia's songs see F. W. Sternfeld's *Music in Shakespearean Tragedy* (London, 1963).

25 *cockle hat.* A hat with a cockle-shell on it signified that the wearer had made a pilgrimage to the shrine of St James at Compostela (in north-west Spain), famous medieval place of pilgrimage.

staff pilgrim's walking-staff

26 *shoon* (archaic plural) shoes

28 *Say you?* what do you say?

38 *Larded* garnished

39 *ground.* F and Q1 read '*graue*' ('grave'), which many editors prefer.

did not go. It has been suggested that the original song had 'did go' (which would give an easier rhythm) and that Ophelia inserts *not* because of her father's not having received an adequate funeral ceremony (*In hugger-mugger to inter him,* line 85 below).

40 *showers* (of tears)

42 *God dild* may God reward ('yield')

42-3 *They say the owl was a baker's daughter.* This may refer to a folk-tale in which Christ begged for a loaf of bread and punished the baker's daughter, who insisted on his being given only a small one, by transforming her

312

into an owl. Perhaps Ophelia is trying to say that she knows she is changed from what she was but is not so badly done by as that other wicked daughter.

43–4   *we know . . . may be.* Presumably this is a comment on the transformation of the baker's daughter.

44   *God be at your table!* Perhaps the emphasis is on *your*: 'The benediction before eating may save you from such a fate as that of the inhospitable baker's daughter.'

45   *Conceit upon her father* – these imaginings of hers about her father – (Claudius is interrupted by Ophelia). Or perhaps this is an aside, spoken in anxiety about what Ophelia may reveal. Or it may be addressed to the Queen, a kind of warning about her son's dangerous violence.

48–67   *Tomorrow is . . . bed.* The song seems to be prompted by her imagining herself to have been disobedient to her father about associating with Hamlet.

48   *Saint Valentine's day.* 14 February, when the birds choose their mates, according to popular tradition. There were also folk-customs: the first girl seen by a man was his 'Valentine'.

49   *betime* early

53   *dupped* opened (by lifting *up* the latch)

57   *la* (a very mild substitute for an oath)

57–8   *make an end on't* finish the song (in spite of its in modesty)

59   *Gis* Jesus
      Saint Charity (the personification of the virtue)

62   *Cock* God (probably with a quibble on the popular name for the penis)

63   *tumbled me* took my virginity

72   *Come, my coach!* Perhaps she imagines herself to be a stately princess or Hamlet's queen.

73   *ladies . . . Sweet ladies.* The only female present is the Queen (unless she has attendants).

75   *Follow her . . . you.* There is no indication whom the King is addressing; but except for Gertrude (and,

possibly, unspecified attendants) Horatio is the only other character on stage, and editors usually leave the King and Queen alone for their obviously private conversation.

76–7   *It springs | All from her father's death.* Claudius does not consider – or wish Gertrude to consider – that Ophelia's love for Hamlet has anything to do with her madness.

81   *author* originator

82   *remove* removal

muddied turbulent with suspicion (stirred up, as a pool of water becomes muddy)

83   *Thick and unwholesome* (like bad blood)

whispers malicious gossip

84   *greenly* in an inexperienced way

85   *In hugger-mugger* with haste and in secrecy. The King could not allow an inquiry into the circumstances of Polonius's death, exposing Hamlet's guilt; for he knows that Hamlet has the secret of the fratricide. To the Queen he must pretend that his actions are prompted by a desire to protect Hamlet from the consequences of his crime.

87   *pictures or mere beasts* (that is, lacking a soul)

88   *as much containing* quite as important

89   *come from France.* This indicates the passage of some time since the night of Polonius's death and the morning of Hamlet's departure (IV.4).

90   *Feeds on his wonder* nurses his shocked grievance (perhaps). For *his* Q2 reads 'this', which is even more difficult; it can hardly refer to Ophelia's distraction (and in any case it is implied that Laertes does not know of it until he sees her at line 155); and the *hugger-mugger* funeral of Polonius is grammatically too far away to be referred to by 'this'.

keeps himself in clouds holds himself sullenly aloof

91   *wants* lacks

buzzers rumour-mongers

314

93-4   *Wherein necessity . . . arraign* in this gossip, as the speakers have nothing definite to go on, they are obliged to invent things and so do not scruple to spread accusations against me

95   *In ear and ear* in many ears one after the other

96   *murdering-piece* (mortar or cannon which scattered a variety of lethal small shot and pieces of metal instead of a single shot)

99   *Attend* (a call to his guards, imagined as just off stage)
  Switzers. Swiss mercenary soldiers were employed in many European courts to form a royal bodyguard (they survive in the Vatican). Their mention here implies that Claudius is usually well guarded; so Hamlet's task is not easy.

101   *overpeering of* rising above
  list boundary, barrier (perhaps the shore)

102   *Eats not the flats.* Shakespeare is doubtless thinking of the advancing tide of such places as the Essex coast and the Thames estuary, where it moves a considerable distance in a short time.
  impiteous. Probably this is another form of 'impetuous', influenced by the meaning of the word 'piteous'. But perhaps Shakespeare uses it to mean 'pitiless'.

103   *head* onset

104   *officers* household servants and guards

105   *as the world were now but to begin* as if civilized life were only now to be created (instead of having been in existence from time immemorial)

107   *The ratifiers and props of every word.* Traditional practices, inherited from earlier times, are the things which give authority and stability to society. This leisurely comment hardly suits the excited tone of the speech. Editors have often emended *word*. It may mean 'pledge, honourable undertakings according to promise', or 'oath of allegiance', or 'title of rank'. But all these interpretations are strained.

108   *Choose we! Laertes shall be king!* Claudius had intima-

ted that Hamlet was the people's favourite (IV.3.4–5). The fickleness of the *multitude* is illustrated by their support for Laertes when the opportunity is offered. The demand *Choose we!* is remarkable. It implies that the election of Claudius was an oligarchic move, not a popular one. But Laertes soon comes to terms with Claudius, and this hint of a democratic revolt is immediately forgotten.

109   *Caps* (which they wave or throw into the air)

111   *How cheerfully on the false trail they cry!* Gertrude, with unusual bitterness of language, imagines the intruders as a pack of baying hounds pursuing a false scent (*false* because the King is not guilty of Polonius's murder).

112   *counter* hunting the trail backwards (like hounds going in the direction contrary to the game). The Danes elected Claudius as their king, and now are going back on their oaths of allegiance.

        you false Danish dogs! Presumably Shakespeare took it for granted that the queen-consort of the monarch was a foreigner.

        false perfidious

117   *Keep* guard

118   *Give me my father.* Apparently Laertes does not yet know that it was Hamlet who killed Polonius.

121   *the chaste unsmirchèd brows.* See the note to III.4.43–4.

122   *true* faithful in marriage

124   *fear our* fear for my royal

125   *divinity* (alluding to the doctrine of kings as divine representatives on earth, the Lord's anointed). Claudius's brave assertion of this doctrine in order to intimidate Laertes comes ironically from one who is himself a regicide.

        hedge protect as with a rampart

126   *peep to.* Claudius's language belittles the power of treason by supposing it to peer furtively out of, or over, its hiding place or *hedge*.

127   *Acts little of his will* (and) performs little of what it intends

132   *juggled with* deceived

134   *grace* the grace of God

135   *To this point I stand* I have gone so far as this

136   *both the worlds I give to negligence* I care nothing of what happens to me in this world or the next

138   *throughly* thoroughly

139   *My will, not all the world's* nothing in the world shall stop me, except my own decision (when my desire for revenge is satisfied)

140–41 *for my means . . . little* I will employ my resources so economically that I shall be able to make them go a long way

142–3 *certainty | Of* truth about

143   *writ* specified

144   *swoopstake* (a gambling term used when a winner took the stakes of all his opponents)
       draw take from

148   *life-rendering* giving life to its young. The pelican was supposed to feed its young with the blood that flowed from self-inflicted wounds upon its breast. No one, as far as I can discover, has yet suggested that Laertes, with his arms stretched out in the form of a cross and with the blood flowing from his wounded breast, is a Christ figure. Yet the religious metaphor seems clear: Laertes's image of himself feeding his father's friends with his own blood is offensive bombast, typical of the man.

149   *Repast* feed

152   *most sensibly* with very intense feeling

153   *level* plain (like a path on the level)
       'pear appear. Q2 reads 'peare', which some editors have interpreted as 'peer'. F reads 'pierce'.

155   (stage direction) *Enter Ophelia.* Presumably Ophelia behaves in such a way as reveals immediately to Laertes that she is mad. It is not clear whether she still

carries her lute or whether she now has a bunch of flowers instead. Perhaps it is intended that she has gone to collect the flowers for her father's grave (lines 178–85). Q1 has '*Enter Ofelia as before*', but this may refer only to her madness. In her first speech in Q1 she says 'I a bin gathering of floures'.

156 *heat, dry up my brains.* Laertes is probably referring to his own fiery anger.

157 *Burn out the sense and virtue* (let scalding tears) destroy the sense and power

158 *paid with weight* paid for in full measure

159 *our scale turn the beam.* (His revenge will weigh heavier than Ophelia's madness.)
      beam horizontal bar of a balance
      rose of May. The English wild rose first flowers in May; Ophelia is in her early bloom.

163–5 *Nature is fine . . . loves* filial love is, by nature, very sensitive; and such is its sensitivity that it sends some most precious token of itself to the object of its love – in this case, Ophelia's sanity departs with her father Polonius. Laertes's language is typically strained. These three lines are not in Q2.

169 *my dove* (perhaps Laertes)

171 *move thus* persuade me as strongly as your madness does

172–3 *A-down a-down, and you call him a-down-a.* Perhaps Ophelia is thinking of Polonius as having been called *down* to his grave, and therefore says that this is a preferable refrain to *Hey non nony* . . . It is possible that the correct reading is 'You must sing "A-down a-down", and you call him a-down-a' (if you refer to Polonius as being dead).

173 *wheel.* Perhaps the spinning-wheel, to which she imagines she is singing the song; or perhaps *wheel* means 'refrain' ('how appropriate is that refrain "A-down a-down" to my song of woe!'); or perhaps it is a movement in her dance.

173-4   *the false steward, that stole his master's daughter.* This story (perhaps a ballad) is unknown. It may be that the three lines sung by Ophelia at 166-8 above are from the ballad, of which she is here giving the title or subject.

175   *This nothing's more than matter* this nonsense has more significance than any coherent sense could have

176-85   Presumably these flowers are distributed by Ophelia to be taken to her father's undecked grave. We can only guess who are the recipients, nor do we know whether the flowers are intended to be real or fantasies of Ophelia's disordered brain.

176-8   *rosemary . . . for remembrance . . . pansies . . . for thoughts.* These are probably gifts to a lover. Perhaps she imagines Laertes to be her lover, and gives these flowers to him.

177-8   *pansies . . . thoughts.* The name comes from French *pensées*.

179   *document in madness* something from which one can gain instruction in the study of madness

179-80   *thoughts and remembrance fitted.* By *thoughts* Laertes probably means 'melancholy thoughts': 'she appropriately brings together melancholy and memories (of happier things)'.

181   *fennel* suggests flattery and *columbines* ingratitude or marital infidelity. Perhaps these are given to the King.

182   *rue.* Perhaps she gives this to the Queen, as suggesting contrition, and then to herself, as suggesting sorrow.

183   *herb of grace o'Sundays.* As 'herb (of) grace' is an ordinary name for *rue*, the idea that such a pious-sounding name is appropriate for use on Sunday seems to be a mere fancy.

184   *with a difference.* The heraldic phrase refers to an alteration or addition to a coat of arms to distinguish one branch of a family from another. But it is only remotely, if at all, applied here: the rue has a different significance for each of the wearers.

184   *daisy* (the flower of dissembling; perhaps given to the Queen)

185   *violets*. These represent faithfulness in love, and Ophelia now has none to give. Perhaps in her fantasy she gives them to Hamlet – all faith in love has disappeared after the murder of Polonius.

185–6   *They say 'a made a good end.* If she is thinking of Polonius, the statement is strikingly untrue; he was killed suddenly, with no opportunity for contrition and for receiving the sacraments.

187   *For bonny sweet Robin . . . joy.* The words of this song, probably relating to Robin Hood, are lost; but the tune, which was exceptionally popular, survives.

188   *Thought* gloomy thought
passion suffering
hell itself (presumably 'torment of soul')

189   *favour* beauty

196   *flaxen was his poll* his head was pale like flax

198   *cast away moan* are wasting our time in grieving

201   *Do you see this? O God!* Q2 reads 'Doe you this ô God'. F reads 'Do you see this, you Gods?' F's 'Gods' is unsuitable in a Christian play, especially immediately after Ophelia's exit-line; but its *see* is probably right. There is no punctuation in Q2 to help us decide whether Laertes, in an expostulatory tone, is asking God to observe what is going on here on earth ('Do you see this, O God?') or whether he is making two broken-hearted utterances, first a general appeal and then an anguished interjection. On the whole the second seems more likely. Perhaps *you* refers to the King, who responds.

202   *commune with your grief* have your grief in common with you
commune (accented on the first syllable)

204   *whom* whichever among

206   *collateral hand* indirect agency

207   *touched* infected with guilt (of the murder of Polonius)

209   *in satisfaction* as recompense

210   *lend your patience to us* be patient for a while at my request

213   *His means of death* the manner of Polonius's death
      obscure (accented on the first syllable)

214   *trophy, sword . . . hatchment*. Memorial emblems, such as the knightly sword and the coat of arms, accompanied the coffin in the funeral procession. The *hatchment* (or 'achievement') was an escutcheon blazoning the arms of the dead person. Many of these old painted escutcheons still hang in churches in England.

215   *ostentation* ceremony

217   *That* so that
      call't in question demand an explanation of it

218   *where th'offence is, let the great axe fall*. The Queen can hardly fail to hear this threat to Hamlet. But Claudius is doubtless thinking of his secret instructions to the King of England *not to stay the grinding of the axe* but Hamlet's *head should be struck off* (V.2.24–5). He comes to terms with Laertes for his own safety. Not until IV.7.43 does the news come that Hamlet, contrary to expectations, is returning to Elsinore; and then Claudius sees the advantages of allying himself with Laertes against Hamlet.

IV.6 6   *greeted* addressed in a letter

      10   *th'ambassador*. The sailor does not name Hamlet, presumably as a disguise. He can hardly be unaware of his identity.

      14   *overlooked* looked over
          means (of access)

      16   *appointment* equipment

      17   *put on a compelled valour* decided to assume an appearance of courage, because we had no alternative

      20   *of mercy* merciful. There seems to be a slight allusion

to the thieves crucified with Christ, as is supported by the phraseology of *they knew what they did*.

20–21   *knew what they did* (were aware that Hamlet was a prince, who would have influence to get them pardoned if they treated him well)

22   *repair* come

25   *much too light for the bore of the matter* weak in comparison with the importance of the matter, like a small projectile in a gun with a large *bore*

26   *will bring thee where I am.* This may suggest that Hamlet is in hiding, but the idea is not developed.

31   *I will give you way for these your letters.* Compare IV.7.39–41.

IV.7   This scene continues the talk between the King and Laertes which was broken off at the end of IV.5. In the interval, the King has been able to give Laertes an account (which the audience does not need) of Hamlet's misdeeds.

1   *my acquittance seal* confirm my acquittal (as guiltless of the misdeeds you had attributed to me)

3   *with a knowing ear.* (Laertes is an intelligent listener, says the ingratiating King.)

6   *feats* deeds

7   *capital* punishable by death

8   *your safety* your care for your own safety
greatness. This word is omitted in F, probably in order to reduce the line to ten syllables.
wisdom political prudence

9   *mainly* strongly
two special reasons. The King omits the really powerful reason: if he were to take public proceedings against Hamlet for the murder of Polonius, Hamlet would be likely to reveal the fratricide. The King is confident in dealing with Laertes because he expects shortly to receive from England the news of Hamlet's death.

10   *unsinewed* without strength

13   *My virtue or my plague, be it either which* whether it is a good side of my character or a serious misfortune (that I have these feelings contrary to my self-interest)

14   *conjunctive* closely united (also an astronomical term, and so leading to the image in the next line)

15   *the star moves not but in his sphere.* In astronomy before Copernicus, the earth, at the centre of the universe, was believed to be surrounded by a series of hollow transparent concentric spheres. On the surface of each a planet was fixed. The sphere revolved around the earth and carried the planet with it.

16   *I could not but by her* (because she is, as it were, my sphere, and with her motion I move) I could not live without her

17   *count* trial

18   *general gender* common people

20   *Work* act
     the spring that turneth wood to stone. Several of these lime-laden springs, able to 'petrify' (with a limestone deposit) objects placed in them, were known in Shakespeare's time.

21   *Convert his gyves to graces* would make the fetters he wore as a prisoner seem to be emblems of his personal honour

22   *Too slightly timbered for* too light in weight to be effective in
     loud (suggesting popular clamour on Hamlet's behalf)

23   *reverted* returned

26   *desperate terms* a condition of despair

27   *if praises may go back again* if one may praise what has been and is now no more

28   *Stood challenger . . . of all the age* was able to challenge all competitors in the world nowadays
     on mount conspicuously, for all to see. An alternative reading is 'challenger-on-mount' ('a challenger mounted and ready in the lists'), but this usage is difficult to parallel.

30   *Break not your sleeps for that.* Laertes need not worry about taking vengeance for his father's murder, for the King has already arranged for Hamlet's death. He is, up to this point, only concerned with pacifying Laertes, not with arousing him to revenge.

32   *let our beard be shook with danger* allow such insulting behaviour to come close to me

33   *You shortly shall hear more.* Claudius has in mind the news he expects of Hamlet's execution in England. But soon quite different news arrives.

37   *This to the Queen.* No more is heard of this letter.

40   *Claudio* (an odd name for Shakespeare to use, as the King's name is Claudius)

41   *you shall hear them.* The King is showing off his confidence in Laertes, and his openness: he will read the letter without previously examining its contents.

43   *naked* (without resources, or unarmed, rather than without clothes)

44   *Tomorrow.* The time-scheme of the play scarcely allows this. Some interval of time is assumed between the end of this scene and V.1, allowing for the inquest on Ophelia. See the headnote to V.1.

46   *more strange* (than *sudden*)

48   *What should this mean?* The King receives the news with consternation, as it shows that his English plot has failed. But Laertes is delighted.
      all the rest (Rosencrantz, Guildenstern, and others in the party for England)

49   *abuse* deception

50   *character* handwriting

51   *alone.* Perhaps Hamlet is avoiding suspicion of having raised support for himself.

52   *devise me* explain it for me. The King is surprised, but is thinking rapidly, and by line 58 has made up his mind about his next move.

53   *lost in* perplexed at

56   *didest.* Q2 has 'didst', possibly a misreading of 'diest'.

it (Hamlet's return, rather than Laertes's impulse to revenge)

57 *how should it be so? How otherwise?* The King is almost incredulous of Hamlet's return, yet the evidence of the letter is strong.

58 *Will you be ruled by me?* The King has recovered his equilibrium. Now he must stir Laertes to revenge against Hamlet.

59 *So you will not* provided that you do not

60 *thine own peace* (peace of mind achieved by taking full vengeance, not the 'reconciliation' rejected by Laertes in the previous line)

61 *As checking at* because he has turned aside from (like a hawk swerving aside from its prey and pursuing some inferior object)
    that if

63 *ripe in my device* matured in my invention

66 *uncharge the practice* be unable to make any accusation as a consequence of our plot (or 'not suspect a plot')

69 *organ* agent

72 *Your sum of parts* all your talents put together

75 *siege* rank

76 *A very riband in the cap of youth* a typical accomplishment of a young man, like a ribbon worn as an ornament in his hat

77 *needful* (it being a necessary accomplishment for a man to defend himself with his sword)
    no less becomes is no less suited by

78 *livery* garments

79 *his sables and his weeds* its (dark) fur-lined garments

80 *Importing health* indicating a care for health (or perhaps *health* means 'prosperity' in general: 'giving an impression of being well-to-do')

81 *Normandy.* As the play is vaguely set in late Anglo-Saxon times, the introduction of a Norman is appropriate enough.

83 *can well* are very skilful

84   *in't* (in his horsemanship)

86   *As had he* as if he had

86-7   *incorpsed and demi-natured | With the . . . beast* grown to
        have one body with the horse, and so half-man and
        half-beast. Shakespeare is doubtless thinking of the
        centaurs.

87   *topped my thought* surpassed my estimate

88-9   *I, in forgery of shapes and tricks, | Come short of what he
        did* whatever I am able to describe as figures and tricks
        (in managing a horse), he exceeded in actual execution

91   *Lamord.* F reads 'Lamound', which editors often spell
        as 'Lamond'. If *Lamord* is accurate, it is curiously
        ominous (*mort*, 'death'), especially when accompanied
        by the oath *Upon my life*.

92-3   *brooch . . . gem* ornament . . . jewel

94   *made confession of you* felt compelled, although he was a
        Frenchman, to acknowledge the truth about you

95   *masterly report* report of your masterly skill

96   *For art and exercise in your defence* in respect of your
        knowledge and skilful practice in the use of your sword

99   *one could match you* an equal opponent could be found
        for you
        scrimers (pronounced to rhyme with 'rhymers') fencers

100   *motion* attack (as distinct from *guard*, 'parrying')

101-4   *this report . . . with you.* There is no other mention in
        the play of Hamlet's envy of Laertes. It sounds like a
        ruse of Hamlet, giving himself an excuse for improving
        his swordsmanship. Or perhaps the actor can convey
        that the whole thing is an invention of the King's.
        Compare *Since he went into France I have been in con-
        tinual practice* (V.2.204-5).

104   *sudden* immediate
        play fence
        you. Grammatically we might have expected 'him'
        (which is, in fact, the F reading).

109-22 This discourse of the King on the effects of time upon will-power is an interesting and ironical comment on Hamlet's situation. Hamlet had given his view of the matter at IV.4.32–66, and had acknowledged to the Ghost that he, *lapsed in time and passion, lets go by | The important acting of your dread command* (III.4.108–9). Claudius seems, moreover, to be repeating the assertion of the Player-King in III.2.198–225, that *Purpose is but the slave to memory.*

110   *love is begun by time* circumstances give rise to love (and they change)

111   *in passages of proof* by definite incidents that prove the truth of what I am saying

112   *qualifies* moderates

114   *snuff.* The image is that of a candle; the *snuff* is the charred part of the candle wick, which, if neglected, spoils and eventually puts out the flame.

115   *is at a like goodness still* remains at the same constant level of goodness

116   *pleurisy* excess. The word is spelt 'plurisy' in the early texts, by association with Latin *plus*, 'more', and not with Greek *pleura*, 'rib', from which is derived modern 'pleurisy', inflammation of the pleura (coverings of the lungs).

117   *his* its

117–18   *That we would do | We should do when we would* when we want to do something, we should do it immediately we know we want to do it

119   *abatements* diminutions of energy

120   *As there are tongues, are hands, are accidents* as the ways in which we are influenced by what people say, and by what they help us to do or restrain us from doing, and by the mere chances of life

121–2   *this 'should' is like a spendthrift sigh, | That hurts by easing* a sigh is a relief to our feelings, though it also harms us (alluding to the belief that with every sigh a drop of blood was lost); likewise, when we say 'I know what I ought to do', it may ease the conscience but the self-reproach also weakens our will-power. (This is the probable explanation of a difficult passage.)

122 *the quick o'th'ulcer* (that is, the main point)

124-5 *in deed . . . More than in words* (contrasting with Hamlet)

125 *cut his throat i'th'church.* Laertes's words contrast strongly with Hamlet's unwillingness to kill the King while he was at his prayers (III.3.73-96).

126 *No place . . . should murder sanctuarize* for a murderer (such as Hamlet) there should be no rights of sanctuary; so there would be no objection to your killing him anywhere, even in church

127 *Revenge should have no bounds.* This is Hamlet's doctrine, expounded by him at III.3.73-96.

128 *keep close within your chamber.* Presumably the King is guarding against the possibility that Hamlet might win Laertes over to his side.

130 *We'll put on those shall praise* I will arrange that some persons shall praise

132 *fine* conclusion

133 *remiss* careless (as not expecting any treachery)

134 *Most generous, and free from all contriving.* Claudius is not speaking the truth, for he knows that Hamlet has already engaged in a complicated contrivance, *The Mousetrap.*

135 *foils* (blunt-edged swords with buttons on the point for use in fencing)

136 *a little shuffling* some little trick of substitution

137 *unbated* without a button on the point
in a pass of practice. This probably means 'in making a treacherous thrust at him', rather than 'while playing a practice-bout' or than 'while making a pass in which you are well practised'. But perhaps the King is deliberately ambiguous.

139-47 Part of the treacherous plan comes from Laertes; in Q1 the proposal to poison the sword comes from the

King himself. This may represent what happened in a performance earlier than the Q2 text, the change being intended to indicate the deterioration of Laertes under the King's influence. At V.2.307–14 Laertes does not confess that the envenoming of the sword was his own idea.

140 *unction* ointment

of a mountebank from a quack doctor (or itinerant drug-seller)

142 *cataplasm* poultice

143–4 *Collected . . . Under the moon.* It was believed that herbs were especially efficacious when gathered by moonlight (see III.2.266). But perhaps *Under the moon* goes with *have virtue* and merely means 'anywhere on earth'.

143 *simples* medicinal herbs

146 *gall* graze

148–9 *Weigh what convenience both of time and means | May fit us to our shape* consider carefully what arrangements of time and of opportunity may suit us in assuming the roles we have decided to act

149 *shape* role

150 *drift* intention, plan

look through become visible

151 *assayed* attempted

152 *back* support

hold stand firm

153 *blast in proof* (like a gun exploding when it is tested by being fired)

154 *cunnings* respective skills in fencing

157 *As* and therefore

158 *preferred* proffered. This seems to be the meaning of Q2's reading, 'prefard'. But F reads 'prepar'd', which may well be right.

159 *chalice* (a special ceremonial cup)

nonce occasion

160 *stuck* thrust

329

161   *may hold there* will be achieved by that

161-2 *But stay, what noise? | How, sweet Queen!* Q2 has only
       the first sentence, F only the second. One or other may
       be an accidental omission. It seems best to include both
       in the text; a director can choose either or both.

165   *O, where?* Presumably these words represent a numbed
       reaction to the deeply felt calamity. Or Laertes may
       speak as if about to run to her.

166   *willow* (the emblem of forsaken love, appropriately)
       askant sideways, leaning over. F has 'aslant', a more
       usual word.

167   *shows his hoar leaves in the glassy stream.* The under-
       side of the willow leaf is greyish, and this, not the
       green upper side, would be reflected in the *glassy stream*
       underneath.

168   *Therewith* (of the willow). F reads 'There with', and
       alters *make* to 'come'.
       fantastic extravagant

169   *crowflowers* buttercups
       long purples purple orchises

170   *liberal* free-spoken
       grosser more obscene

171   *cold maids* (distinguished from *liberal shepherds*; the
       maidens are chaste and therefore ignore obscene names
       for flowers)
       dead-men's-fingers (so named from the pale tuber-like
       roots of some kinds of orchids)

172-3 *There ... | Clambering to hang.* As one forsaken in love,
       Ophelia tries to hang her garland on a willow tree. Or
       perhaps she imagines herself to be decorating her
       father's monument.

172   *crownet weeds* garlands made of weeds

173   *an envious sliver broke.* There is no word here of
       Ophelia's death's being suicide, though the strong
       suspicion of this is voiced in the next scene (V.1.1–25
       and 223–34).
       envious malicious

sliver branch

175   *clothes.* Ophelia is imagined as wearing the elaborate farthingale of an Elizabethan court lady.

177   *tunes.* Q2 has 'laudes', a strange word in this context, but just possible, referring to parts of the Psalms sung at the service of Lauds. The F reading 'tunes' is supported by Q1, 'Chaunting olde sundry tunes'.

178   *incapable of* unable to comprehend

179–80   *indued* | *Unto that element* having the qualities appropriate for living in the water

182   *lay* song

187   *our trick* the way of us men

187–8   *Nature her custom holds,* | *Let shame say what it will* Nature follows her usual course, even though our shame (at being unmanly) rebukes us

188–9   *When these are gone,* | *The woman will be out* after my tears are over, the woman-like side of my human nature will cease to appear

191   *this folly* these foolish tears

       drowns. So Q2; F reads 'doubts', which could be interpreted as 'douts' (puts out).

192   *calm his rage* (not a true statement of what has happened)

V.1   It seems that this remarkable scene was an afterthought. V.2 would follow naturally upon IV.7, where we are told (line 44) that Hamlet will arrive at the court *Tomorrow*. V.2 opens with Hamlet's narration to Horatio of what had happened to bring him back to Elsinore.

       (stage direction) *Enter two Clowns.* This is the direction in Q2 and F. But Q1 has '*enter Clowne and an other*'. This probably indicates the principal comic actor and his 'feed', who appear as rustics ('clowns'). The First Clown plays the part of a gravedigger: he is addressed as *Goodman Delver* (line 14) and called a *sexton* (lines

88 and 160) and *grave-maker* (line 140). It would be wrong to regard the Second Clown as another; for two men cannot easily dig the same grave.

1   *in Christian burial* with the authorized funeral services of the Church and in consecrated ground (as was not permitted to suicides)

2   *salvation.* He presumably should say 'damnation', but he has muddled notions of her presumptuousness in dying and going to heaven before her due time.

4   *straight* straightaway

4–22   *The crowner . . . law.* The Clowns give a burlesque of the arguments in the coroner's court over Ophelia's death.

4   *crowner* coroner. This colloquial form occurs in common Elizabethan usage, and not only in uneducated speech.
    sat on her conducted an inquest into the cause of her death

4–5   *finds it* has given his verdict that the cause of her death does not prohibit

8   *'tis found so* this verdict has been given by the coroner

9   *se offendendo.* He means '*se defendendo*' ('in self-defence'), the phrase used in a plea of justifiable homicide. But it is, of course, comically misapplied in a case of suicide. Q2's reading, 'so offended', may be a further comic corruption of the phrase, rather than a misprint.

11   *branches* divisions of an argument. Shakespeare is doubtless making fun of the over-systematic distinctions and quibbles of lawyers.

12   *Argal.* The Clown is attempting the Latin *ergo*, 'therefore'.

14   *Goodman* (a polite form of address to a working-man)
    Delver gravedigger

17   *will he nill he* willy-nilly

22   *crowner's quest law* (that is, according to the formalities governing a coroner's inquest (*quest*))

26   *there thou sayst* what you say is true

27–9   *great folk . . . even-Christian.* This looks forward to the

Priest's remarks at lines 223–34, including the revealing information that *great command o'ersways the order*.

27   *countenance* social and legal privilege

28–9   *even-Christian* ordinary fellow-Christians (who are all equal, whatever their social rank, in the sight of God)

31   *hold up* continue

33   *arms* (both 'a coat of arms' and 'arms to hold a spade with')

34   *none* (no coat of arms)

36   *the Scripture* (Genesis 2.15 and 3.19)

37   *Could he dig without arms?* This mocks the absurd claims of writers on heraldry about the antiquity of their branch of knowledge

39   *confess thyself* – (to be a fool. Or perhaps this is the first half of the proverb 'Confess yourself and be hanged', which may prompt the Second Clown to guess *gallows-maker* (line 43) as the answer to the riddle.)

40   *Go to!* (an interjection of impatience: 'come on!')

43   *frame* (the 'framework' of the gallows)

52   *unyoke* (after this great effort, you can have your yoke taken off, like a beast of burden whose day's task is done, and can give your brain a rest)

55   *Mass* by the mass

60   *stoup* (pronounced like 'stoop'; a flagon containing two quarts)

61–119   *In youth . . . meet.* The Clown sings three garbled stanzas of a well-known poem attributed to Thomas Lord Vaux (1510–56), first printed in the book of *Songs and Sonnets* (by the Earl of Surrey and others) published by Tottel in 1557, with the title 'The Aged Lover Renounceth Love', and printed separately as a ballad in 1563.

63   *O . . . a* (presumably grunts made by the digger at his labours rather than interpolated vowels in the song)
        behove (that is, 'behoof') benefit, advantage

65   *feeling of his business* response to the sombre nature of his job

333

67-8   *in him a property of easiness* natural for him to carry out his distressing task without any painful sensations

70   *hath the daintier sense* is more fastidious (than the hard hand of a working man)

74   *such* (as I was in my youth)

76   *jowls* thrusts or knocks forcibly (presumably with a play upon *jawbone*)

77   *Cain's jawbone, that did* the jawbone used by Cain, who committed. According to legend, he used an ass's jawbone to murder his brother Abel. Hamlet's mind reverts to fratricide, as does the King's (III.3.37-8).

78   *politician.* This word generally had a derogatory meaning: 'schemer'.
      this ass (the gravedigger)
      o'erreaches gets the better of (perhaps with a pun on the sense 'reach over')

79   *circumvent* outwit

83-4   *praised my Lord Such-a-one's horse when 'a meant to beg it.* Shakespeare gives an instance of this kind of deviousness in *Timon of Athens*, I.2.210-16.

87   *my Lady Worm's* it belongs to my Lady Worm

87-8   *chopless* without the lower jaw

88   *mazzard* skull (the upper part)

89   *revolution* reversal of fortune brought about by time

89-90   *trick to see* knack of seeing

90   *cost no more the breeding but* cost so little to raise that men are willing

91   *loggats* (a game played by throwing pear-shaped pieces of wood – *loggats* – at wooden pins stuck in the ground)
      Mine (my own *bones*)

93   *For and* (an emphatic form) and

97   *quiddities* subtleties
      quillets small distinctions

98   *tenures* (modes of holding property from a superior owner, or periods of time during which it may be so held)

100   *sconce* head

101   *action of battery* suing for physical violence upon himself

102   *statutes* (legal documents acknowledging debts, by which creditors acquired rights over the debtors' lands and goods)

102-3 *recognizances* (certain kinds of statutes)

103   *fines* (legal documents by which entailed property was changed into freehold possession)
      double vouchers (persons (generally two) who played their part in the legal devices of *recoveries*)
      recoveries (the process including *fines*)

104   *fine of his fines* end of his *fines* (as in line 103). In this sentence Hamlet achieves four puns on the word *fine*.
      recovery successful attainment

106   *vouch him . . . of* guarantee his legal title to

107-8 *the length and breadth of a pair of indentures.* (Two of his legal documents would together be of the same size as his grave.)

108   *indentures* joint agreements. The document was cut or torn into two parts so that the exact fitting together of the irregularly indented edges was a proof of genuineness. Perhaps Hamlet is punning, referring to the two teeth-bearing jaws.

108-10 *The very conveyances . . . more* the documents themselves, symbols of ownership, are too bulky to go into this grave (or coffin), and must the owner of all these lands occupy no more space

108   *conveyances* (documents legalizing the transfer of ownership of property)

109   *box* (grave, or coffin, compared to the box in which a lawyer keeps his documents)
      inheritor owner

114   *sheep and calves* foolish fellows

114-15 *assurance* security (with a pun on the legal sense, 'documentary conveyance of property')

115   *in that* (by trusting to legal documents, which are only made of parchment)

115–16 *Whose grave's this.* Horatio, as well as Hamlet, is ignorant of Ophelia's death, having left the court at the end of IV.6.

120 *thou liest.* Hamlet jestingly uses the formula of insult among gentlemen.

126 *a quick lie* a lie that will return from me to you quickly

126–7 *'Twill away again from me to you* (the Clown 'gives him the lie' back again)

135 *absolute* positively precise (in language)

135–6 *by the card* precisely, as if according to the directions given on a seaman's chart or on his compass (divided into thirty-two points)

136 *equivocation* deliberate use of ambiguity in words. It was notorious in Shakespeare's time as a device, attributed to the Roman Catholics, for taking oaths with mental reservations and double meanings.

137 *the age* our contemporaries of all classes (both *peasant* and *courtier*)

138 *picked* over-refined

138–9 *the toe of the peasant comes so near the heel of the courtier* (a curious echo of the Queen's image at IV.7.163: *One woe doth tread upon another's heel*)

139 *kibe* chilbain

145 *that very day that young Hamlet was born.* There seems to be a curious symbolism in the gravedigger's having entered upon his occupation at the same time as Hamlet entered into being, as if preparation for death began from the day of birth.

158 *Upon what ground?* from what cause? (But the Clown chooses to take *ground* literally.)

160 *thirty years.* This seems conclusive that at this point Shakespeare intended Hamlet to be aged thirty. See the notes to I.1.171 and lines 170–71 below.

163 *pocky corses nowadays.* The ravages of the 'great pox' (venereal diseases) were serious in Elizabethan England.

164 *hold* last out

169   *sore* (an intensifying epithet: 'terrible')

170   *lien* (an old form) lain

170–71 *three-and-twenty years.* Q1 has a passage which combines lines 139–46 and 170–71 and gives about twelve years since Yorick's death, so that in Q1 Hamlet could be in his late teens.

177   *Rhenish.* See the note to I.4.10.

178   *Yorick.* This (like 'Osrick' in V.2) is a Scandinavian-sounding name, suggesting Jörg (George) and Eric.

182   *fancy* imagination

183–9 *He hath . . . grinning.* This passage is a wonderful glimpse of the privileged position of the jester in a great Elizabethan household.

189   *grinning* (as a skull appears to be)

        chop-fallen with the lower jaw hanging down (as if miserable)

189–90 *get you to my lady's table.* There were engravings of Death (represented by a skeleton) coming into a young lady's bedchamber while she sits at her toilet-table. For *table* F reads 'Chamber', which may be right; *table* could be due to a repetition from line 188.

190–91 *paint an inch thick* (the frequent hostility to face-painting; compare III.1.51 and 143–5)

191   *favour* facial appearance

194   *Alexander* (the Great)

202   *too curiously* with unreasonably minute attention

203   *follow him* (in imagination)

204   *with modesty* moderately and reasonably (that is, not *too curiously*, which would make the idea improbable)

207   *loam* (mortar or plaster made of clay and straw)

209–12 *Imperious Caesar . . . winter's flaw.* Perhaps this impromptu verse-epigram (a characteristic specimen of its kind) serves, like the love poem to Ophelia (II.2.115–18), to identify Hamlet as a 'university wit'.

209   *Imperious* imperial

211   *earth* (piece of earth, that is, Caesar's remains)

212   *expel the winter's flaw* keep out a sudden gust of winter wind

215   *maimèd* incomplete

217   *Fordo* undo, destroy
        it its
        some estate rather high social station

218   *Couch we* let us lie down and so be concealed

219   *What ceremony else?* Laertes irritably repeats his
        question, following an embarrassed or indignant silence
        by the Priest.

222   PRIEST. For his two speeches Q2 has the heading
        '*Doct.*'. This presumably means 'Doctor of Divinity'
        and would point to a Protestant rather than a Catholic
        cleric. But Laertes calls him a *priest* at line 236.
        enlarged extended

223   *warranty* authorization
        doubtful (owing to the suspicion of suicide. There was
        nothing, however, in the Queen's description of
        Ophelia's death (IV.7.166–83) to suggest that it was
        suicide; and we are told at V.1.4–5 that the coroner
        gave his judgement that it was to be *Christian burial*.)

224   *great* (that is, of the King)
        order regulations prescribed by the ecclesiastical
        authorities

226   *For* instead of

227   *Shards* broken pieces of pots

228   *crants* (an unusual and foreign word, apparently
        Germanic, whose use may be a bit of local colour)
        garlands

229   *strewments* flowers strewn on the grave or coffin
        bringing home. Ophelia's funeral has followed the usual
        custom of being made to resemble a wedding festival.
        Instead of being taken to her husband's house, she is
        brought to her 'last home'.

230   *Of* with
        burial burial service

234   *peace-parted souls* those who die piously in peace ('Lord,
        now lettest thou thy servant depart in peace', Luke
        2.29)

338

238   *howling* (as a damned soul in hell)

244   *Whose wicked deed* (the killing of Polonius, to which alone Laertes seems to attribute Ophelia's loss of reason)

        ingenious sense naturally quick (or perhaps 'noble') powers of mind

246   *caught her . . . in mine arms.* This implies an open coffin.

249   *Pelion* (a mountain in Thessaly; presumably it is *old* because of its reputation in ancient literature)

250   *blue* (presumably like a distant mountain)

252   *Conjures* puts a magic spell upon

        wandering stars planets (contrasted with the 'fixed stars')

        stand stand still

253   *wonder-wounded* awe-struck

        This is I. Presumably he throws off his cloak or *sea-gown* (V.2.13).

254   *Hamlet the Dane* (a defiant way of describing himself, asserting his princely rank or his claim to the throne)

        The devil take thy soul! Perhaps with this Laertes leaps out of the grave and flies at Hamlet. Before it, Q1 has the direction '*Hamlet leapes in after Leartes*', but this turns Hamlet into the physical aggressor, though the text (lines 256 and 259) indicates otherwise.

257   *splenitive* of an angry temperament. In sixteenth-century physiology the spleen was regarded as one of the seats of emotion, particularly of choler.

259   *Which let thy wisdom fear* which your good sense should cause you to fear

263   *wag* (not a ludicrous word) move. The movement of the eyelids is among the last visible ones to cease in a human being.

265   *I loved Ophelia.* Hamlet is shown briefly as having lost most of his self-consciousness and as being moved by serious feelings. Or perhaps it is another self-dramatization?

265   *Forty* (its use as an indefinitely large number seems to derive from its frequent biblical use)

266   *quantity* (comparatively small quantity)

269   *forbear him* refrain from conflicting with him (Hamlet)

271   *Woo't* wouldst thou

272   *eisel* vinegar. This is the common emendation of the word 'Esill' in Q2 and '*Esile*' (italicized, as if the printer thought it might be a proper name or a foreign word) in F. The difficulty is that something more violently absurd may be expected than the notion of eagerly drinking vinegar. This has prompted such conjectures as 'Nilus' (the river Nile – which might have suggested *Eat a crocodile*), 'Yssel' in Flanders, 'Weissel' (Vistula), which flows into the Baltic, and others.

        crocodile (regarded as a venomous beast; perhaps alluding also to its hypocritical trick of counterfeiting tears)

275   *quick* alive

278   *burning zone* (part of the sky representing the path of the sun between the tropics of Cancer and Capricorn)

279   *Make Ossa like a wart.* Hamlet derides Laertes's mention of *Pelion* (line 249) by naming the other mountain of Thessaly, always associated with Pelion: when the giants made war upon the gods of Olympus they tried to scale heaven by piling Pelion upon Ossa.

280   *mere* pure

282   *Anon* soon afterwards

        dove (symbol of peace and quiet)

283   *golden couplets.* The newly hatched two chicks of a dove are covered with a yellow down.

        disclosed hatched

285   *use* treat

288   *cat . . . dog.* Presumably Hamlet is comparing Laertes to a cat for his whining lamentation and to a dog for his snarling. But perhaps *dog will have his day* refers to Hamlet: 'My turn will come soon'.

290 *Strengthen your patience in our last night's speech* let thoughts of our conversation last night enable you to preserve your patience (under such provocation by Hamlet)

291 *the present push* an immediate test

293-5 *This grave shall . . . be.* The King speaks these lines publicly, but they have an additional meaning for Laertes, as continuing lines 290-91: Hamlet will soon be in his grave, too, and then we can rest safe; but meanwhile, looking forward to the duel, we can remain patient.

293 *living monument* enduring memorial (but the King knows that Laertes will take his remark ironically)

294 *An hour of quiet shortly shall we see.* The King expects that Hamlet's death, which he has plotted, will solve his anxieties. But he himself will soon find *quiet* in death.

V.2. 1 *this.* Possibly the letter to England given to Hamlet, *the other* being the *commission* given to Rosencrantz and Guildenstern (line 26); the contrast shows the King's treachery.

4 *fighting* agitation

5-6 *Methought I lay | Worse than the mutines in the bilboes* it seemed to me that I felt more uncomfortable in my bed than do mutineers in their iron fetters

6 *Rashly . . . .* After five lines of interpolation, the sentence is resumed, not quite logically, at line 12: *Up from my cabin.*

7 *praised be rashness.* The praise of impetuous conduct and the confidence in divine providence are ill connected logically. Hamlet speaks eloquently, but without philosophical competence, of the old dilemma of human action and reliance on the will of God. At V.1.257 he boasted *I am not splenitive and rash.*

8 *indiscretion* lack of judgement

9   *pall* fail
       learn teach

10–11   *There's a divinity . . . will.* This is the first evidence of Hamlet's new piety or Christian patience, preparing us for lines 213–18. Perhaps Shakespeare is interesting the audience by showing, after the excited reasoning of IV.4.32–66, the meditative force of V.1.65–212, and the anxieties of V.1.250–88, a new kind of irresponsibility in Hamlet.

11   *Rough-hew* (like a piece of timber)

13   *sea-gown* (described in the 1611 dictionary of Cotgrave as 'a coarse, high-collared, and short-sleeved gown, reaching down to the mid-leg')
       scarfed about me wrapped around me like a sash. He had not dressed properly, but merely put his gown around him without using the sleeves.

14   *them* (Rosencrantz and Guildenstern)

15   *Fingered* stole
       in fine finally

18   *grand* (sarcastic)
       commission (the *commission* of III.3.3 and the *letters sealed* of III.4.203. See the note to IV.3.58.)

20   *Larded* garnished
       many several a variety of different

21   *Importing* deeply concerned with

22   *bugs and goblins* terrors and dangers (spoken contemptuously, for Hamlet believes them to be imaginary)
       bugs (literally) bogies, bugbears
       in my life if I am allowed to live (or perhaps 'in my daily behaviour')

23   *supervise* viewing
       no leisure bated without any delay being permitted

24   *stay* wait for

26   *Here's the commission.* Presumably he hands it to Horatio.

29   *be-netted* ensnared

30   *Or* before

make a prologue to my brains go through the initial
steps of submitting the problem to my intelligence (as
often with Hamlet, a theatrical metaphor)

31   *They* (his *brains*, without his conscious will)

32   *fair* (in a clear hand, like a professional scrivener)

33   *statists* men involved in business of state

34   *A baseness to write fair* evidence of ungentlemanly
birth to have a clear handwriting, like a professional

36   *yeoman's service* (the kind of admirably loyal and
reliable military service which an English yeoman
rendered to his feudal lord)

37   *effect* import

38   *conjuration* appeal or injunction (as from a person able
to rely upon some special authority)

40   *As* so that (whereas the *As* in line 39 means 'because')
like the palm might flourish. Hamlet is mocking the
high-flown style of diplomatic correspondence, which
borrowed biblical phrases: 'The righteous shall flourish
like the palm tree', Psalm 92.12.

41   *wheaten garland* (emblematic of *peace*)

42   *comma*. This, the reading of both Q2 and F, is difficult.
Perhaps it is used in the sense 'a short part of a sentence'. But the word may be wrong. The suggested
emendations ('commere', 'cement', 'column', 'concord',
'calm', 'compact', etc.) are unsatisfactory.
amities. Perhaps Hamlet is ironical; for England's
cicatrice looks raw and red | After the Danish sword
(IV.3.62–3), and Shakespeare could hardly have been
ignorant of the terrible conflicts between the Anglo-
Saxons and the Danes.

43   *as's of great charge*. Hamlet characteristically puns on
'asses bearing heavy burdens'.

44   *That* (follows *conjuration*, line 38)

46   *those bearers* (Rosencrantz and Guildenstern)

47   *shriving time* (a period of time for confession and
absolution before execution)

48   *ordinant* in control (compare lines 10–11)

49   *signet* seal

50   *model* replica

      that Danish seal (probably pointing to the seal on the commission now in Horatio's hand). Hamlet seems to be saying that, by good luck, he had his father's seal, and, equally luckily, the Danish seal of state of the new monarch was not (as one would expect) different from that of his predecessor.

52   *Subscribed it* (by forging King Claudius's signature)
      impression (of the seal)

53   *changeling* (like a human child taken by the fairies and replaced by one of their own)

53-4 *the next day | Was our sea-fight* .... Shakespeare makes it clear that Hamlet's substitution of the *commission* to be carried to England had nothing to do with his accidental return to Denmark.

54   *our sea-fight.* This is described in IV.6.15 as *Ere we were two days old at sea.* So the substitution of the commission took place during the first night aboard ship.

56   *to't* to their death

57   *did make love to this employment* were willing and active collaborators in Claudius's schemes against me

58   *defeat* destruction

59   *insinuation* intrusive intervention

61   *pass* thrust (of the rapier)
      fell incensèd points fiercely angered sword-points

62   *mighty opposites* (Hamlet and Claudius)

63   *Does it not . . . stand me now upon* is it not now my duty

66   *angle* fishing-hook
      my proper life my very life

67   *cozenage* cheating by inspiring confidence in one's victim
      is't not perfect conscience may I not with a clear conscience

68   *quit* pay back
      be damned act sinfully

69   *canker* cancer, ulcer

nature (human nature)

69–70   *come | In* grow into

74   *a man's life's no more than to say 'one'.* The probable meaning is that the *short* time will be enough: he needs only a single successful thrust of his rapier into Claudius to end his life (*one* is the swordsman's claim to have hit is opponent's body). But perhaps it is another of Hamlet's newly acquired fatalistic generalizations, like *There's a divinity* . . . (line 10) and *The readiness is all* . . . (line 216), and so refers to his own life, not the King's.

78   *favours* friendship

79   *bravery* bravado

80   (stage direction) *Osrick.* The first form of the name in Q2 is '*Ostricke*', and this is used for his speech headings in the duel scene. In view of the many references to birds in this episode, it is tempting to suppose that 'Ostrick' was Shakespeare's original intention. But at lines 343–4 Q2 has '*Osrick*', and F has '*Osricke*' ('*Osr.*') throughout. Q1 has '*Enter a Bragart Gentleman*', which indicates how he appeared on the stage. Hamlet's easy wit in ragging poor Osrick, showing a mind free from vacillation and anxiety, confirms the change of mood revealed in the earlier part of the scene.

83   *waterfly* (vain and meddlesome creature)

85   *state* (of soul)

    more gracious happier (as being in a state of grace)

87   *Let a beast be lord of beasts, and* if a man, however contemptible he may be, owns large flocks and herds and is therefore rich (he will be received at the royal court). Wealth brings its position at court, regardless of merit.

    crib manger

88   *mess* (a division of the company at a banquet)

    chough jackdaw (which is able to make a chatter resembling human speech)

89   *spacious in the possession of dirt* the owner of many acres of land

92   *diligence of spirit* attention. Hamlet begins to mock Osrick's style of speech.

93   *Put your bonnet to his right use.* It was customary to wear hats indoors. Probably Osrick's excessive cap-doffing was an affectation of respect. But he politely pretends he has taken his hat off for his comfort in the hot weather.
    bonnet (any kind of headwear)
    his its

97   *indifferent* fairly

98-9   *for my complexion.* This is F's reading. Q2 has 'or' instead of *for*; this could be right if one puts a dash after *complexion* and supposes that Hamlet is interrupted by Osrick before he can finish his sentence with 'judges it wrongly' (or something of the sort).

99   *complexion* bodily state

105   *Nay . . . .* Osrick apparently wins, and does not put on his hat until he departs at line 179.

107-11   *an absolute gentleman . . . see.* Osrick's panegyric has been arranged by the King (IV.7.130).

107   *absolute* perfect
    differences distinguishing qualities

108   *soft society* sociable disposition
    great showing impressive appearance

109   *card* accurate guide, to be used as a seaman uses his chart or compass (see V.1.135-6 and note)
    calendar directory which one may consult for information
    gentry gentlemanliness

110   *continent* embodiment

110-11   *what part a gentleman would see* every quality a gentleman would like to see

112   *his definement suffers no perdition in you* he loses nothing by being described by you

113   *divide him inventorially* list his qualities one by one

113-14   *dizzy th'arithmetic of memory* (the number of his qualities would be so large that one's memory would become confused in trying to remember them)

346

114   *yaw* move unsteadily (of a boat)
        neither for all that

115   *the verity of extolment* praising him truly

116   *article* importance
        infusion mixture of good qualities

117   *dearth and rareness* 'dearness' (preciousness) and rarity
        make true diction of speak truthfully about

118   *his semblable is his mirror* the only thing that resembles
        him is his own image in a mirror
        who whoever

119   *trace* follow in his footsteps (that is, imitate)
        his umbrage (is) a shadow of him

120   *infallibly* accurately

121   *concernancy* (apparently a word invented for the
        occasion) purpose of all this

122   *more rawer breath* too little refined way of speech

125   *You will to't* you can succeed, if you try

126   *imports the nomination of* is your purpose in naming

134   *approve me* demonstrate the truth about me (or perhaps
        'be to my credit')

137   *compare* vie

138–9   *to know a man well were to know himself.* This exercise in
        logical nonsense seems to be based on an extension of
        'Judge not, that you be not judged' (Matthew 7.1). It
        would be wrong for Hamlet to judge Laertes's excel-
        lence, unless he were to consider himself worthy to be
        judged to be of equal excellence, and that would be a
        presumptuous self-opinion, for he cannot really *know*
        himself; therefore he cannot really know (or estimate)
        Laertes's excellence.

139   *himself* oneself

140   *for* with

140–41 *imputation* reputation

141   *by them* by people in general. Some editors, following
        Q2's punctuation, read 'by them in his meed' ('by
        those who are in his pay, his retainers'), but this seems
        to indicate an irony that is beyond Osrick.

141   *meed* merit (probably, but the word is difficult)
      unfellowed without a rival

145-6   *Barbary horses*. North African horses were much
        esteemed.

146   *he has impawned* Laertes has wagered

147   *poniards* daggers
      assigns appurtenances
      as such as

148   *hangers* straps by which the sword (or its scabbard)
      was attached to the man's belt (*girdle*)
      carriages (an affected word for *hangers*)

149   *very dear to fancy* (probably 'delightful to think about')
      responsive to (perhaps 'matching' or 'in keeping with';
      the two items 'go well together')

150   *delicate* finely wrought
      of very liberal conceit (perhaps) tasteful in design and
      decoration

152-3   *I knew you must be edified by the margent* I expected that
        you would fail to understand something he said and
        have some word or phrase explained. (Explanations of
        difficult words or phrases were usually printed in the
        margent (margin) rather than at the foot of the page.)

152   *edified* enlightened

155-6   *germane to the matter* appropriate to the thing itself (*the
        matter* contrasts with *The phrase*)

156-7   *I would it might be 'hangers' till then* I had rather we
        kept the word 'hangers' until that time comes (when
        we can carry cannons at our sides and not merely
        rapiers)

162   *laid* wagered

162-4   *in a dozen passes . . . he shall not exceed you three hits. He
        hath laid on twelve for nine*. These odds are difficult to
        interpret, but must have been immediately intelligible
        to Shakespeare's audience, familiar with the art of
        fencing and with the conventions of fencing matches.
        It seems that the King wagers that, in twelve bouts or
        rounds, Laertes's score will not exceed Hamlet's by

three. That means that if the score were Laertes 8 and
Hamlet 4, Laertes would win; and that if the score were
Laertes 7 and Hamlet 5, Hamlet would win. This
explanation seems to be supported by Q1, where the
reporter is doubtless remembering what he saw on the
stage. Hamlet asks 'And howe's the wager?' and receives the reply 'Mary sir, that yong Leartes in twelue
venies | At Rapier and Dagger do not get three oddes
of you.' In the event, Hamlet wins the first two bouts
(lines 275 and 280 below). The score of two-nil against
him is serious for Laertes, for it means he must win at
least eight of the remaining ten bouts in order to win
the match. The King thereupon says *Our son shall win*
(line 281). But what is the meaning of *He hath laid on
twelve for nine*? By the natural run of the sentences *He*
would be the King. The actor might convey that *He*
was Laertes. It would be natural to take *twelve for nine*
as being related to Hamlet's 'advantage' of *three hits*.
Perhaps *for nine* means 'instead of nine': Laertes wants
a larger number of bouts than usual, in order to achieve
a lead of at least four hits over Hamlet. Unfortunately
there is no evidence that nine was the usual number of
bouts. Perhaps the wager is that Laertes will not achieve
twelve hits before Hamlet has achieved nine. If so,
they might have to fight as many as twenty bouts; for
the score, after the nineteenth, could be 11 to 8.

163   *passes* (probably means 'bouts' or 'rounds', which
    ended when one of the contestants scored a hit)

165–6   *vouchsafe the answer* accept the challenge. But Hamlet
    deliberately misunderstands the words as merely 'give
    a reply'.

167   *How if I answer no?* (a moment of suspense, when
    Hamlet comes near to spoiling the treacherous plot)

168–9   *I mean . . . in trial*. Osrick assumes that it is unthinkable
    that a gentleman should refuse to respond to a challenge
    of this kind, and so he pretends that Hamlet may have
    misunderstood him.

171   *breathing time* time for taking exercise

174   *the odd hits* my small score of successful hits

175   *re-deliver you* report what you have said

176   *flourish* verbal decoration

178   *I commend my duty.* This is a merely complimentary phrase, and Hamlet's immediate response is conventional too. But after Osrick has left he plays with the words, taking them separately and literally as 'I praise my performance of duty'.

182–3 *This lapwing runs away with the shell on his head.* Presumably Osrick puts his hat on at his departure. The image is of a precocious young bird which, just hatched, starts running away with a piece of its shell still clinging to its head.

184   *comply . . . with his dug* behave with ingratiating good manners towards his nurse's breast ('he was born a courtier')

185   *bevy* covey of birds. Q2 has 'breede', which is acceptable; but the appropriateness of F's 'Beauy' ('bevy') is strongly in its favour.

186   *drossy age* present times, which are worthless
      dotes on makes a cult of

186–7 *got the tune of the time* acquired the fashionable mannerisms of speech

187   *out of an habit of encounter* by practice in having constant conversational contact with other gallants. F reads 'outward habite of encounter' ('exterior manner of address'), which is parallel to *the tune of the time*.

187–8 *yeasty collection* frothy accumulation (of modes of expression)

188   *carries* sustains
      through and through right through

189   *fanned and winnowed* carefully considered. Q2 reads 'prophane and trennowed', which does not make sense. F reads 'fond and winnowed'; but 'fond' is difficult, for the meaning the context requires is the opposite of 'foolish'. The emendation to 'fand', that is, 'fanned'

('sifted'), is commonly accepted, though it is rather close to *winnowed* in meaning. An equally probable emendation is 'profound'.

190   *are out* (soon burst)

192   *attend* await

194   *that* if

196   *his fitness speaks* his (the King's) readiness is declared

199   *In happy time* (a polite phrase) it is an opportune moment

200–   *gentle entertainment* friendliness of attitude
201

204–5   *Since he went . . . continual practice.* This is more or less consistent with the King's words at IV.7.101–4; nevertheless at II.2.296–7 Hamlet told Rosencrantz and Guildenstern that he had *forgone all custom of exercises.*

205   *at the odds* with the advantage given me (at lines 162–4)

209–10   *gaingiving* misgiving

212   *repair* coming

213   *We defy augury* I shall disdain forebodings. For a moment Hamlet becomes almost like his admired Horatio (III.2.75–81 – though Horatio's stoicism has no religious foundation). But it is perhaps felt to be a moment of carelessness, rather than heroism, before the catastrophe of the duel.

213–14   *There is special providence in the fall of a sparrow.* 'And fear ye not them which kill the body, but are not able to kill the soul; but rather fear him which is able to destroy both body and soul in hell. Are not two little sparrows sold for a farthing? And one of them shall not light on the ground without your father. Yea, even all the hairs of your head are numbered. Fear ye not, therefore; ye are of more value than many sparrows', Matthew 10.28–31. The phrase is also influenced by *augury*, which originally meant the foretelling of the future by observing the behaviour of birds.

214   *it* my death

216–17   *The readiness is all. Since no man knows of aught he*

> *leaves, what is't to leave betimes?* Q2 places *knows* after *leaves*. F reads: 'the readinesse is all, since no man ha's ought of what he leaues. What is't to leaue betimes?' Many amendments have been suggested. On the whole, the simplest is to suppose that *knows* in Q2 has got out of place. The meaning is then: 'To be ready (for death) is all that matters. As no one has knowledge of what happens after his death, what does an early death matter?'

218   *Let be* do not try to postpone the fencing match. Alternatively *Let be* may be part of the previous sentence, giving the meaning 'since a man cannot find out from anything on earth (*of aught he leaves*) what is the appropriate moment for his dying, don't bother about it'. The words are in Q2, not in F.

     (stage direction) Q2 and F differ slightly; see collations list 4.

     state (that is, courtly attendants)

220-38   Hamlet is loyally carrying out his mother's request (lines 200-201) and adopts her explanation of his behaviour (V.1.280-84).

222   *presence* royal assembly (or perhaps only the King and Queen)

223   *punished* afflicted

     a sore distraction. The excuse of madness must be regarded as disingenuous. In the episode of the killing of Polonius, Hamlet is conspicuously sane in his discourse and expressly denies to his mother that he is really mad (III.4.140-45).

225   *exception* right to take exception

232   *faction* contending party

237   *That I have* as if I had

238   *my brother*. As Ophelia's brother, Laertes might have been Hamlet's brother-in-law. But the allusion would be awkward, and perhaps, rather, the echoes of the fratricide are heard even here.

     in nature so far as my personal feelings are concerned (but not as regards my position in society)

239   *Whose motive* the impulse from which

240   *terms of honour* condition as a man of honour

241   *will* desire

243   *voice* opinion

       precedent of peace knowledge of a precedent for my making peace with you

245   *receive* accept

246   *will not wrong it.* Laertes's plain speaking is the extreme of treachery.

       embrace welcome

247   *frankly* without ill-feeling

249   *foil* (a characteristic pun: 'the gold-leaf used to set off the brightness of a gem' and 'a blunted sword')

251   *Stick fiery off* shine out brightly in contrast

257   *But since he is bettered, we have therefore odds.* Perhaps *since* means 'since then', giving the meaning 'Since I saw you both fence, Laertes has improved himself. Therefore we are giving three points to Hamlet.' Another suggestion is that the King's stake is so much more valuable than Laertes's that he has asked for favourable odds. But it is difficult to see how this could be communicated to an audience.

       bettered more skilful than you (or perhaps 'improved by his training' in France). Q2 has 'better' for F's 'better'd'.

258   *Let me see another.* This begins the process (also covered by the King's elaborate speech at lines 261–72) through which Laertes secures the *Unbated and envenomed* rapier.

259   *likes* pleases

       a length one and the same length. From surviving rapiers it seems that the length of the blades varied considerably. Hamlet's question increases the suspense by suggesting that he may, contrary to the King's expectation (IV.7.135), inspect the weapons and so discover the plot.

263   *quit in answer of the third exchange* (probably) win the

third bout, which will pay Laertes back for his having won the first and second. The King is thinking of the need to bring into effect his *back or second* (IV.7.152) and to get Hamlet to drink from the poisoned cup as soon as possible.

266   *cup* (the *chalice* of IV.7.159)

union large pearl

268   *Denmark's crown* (presumably that which he is now wearing)

269   *kettle* kettledrum

273   *judges* (of whom Osrick is the only active one)

274   *Judgement* (appealing to the *judges* for a decision)

275   (stage direction) *Drum, trumpets, and shot.* Presumably the King or an official gives the order.

piece piece of ordnance, cannon

276   *this pearl is thine.* Presumably this is the moment when the King throws the poison into the cup, as Hamlet later believes (line 320). We would assume that the King has drunk from the cup first, but the placing of *Here's to thy health* suggests that he throws in the poison and takes a sip before it has time to dissolve; the cup will have been shaken and enough time will have elapsed before it reaches Hamlet.

278   *I'll play this bout first* (presumably a grave discourtesy, a refusal of the King's amity)

281   *He's fat and scant of breath.* The word *fat* (in both Q2 and F) is incongruous. There is slight evidence that it could mean 'sweaty', but the usual meaning was the same as today. Possibly the Queen's tone is bantering, giving expression to her motherly happiness at her now well-behaved son. But the word may be wrong. What the sense needs is something like 'he sweats and scants his breath.' None of the emendations suggested so far (e.g. 'faint', 'hot') is satisfactory.

282   *take my napkin.* This move of the Queen can appear significant: she openly goes over to Hamlet's 'side', leaving the throne and the King. It may be a relic of the

old motivation which appears in Q1: having secretly allied herself with Hamlet against the King, she suspects some treachery and is warning her son.

napkin handkerchief

283   *The Queen* (as well as the King)

284,   *do not drink . . . . It is the poisoned cup. It is too late.* At
286   this sudden turn of events the King, for all his usual skill and promptitude, cannot summon the energy to face the peril of abandoning the plot by saving his Queen.

289   *I do not think't.* Perhaps this is almost a moment of despair in the King, though he retains his self-control as he waits for the Queen to show the effects of the poison.

292   *pass* make your thrusts

293   *make a wanton of me* are playing with me as if I were a child (unworthy of your serious swordsmanship). Perhaps the implication is that Laertes's bad *conscience* is affecting his skill.

296   *Have at you now!* This is usually interpreted as indicating that Laertes suddenly thrusts at Hamlet, without warning, and wounds him, thus apprising him of the treachery.

     (stage direction) Q2 has no stage direction for the exchange of rapiers. F has '*In scuffling they change Rapiers*'. The compiler of Q1 remembered the situation as '*They catch one anothers Rapiers, and both are wounded, Leartes falles downe, the Queene falles downe and dies*'. Probably Burbage displayed a virtuoso piece of swordsmanship as Hamlet. When in a tight corner a swordsman would throw down his own weapon and seize the blade of his opponent's, securing enough leverage to wrench it away. The opponent then had no alternative but to pick up the other weapon, by which time his opponent would have recovered himself.

     Part them. The King wishes to save Laertes.

297   *Ho!* Perhaps this is Osrick's cry to stop the duel in

accordance with the King's instructions. Q2 reads 'howe' here and 'how' at line 305; this was a common spelling of 'ho', though 'how' could be an exclamatory interrogative.

300   *as a woodcock to mine own springe* (a curious echo of Polonius's *springes to catch woodcocks*, I.3.115)

302   *She swounds to see them bleed*. He tries to keep up appearances and to cover the cause of the Queen's collapse. Knowing that the Queen, Hamlet, and Laertes will soon be dead, he can still hope to escape exposure.
        swounds swoons

304   *poisoned*. The terrible word arouses Hamlet's fury.
        (stage direction) *She dies*. There is no indication in Q2 or F; perhaps the Queen, speechless, hears and sees some of the later words and actions before dying. Hamlet's *Follow my mother* (line 321) implies that he knows she is dying, if not dead; his *Wretched Queen, adieu!* (line 327) may be an immediate response, accompanied by some gesture, to her death.

311   *Unbated . . . practice* (an echo of the King's words at IV.7.137)
        practice plot

314   *can no more* can say no more. But in fact Laertes is able to give the first public evidence of the King's guilt.

316   *Then, venom, to thy work*. Hamlet never really becomes a contriving revenger. He kills the King, as he had killed Polonius, on the spur of the moment.

318   *but hurt* only wounded. Perhaps he is intended to suppose that the poison on the sword-point has been used up on Hamlet and Laertes.

320   *Is thy union here?* Hamlet is probably still making a pun, referring to his uncle's *union* in marriage with his mother.

321   (stage direction) *The King dies*. Claudius dies without contrition or forgiveness, unlike Laertes.

322   *tempered* compounded

326   *make thee free* acquit you of the guilt

328 *You that look pale* . . . (the courtiers and attendants)

329 *mutes* actors with wordless parts in a play

330 *as* which I have not, because

    sergeant (an officer of the sheriff, responsible for arrests)

331 *arrest* (doubtless a final pun: death stops him from proceeding with his story)

334 *the unsatisfied* those who are in doubt about my conduct

335 *more an antique Roman than a Dane.* The common notion that, among the Romans, suicide was an acceptable way of escaping from an intolerable situation derived from the many stories in which stoical Roman nobles foiled the dishonour they suffered from wicked emperors. A Christian *Dane* would know that *the Everlasting had . . . fixed | His canon 'gainst self-slaughter* (I.2.131–2). But Horatio's Roman allusion is congruous with the classical education he showed at I.1.113–25. Here he temporarily loses the imperturbability of one who *Fortune's buffets and rewards has ta'en with equal thanks* (III.2.77–8).

338 *wounded name* damaged reputation

339 *shall I leave behind me.* This is the Q2 reading. F has 'shall liue behind me', and Q1 'wouldst thou leaue behinde'. The excellent suggestion has been made that the Q2 reading is a mistake for an original 'shall't leave behind me', which improves the scansion and the meaning.

341 *felicity.* Hamlet refers to the happiness of release from life's miseries (compare III.1.63–4) rather than to the joys of heaven.

343 (stage direction) *and shout within.* This is only in F. Many editors have emended *shout* to *shot* or *shoot*, to connect with the *warlike volley* in line 346.

    Both Q2 and F have an entry for Osrick at the end of the line, though there has been no reasonable point of exit for him. Probably no more is implied than that he comes forward to give his explanation of the *warlike noise*.

344   *with conquest come from Poland*. This is the first news of the outcome of Fortinbras's expedition (II.2.72–80, IV.4).

345   *the ambassadors of England* the Englishmen coming as ambassadors to the King of Denmark (see lines 71–2). The dramatic time has been drastically shortened.

347   *o'er-crows* triumphs over (like the victor in cock-fighting)

349–50   *But I do prophesy . . . Fortinbras.* This does not mean that there is any connexion between *the news from England* and *the election* (to the Danish throne). Rather, Hamlet turns aside from the triviality of the fate of Rosencrantz and Guildenstern to his serious concern for the future of the Danish crown. Perhaps some stage business is required: he is handed the crown of Denmark (taken from the dead Claudius), and his dying thoughts, self-forgetful and calm, are upon its inheritance by a worthy successor.

    Shakespeare does not intend us to regard Fortinbras as a tyrant, or his assumption of power as arbitrary. The praise bestowed on him by Hamlet (*a delicate and tender prince*, IV.4.48) is important, confirming the good impression of Fortinbras given throughout the play (II.2.68–80 and IV.4.1–8). In many respects Fortinbras seems to embody Hamlet's ideal of kingship. *lights | On* alights upon

350   *voice* vote

351   *occurrents, more and less* incidents, great and small

352   *solicited* – incited me to – . Probably Hamlet breaks off in mid-sentence, intending to continue with something like 'my various actions over the last few months'.

    silence. F somewhat incongruously adds 'O, o, o, o' (presumably indicating the actor's dying groans).

354   *flights of angels sing* may companies of angels sing

355   (stage direction) *his train.* As there are now four dead

bodies on the stage, requiring at least eight men for their simultaneous removal, Shakespeare has good reason to bring on a stage-army. It provides a splendid military finale.

drum drummer

colours military ensigns

358   *quarry cries on havoc* heap of dead proclaims that the hunters have carried out their slaughter (rather than '... cries out for revenge')

359   *toward* in preparation

thine eternal cell (the grave)

361   *dismal* (a strong word) calamitous

363   *The ears* (Claudius's)

366   *Where should we have our thanks?* The Ambassador seems to be politely inquiring about the succession to the throne of Denmark.

his (Claudius's)

367   *Had it th'ability of life* even if it could utter words

369   *jump* exactly

question conflict

371   *give order* (presumably addressed to Fortinbras, who has his military power with him)

372   *stage* platform

373   *let me speak.* Horatio is proposing to speak to the people, rather like Mark Antony in *Julius Caesar*, III.2.

375   *carnal, bloody, and unnatural acts* (the murder of King Hamlet by his brother Claudius and the Queen's re-marriage; the plot against Prince Hamlet which was to lead to his execution in England)

376   *accidental judgements, casual slaughters* (the unpremeditated killing of Polonius behind the arras; Ophelia's drowning; the Queen's unintended death by poison; the killing of Laertes by his own *Unbated and envenomed* sword)

377   *deaths put on by cunning and forced cause* (the intended death of Hamlet by execution in England; the consequent deaths of Rosencrantz and Guildenstern)

377 *put on* instigated
   forced not genuine

378 *in this upshot* as a final result of this

378–9 *purposes mistook | Fallen on th'inventors' heads* (the
   death of Laertes by the unbated sword intended for use
   on Hamlet; the Queen's death by the poison intended
   for Hamlet; the King's death by the poisoned sword
   and drink)

383 *I have some rights of memory*. Fortinbras's claims to the
   Danish throne have not hitherto been mentioned, nor
   are we told what they are. But we remember that old
   Fortinbras forfeited his personal lands to old Hamlet
   (I.1.80–104 and I.2.17–25) and so his son might regard
   himself as the residual heir to the throne after the
   expiring of the Hamlet lineage. It is notable that
   Fortinbras speaks only of *rights of memory* in Denmark.
   He is not like Malcolm in *Macbeth* or Richmond in
   Richard III, the rightful heir to the throne who ousts a
   regicide and usurper and so can cleanse the kingdom of
   corruption. A peaceful transfer of the throne to a
   strong, worthy, and rightful claimant, and so an
   avoidance of political disorder, is what the ending of this
   tragedy requires (and perhaps supplies).
   of memory ('not forgotten' (by you) or 'ancient' (claims).
   Perhaps both meanings are implied.)

384 *Which* (this kingdom)
   my vantage good fortune

386 *from his mouth*. See lines 350–51.
   whose voice will draw on more. Denmark being an
   elective monarchy, Fortinbras's claims will be dependent upon his winning support. The approval of him
   by the popular Prince Hamlet as he died will win him
   many votes in the election.

387 *this same* (Horatio's proposal that he give *to the yet
   unknowing world* a full account, which will include
   Hamlet's recommendation of Fortinbras)
   presently immediately

389   *On plots and errors* on top of the plots and misjudge-
       ments. Horatio fears disorder as a result of the disasters
       to the ruling house.

391-2 *he was likely, had he been put on,* | *To have proved most*
       royal. The tribute over the dead body of the tragic hero
       is conventional. It does not necessarily cast a light over
       the whole of the preceding play. A similar problem
       faces us in *Julius Caesar*, where Mark Antony praises
       Brutus as 'the noblest Roman of them all' (V.5.68–75),
       and in *Coriolanus*, where Aufidius praises Coriolanus:
       'he shall have a noble memory' (V.6.155). But Fortin-
       bras's strong words are consistent with Ophelia's *Th'*
       expectancy and rose of the fair state (III.1.153).

391   *put on* put to the test (by his accession to the throne,
       rather than by following a career as a soldier)

392   *passage* (from this life to the other world)

393   *The soldiers' music and the rites of war.* A military
       funeral is described by Aufidius at the end of *Coriolanus*,
       V.5.149–52:

                            Take him up.
          Help three o'th'chiefest soldiers; I'll be one.
          Beat thou the drum, that it speak mournfully.
          Trail your steel pikes.

394   *Speak* ('let them speak')

396   *field* battlefield

397   *shoot . . . a peal of ordnance is shot off.* This again re-
       minds us, unhappily or ironically, of Claudius's
       partiality for gunshot (I.2.124–8, I.4.8–12, and V.2.269–
       72).

AN ACCOUNT OF THE TEXT

Hamlet was entered in the Register of the Stationers' Company on 26 July 1602 to James Roberts as 'A booke called the Revenge of Hamlett Prince Denmarke as yt was latelie Acted by the Lo: Chamberleyn his servantes'. But it first appeared in print from the press of Valentine Simmes, in 1603. It was then described on the title-page as *The Tragicall Historie of Hamlet Prince of Denmarke By William Shake-speare*, and was said to be 'As it hath beene diuerse times acted by his Highnesse seruants in the Cittie of London: as also in the two Vniuersities of Cambridge and Oxford, and elsewhere'. This edition, printed in quarto (that is, on sheets of paper folded twice), is an unauthorized text which appears to derive not from Shakespeare's manuscript, or even from a good copy of it, but from a manuscript reconstructed from memory by one or more of the actors of Shakespeare's company. The performer of Marcellus, whose role is exceptionally well reported, is particularly open to suspicion.

The text of the first, or 'bad', quarto (hereafter referred to as 'Q1') is seriously corrupt. It contains only about 2200 lines, whereas there are about 3800 in the good quarto. The reporter's memory is often imperfect, as may be seen from his garbling of part of 'To be, or not to be' (III.1.56–88):

> To be, or not to be, I there's the point,
> To Die, to sleepe, is that all? I all:
> No, to sleepe, to dreame, I mary there it goes,
> For in that dreame of death, when wee awake,
> And borne before an euerlasting Iudge,
> From whence no passenger euer retur'nd,
> The vndiscouered country, at whose sight
> The happy smile, and the accursed damn'd.

At other times the reporter remembered little more than the dramatic situation, and seems to have composed his own verse,

362

with occasional echoes of the original wording, as in Hamlet's 'pictures' speech (III.4.54-89):

> ... behold this picture,
> It is the portraiture, of your deceased husband,
> See here a face, to outface *Mars* himselfe,
> An eye, at which his foes did tremble at,
> A front wherin all vertues are set downe
> For to adorne a king, and guild his crowne,
> Whose heart went hand in hand euen with that vow,
> He made to you in marriage, and he is dead.
> Murdred, damnably murdred, this was your husband,
> Looke you now, here is your husband,
> With a face like *Vulcan*.
> A looke fit for a murder and a rape,
> A dull dead hanging looke, and a hell-bred eie,
> To affright children and amaze the world.

Other plays by Shakespeare, such as *Romeo and Juliet*, *Henry V*, and *The Merry Wives of Windsor*, also exist in 'bad' quartos; and Q1 of *Hamlet* shares some of their characteristics. But also, and more puzzlingly, it shows signs of deriving from a version of the play significantly different from that which we know today. Polonius is called Corambis; Reynaldo, Montano. Hamlet's madness is much more pronounced, and the Queen's innocence of her husband's murder much more explicitly stated. (In these respects, the earlier play corresponds more closely with the original story.) The Queen is represented as concerting and actively co-operating with Hamlet against the King's life. And there are structural differences; the 'nunnery' scene (III.1.56-150) comes earlier than in the accepted text, and a scene in which Horatio tells the Queen of Hamlet's return to Denmark from England replaces those in which Horatio receives Hamlet's letter (IV.6) and the episode in which Hamlet and Horatio discuss the events of the voyage (V.2.1-74). The 'bad' quarto, then, arouses suspicions that the play may have been performed soon after it was written in a text that has otherwise not come down to us, possibly an earlier version, possibly a shortened form of what we now regard as the authentic text, made conceivably for a touring company.

For all its faults, Q1 is occasionally useful to the editor. Once or twice, it is the only source of what seems an authentic reading (as at III.2.261; see the Commentary). It provides supporting evidence for other readings. Its stage directions, scanty though they are, are of exceptional interest, since they give us information about the early staging of the play which is not available elsewhere (the more interesting of them are given in collations list 7 below). And it reports an expansion of Hamlet's comments to the First Player on 'those that play your clowns' which may well derive from Shakespeare's own theatre, and perhaps from his pen. Our edition is the first to include this passage in the text (III.2.43–55).

The entry of *Hamlet* to James Roberts in 1602, mentioned above, was probably what is known as a 'staying entry', designed, that is, to prevent unauthorized publication. The players may well have wished to keep the play out of print while it was one of their main assets. If so, they failed, but after Q1 was published they appear to have authorized the play's publication; it is pleasant to think that this may have been in an attempt to redeem Shakespeare's reputation. James Roberts was the printer (though not the publisher) of the second quarto ('Q2'), which appeared late in 1604 (some copies are dated 1605), described on the title-page as 'The Tragicall Historie of Hamlet, Prince of Denmarke. By William Shakespeare. Newly imprinted and enlarged to almost as much againe as it was, according to the true and perfect Coppie'. This is the longest single version that we have. The enlargement is mainly in the contemplative and imaginative parts, little being added in the way of action and incident. The play appears to have been printed largely from Shakespeare's own manuscript, with some use of Q1. Unfortunately it is badly printed, with many obvious misprints and errors of omission, transposition, and so on, probably because the manuscript was difficult to read. And the punctuation is chaotic. Moreover, Q2 does not include passages totalling about 95 lines which were later printed in the first Folio ('F'). The two main omissions are II.2.239–69 and 336–61, and slight awkwardnesses in the surrounding dialogue suggest that they were cuts in Q2, rather than later rewritings. Although Q2 is the best single surviving text, it does not tell us all that we need to know.

The good quarto was reprinted several times, without authoritative alteration. The only other early text of the play of importance to an editor is the one included in the collected edition of Shakespeare's plays, known as the first Folio, which appeared in 1623. Here, as at the beginning of the text of Q2, it is called *The Tragedie of Hamlet, Prince of Denmarke*. Again the situation is not straightforward. The printers seem sometimes to have consulted a copy of Q2, but to have taken as their primary source either the prompt copy, or a transcript of it, which bore witness to changes made in the theatre, whether with or without Shakespeare's help and approval. Their text (which, on the whole, is well printed) omits about 230 lines that are found in Q2; most of these are in Hamlet's role, and they include one of his soliloquies ('How all occasions...', IV.4.32–66). A few of the omissions are clearly accidental, but most are deliberate cuts, made presumably to lighten the actor's task. The stage directions are rather more explicitly theatrical than those of Q2, especially in the final scene. And the text includes additions and repetitions of words and phrases unnecessary to the sense, along with indications for sounds 'within', that may be theatrical in origin. There are, then, good grounds for belief that the Folio comes closer than Q2 to representing the play as it was performed by Shakespeare's company. But in some respects it also offers a more carefully prepared, 'literary' version, correcting lacking concord between subject and verb (II.2.20; IV.5.99), regularizing the logic (II.2.216), and correcting words interpreted as being erroneous ('sulleyes' for 'sallies', II.1.39).

The modern editor, then, is faced with three different versions of the play. How can he best provide a single text which will not betray Shakespeare's intentions? When variants are indifferent, Q2 may claim superior authority as the text that is closest to Shakespeare's manuscript. Other variants have to be judged on their intrinsic merits (which usually means literary merits) in the light of all the information available. The Folio has its own kind of authority, both because it corrects many obvious errors in Q2, and because it represents the practice of the playhouse for which Shakespeare wrote. In this edition, changes made in F are admitted into the text when they seem to represent a genuine amendment of a probable error in Q2. When the changes are merely a 'modernization' of grammar or of the form of a word, the Q2 reading is usually retained. The longer passages contained in F but not printed in Q2 are included. So also are many of the repetitions in Hamlet's speech not found in Q2 (for example 'well, well, well' at III.1.92, where Q2 has only 'well'). Although these have sometimes been regarded by recent editors as 'actors' interpolations' and therefore denied a place in Shakespeare's 'authentic text', there is no need to take so derogatory a view of them. *Hamlet* was performed by the company to which Shakespeare belonged, and presumably he acted in it (there is a tradition that he played the Ghost). So changes in the Folio text may represent his own minor improvements to help the actors. We have reason to respect the modifications made in the acting versions of his plays; indeed, a director of the play might find it convenient to use some of F's slightly more theatrical readings that an editor feels obliged to exclude; and he could do so with the confidence that there is a good chance that they indicate Shakespeare's second thoughts.

Few additions have been made to the stage directions; usually the stage business that can be deduced from the text or derived from theatre traditions is discussed in the Commentary. The number of elisions of vowels has been reduced. The practice of the printers in the early texts is inconsistent and unreliable, and any relation to the pronunciation of words on the stage is not known. It seems likely that the scansion of the verse line demands the weakening of syllables, and that the vowels were pronounced lightly, retaining the rhythm of the line, rather than suppressed entirely and so causing uncouth consonant clusters.

In both Q1 and Q2, the play is printed continuously, without division into acts and scenes. In F, only a perfunctory attempt at division occurs, extending no further than II.2. In this edition the traditional division is followed.

COLLATIONS

The collation lists are *selective*. They are arranged as follows: (1) readings of this text derived from F, not Q2; (2) readings derived from Q1, not Q2 or F; (3) readings not derived from Q1, Q2, or F; (4) alterations of Q2's stage directions; (5) readings of F and Q1 not accepted in this text; (6) passages found in Q2 but omitted in F; (7) stage directions in Q1.

Quotations from early editions are unmodernized, except that 'long s' (ʃ) is replaced by 's'.

I

The following readings in the present text of *Hamlet* derive from F, not from Q2. F's reading (as given in this edition) is followed by the Q2 form, unmodernized. The list includes passages found in F only, totalling about 95 lines. In general, F's adoption of more familiar variant spellings and its correction of obvious misprints are not noted here.

I.1.	16	soldier] souldiers
	21	MARCELLUS] *Hora.*
	44	harrows] horrowes
	63	sledded] sleaded
	73	why] with
		cast] cost
	91	returned] returne
	93	covenant] comart
	139	you] your
	176	conveniently] conuenient
I.2.	58	He hath] Hath
	67	Not so] Not so much
	77	good] coold
	83	denote] deuote
	96	a] or
	132	self] seale
	133	weary] wary
	137	to this] thus
	143	would] should
	149	even she] *not in* Q2

	175	to drink deep] for to drinke
	178	see] *not in* Q2
	224	Indeed, indeed] Indeede
	237	Very like, very like] Very like
	257	Foul] fonde
I.3.	3	convoy is] conuay, in
	12	bulk] bulkes
	18	For . . . birth] *not in* Q2
	49	like] *not in* Q2
	68	thine] thy
	74	Are] Or
	75	be] boy
	76	loan] loue
	83	invites you. Go.] inuests you goe,
	125	tether] tider
	131	beguile] beguide
I.4.	2	a] *not in* Q2
	71	beetles] bettles
I.5.	20	fretful] fearefull
	47	a] *not in* Q2
	55	lust] but
	56	sate] sort
	68	posset] possesse
	95	stiffly] swiftly
	116	bird] and
	122	my lord] *not in* Q2
II.1.	28	no] *not in* Q2
	38	warrant] wit
	39	sullies] sallies
	40	i'th'] with
	52-3	at 'friend' . . . 'gentleman'] *not in* Q2
	63	takes] take
	105	passion] passions
	112	quoted] coted
II.2.	43	Assure you,] I assure
	57	o'erhasty] hastie
	73	three] threescore
	90	since] *not in* Q2
	126	above] about

137 winking] working
143 his] her
148 watch] wath
149 a] *not in* Q2
151 'tis] *not in* Q2
189 far gone, far gone] farre gone
210 sanity] sanctity
212–13 and suddenly . . . between him] *not in* Q2
213 honourable] *not in* Q2
214 most humbly] *not in* Q2
215 sir] *not in* Q2
224 excellent] extent
228 over-happy] euer happy
229 cap] lap
236 that] *not in* Q2
239–69 Let me . . . dreadfully attended] *not in* Q2
272 even] euer
278 Why] *not in* Q2
303 What a piece] What peece
305 moving how] moouing, how
admirable, in] admirable in
306 angel, in] Angell in
309 woman] women
320 of] on
323–4 the clown . . . o'th'sere] *not in* Q2
325 blank] black
336–61 How comes . . . load too] *not in* Q2
363 mows] mouths
372 lest my] let me
397–8 tragical-historical, tragical-comical-historical-
pastoral] *not in* Q2
424 By'r] by
428 French falconers] friendly Fankners
442 affectation] affection
445 tale] talke
472 Then senseless Ilium] *not in* Q2
477 reverend] reuerent
479 And] *not in* Q2
502 'Mobled Queen' is good] *not in* Q2

369

	512	husband's] husband
	537	ha't] hate
	551	his] the
	558	the cue] that
	579	O, vengeance!] *not in* Q2
	597	devil . . . devil] deale . . . deale
III.1.	1	And] an
	28	too] two
	32	lawful espials] *not in* Q2
	46	loneliness] lowlines
	55	Let's] *not in* Q2
	83	of us all] *not in* Q2
	85	sicklied] sickled
	92	well, well, well] well
	99	the] these
	107	your honesty] you
	121	to] *not in* Q2
	129	all] *not in* Q2
	138	Go] *not in* Q2
	142	O] *not in* Q2
	143	too] *not in* Q2
	145	lisp] list
	146–7	your ignorance] ignorance
	153	expectancy] expectation
	157	music] musickt
	158	that] what
	160	feature] stature
	189	unwatched] vnmatcht
III.2.	10	tatters] totters
	22	own] *not in* Q2
	25	make] makes
	26	of the which] of which
	29	praise] praysd
	36	sir] *not in* Q2
	99	detecting] detected
	123–4	HAMLET I . . . lord] *not in* Q2
	144	*very lovingly*] *not in* Q2
		She kneels, and makes show of protestation unto him] *not in* Q2

370

146	is miching] munching
151	counsel] *not in* Q2
165	orbèd] orb'd the
173	your] our
178	In neither] Eyther none, in neither
179	love] Lord
200	like] the
209	joys] ioy
233	If, once a widow, ever I be wife] If once I be a widdow, euer I be a wife
262	Pox] *not in* Q2
265	Confederate] Considerat
275	HAMLET What, frighted with false fire?] *not in* Q2
285	two] *not in* Q2
287	sir] *not in* Q2
317	start] stare
326	of my] of
366	thumb] the vmber
375	the top of] *not in* Q2
379	can fret me] fret me not
393-4	POLONIUS I will say so. HAMLET 'By and by' is easily said. *Exit Polonius* Leave me, friends.] Leaue me friends. | I will, say so. By and by is easily said,
396	breathes] breakes
398	bitter business as the day] busines as the bitter day
403	daggers] dagger

III.3.	19	huge] hough
	22	ruin] raine
	23	with] *not in* Q2
	50	pardoned] pardon
	58	shove] showe
	73	pat] but
	79	hire and salary] base and silly
	89	drunk] drunke,

III.4.	5	with him] *not in* Q2
	6	HAMLET ... mother] *not in* Q2
	7	warrant] wait
	21	inmost] most

50 Yea] Ore

53 That . . . index] *spoken by Hamlet*

60 heaven-kissing] heaue, a kissing

89 panders] pardons

90 mine] my very

very] *not in* Q2

91 grainèd] greeued

92 not leave] leaue there

96 mine] my

98 tithe] kyth

140 Ecstasy?] *not in* Q2

144 I] *not in* Q2

159 live] leaue

166 Refrain tonight] to refraine night

187 ravel] rouell

216 foolish] most foolish

IV.2. 2 GENTLEMEN (*within*) Hamlet! Lord Hamlet!] *not in* Q2

6 Compounded] Compound

30–31 Hide fox, and all after] *not in* Q2

IV.3. 42 With fiery quickness] *not in* Q2

54 and so] so

70 were . . . begun] will . . . begin

IV.5. 9 aim] yawne

42 God] good

57 la] *not in* Q2

83 their] *not in* Q2

90 his] this

98 QUEEN Alack . . . this?] *not in* Q2

108 They] The

159 Till] Tell

162 an old] a poore

163–5 Nature . . . loves] *not in* Q2

167 Hey . . . nony] *not in* Q2

183 O, you must] you may

196 All] *not in* Q2

200 Christian] Christians

I pray God] *not in* Q2

201 see] *not in* Q2

IV.6.   9   an't] (and't); and
         21   *good*] *not in* Q2
         25   *bore*] bord
         29   *He*] So
         31   give] *not in* Q2
IV.7.   6   proceeded] proceede
         14   conjunctive] concliue
         22   loud a wind] loued Arm'd
         24   And] But
              had] haue
         36   How . . . news] *not in* Q2
              Letters . . . Hamlet] *not in* Q2
         45   *your pardon*] you pardon
         46   *and more strange*] *not in* Q2
         47   *Hamlet*] *not in* Q2
         55   shall] *not in* Q2
         56   didest] didst
         61   checking] the King
         87   my] me
        133   on] ore
        139   that] *not in* Q2
        155   ha't] hate
        162   How, sweet Queen] *not in* Q2
        167   hoar] horry
        171   cold] cull-cold
        177   tunes] laudes
V.1.   9   *se offendendo*] so offended
         12   and to perform. Argal,] to performe, or all;
       34-7   SECOND CLOWN Why . . . arms?] *not in* Q2
         43   frame] *not in* Q2
         60   stoup] soope
         84   meant] went
         88   mazzard] massene
      104-5   Is . . . recoveries] *not in* Q2
        106   his vouchers] vouchers
        107   double ones too] doubles
        118   O] or
        119   For . . . meet] *not in* Q2
        141   all] *not in* Q2

163 nowadays] *not in* Q2
170–71 three-and-twenty] 23
181 Let me see] *not in* Q2
204 as thus] *not in* Q2
212 winter's] waters
222, 231 PRIEST] *Doct.*
225 have] been
227 Shards] *not in* Q2
257 and] *not in* Q2
273 thou] *not in* Q2
281 thus] this
294 shortly] thereby
V.2. 6 bilboes] bilbo
9 pall] fall
17 unseal] vnfold
43 as's] (Assis); as sir
52 Subscribed] Subscribe
57 Why . . . employment] *not in* Q2
68–80 To quit . . . here] *not in* Q2
93 Put] *not in* Q2
98 sultry] sully
 for] or
101 But] *not in* Q2
148 hangers] hanger
154 carriages] carriage
160 impawned, as] (impon'd as); *not in* Q2
175 re-deliver] deliuer
 e'en] *not in* Q2
179–80 Yours, yours. He] Yours
184 comply] so
185 bevy] breede
187 yeasty] histy
189 winnowed] trennowed
203 this wager] *not in* Q2
206 But] *not in* Q2
209–10 gaingiving] gamgiuing
214 now, 'tis] tis
234 Sir, in this audience] *not in* Q2
244 keep] *not in* Q2

374

till] all
248 Come on] *not in* Q2
257 bettered] better
266 union] Onixe
280 A touch, a touch] *not in* Q2
293 afeard] sure
307 Hamlet. Hamlet,] *Hamlet,*
310 thy] my
319 murderous] *not in* Q2
320 thy union] the Onixe
345 the] th'
358 proud] prou'd
373 th'] *not in* Q2
377 forced] for no
386 on] no
393 rites] right

2

The following readings in the present text derive from Q1, and not from Q2 or F. Q1's reading (as given in this edition) is followed by the Q2 and F forms, unmodernized.

I.2. 209 Where, as] Whereas Q2, F
III.2. 43–55 And then you . . . Well] *not in* Q2, F
261 must take] mistake Q2, F

3

The following readings in the present text are emendations of the words found in Q1 (for III.2.45), Q2, or F (which are printed, unmodernized, after the reading of this edition, with where appropriate the forms found in other early texts). A few of these alterations were made in the later quartos or folios. Most of the other emendations were made by the eighteenth-century editors.

THE CHARACTERS IN THE PLAY] *not in* Q2, F
I.1. 94 designed] desseigne Q2; designe F
121 feared] feare Q2

I.2.   82   shapes] chapes Q2; she wes F
       129   sullied] sallied Q2; solid F
I.3. 109   Running] Wrong Q2; Roaming F
       130   bawds] bonds Q2, F
I.4.   27   the] their Q2
        36   evil] eale Q2
        70   summit] somnet Q2; Sonnet F
I.5.   43   wit] wits Q2, F
II.2. 324   tickle] tickled F
       341   berattle] be-ratled F
       348   most like] like most F
       493   fellies] follies Q2; Fallies F
       517   whe'er] where Q2, F
       581   father] not in Q2, F
III.2. 45   quote] quotes
       229   An] And Q2
III.3.   6   near us] neer's Q2; dangerous F
        17   or 'tis] or it is Q2; It is F
III.4. 170   master] not in Q2
IV.1.   40   So haply slander] not in Q2, F
IV.2. 17–   like an ape an apple] like an apple Q2; like an
        18   Ape F
IV.5.   16   QUEEN Let her come in] spoken by Horatio in Q2;
             printed in italic as part of a stage direction in F
       121   brows] browe Q2; brow F
       144   swoopstake] soopstake Q2; Soop-stake F
       154   VOICES (within) Let her come in] spoken by
             Laertes in Q2; F substitutes the stage direction 'A
             noise within. Let her come in.'
IV.7. 121   spendthrift] spend thrifts Q2
V.1. 272   eisel] Esill Q2; Esile F
V.2.   19   Ah] A Q2; Oh F
        29   villainies] villaines Q2, F
        73   interim is] interim's F
        78   court] count F
       109   feelingly] sellingly Q2
       140   his] this Q2
       141   them, in his meed he's] them in his meed, hee's Q2
       189   fanned] prophane Q2; fond F

217 knows of aught he leaves,] of ought he leaues,
     knowes Q2; ha's ought of what he leaues. F

4

The directions in this edition are based on those of Q2, with
some additions from F. The original directions have been
normalized and clarified. Further directions have been added
where necessary to clarify the action. There are no directions
for speeches to be spoken aside or addressed to a particular
character in Q2 or F, except that Hamlet's interjections in the
play scene (III.2.191 and 234) are printed to the right of the
dialogue in Q2, as if to indicate their special nature. Below are
listed some of the more important additions and alterations to
Q2's directions. When these derive in whole or part from F,
this is noted. The list also includes the more interesting F
directions not accepted in this edition. Minor alterations to
Q2, such as the addition of a character's name to *Exit*, the
change of *Exit* to *Exeunt* or *Song* to *sings*, the normalization of
character names, and the provision of exits and entrances
where these are obviously required, are not listed here.

I.1. 127   *He spreads his arms*] *It spreads his armes.* Q2; *not
            in* F
I.2.   0   *Flourish. Enter Claudius, King of Denmark, Ger-
            trude the Queen, and the Council, including Polonius
            with his son Laertes, Hamlet, Voltemand, Cornelius,
            and attendants*] *Florish. Enter Claudius, King of
            Denmarke, Gertrad the Queene, Counsaile: as
            Polonius, and his Sonne Laertes, Hamlet, Cum
            Alijs.* Q2; *Enter Claudius King of Denmarke,
            Gertrude the Queene, Hamlet, Polonius, Laertes, and
            his Sister Ophelia, Lords Attendant.* F (F directs
            Voltemand and Cornelius to enter after line 25)
II.1.   0   *Enter Polonius, with his man Reynaldo*] *Enter old
            Polonius, with his man or two.* Q2; *Enter Polonius,
            and Reynoldo.* F
II.2. 76   *He gives a paper to the King*] *not in* Q2, F
      167   *Enter Hamlet*] Q2; *Enter Hamlet reading on a
            Booke.* F

377

170 *Exeunt the King and Queen] Exit King and Queene.*
   Q2 *(after line 169); Exit King & Queen.* F *(after*
   'Ile boord him presently')

III.1. 42 *Exit the Queen] not in* Q2, F

III.2. 0 *Enter Hamlet and the Players] Enter Hamlet, and*
   three of the Players. Q2; *Enter Hamlet, and two or*
   three of the Players. F

  101 *Danish march. Flourish. Trumpets and kettledrums.*
   Enter the King and Queen, Polonius, Ophelia,
   Rosencrantz, Guildenstern, and other lords attendant,
   with the guard carrying torches] Enter Trumpets and
   Kettle Drummes, King, Queene, Polonius, Ophelia.
   Q2; *Enter King, Queene, Polonius, Ophelia, Rosin-*
   crance, Guildensterne, and other Lords attendant,
   with his Guard carrying Torches. Danish March.
   Sound a Flourish. F

  144 *The trumpets sound]* Q2; *Hoboyes play.* F

  269 *He pours the poison in the King's ears] not in* Q2;
   Powres the poyson in his eares. F

  352 *Enter a Player with recorders] Enter the Players*
   with Recorders. Q2; *Enter one with a Recorder.* F

III.4. 8 *Polonius hides behind the arras] not in* Q2, F

  25 *He makes a thrust through the arras and kills*
   Polonius] not in Q2; *Killes Polonius.* F

  31 *He sees Polonius] not in* Q2, F

  218 *Exeunt Hamlet, tugging in Polonius, and the Queen]*
   Exit. Q2; *Exit Hamlet tugging in Polonius.* F

IV.2. 4 *Guildenstern] not in* Q2

IV.3. 11 *Guildenstern] not in* Q2

IV.6. 0 *Enter Horatio and a Gentleman] Enter Horatio and*
   others. Q2; *Enter Horatio, with an Attendant.* F

  4 *Exit the Gentleman] not in* Q2, F

V.1. 64 *Enter Hamlet and Horatio]* Q2; *Enter Hamlet and*
   Horatio a farre off. F *(after line 55)*

  74 *He throws up a skull] not in* Q2, F

  95 *He throws up another skull] not in* Q2, F

  213 *Enter the King and Queen, Laertes, and the corpse*
   of Ophelia, with lords attendant and a Priest] Enter
   K. Q. Laertes and the corse. Q2; *Enter King,*

Queene, Laertes, and a Coffin, with Lords attendant.
F; *Enter King and Queene, Leartes, and other
lordes, with a Priest after the coffin.* Q1

218   *He withdraws with Horatic] not in* Q2, F
239   *She scatters flowers] not in* Q2, F
246   *He leaps in the grave] not in* Q2; *Leaps in the
       graue.* F

V.2. 80   *Enter Osrick] Enter a Courtier.* Q2; *Enter young
           Osricke.* F
104   *He invites Osrick to put on his hat] not in* Q2, F
218   *Trumpets and drums. A table prepared, with flagons
       of wine on it. Enter officers with cushions, and other
       attendants with foils, daggers, and gauntlets. Enter
       the King and Queen, Osrick, Laertes, and all the
       state] A table prepard, Trumpets, Drums and
       officers with Cushions, King, Queene, and all the
       state, Foiles, daggers, and Laertes.* Q2; *Enter King,
       Queene, Laertes and Lords, with other Attendants
       with Foyles, and Gauntlets, a Table and Flagons of
       Wine on it.* F
219   *He puts Laertes's hand into Hamlet's] not in* Q2, F
260   *They prepare to play] not in* Q2; *Prepare to play.* F
       (after line 259)
274   *They play]* F; *not in* Q2
275   *Drum, trumpets, and shot. Flourish. A piece goes off]*
       Q2; *Trumpets sound, and shot goes off.* F *(after
       line 277)*
279   *They play] not in* Q2, F
285   *She drinks]* Q1; *not in* Q2, F
294   *They play] not in* Q2; *Play.* F
296   *In scuffling they change rapiers, and both are wounded
       with the poisoned weapon] not in* Q2; *In scuffling
       they change Rapiers.* F
297   *The Queen falls] not in* Q2, F
304   *She dies] not in* Q2, F
316   *He wounds the King] not in* Q2; *Hurts the King.* F
320   *He forces the King to drink] not in* Q2, F
321   *The King dies] not in* Q2; *King Dyes.* F
325   *He dies] not in* Q2; *Dyes.* F

343   *A march afar off, and shout within*] *A march a farre off.* Q2; *March afarre off, and shout within.* F

352   *He dies*] not in Q2; *Dyes* F

354   *March within*] not in Q2, F

355   *Enter Fortinbras, with the Ambassadors and with his train of drum, colours, and attendants*] *Enter Fortenbrasse, with the Embassadors.* Q2; *Enter Fortinbras and English Ambassador, with Drumme, Colours, and Attendants.* F

397   *Exeunt marching; after the which a peal of ordnance is shot off*] F; *Exeunt.* Q2

5

The following are some of the variant readings and forms of words more commonly found in other editions (especially nineteenth-century ones). The reading of this edition, with its origin, is given first, followed by the rejected variant. (Emendations proposed by other editors but not adopted here are discussed in the Commentary to I.4.33, II.2.255, III.3.7, III.4.4, 122, 163, and 170, IV.4.25–6, IV.5.39, and V.2.42 and 281.)

I.1. 33   have two nights] Q2; two Nights haue F
     87   heraldy] Q2; Heraldrie F
     88   these] Q2; those F
   141   strike] Q2; strike at F
   162   stir] Q2; walke F

I.2. 11   an ... a] Q2; one ... one F
    24   bands] Q2; Bonds F
    50   My dread lord] Q2; Dread my Lord F
    85   passes] Q2; passeth F
   127   heaven] Q2; Heauens F
   198   waste] Q2, F; vast Q1
   213   watch] Q2; watcht F

I.3. 26   particular act and place] Q2; peculiar Sect and force F
    63   unto] Q2; to F
    65   courage] Q2; Comrade F
    77   dulleth] Q2; dulls the F
   123   parle] Q2; parley F

I.4. 49 interred] Q2; enurn'd F

I.5. 33 roots] Q2; rots F

  62 hebona] Q2; Hebenon F

  112–13 *Enter Horatio and Marcellus* HORATIO My lord, my lord!] Q2; *Hor. & Mar. within.* My Lord, my Lord. | *Enter Horatio and Marcellus.* F

  132 I will] Q2; Looke you, Ile F

II.2. 20 is] Q2; are F

  97 he's] Q2; he is F

  142 prescripts] Q2; Precepts F

  203 yourself] Q2; you your selfe F

  203–4 shall grow] Q2; should be F

  216 will not] Q2; will F

  278 anything but] Q2; any thing. But F

  446 when] Q2; where F

  454 heraldy] Q2; Heraldry F

  522 abstract] Q2; Abstracts F

  556 her] Q2; *Hecuba* F

  585 stallion] Q2; Scullion F

III.1. 1 conference] Q2; circumstance F

  19 are here] Q2; are F

  33 We'll] Q2; Will F

  72 despised] Q2; dispriz'd F

  145 and amble] Q2; you amble F

  148 marriage] Q2; Marriages F

  159 time] Q2; tune F

III.2. 79 commeddled] Q2; co-mingled F

  191 That's wormwood] Q2; Wormwood, Wormwood F

  328 ROSENCRANTZ] Q2; *Guild.* F

III.3. 15 cess] Q2; cease F

  25 about] Q2; vpon F

III.4. 23 Help] Q2; Helpe, helpe F

  24 Help] Q2; helpe, helpe, helpe F

  38 brassed] Q2 (brasd); braz'd F

  51 heated] Q2; tristfull F

  180 This] Q2; Thus F

IV.3. 15 Ho! Bring in the] Q2; Hoa, *Guildensterne*? Bring in my F

  66 congruing] Q2; coniuring F

IV.5.   39   ground] Q2; *graue* F

        99   is] Q2; are F

      158   paid with] Q2; payed by F

      201   O God] Q2; you Gods F

IV.7.   7   criminal] Q2; crimefull F

         8   safety, greatness,] Q2; Safety, F

       20   Work] Q2; Would F

       52   devise] Q2; aduise F

       91   Lamord] Q2; *Lamound* F

     104   you] Q2; him F

     124   in deed your father's son] Q2; your Fathers sonne indeed F

     158   preferred] Q2 (prefard); prepar'd F

     166   askant] Q2; aslant F

     168   Therewith ... make] Q2; There with ... come F

     191   drowns] Q2; doubts F

V.1.   60   in] Q2; to *Yaughan* F

      65   'A] Q2; that he F

      73   into] Q2; *intill* F

   86–7   chopless] Q2; Chaplesse F

     170   now hath lien you] Q2; now: this Scul, has laine F

     183   bore] Q2; borne F

     190   table] Q2; Chamber F

     233   a] Q2; sage F

     243   double] Q2; trebble F

     259   wisdom] Q2; wisenesse F

V.2.   63   think] Q2; thinkst F

     105   my ease] Q2; mine ease F

     187   out of an] Q2; outward F

     339   I leave] Q2; liue F

     352   silence.] Q2; silence. O, o, o, o. F

6

The following are the more important passages found in Q2 but omitted in F. They total about 230 lines. Odd words and insignificant phrases are not included here.

I.1.108–25 BARNARDO I think ... countrymen
I.2.58–60 wrung ... consent

I.4.17–38 This heavy-headed ... scandal
75–8 The very ... beneath
II.2. 17 Whether ... thus
443–4 as wholesome ... fine
463 So, proceed you
III.2.176–7 women fear ... And
181–2 Where love ... there
228–9 To desperation ... scope
III.4.72–7 Sense sure ... difference
79–82 Eyes without ... mope
162–6 That monster ... put on
168–71 the next ... potency
181 One word more, good lady
203–11 There's letters ... meet
IV.1. 4 Bestow ... while
41–4 Whose whisper ... air
IV.3.25–7 KING Alas ... that worm
IV.4.9–66 Enter Hamlet ... worth
IV.7.67–80 LAERTES My lord ... graveness
99–101 the scrimers ... opposed them
113–22 There lives ... ulcer
V.2.106–41 Sir, here is ... unfellowed (replaced by 'Sir, you are not ignorant of what excellence Laertes is at his weapon')
152–3 HORATIO ... I knew ... done
190–202 Enter a Lord ... Exit the Lord
218 Let be

7

The following are the more interesting of the stage directions in Q1. Some of them probably indicate impressions drawn from a contemporary performance of the play. The line references are to this edition.

I.1. 0 Enter two Centinels.
I.2. 0 Enter King, Queene, Hamlet, Leartes, Corambis, and the two Ambassadors, with Attendants.
I.5. 149 The Gost under the stage.
II.1. 0 Enter Corambis, and Montano.

II.2.   0   *Enter King and Queene, Rossencraft, and Gilder-stone.*

       39   *Enter Corambis and Ofelia.*

     378   *The Trumpets sound, Enter Corambis.*

III.2. 144   *Enter in a Dumbe Shew, the King and Queene, he sits downe in an Arbor, she leaues him: Then enters Lucianus with poyson in a Viall, and powres it in his eares, and goes away: Then the Queene commeth and findes him dead: and goes away with the other.*

    163   *Enter the Duke and Dutchesse.*

III.3. 72   *hee kneeles. enters Hamlet*

III.4. 103   *Enter the ghost in his night gowne.*

    218   *Exit Hamlet with the dead body.*

IV.4.   0   *Enter Fortenbrasse, Drumme and Souldiers.*

IV.5. 20   *Enter Ofelia playing on a Lute, and her haire downe singing.*

    155   *Enter Ofelia as before.*

V.1.   0   *enter Clowne and an other.*

    213   *Enter King and Queene, Leartes, and other lordes, with a Priest after the coffin.*

    246   *Leartes leapes into the graue.*

    253   *Hamlet leapes in after Leartes*

V.2. 80   *Enter a Bragart Gentleman.*

    296   *They catch one anothers Rapiers, and both are wounded, Leartes falles downe, the Queene falles downe and dies.*

    355   *Enter Voltemar and the Ambassadors from England. enter Fortenbrasse with his traine.*